Finding Home

Lauren Westwood writes romantic
women's fiction, and has also written
an award-winning children's book.
Originally from California, she now
lives in England in a pernickety old
house built in 1602, with her partner
and three daughters.

Finding Home

Lauren Westwood

First published as an ebook in 2016 by Aria,
an imprint of Head of Zeus, Ltd.

First published in print in the UK in 2017 by Aria.

9 7 5 3 1 2 4 6 8

A catalogue record for this book is available from
the British Library.

ISBN (PB): 9781788540988
ISBN (E): 9781784975883

Typeset by Divaddict Publishing Solutions Ltd.

Printed and bound by CPI Group (UK) Ltd, Croydon, CR0 4YY

Head of Zeus Ltd
First Floor East
5–8 Hardwick Street
London EC1R 4RG

WWW.HEADOFZEUS.COM

To mom and dad – with love and thanks

Finding Home

Part One

The cup of tea on arrival at a country house is a thing which, as a rule, I particularly enjoy. I like the crackling logs, the shaded lights, the scent of buttered toast, the general atmosphere of leisured cosiness.

~ PG Wodehouse – *The Code of the Woosters*

'Is Thornfield Hall a ruin? Am I severed from you by insuperable obstacles? Am I leaving you without a tear—without a kiss—without a word?'

~ Charlotte Brontë – *Jane Eyre*

Prologue

October, London, NW—

On paper, the flat looks perfect.

I rummage in my bag and uncrumple the printout of the particulars. The blurb describes it as a 'bolthole', 'with lots of potential' in an 'up-and-coming area', 'close to transport'. However, in the short time that I've been flat-hunting, I've learned that 'estateagentspeak' is a whole different language from the Queen's English. I'm pretty sure that 'bolthole' means tiny, and 'lots of potential' means bad plumbing, a grotty kitchen, and no central heating. The 'up-and-coming area' means no Starbucks for miles, and the blister on my heel is testament to the fact that 'close to transport' means that in the wilds of Zone 3, the Tube is a twenty-minute walk, but you can park a car in the street without a resident's permit.

I double-check the map and put the papers back in my bag. After walking for miles down the busy road from the Tube, I'm finally getting closer to the arrow that marks Thornton Gardens. I like the name because it reminds me of Thorn*field* – the house where Jane Eyre met Mr Rochester. The sign for the road is half-hidden behind a flame-coloured Boston ivy on the corner house. Turning down the road, I instantly leave behind the squeal of bus brakes and the smell of fried chips, and enter what feels like another world.

Thornton Gardens is lined with parked cars and London plane trees, and as I crunch through the yellow leaves on the pavement, I spot not one, but two blue plaques on the houses of the slightly down-at-heel Victorian terrace. I've never heard of either the composer or the Crimean war journalist that apparently lived there, but I sense a sudden crackling of electricity in the air – an undercurrent of history that seems like a good omen for my new job teaching English literature at the college.

Near the end of the terrace there's a 'for sale' sign shaped like a giant lollipop propped against the steps. I make my way towards the house. From afar, I can see that the paint on the windowsills is chipped and the brickwork needs repointing. But something flickers inside my chest as I crane my neck and look upwards at each floor of the tall, red-brick house. The flat for sale is at the very top. From the frieze of cherubs over the door to the pigeons swirling in the sky high above the Dutch gable, I have a strange feeling that I've been here before. That I'm meant to be here now.

While I'm waiting for the estate agent to arrive, I mentally rehearse how I'm going to convince my boyfriend, Simon, to come and have a look. Even with some ticks against it, the flat is still over our budget. Whilst I'm content to find a place that 'just feels right', Simon will want to crunch the numbers. I'll tell him that between cycling to work and climbing all those stairs, I won't need to pay for a gym membership to keep fit. And we can do loads of the work ourselves – it will be so much fun to strip wallpaper, sand floorboards and choose paint colours together, not to mention scouring little antique shops for period furniture. Maybe I can take a weekend course in upholstery or sewing and make the curtains and cushions myself...

The fragile autumn sun goes behind a cloud and the sudden chill jars me back to reality. I look around for the estate agent – he's a few minutes late. To be honest, I'm a little nervous to meet him. When we spoke on the phone, he hadn't sounded overly impressed with my budget or the fact that I've spent the last seven years doing my PhD. In the end, I found myself exaggerating ever so slightly about my salary and Simon's promotion prospects at the bank where he works. Surely finding the perfect home is about more than facts and figures; noughts of a bank balance. It's about finding that place you've been looking for all your life without even knowing it; a safe little nest; an island in a turbulent sea. My mum always says that 'every pot has a lid'. I can only hope that she's right.

A dark green Mini with a racing stripe down the bonnet turns into the road and nips into a tiny spot on a double yellow. A man with spiky gelled hair wearing a pinstriped suit jumps out. His eyes flick past me, and I wish I'd worn a smart suit and heels rather than a vintage skirt from Camden Market and ballet flats left over from my student days.

'Hello?' I say.

Realising that I must be the client, he breezes over to me. 'Sorry I'm late,' he says, all charm. I recognise his drawled vowels and nasal intonation from the phone. 'I'm Marcus Hyde-Smythe. And you must be...'

'Amy Wood.' As we shake hands, I'm instantly annoyed with myself for forgetting the *Doctor* Amy Wood part.

'Are we waiting for anyone else, or are you on your own today?' He gives me a little wink.

'Just me today. When I find the right place, I'll bring my boyfriend round. We've been renting for a few years, but now we're hoping to buy.'

Or, I am, I don't tell him. Because when I told Simon that I'd registered us at a few local estate agents, 'just in case something comes up', he hadn't actually sounded too keen. He was even less keen when he started receiving a daily barrage of text messages with particulars of every available flat in a five-mile radius. Sometimes I worry that to him, the rented ex-council flat in Docklands with the leather and chrome three-piece suite and the 50-inch 3D TV feels a little *too* much like home.

'Good good.' Marcus Hyde-Smythe's thin lips curve into a smile. 'Now do remind me again, are you looking for modern or a fixer-upper?'

'Oh – nothing too modern. I'd love to find a place with lots of character and original features.' Turning away, I look again at the front of the house. I can almost picture the women who might have lived here in the past: their long silk skirts rustling as they come out of the front door; hailing a Hansom cab, rushing off to attend a fitting for a new hat on Regent's Street, followed by tea at Fortnum and Masons... 'In fact,' I say dreamily, 'from the outside, this house seems perfect.'

'Original features.' His long nose flares at the words like there's a foul smell. 'Good good.' He checks an over-sized gold watch on his wrist. 'Well, let's go up then. The other viewing should be just about finished.'

'Other viewing?'

'This flat is listed with a few different estate agents. I've been told that another couple is viewing it before you.'

'Oh.' Worry clumps in my chest. Unfortunately, my perfect flat might be someone else's perfect flat too – lots of people's, in fact. People with a lot more noughts on paper than Simon and me. But I can't think about that now. 'Great,' I say briskly. 'Let's go up.'

He fishes out a bundle of keys from his pocket and opens the door. I step inside reverently. The foyer is littered with junk mail, but underneath there's an original red and black tile floor in a geometric pattern. At the rear, a staircase with a railing painted in layers of white gloss rises upward below a cracked moulding of intricate plaster fruit. I breathe in the smell of Mr Sheen, old house, and a slight undernote of wet dog. It's an unfamiliar smell, but one that I could definitely get used to.

From somewhere above there's a clip-clop of heels. A moment

later, a ginger-haired woman in a red trouser suit with a clashing fake-tanned face appears on the stairs.

'Hello, Florence,' my estate agent smarms. 'Good viewing?'

The ginger-haired woman rolls her eyes. 'Give them a few more minutes,' she says. 'They can't keep their hands off each other. They like the flat so much that I think they're about to try out the bedroom before the offer's even gone in – or any furniture.'

The breath freezes in my lungs. Have I lost the flat before I've even seen it? 'Um, I'd still like to view it, if that's okay,' I say.

My estate agent gives me a look like he's a bit sorry for me. But I'm determined not to be put off by the competition. Before anyone can suggest otherwise, I march up the stairs.

There are several other flats in the building off the first and second floors, with doors painted in different colours of caked-on gloss. The final flight of stairs that goes up to the attic flat is narrow and rickety. From behind the shiny black door at the top I can hear high-pitched laughter that devolves into a passionate squeal. All of a sudden, I'm reminded of the scene where Jane Eyre discovers Mr Rochester's nasty little secret locked away up in the attic and her ill-fate is sealed. My resolve begins to waver. Maybe I should come back another day...

'Do you want me to go first?' My estate agent comes up beside me. 'Make sure they're decent?' He gives me another irritating wink.

Ignoring the smarm, I steer him back to business. 'So can you tell me how this works?' I say. 'If I love the flat can we put in an offer today, or what?' I'm counting on the *or what* option since I'll need to get Simon on board first. As we reach the top of the stairs, I take out my phone and draft him a one-line text. If he can meet me after work to view the flat, then we might have a better chance of getting in before there's a bidding war.

'One step at a time,' Marcus Hyde-Smythe says, somewhat

condescendingly. 'Let's make sure you really do love it first, okay?'

'Okay.' My thumb hovers over the send button.

I turn the brass knob and gently push open the door. One glance and I just *know*. It's the right home for Simon and me; the perfect canvas for our new life together. My heart curls up inside me like a contented cat in front of a fire. I step inside a lovely little reception room with a polished wooden floor. On one wall there's a cosy cast-iron fireplace with blue and white tiles. Beyond that, under the eaves, is a perfect corner for me to set up my desk – just below the row of sash windows that flood the flat with pink and orange autumn light. I can just see us living here: me holding little soirees for my book group; Simon having a dinner party for his workmates. I picture us standing together at the window, clinking our wine glasses and watching the sky grow dark and hazy over the chimney pots of London.

The sound of footsteps and cooing voices coming from the kitchen shatters my daydreaming. Hopefully the lovey-dovey couple will get a room for a few hours so I can get Simon here and start the process of putting in an offer. I quickly hit 'send' on the text I've drafted.

'Let's look at the bedroom again!' the woman says. For a split second I see a flash of blonde hair at the door to the kitchen. From inside, there's the sound of a phone beeping with a text message.

'Oh bugger,' a man's voice. 'Just a second.'

The man comes to the kitchen door.

Our eyes meet.

The moment freezes into slow motion.

'Simon?' I gasp.

'Amy?' he gasps.

Everything speeds up again as the terrible truth registers. The rising nausea in my stomach; the guilty look on Simon's face; the weight of the phone in my hand; and then the lightness

8

as I swing back my arm and let go; the phone flying through the air, bridging the gap between us. And then the horrible little thud as the throw goes wide and my iPhone makes contact with the woman's pert little upturned nose. And she screams, and I scream; and I turn and run down the stairs; as the walls of my life come crumbling down around me.

Letter 1 (Transcription)

Rosemont Hall
April 10, 1952

Dear Henry,
I trust that you are studying hard in your last few weeks at university. Soon you will return home to Rosemont Hall. I fear you will find it changed for the worse.

Yesterday I sold the Gainsborough that hung in the green salon. For me, it was like losing your mother all over again. The house is diminished: the walls stark and empty, the room devoid of the life and laughter it once held. It is little consolation that the beams in the attic may now be replaced, the boiler fixed, and the rose bedroom repapered. I know what you would say to me were you here – 'the house is just a house; a painting just a painting'. And we would argue about it and agree to disagree.

But now, my indulgence has ended. It is time for you to make something of yourself. I have a plan that will end this sorry plight and restore the fortunes of our family and our proud heritage. By the time you return, the arrangements will be in place. Until then, I remain...

Your father

One

The car sputters as I pull into the driveway of the bungalow, as if it doesn't want to be seen outside. I find third gear instead of first, and everything clunks to a halt. Mrs Harvey, the neighbour next door, twitches the curtains at her kitchen window and gives me a little wave. I force myself to smile back at her until she disappears again, no doubt off to phone her friends at the Scrabble club to tell them that not only is Amy Wood back at home living with her parents, but she can't drive properly either.

I open the car door but can't quite muster the will to get out. Leaning against the headrest, I close my eyes. Everything that happened on that horrible afternoon – was it really a month ago already? – comes rushing back. The horror, the crushing panic, the jealous disbelief at seeing my boyfriend of seven years standing there in that quaint little flat, canoodling with another woman. It was only afterwards that I realised that I knew her – 'Ashley', the P.E. teacher at the sixth-form college where I taught – a little blonde, American thing who's also some kind of Olympic athlete. Now with a wonky nose, thanks to me and my poor aim.

But worst of all was the aftermath... The chairman of the department's voice: 'I'm sorry, Ms Wood, but the Board of

12

Governors cannot condone a teacher-on-teacher assault – no matter what the circumstances.' My tears and protestations, and his further reply: 'Yes, I'm sure the flat did have the most wonderful original features...'

'You okay, Princess?'

I blink back to reality. My dad is standing on a ladder at the front of the bungalow, tussling with a wisteria vine that's drooping over the window. I force myself to get out of the car and walk over to him. The bungalow was built in the 70s – all red-brick, pebble-dash and stained wood, identical to every other one on the road. When my parents decided to sell the little half-timbered cottage I grew up in and move to town, I felt like a little plant uprooted from my plot of earth and plopped into a plastic pot in a DIY store. I hated the bungalow; everything – from the orange pile carpet and avocado bathroom suite, to the view of the lightening-blackened oak tree out my bedroom window – felt *wrong*.

But to be fair, over the years, Dad has worked hard on the place. The bungalow always has a fresh coat of white paint around the door, and the garden still looks lush in the pale November sun. To them, *home* is being walking distance from the shops and the local church, and down the road from the pub where they play Scrabble and bridge every week. It's a comfortable, friendly place for their retirement, and I really can't argue with that.

Dad sets down his ball of twine on the top rung, and it promptly rolls off and unwinds.

'Yes Dad, I'm fine.' I accept the sudden reversion to infancy that my parents have inflicted on me ever since the night I turned up on their doorstep almost exactly a month ago, tearful and incredulous at having lost my boyfriend, the perfect flat, and my dream job all in less than 24 hours. I pick up the ball of twine. 'Do you need a hand?'

'Sure.'

Dutifully, I snip a piece of twine and hold it out to him. He ties the recalcitrant tendril to the trellis. It's the first time I've felt useful all day. I cut two more pieces and hand them to him.

'Have you been out shopping or something?' Dad asks.

'No, I went to see about a job.'

'A job!' He comes a few steps down the ladder and shakes my hand like he's amazed I would do something so grown-up. 'What is it? No, don't tell me… Let's see… Badminton Girls School? Teaching impressionable young ladies about the dangers of corsets?'

'Actually, it was a comprehensive in Bridgwater. And unfortunately, it turns out that they're not hiring.' *Me*. They're not hiring me. Nor are any of the other colleges and secondary schools within a 30-mile radius of Bristol that I've tried over the last month. Not even to teach an evening course.

'Well,' he scratches his receding hair, 'chin up. You'll find something.'

'Yeah, Dad.' I smile bravely. 'I will.' *But what*? I've even started checking the ads on Gumtree twice a day. Everything in the local area seems to involve cleaning toilets at a pub or stacking groceries at Tesco. And just like below-stairs in Victorian times, even those places probably wouldn't hire a mobile-phone-throwing trouble-maker who's been sacked without a character reference.

'That should do it.' Dad ties the last piece of twine and climbs down the ladder. 'I'll take it from here.'

'Sure, Dad. I'm going inside to change.'

The screen door slams behind me as I enter the house and peek inside the kitchen. Mum is standing at the stove wearing a Wallis and Gromit apron that one of her reception kids gave her last Christmas. She's cooking a huge pan of sausages. The grease sizzles and spits in the pan and splatters against Wallis – or Gromit? – as Mum painstakingly adds the onions and leeks. My stomach roils. Ever since I was little, I've hated sausages. But I wouldn't want to hurt Mum's feelings by actually saying so.

'Smells good, Mum.'

Mum glances at me over her shoulder and frowns. 'The top button on your jacket is hanging by a thread. Do you want me to sew it back on?'

The top button does seem loose, I notice, as I peer down at my 'go-to' black suit jacket. I wish I could blame my failure at the interview on looking bedraggled, but I know that's just wishful thinking. 'That's okay, Mum. I'll do it later.' I walk off towards my bedroom.

'How was the interview?' Mum says.

I stop and turn back. 'It wasn't exactly an interview – it was an informational interview. You know, like an enquiry.'

'Oh.' She turns over the sausages with a fork. 'So you didn't get the job.'

'No.' I sigh.

She turns the heat down on the hob and covers the foul-smelling concoction. 'Well, if you're as keen to get a job as you say you are, Mrs Harvey from next door might be able to set you up. Her niece is pregnant and her office is looking for a temp.'

'A temp?'

'Just until you get back on your feet.'

'A temp what?' I practically choke. 'In an office?'

'It's in Bath – that's all I know. But I can get the details from her.' Mum dishes out the sausages, heaping spoonfuls of congealed grease onto three plates.

'I don't really think that's quite the thing I'm looking for. I mean, I spent years at uni getting a first and doing my doctorate...' The words dissolve on my tongue. I may have been good at doing research and writing clever little essays for scholarly journals – I wrote a thesis on 'Houses as Characters in 19th Century Fiction' that won a prize. As a teacher, I prided myself on my ability to bring to life some of the great literary classics for my flock of university-bound students – together we explored every nuance of Mr Darcy's behaviour through the eyes of Elizabeth Bennet in *Pride and Prejudice*; studied each fluttering heartbeat of Jane Eyre's descent into love with her troubled employer, Rochester, in *Jane Eyre*; jumped at sinister shadows on every page at Manderley along with the second Mrs de Winter in *Rebecca*. But let's face it – those aren't exactly real-world skills.

'Suit yourself.' Mum shrugs.

I hang my head. 'I guess it couldn't hurt to have the details – just in case nothing else comes along.'

Mum smiles a little too smugly. 'That's my girl. When the going gets tough, the tough get going...'

'Yeah, Mum.' I give her a half-hearted high five. 'Stiff upper lip and all that.'

Mum seems almost gleeful as she phones Mrs Harvey next door and gets the details. The details consist only of an address and the name of a firm in Bath: *Tetherington Bowen Knowles*. As soon as I hear the name, I take heart. It sounds like an ultra-respectable firm of solicitors, or maybe an accountancy office. Someplace with comfortable sofas and brass lamps with green glass shades that smells of ancient cigar smoke, leather-bound books and yellowing papers. My parents don't have internet access, so I can't find out for sure.

'She says you should go tomorrow,' Mum says. 'Apparently her niece is "about to pop".'

I grimace at the image. 'Okay, I will.'

*

At dinner, I douse the sausages with mustard and pick at them, half-listening to Mum and Dad gossiping about their neighbours, the church-roof fundraiser, and the merits of

Aldi vs Lidl. Afterwards, we spend a quiet evening in front of the television watching *Celebrity Antiques Road Trip*, and *Mastermind*. When Dad puts on a recording of *Autumnwatch*, I excuse myself on the grounds that I want to 'see about the temp job' first thing the next morning. Dad looks impressed. 'Okay Princess,' he says. 'We'll be here cheering for you.'

'Great Dad,' I say. 'That's nice to know.'

'And make sure you sew on that button,' Mum says as I leave the sitting room.

I go into the bathroom, rub on my five-minute facial mud mask, and stick cucumber slices over my eyes. Sitting on the edge of the bathtub, the more I try not to think about the past, the clearer it is in my mind. Simon is there in vivid colour – sitting two rows behind me in the lecture hall where we first met. We got to talking and found that we shared the same night bus home. Great love stories through the ages are built on less, I suppose. One thing led to another, and pretty soon, Simon was over at my little basement flat so often that, in his words, it was 'mad to throw away money renting two flats'. Not, admittedly, the most romantic reason ever given for moving in together. Still, I dutifully moved my books, my clothing, and myself into his bachelor pad in Docklands – that was already complete with free weight set, Xbox, nose-hair trimmer, and trouser press. I always felt slightly out of place there – like I never truly made my mark. At night, I used to dream about the day when we could finally afford a real 'together home'.

Although the living situation wasn't perfect, Simon was a model boyfriend. I could always count on the odd token of affection: a bouquet of 50% off flowers from the Whistlestop at Waterloo Station; my favourite falafel wrap with no onions brought home when he was working late; text messages that he was sitting in another boring meeting with Saudi investors and would rather be home with me watching *University Challenge*. After a year or so, the tokens dwindled, and the lean years began: me working round the clock on my thesis; him working round the clock at the investment bank. But we still had the weekends, mostly spent curled up together on the orange crush velvet sofa that we found in a skip in Wapping and together managed to upend through the window of the flat. We ate a lot of takeaways, drank a lot of wine, watched a fair few films, and when we weren't too tired, had sex in the narrow double bed decorated with the crocheted duvet cover I bought at Petticoat Lane market. All in all, it was a nice existence rather than a great love story – but in the real world, there's nothing wrong with nice. And in the last few months, things had been looking up: I began teaching English literature at the college, and the bank promoted Simon to vice president of emerging markets. My life, signed, sealed and delivered. My life...

I pick off one of the cucumber slices and eat it. Around me, the sight of wall-to-wall Artex and avocado bathroom suite make my stomach give a little lurch. Why am I here when I should be standing at the head of a table filled with clever and interested students, engaging in intelligent debate about 'The myth of feminist identity in Jane Austen'? What happened to the future that 'might have been': a scene in a romantic restaurant, wine and candles; Simon taking something from his pocket, down on one knee, everyone else stopping their conversations and turning to watch. I imagine the ring – he knows I like antiques, so maybe it will be something vintage – Victorian with seed pearls and tiny diamonds. And instantly, I will have joined the sisterhood of women who, after going through toil and hardship, finally get a happy ending.

A happy ending. Was I so wrong to want one?

I wash the mud off my face and look in the mirror. The woman who stares back is a little thinner than a month ago, with what a novelist might glibly describe as a heart-shaped face and porcelain skin. Her shoulder-length hair is thick and dark, and cut in a long bob. Only her eyes seem to have lost a little of their sparkle. While the sting of being usurped by the perfect 'Ashley' ('I'm really sorry, Amy, but when I met her at that little "do" for new teachers, I just knew it was destiny') has begun to numb slightly, the ache of what the hell I'm going to do now lingers on. A temp job is not what I had in mind. But I have to do something – anything – to get back on my feet, even though my knees still feel like jelly. I do a few facial exercises in the mirror and practice my best 'interview' smile. It's always nerve-wracking trying for a new job, but really, how bad can it be?

I brush my teeth and don my fuzzy slippers. Before leaving the bathroom, I poke my head into the hallway to check that the coast is clear. The TV is off and there's a light on under my parents' door. I venture down the hall to the airing cupboard in search of Mum's sewing kit, but it isn't there. Hurrying back to my own bedroom, I pop in a pair of blue foam earplugs bought last week following a nocturnal emergency – noises coming from my parents' room in the middle of the night. I cross my fingers that I'll get a job quickly, earn some money, and soon be able to afford 'a room of my own'.

But until then, all I can do is lie down in the narrow bed, crawl under the duvet, and pull the pillow tightly around my ears.

Two

Two little words.

My heart plummets as I stand on the pavement outside the golden Bath-stone office of *Tetherington Bowen Knowles*, debating whether to go inside or jump back on the train never to return. This isn't an ultra-respectable firm of solicitors or an accountancy office. It isn't a doctor's surgery or a career consultancy. The office where, if I'm lucky, I might be able to get a temp job, is none other than an...

Estate agent.

Estate agents – the profession that everyone loves to hate. For me, it's the profession that I'll forever associate with the scene of my ultimate humiliation. The memory of that look on my estate agent's face after I threw the mobile phone at Ashley – his fleshy stiff-upper lip, ever so slightly amused – is permanently etched onto my brain. The unfurling of a spotty silk handkerchief when he came to the rescue of the damsel with the bloody nose. His parting words to me as I ran down the stairs to the street, my dreams in tatters, my face puffy and tear-streaked: 'So, Miss Wood, can I assume you won't be putting in an offer?'

I take a deep breath to steel myself as the button on my jacket begins to strain across my chest. The only way I'm going to get out of the hole I've fallen into is to get a job – any job. I have to keep my eye on the prize – moving out of my parents' house and into a flat that I can make my own. I have to go inside.

A little bell tinkles as I push open the door. Instantly, everyone inside the open-plan space is abuzz with activity and energy. At one desk, a spiky-haired man in an impeccable suit is laughing into a phone cradled on his shoulder and gesturing with a pen. At the back of the room, an older woman in tweed flashes me a coral-lipped smile as she pours milk into her coffee cup, and even the heavily pregnant woman at the first desk as I enter – Mrs Harvey's niece, I presume – looks up from her computer screen grinning through teeth gritted like a Cheshire Cat. I seem to be the only one who can't make my lips curve upwards.

I approach the niece. Everyone leans in like plants growing towards the sunlight.

'Hi, uhh, I'm Amy Wood. Your aunt was going to ring this morning. About the job for maternity-leave cover?'

Instantly, the electricity in the room fizzles out. Everyone falls back into their various tasks like marionettes with broken strings. The niece looks at me with disdain.

'Take a seat. Mr Bowen-Knowles is on a conference call.'

I skulk my way over to the waiting area that's, in a word, beige. Needless to say, there are no leather-bound books or cheery brass lamps. I sit down on the edge of a firm beige sofa with chrome arms that's flanked with potted palms. The beige-wood coffee table is covered with piles of property particulars. One pile is an advertisement of available properties in an estate of new-build mansions. I recognise some of the mysterious lexicon: 'top-quality fixtures and fittings to suit' – referring, I surmise, to the fake marble pilasters, white carpet, and shiny black kitchens in the photo. The other pile contains a mixture of one-bed flats and village semis in the greater Somerset area – many of them in 'charming villages' (no supermarket for miles); or 'easy commuting distance' to places as far away as London and Cardiff. I peruse the particulars for a one-bed flat in a newly gentrified part of Bristol, and gasp at the 'newly reduced!' price. Even if I hadn't been categorically sacked from my teaching job, I'd still have trouble affording the down payment on even a small flat on my own. My shoulders begin to droop—

'Amy Wood?'

'Yes, that's me.' As I stand up, the button on my jacket heralds my grand entrance by popping off onto the floor and bouncing like a flat rock skimming the surface of a placid lake. And unfortunately, the man standing at the door of a tiny beige-walled office is *not* smiling. His eyes follow the progress of the button until it lands petulantly under the niece's desk.

His gaze moves to the tiny wrinkle of black lace at the top of my bra that I'm aware is now peeking out of the V of my blouse. All I can do is wait – for his eyes to reach my face just as my cheeks flush bright red.

'Come into my office. I'm Alistair Bowen-Knowles.'

He ushers me inside. The large desk that takes up most of the office is unnaturally tidy. On the walls are architects' drawings of modern houses and six framed 'Salesman of the Year' certificates, all arranged to the millimetre. Mr Bowen-Knowles is wearing a starched pink shirt with cufflinks, pin-striped trousers and a purple and silver tie. His eyes are set too closely together, his nose long and wolf-like.

Mr Bowen-Knowles steeples his fingers. 'So, Miss Wood. What can I do for you?'

Smiling, I launch into my prepared answer. 'I understand you might have a job opening in your office. I'm looking for work and I thought I'd make a good... uhh... fit.' I hand him my one-page CV (highlighting my education, and downplaying the fact that I have absolutely no relevant experience). He takes it from me and scans it, his eyes narrowing.

'Are you sure you're in the right place?' His lip twists in disdain. 'The bookstore's down the street.'

I shift in my chair, ready to make a dignified exit. Things

have been hard enough without adding Mr Salesman-of-the-Year to my woes. My eyes settle on the white business cards neatly displayed in a Links of London holder. Beneath the script words *Tetherington Bowen Knowles* is a line of small print that I hadn't noticed before: '*Specialists in unique and historic properties.*' I take one of the cards from the holder.

Unique. Historic. Two little words...

And just like that, the noxious mist clears from my mind.

'You may look at my CV and think that I'm overqualified.' I sit up a little straighter. His right eyebrow twitches upwards like he'd had no such notion.

'But the truth is, academia was a bit stodgy. I've read a lot of classic English books that feature "unique and historic properties". And I think I'd be the perfect person to sell them. Your agency's speciality is right "up my street" – so to speak.' I smile, really warming up now.

The niece waddles in, her smile now looking more like a grimace, and puts a cup of coffee on the desk in front of me. I ignore it.

'In fact, I've loved old properties ever since I was a girl and my dad did up our cottage. It was full of character and quirks – just like a person. I adored it – and was gutted when they moved.' I lean forward. 'I'm sure I'll be able to sell lots of unique and historic properties and find lots of people their perfect home. Maybe be... uhh... Salesman of the Year – like you.' I laugh nervously. 'Saleswoman, I mean.'

Satisfied with my 'pitch', I sit back. Instead of looking duly impressed, Mr Bowen-Knowles is fiddling with his right cufflink.

'Are you finished?' he says curtly.

'Yes.' I shrink in the chair.

'Good.'

He picks up his BlackBerry and frowns at the screen. The silence is painful as he begins tapping a message on the tiny keys.

'How old are you?' he says, without looking up.

'I just turned thirty... one.'

'And where did you go to school?'

'I did my D.Phil in history and literature at UCL.'

'Before that?'

'Willowdale Comprehensive. In Wookey Hole.'

'It shows.'

'Sorry?'

Mr Bowen-Knowles sets down his BlackBerry with an irritated sigh. 'Ms Wood, *Tetherington Bowen Knowles* has a very exclusive clientele. Our buyers demand taste, refinement, and discretion.' He looks down his nose at me. 'I'm sure it's impressive that you've read books about historic houses, and that your father "did up" an old cottage.' He shakes his head and tsks. 'But frankly, I question whether you have the right demeanour to work here. This is a business – it's about numbers and commissions; not some kind of pie-in-the-sky matchmaking service. We expect the refinement and gravitas of Cheltenham Ladies College; not Wookey Hole.'

The styrofoam cup pops in my hand, startling both of us. I'm not sure whether to laugh in his face, or stand up and storm out. Maybe I have been blathering a bit and obviously, I don't have any sales experience. Maybe he's testing me, or maybe he's just rude. All I know is, now that he's telling me that I'm not worthy to be an estate agent – even a temporary one – I'm determined to prove him wrong.

'Mr Bowen-Knowles...' I lift my chin and sit rigid in the chair, 'I understand your concerns. But if you hire me today, you won't regret it, I promise. I'm smart and enthusiastic, and I learn quickly. Plus, I know Somerset, Wiltshire and Gloucester like the back of my hand. I'm asking you to give me a chance...'

Give me a chance – I'd said that to Simon when he came back to the flat we shared in Docklands to officially break up with me. Give me a chance to learn to cook. Give me a chance to clean up my papers, books, and clutter. Give me a chance to watch Sky Sports with you on Sunday nights instead of *Antiques Roadshow*. Give me a chance...

Did I really say those things? How pathetic.

Mr Bowen-Knowles doesn't bother to respond. He picks up his BlackBerry again and checks the screen.

I stand up, sighing inwardly. If I've learned anything from surviving the worst month of my life, it's that there's no point sticking around to be humiliated further. I'll just thank him politely, walk out with my head held high, and forget I ever set foot—

All of a sudden, there's a commotion in the outer office.

'Shit, Sally!' someone male yells.

'It's not shit, it's my waters breaking,' wails a female voice.

'Shit!' Mr Bowen-Knowles echoes, his lip twisting in annoyance.

I fling open the office door. The pregnant niece – Sally – is standing next to her desk, with gooey fluid running down her leg and puddling at her feet. The other woman I saw earlier is nowhere to be seen, and the spiky-haired man has a look of disgusted horror on his face.

I rush forward, strip off my jacket, and push up the sleeves of my ivory silk blouse. Only then do I realise that I don't have a clue what to do. Sally's body tenses and she begins to moan. The sound crescendos into a deep groan and rises in pitch, climaxing into a shriek.

'Oh God, it hurts! Fuck!'

I put one hand on her back to steady her. She leans over the back of her chair and somehow manages to knock my jacket into the pool of goopy fluid at her feet. Biting my lip, I reach across her to the desk phone. I may never have worked in an office before, but even I know how to dial 999. Sally begins to breathe again as the pain seems to pass.

'I think it's coming,' she gasps.

'What? Now?'

'I've had the pains since last night. Oh… fuck!' She doubles over again.

With forced calm, I try to explain what's happening to the emergency services operator: pains since last night, waters oozing over my jacket and the posh parquet floor of *Tehtherington Bowen-Knowles: Estate Agents and Specialists in Unique and Historic Properties*. I give them the address. No, I'm not her friend or her doula. No, I'm not a colleague. I'm just an interviewee who was about to be shown the door when—

'Oooohhh! Fuck!!!'

'Five minutes? Okay, thanks.'

'Can you type?'

I put down the phone and wheel around, startled. Mr Bowen-Knowles has come out of his office and is standing uncomfortably close to me. His eyes skim to my chest, and I'm suddenly aware how sheer my blouse is.

'Sorry?'

'Type, Ms Wood – as in, on a computer.' His eyes return to my face and he mimes a keyboard.

'Yes, of course. One hundred words a minute.'

'Fucking help me!' Sally cries.

Mr Bowen-Knowles flicks his hand at Sally, keeping his distance. 'Obviously I'm not going to have time to do any more interviews. So you can come in if you like – as temporary admin support.'

'Admin support?'

He looks at me like I'm an idiot. 'Sally's the receptionist. You don't think we'd actually trust her with anything more than that, do you?'

'Oh, well, I don't really know…' He must have thought I was a complete moron spouting off about selling historic properties when the only job opening was for a temporary receptionist.

He shrugs at my clear disappointment. His eyes roam downwards again. 'I'll tell you what. Since you're so – keen—'

he grins wolfishly, 'if you earn your spurs, I might let you do the odd viewing. We've got more rich Londoners down here at the weekend than we know what to do with. You don't deal with any other aspect of the purchase and sale. *And* only if none of the other agents are available.'

'Viewings? That sounds interesting.' Certainly, the one and only viewing that I went on in London was all that and more. But at least this time, I'd be on the other side of the fence. And doing more than just admin.

'Oh God, it's coming!'

Outside, a siren wails.

I switch back into crisis management mode as Sally leans over the desk and hikes up her skirt. I'm vaguely aware of the two men standing behind me, their faces paralysed in horror. I grab her hand and squeeze it. 'Just hang in there,' I yell to Sally. 'You're doing great!'

The door bursts open and two paramedics arrive. They lift my predecessor onto a stretcher, ply her with tubes and monitors, and give her a gas mask to breathe into.

'I want an epidural!' Sally yells, gasping.

'Too late for that.'

'What? Fuck. No!'

The paramedics wheel the screaming woman out of the office. I hold the door for them to go through, and then turn, sweaty and rumpled, to face my new employer.

Mr Bowen-Knowles frowns so deeply you could almost germinate seeds in his brow. 'Well, Ms Wood,' he says. 'You want the job, right?'

'Yes, but—'

'So don't just stand there.' He points to the mess on the floor. 'Take some initiative.'

'Yes, Mr Bowen-Knowles,' I say through my teeth. I pick up my soggy jacket, and head to the back of the office to look for a loo and a mop.

Three

By mid-morning, I feel like a veteran of foreign wars. In the span of a few short hours, I've got a job, played maternity nurse, mopped the floor, taken my jacket to the dry cleaners, and when I get back, I find that I've become the 'face' of *Tetherington Bowen Knowles* – the other estate agents are out on viewings and Mr Bowen-Knowles is closeted in his office with the door firmly shut – so I'm on my own. As it's fairly obvious that I won't be getting an induction, I use the time to explore the office. In the back there's a disabled loo with a 'salesman of the month' chart tacked to the door (someone has crossed out 'man' with a red pen and written 'person' instead), a stationery cupboard, and a coffee machine that looks like something out of Dr Jekyll's laboratory percolating a black, poisonous sludge. I settle for a cup of freezing water from the cooler.

My new desk is covered in pink objects of all description: rose-coloured stickies, soft toy bunny rabbits, floral-toned make-up and nail polish, a clock shaped like Cinderella's glass slipper, and a pink mug with frolicking teddy bears. Sitting down in the swivel chair, I whisk everything into a desk drawer that's already overflowing with chocolate, baby magazines, and used tissues with blotted pink lipstick. A clean desk equals a clean slate. As an afterthought, I open the drawer and take out Cinderella's glass slipper. I've never had a clock on my desk before, but somehow it seems appropriate.

Next, I look over the stickies that Sally has pasted around the computer screen. I'm relieved to find the name and number of an IT consultant. I call the number to find out how to log in to the computer system. The consultant sets me up with my very own email address: amy.wood@tbk.com. I hang up the phone feeling confident for the first time in weeks. I have a desk, a computer, and an email address. I have a job – in an office. In a few weeks, I'll have my first pay cheque. Things are definitely looking up—

But the next instant, I notice a couple lurking outside the window looking at the placards. They're both bundled up in layers of tattered winter clothing that's definitely past its sell-by date. I hold my breath... they're at the door... they're coming inside.

Having a desk and an email address is one thing – having actual clients is quite another!

The man guides the woman inside with a hand on her back. His eyebrow twitches like he's almost as terrified as I am.

'Hello!' I spring to my feet with a welcoming smile, like I imagine Kirsty Allsopp would do. I've watched every episode of her vintage home show, and she really knows how to make people feel at ease.

'I'm Amy Wood. May I help you?'

'Uhh...' the man looks at the woman. She twiddles with the paisley scarf around her neck. 'We're looking for a new house.'

'Great, we've get lots of lovely properties that I can show you. What kind of home are you looking for? Period or modern, or...' I hesitate, suddenly remembering that I'm only supposed to be doing admin. 'Or maybe you want to take a seat and wait for my colleagues—' I cut off. 'I mean... can I take your details?'

Looking confused, they sit down on the beige sofa. I perch on the edge of the coffee table on top of some home decorating magazines. I scribble my pen in the notebook to get the ink flowing.

'Your name, please?'

'Mary Blundell,' the woman says. 'And this is Fred.'

'Pleased to meet you,' I say. 'And your budget?'

'Three million.'

I sit back and look at her, stunned. Three million? Pounds? Sterling? I'd had them pegged as first-time buyers who'd be after a higgledy-piggledy little cottage in Pucklechurch – or something. My instincts as an estate agent are rubbish!

'Well...' Mr Blundell seems worried by my hesitation. 'I guess we can stretch to 3.2 for the right place, you know?'

'Absolutely.' I stand up. 'Let me get you some brochures and—'

A door slams in the back. As I reach my desk, the spiky-haired man who did absolutely nothing to help out with the baby birthing has returned. I expect everything to be all smiles again, and if I'm Kirsty, then maybe he can be Phil Spencer. But when the man catches sight of me, he immediately glares in the spitting image of Mr Bowen-Knowles. My fantasy of happy colleagues fizzles like a dud firework.

'What do you think you're doing?' His accent is like cut glass.

I glance towards the couple on the sofa. Counting them and the newcomer, three people are looking at me like I have two heads.

'These people are looking for a new home. No one else was here, so I took their details. Mr and Mrs Blundell.' I gesture towards the couple.

When Spiky-hair turns to the prospective clients, his demeanour changes completely. His face erupts into an obsequious grin. Pushing past me, he approaches the couple.

'Sorry for the confusion – she's new,' he schmoozes. 'I'm Jonathan Park-Spencer. Please come into my office and I'll help you right away.'

The couple stand up, looking bewildered.

'It's fine,' I say, secretly seething. 'Jonathan can take it from here.'

The three of them disappear through a door next to Mr Bowen-Knowles's office.

I sit back down at my 'de-pinked' desk. Obviously, as I have no experience, it was right for Jonathan to take charge of the clients, but I should have asked to sit in and listen so that I can start learning the ropes for when I'm called upon to do viewings. I stare at the door, listening to the muffled voices behind it, but I can't make out what they're saying. To make myself more useful for next time – if there is a next time – I grab a pile of glossy property brochures from a nearby desk and flip through them to familiarise myself. New-builds, modern flats, development sites, office space for lease, a few semis; my eyes glaze over. Where are the 'unique and historic' properties that this place is supposed to specialise in? If I had a budget of three million (three million!) pounds like Fred and Mary Blundell, I wouldn't come to *Tetherington Bowen Knowles* based on the placards in the window. For that kind of money they could buy themselves a Thornfield, a Pemberly, a Manderley. In so many classics that I've loved since my girlhood, there's a notable house – grand, quirky, sometimes even a little bit sinister – and I love all of their fictional idiosyncrasies. My heart momentarily flutters with excitement. How lovely it would be to find a buyer for a historic home; a kindred spirit to chat with over Earl Grey tea, currant scones and cucumber sandwiches. Maybe I could help them find craftspeople to help with any needed restoration, and even help them source antiques for the place. Or I could do research on the history of the house or—

The door in the back slams again. An attractive Asian woman with shiny bobbed hair comes in, looking daring in a teal satin suit and matching heels. She sets her handbag on the desk opposite mine and actually smiles at me.

'Hi, I'm Amy Wood – new here today.' I lean over my desk and proffer my hand.

'Claire Kumar.' She shakes my hand firmly. 'Is he back?' She nods her head at Jonathan's desk.

'Some clients came in. He took them to the spare office.'

'Typical.' She shakes her head. 'The one day I'm late, Uriah Heep gets all the action.'

The literary reference makes me like her instantly. Before I can muster up my own Dickensian reply, the door to Mr Bowen-Knowles's office bangs open.

'Wood,' he yells, 'where's my coffee? I always have it at half eleven. And Kumar...' he makes a show of checking his garish gold watch, 'nice of you to join us. You'll be pleased to hear that there's a viewing at two for that dump in Chipping Sudbury. You know the drill – it's a "character property brimming with potential, in need of a little TLC".' He wrinkles his nose. 'Make sure you whisper in their ears that the vendor's desperate to sell and will probably pay some poor sod to take it off his hands. Just don't mention the subsidence – or the roof, or the new chicken shit plant, or the frackers or...' he scratches his head, 'anything really. I want that place under offer in a fortnight.'

'But Alistair, that listing is Jonathan's.' Claire sounds incensed. 'He should be handling it—'

'Save that for your barrister course – if you get there. And at this rate...' he flashes her a vulpine smile, 'your hair will be grey by then and you won't have to bother with a wig.'

With that, he returns to his office and slams the door.

'Ugh,' Claire says. 'That man is insufferable.'

'Are you studying to be a barrister?'

'Yeah. And as soon as I can get a pupillage, I'm out of here.'

A less than ringing endorsement of my new place of employ, but I'm hardly surprised. Mr Bowen-Knowles's outburst has shaken the chat out of her. She stares at her computer screen and begins typing. I clear my throat. 'Um, I was wondering – could you show me how to use the coffee machine?'

'Sure.' With a sigh she stands up and we walk to the kitchen. I stand aside and watch as she disembowels the machine, puts in a filter and a packet of coffee, empties the sludge from the pot, fills it with water, and presses a series of buttons. I think about how in the staffroom at the college, all the coffee is instant. Memories of the chalky, acidic taste triggers a little pang of loss.

'The boss likes his with no milk and two sugars,' she says as the machine begins to sputter and gurgle. 'And his special mug is in here.' She opens a cupboard and takes out a huge white and green mug with the words 'I'd rather be... GOLFING!' scrawled in black across it. Instantly, I recoil. In hindsight, I realise that in my relationship with Simon, I missed plenty of warning signs that something rotten was lurking beneath the surface. Like the fact that we used to do the Saturday *Telegraph* crossword together in bed, but he suddenly started buying the *Times*. Or the fact that he went to work at an investment bank instead of finishing his theology thesis. Or that every other week on Sunday afternoons, he liked to play golf. It's not that I have anything against golf per se, but it's one of those things that just seems so *male*. Secretly, I've always agreed with Mark Twain: that 'golf is a good walk spoiled'. As such, I always found an excuse never to go with Simon – even to watch. One of my many mistakes, perhaps. I imagine 'Ashley' in a little white golf skirt and polo shirt, dangling her long, tanned legs over the side of the golf-cart and pursing her bee-stung lips anxiously as Simon tees off with his prized 3 wood. My hand trembles a little and I almost drop the mug.

'No milk, two sugars,' I repeat lamely.

Claire returns to her desk and I bring Mr Bowen-Knowles his mug of coffee. Luckily he's on the phone when I go into his office, and other than his frown lingering a good eight inches below my chin, I escape unscathed. As I close the door, Jonathan's be-pinstriped, be-hair-gelled personage emerges from the spare office. The Blundells trail after him, looking positively downtrodden.

'Goodbye,' I say as they walk past me. 'I hope you find the perfect home.'

'Oh, we will.' Mary Blundell smiles at me. I smile back, hoping that I see them again. There's a twinkle in her eye and I get the distinct idea that she's not actually cowed by Jonathan's power-of-posh. Nor should she be – after all, they're the ones with the budget of three million (three million!) pounds.

As the Blundells are leaving, the older woman who I saw earlier, Patricia, arrives. As soon as she opens her mouth to greet the others, I peg her as the Cheltenham Ladies College ringer: Camilla Parker Bowles suit, hot-curlered hair, horsey laugh, calls people 'Dahling'. Everyone but me, that is. When I introduce myself, she gives me a pained wince and turns to Jonathan to talk cricket.

*

The hours tick by on Cinderella's glass slipper. I realise that in academia, I was never really conscious of time passing – or in this case, not passing. Claire leaves for her viewing, and returns looking down in the mouth, like it was all a waste of time. No other clients come through the door, and except for the odd moment of everyone perking up whenever someone hovers on the pavement outside, the atmosphere is one of varying degrees of boredom.

'Can I help out with anything?' I ask each of them in turn. I'm answered with shaken heads all around. I shuffle through the brochures again. There are so many books I could be reading; young people I could be teaching. Sitting here, I feel like one of the many nameless women that history has forgotten – without any sort of meaningful status or occupation. The only consolation is that, looking around at the others, I can imagine that they might be feeling the same way.

The office phone rings and suddenly everyone sits up at attention. Patricia answers it and we all hang on her every word: 'Yes... that's right... yes we do... you've come to exactly the right place.'

She puts her hand over the phone: 'New instruction!' she whispers excitedly.

Everyone exchanges excited glances. Jonathan actually leaps to his feet.

We all watch her face as she listens to the voice at the other end. Her smile begins ever so slowly to melt. 'Please hold for a moment,' she says.

'It's a probate,' she announces grimly. 'They're popping their clogs right and left around here. But I did the Harris estate – it's someone else's turn.'

'Not me, I'm afraid.' Jonathan plunks back down with his elbows spread behind his head. 'I'm shooting off now to do that Weston-super-Mare valuation. No time to talk to a long-winded solicitor. You do it, Claire – it's good practice for being a mouthpiece.'

'I'd love to,' Claire replies, 'but the childminder just texted.' She gives an unapologetic little shrug. 'I've get to go get Atul a bit earlier today.'

A silence ensues. Patricia taps her fingers on the desk, her equine face more closely resembling a stubborn mule.

'I'll do it,' I say in a small voice, wondering what I've just agreed to do; vainly hoping that someone will fill me in.

'Line two,' Patricia says. 'Mr Kendall.'

I fumble with the phone headset, and get my pen and paper ready. I'm conscious that everyone is watching me. Judging...

One button on the phone is lit. Taking a breath, I press it.

'*Tetherington Bowen Knowles*, Amy Wood speaking. How may I help you?'

... And the solicitor on the other end speaks quickly and with purpose.

... And I furiously scribble down notes: Mr Kendall represents the estate of an old woman who has just died. The house needs to be sold. But it's not just any house. My heart begins to thrum with excitement.

'... Rosemont Hall, a Palladian-style Georgian manor house with 120 acres.'

'... historical gem that's been in the family for 200 years.'

'... partially derelict and needs total modernisation...'

'If your valuation is adequate, we'll give you the exclusive listing...'

'Miss Wood?'

... And I've been writing so quickly that I barely realise that Mr Kendall is addressing me. 'So, can you send someone round for the valuation?'

'Absolutely,' I say. 'How about tomorrow?'

'Tomorrow's Saturday. Can you come round on Monday, 3 o'clock?'

'Monday, 3 o'clock.' My hand is trembling with excitement as I write down the time and the address for my first viewing. 'Great. I'll definitely see you then.'

Four

When I arrive at the bungalow that evening, my mind is overflowing with possibilities. I keep replaying all of the events of the day, especially every word of the phone call I took about Rosemont Hall. I have a strange feeling – a premonition almost – that for me, everything is about to change. It's almost like a house from the books I love has jumped off the page and landed in my lap. Surely it's fate that I took the call – one that no one else could be bothered with. Now I just have to convince Mr Bowen-Knowles to put me in charge of the viewings.

Mum and Dad are already eating dinner when I come inside – chicken casserole. I sit down at the table, suddenly ravenous. 'Guess what!' I say. 'I got the job.'

'Well done, Princess.' Dad devours a Brussel sprout, takes a gulp of wine, and gives me a proud smile.

Mum looks up. 'That blouse is practically see-through. Your bra is showing. What happened to your jacket?'

'It's a long story.' I pull the edges of my blouse together. Not that it helps.

Mum raises an eyebrow. 'And what exactly is the job?'

'It's at an estate agent's,' I say. 'They're called *Tetherington Bowen Knowles*.'

'An estate agent's!' Dad's forkful of peas seems to go down the wrong way. 'I thought it was a solicitor's or something.' He looks at Mum.

'No wonder Mrs Harvey never said.' Mum pours gravy over her potatoes.

I put down my fork, alarmed. 'But I thought... I mean – you said I should try for it.'

'Well, you sounded desperate.'

'I wouldn't say that. And anyway, there's absolutely nothing wrong with it. Is there? Just think of Kirsty and Phil, or Sarah Beeny – or Kevin on *Grand Designs*. I know you watch all those shows. Everyone does.'

'Well maybe once or twice.' Dad scratches his mop of greying hair. 'Becca, what was the name of that estate agent who sold us our house?'

'Frank Knightly or something like that. He told us the boiler was new and then "bang" – within six months it needed a total replacement.'

'Two thousand quid!' Dad chimes in, as if I'm personally responsible.

'And then there's the school extension practically in the back garden,' Mum shakes her head. 'Literally – not a mention. And now the kids are so close they can virtually see into our loo.' She gives me the tsk reserved for her most indolent students.

'I guess everyone has their horror stories.' I clench my teeth. 'But at least it's a job. And I'll mostly be doing... uhh... admin and office-manager stuff. And some viewings at the weekend. Country retreats – for rich Londoners.'

Dad pushes away his plate like he's suddenly lost his appetite. 'Londoners are pricing local people out of the market. I'm not sure we should be supporting that—'

I throw up my hands. 'Look, I'm sorry my new job does not involve developing a cure for cancer or helping underprivileged children, or teaching teenagers about the plight of wronged literary heroines through the centuries. I'm sorry that I can't get a teaching job, and that even Tesco and McDonald's might not have me. Never mind that in actual fact, I spent the morning practically delivering a baby on an office floor. Then later on I took a call about selling an amazing Georgian house – a "historical gem" with "bags of potential". I was starting to feel good about things.'

There's a moment of awkward silence around the table. 'Don't worry, honey,' Dad says. 'We're very proud of you.'

I turn away so he can't see the tear leaking from the corner of my eye. I'm grateful that he's bothered to lie, and sorry that he has to.

'Worse things happen at sea,' Mum says.

I nod silently.

Mum peers over at my plate. 'You haven't eaten a thing. If you don't like the casserole, there are some sausages left over from last night.'

'Thanks Mum, but I'm not hungry.' I push away the plate of casserole and stand up. 'And just so you know – I actually hate sausages.'

Leaving them to look at each other in shock, I make my exit from the kitchen.

Alone in my bedroom, I remove my world-weary blouse, lie down on my bed and stare up at the ceiling. My parents may be unimpressed with my new job, but I can't let that defeat me. Even if there are a few bad apples in the barrel, it doesn't mean that every estate agent is like that. And anyway, I can be different from the rest. Thinking about it objectively, there are lots of positives to my new job. I'll get to meet new people, learn new skills, and maybe – once I'm no longer 'only admin' – find someone their perfect home. That's an exciting prospect, surely.

I let out an inevitable sigh as thoughts of Simon creep out of the shadows beyond the circle of lamplight. His features are beginning to blur in my mind, but I can still picture every detail of the darling little flat in the terrace with the blue plaques. Did Simon and 'Ashley' buy the flat together? Are they there together now, limbs coiled in an ornately scrolled brass bed with a cover that she quilted herself? I change my clothes and concentrate on pushing all thoughts of it from my mind. For me, that future wasn't meant to be. Which means that somewhere out there is a new way that I'll have to forge myself. I've taken the first step – if I can work for a few months at the estate agency, at least I'll be able to pay the minimum on my student loans until a teaching job comes along. And once I 'earn my spurs' doing admin and viewings, maybe I'll even earn some commission. When at last I've saved enough for my own flat, I know that Mum will help me scour charity shops for old china and furniture to 'upcycle', and Dad will be able to help out if it needs redecoration. I'll have wall-to-wall bookshelves and a comfy sofa, and maybe a little fireplace if I'm really lucky… And working at an estate agency, maybe I'll even get an inside track on anything in budget that comes on to the market. When the next 'right' home for me comes along, I'll need to be ready.

I get up and walk over to the bookshelf. On the top shelf there's a framed photo of me sitting on Dad's old ride-on lawn-mower at the cottage where I grew up. The cottage was in the middle of nowhere – miles away from school or any girls my age. It smelled of Mum's home-made bread on a Saturday morning, linseed oil on the wooden panelling, and Dad's cigars. It smelled of home, because that's what it was. It may not have been flesh and blood, but it had a living, beating heart. One that resonated with mine.

Once, I asked Dad why they sold the cottage after he'd spent so much time doing it up with his own two hands. 'I did love that place,' Dad had admitted. 'But to be honest, when we knew you'd be leaving to go to uni, there didn't seem any point to staying there. It wouldn't have been the same without you.'

The living and beating heart of the house.

I take a well-thumbed copy of *Jane Eyre* off the shelf. It's been my favourite book ever since I was a girl. At night, curled up in my little bed under the beams, Jane was like the best friend I didn't have. The book was much more than words on a page – reading it made me feel like I'd breathed her every breath, lived her every moment. And some of her moments – as she falls in love with Rochester – were, in hindsight, the closest I've ever come to finding that one true love that every girl dreams about.

I turn on my reading light and get into my bed. The book falls open to one of my favourite passages – where Jane meets Mr Rochester on the moor:

> 'You live just below—do you mean at that house with the battlements?' pointing to Thornfield Hall, on which the moon cast a hoary gleam, bringing it out distinct and pale from the woods that, by contrast with the western sky, now seemed one mass of shadow.

I read a little more, then close the book, and turn off the light. 'Rosemont Hall,' I whisper into the darkness. *Rosemont Hall.*

Letter 2 (Transcription) (unsigned)

Rosemont Hall
May 8ᵗʰ 1952

Dearest A

  My exams have finished and I arrived home last night. When can I see you? Will you meet me tomorrow night in our old place? I have so much to tell you.

  I'm sorry to say that my father is much changed for the worse. When I came into the house, he was wandering through the halls, staring at the blank spaces on the walls; mumbling to the absent ghosts. At first, I thought he hadn't seen me. But then, he spoke. 'I've put things in motion,' he said. 'It's time you made something of yourself.' I recognised that cold gleam in his eye. Whatever he's planning, I want no part in it.

  I also know that if I am ever to 'make something of myself', I need you by my side. It's time that we talked of our future, my love. My dream is for our children to chase each other through the corridors of this old house, to slide down the banisters, and play hide-and-seek in the secret rooms behind the panelling! And even if the roof leaks, and the plaster cracks, and the paint peels, we will be happy here. Together we will fill this sad place with laughter once again.

Five

On Monday morning I get up early and drive to Bath. I'm armed for my day at the office with: a packed lunch (chicken sandwich and Mum's home-baked banana bread), my 'Reader, I married him' mug that I bought at Portobello market, a brand-new No.7 lipstick, and just in case any more babies need birthing, an extra jacket with all the buttons intact. I'm wearing the best specimens of my limited 'office' wardrobe: a primly cut black skirt, pink twinset with pearl buttons, black patent courts, and my favourite rose-coloured pashmina.

The office is located in a Georgian parade not far from the Pump Rooms. The car park is mostly empty (secretly, I was hoping to be issued a Mini Cooper with a racing stripe like the estate agent drove in London). The back door is locked, and no one answers when I knock. I find a narrow alleyway that leads to the main street, and walk along admiring the lovely golden Bath stone bathed in winter sunlight. I grab a skinny pumpkin spice muffin from Starbucks and go into the office through the front door.

The other three estate agents are already at their desks. Everyone instantly sparks to life, and then fizzles when they see that it's only me. Mr Bowen-Knowles's door is shut, but I can hear his voice through the door. In a way, I'm relieved. I need to tell him about the call I took on Friday afternoon, but I'm hoping to galvanise myself with a coffee first.

Feigning a confidence I don't feel, I go to my desk, plunk

down my bag, and greet Claire sitting opposite with a warm 'Hi, how was your weekend?'

At first she looks puzzled by my friendly manner, but quickly smiles back. 'It was good,' she says. 'It was my son's birthday.'

'Lovely,' I say. 'How old is he?'

'Twelve.'

Twelve! It always amazes me when someone who looks about my age has a twelve-year-old child. I'd never even *thought* about having children until things broke down with Simon, and even then, I can't swear with hand on heart that it was my biggest regret about losing my boyfriend.

Claire looks at me like she's expecting a response.

'Oh,' is all I can manage. 'And is there any word about Sally and the baby?' I quickly change tack.

Claire shrugs. 'Fine as far as I know.'

'That's good.' I give a little laugh. 'It was quite an eye-opener for my first day—'

Mr Bowen-Knowles chooses that moment to come out of his office and yell for some coffee. Or that might have been his original reason for bursting onto the main floor, but as soon as he sees me, his face morphs into something reptilian. He gestures curtly for me to go to his office. I stand up, tuck my hair behind my ears, and get ready to march to the gallows. He sits down at his desk and steeples his fingers, and I know I must be in trouble because his close-set eyes never leave my face.

'I understand you took a phone call on Friday afternoon,' he says.

'Yes, that's right,' I say brightly. 'It's a Georgian mansion – sounds like something really special. The solicitor wants a valuation this afternoon. At 3 o'clock. I said I thought that would be okay.'

He scratches his head, fiddles with the clasp on his cufflink, leans forward, and glares at me. 'Just when were you going to tell someone about this? Or did you think you'd just go there on your own and pull some valuation out of your pert little arse?'

I bite my tongue. Hard. I force myself to stare back at him pleasantly. 'I was just about to come and tell you. It's like you read my mind.'

He takes out his BlackBerry and looks at the screen.

'Be ready to go at half two,' he says.

'You mean...? Yes, of course,' I manage. Before he can change his mind, I excuse myself and close the door of his office behind me.

Back at my desk, I can't stop beaming.

'What's up?' Claire asks, looking somewhat concerned.

'It was about that probate call I took on Friday.' I say. 'Mr Bowen-Knowles is going today to value the property, and he's agreed to let me tag along for the experience.' I give a little laugh. 'I was worried that he would say no.'

Out of the corner of my eye, I see Patricia and Jonathan exchange knowing looks. Claire raises her eyebrows, but says nothing.

'What? Did I say something wrong?'

Jonathan smirks behind his hand, looking like a guilty public-school boy who's made a mess of the toilet on Parents' Day. Ignoring him, I focus on Claire. She doesn't seem that tight with the rest of them, but clearly I haven't won her over yet.

'Are you married, Amy?' she asks.

'No. Why?'

'Umm, no reason.'

It's obvious that there *is* a reason, but that no one wants to tell me. So that's how they want to play it, then? Fine. Without another word, I grab my mug and go off to the kitchen. I lean against the sink, my fists clenched. 'Temporary,' I mouth to myself. 'This job is just temporary.'

A moment later, Claire joins me. She takes one look at me, and puts a finger to her lips. 'The walls have ears,' she whispers.

'Not to mention gaping gobs. But some night after work, maybe we can go to the pub. I'll fill you in on the gory details.'

'Okay.' My anger ebbs. 'Let's do it.'

It's as if we've silently made a pact over our cups of luke-warm, bitter coffee. I return to my desk and log onto the computer, pleased that I actually have a few emails (a system-generated welcome message and some spam). I still have no work, but that seems, at most, a technicality. Instead, I google Rosemont Hall. I know it's not exactly trawling the archives of the British Library, but still, it feels good to be doing some 'research'.

The first entry I find is on a website about 'England's Heritage at Risk'. According to the site, hundreds of country houses fell to ruin after the war and were demolished prior to the 1970s. Of the ones that are left, thousands are at risk of becoming derelict or are already in ruins. One of them is Rosemont Hall. There's a brief article that I read through carefully.

The house was originally built in 1765, and is considered one of the finest examples of Georgian Palladian-style architecture in the South West. The original owner made his money in the slave trade. He lost the house in a game of whist to a small-time gambler called William Windham. Windham became a Lord, and commissioned his own family crest – a dog and unicorn – symbolising fidelity and virtue.

The house was passed down in the Windham family for generations. In the twentieth century, the most illustrious owner was Sir George Windham, a war hero who made a name for himself as an art dealer and collector. The house fell into disrepair after World War II, and Sir George was forced to sell off his art collection to pay for repairs. The East Wing of the house burned down in the early 1950s and Sir George died soon afterwards. The house was passed to his son, Henry Windham. The family fortunes diminished, the East Wing was never rebuilt, and the house slid into further decline.

The more I read, the more the images of the house and its past begin to take shape in my mind. Slave traders, gamblers, war heroes – straight from the pages of a romantic novel. And the unmentioned women who were no doubt there too – somehow they all found a home at Rosemont Hall. What lives and loves has it witnessed, what secrets have its walls overheard? The final line of the article gives me goosebumps: 'Now in a perilous state, this important house has an uncertain future.'

I sit back in my chair and consider things with new clarity. Last week, my getting this job was all about earning money to afford my own flat. But now, suddenly, an important and imperilled piece of history is about to be placed in my care. How well I do my job will influence its fate – maybe even its continued existence. *If* I can convince Mr Bowen-Knowles to put me in charge.

I jot down the key details about the house so that I can trot them out later for Mr Kendall, the solicitor. I lose myself in the work, concentrating so hard that I completely fail to notice the long shadow of Mr Bowen-Knowles frowning over my desk.

'It's almost half two,' he announces. 'You coming?'

'What? Now?' I quickly close my notebook. 'I mean, yes, I'm ready.' Everyone in the office watches as I find the address details. Mr Bowen-Knowles checks his watch with an irritated sigh, then heads out the door. I grab my coat and handbag and mouth a quick goodbye to Claire. She wishes me luck, then turns away to chat with the rest of them now that the boss (and/or the new girl) is leaving.

In the car park, Mr Bowen-Knowles points to a gunmetal-grey BMW. I hesitate. 'Maybe I can follow behind you,' I suggest. 'The house is on my way home, actually.'

'Where's your car?' he asks coldly. I point to the slightly battered Vauxhall Corsa that I picked up at Car Giant before I left London.

Mr Bowen-Knowles snorts. 'I don't want that thing within two miles of any of our clients, do you understand? Get in.' He pings open the automatic locks. I get in the passenger side with my head hung low. I picture him making another mental tick against me: wrong accent, wrong car, wrong – everything. But I *will* persevere.

I sit in silence as my boss punches the address into his satnav. We pull out of the car park with *Talk Sport* blaring on the radio. I try to think of something intelligent to say about whatever the current caller – 'Jim from Newcastle' – is banging on about: a referee's decision not to give Newcastle a penalty against Arsenal...

Arsenal. Simon's team. As we drive on in awkward silence, a cloud of sadness engulfs me.

He switches off the radio. 'Check under the seat, will you?' he says. 'I've got a printout of local prices in here somewhere.'

'Okay, sure.' I dig under the seat and pull out a stack of papers. I flip through them, hoping that in the half-hour or so before we arrive at our destination, he'll explain to me all the tricks of the trade.

Tricks of the trade.

Silly me.

I discard a few old property brochures and a printed Google map. Underneath the map, in all its glory, is yesterday's *Sun* folded open to the page 3 girl. I stare at the assets of Amanda, age 18, from Huddersfield (enjoys diving, candlelit dinners, and netball) who is gracing the page, and see out of the corner of my eye that Mr Bowen-Knowles is looking right at me. He meant for me to find it!

He grins wolfishly and switches the radio back on. 'Never mind – maybe it's in the boot. And by the way, when we get to the house, just stand there and look pretty – I'll do the talking.'

'You have reached your destination,' the electronic voice drones. I forget all about my infuriating boss as we turn off the main road and head through a pair of ancient stone pillars each with a weathered urn on top. Twisted wrought-iron gates sag under their own weight, half-hidden by twining blackberry thorns and nettles.

A sense of anticipation expands inside my chest as we make our way up the curving drive, flanked by a thick woodland of beech, silver birch, and the odd giant rhododendron. Flame-coloured leaves swirl in the air and settle onto the road. Eventually, the trees thin out to rolling fields dotted with sheep.

The car tops a little hill and suddenly, it's there before us – Rosemont Hall. It stands four stories tall, with a main section and two symmetrical wings on either side. The centre section is made of red brick and cream stone, and graced by Palladian-style pilasters. At the pinnacle of the roof, a huge round window stares out at the parkland and the surrounding countryside like an ever-vigilant eye.

And the moment I see it, I experience a powerful sensation almost like déjà vu. My pulse amplifies in my chest.

'What a dump,' my boss says. He points to the right side of the house. 'Looks like it's about to collapse.'

I bite my tongue and look where he's pointing. The wing on the right is a total ruin. Huge burned timbers cut across the sky and there are weeds growing along the top of the remnants of the wall. The bricks are smoke-stained around the empty window frames, and streaks of damp darken the wall like tears. It looks so sad, and yet also, hopelessly romantic; standing silent and stalwart against the ravages of time, neglect, and the English climate.

The drive curves around a circular forecourt, and a sweeping set of stone stairs leads up to the front door. We park next to a decrepit stone fountain in which algae-covered nymphs frolic in a trickle of water. I jump out of the car, craning my neck to take in the full height of the house. Above me, the stone lintels and window cornices are cracked and decayed, and mortar is crumbling between the stone quoins and bricks. I snap a few quick photographs on my mobile. Visions creep into my mind about how it must have looked in its heyday: armies of servants in prim black and white lining up to greet the master on his return home from a hunt; ladies sweeping out of a carriage in their dresses of silk, taffeta and velvet purchased on a shopping trip to Mayfair; the gravel drive neatly raked; the hedges trimmed in fantastical shapes in the formal gardens, the fountain clear and bubbling, the imposing front door black and glossy with fresh paint.

A drop of water falls on my nose, and the vision evaporates. Water is trickling down from a carved stone pediment above the door. I can just make out the family crest – a dog and a unicorn – fidelity and virtue. It's so cracked and weathered that I fear it might topple down on us.

I may be new to the job, but even I can tell that Rosemont Hall is in peril.

The weak yellow sun goes behind a cloud, leaving the face of the house in shadow. Another car – a blue BMW – is coming up the drive. As it parks next to its grey twin, Mr Bowen-Knowles stands at the ready with a small spiral notebook in hand.

'Must be Mr Kendall,' I state the obvious.

'Remember what I said.' His grin is disturbing like he's having a flashback to the newspaper under the seat. But I can't worry about that now. I'm completely focused on the house and the task at hand. The newcomer gets out of the car. He's mid-fifties, with greying hair and a kindly, almost grandfatherly face. He looks smart in a grey suit, blue tie, and grey woollen overcoat.

'Mr Kendall, I presume?' Mr Bowen-Knowles instantly smarms all over him. 'I'm Alistair Bowen-Knowles – please call me Alistair.' He holds out his hand sheepishly, like they should be greeting each other with a Bullingdon Club secret handshake instead of meeting like complete strangers. 'Such an amazing place. Such history! It'll be such a pleasure to work with you on this err... project.' He twists his right cufflink.

'Yes... uhh... Mr Alistair, pleased to meet you. I'm Ian Kendall.' He looks awkwardly at me as they shake hands.

'Hello,' I say, stepping forward. 'I'm Amy Wood. We spoke on the phone.'

'Nice to meet you.' He shakes my hand firmly and gestures towards the house. 'Shall we go inside?'

We follow him up the steps to the front door. Mr Kendall takes out an ancient bundle of keys that looks like they might unlock the Bastille. It takes several tries before one turns in the corroded lock.

We step inside into a vestibule that opens onto an enormous main hall. I'm vaguely aware of my boss making the appropriate noises of appreciation – whereas I'm genuinely awestruck. The double-height hall is gracefully oval-shaped, with a chequerboard floor of grey and white marble. Faux Ionic columns and empty statuary niches adorn the cool white marble walls. The ceiling is decorative plaster with a painting in the middle depicting various *in flagrante* Greek gods and goddesses.

At the back of the hall, a staircase sweeps upwards and divides, creating two symmetrical galleries that overlook the main hall. Huge latticed windows trap the sunlight.

But just like on the outside, neglect and decay have taken residence everywhere. Spots of damp mottle the ceiling; wide cracks gape in the walls and floor. The cavernous room is freezing, and silently devoid of life. Its heart has stopped, or at least, needs a major kick-start.

'The house has been in the Windham family for six generations,' Mr Kendall explains as we walk through a suite of rooms off the hall. 'The last of the Windhams – Henry and his wife Arabella – were married for almost forty years. Henry died over a decade ago. Arabella passed on two weeks ago.'

'That explains it then,' Mr Bowen-Knowles smirks, gesturing at the mounds of clutter, lattice of cobwebs and threadbare furniture. 'We see it a lot. A lifetime's worth of stuff that no one wants and no one knows what to do with.'

'It's like a time warp,' I say, rapt with fascination. The rooms we go through are faded but elegant: the green salon, the library, the yellow dining room. 'The Windhams must have been very happy here.'

Mr Kendall smiles faintly. 'Perhaps. Though, they never did have any children. The heirs – Mr Jack and Ms Flora – are distant relatives. They're American.'

'It must have been amazing for them to inherit a spectacular English country house,' I say.

Mr Kendall shakes his head. 'Neither of them has ever visited the house. And they aren't planning to. They're very keen to sell as quickly as possible.'

'Then you've come to the right place,' my boss chimes in.

I shake my head, astounded. Why wouldn't the heirs even want to see the house that they'd inherited? To be handed Rosemont Hall on a silver platter would be a dream come true for someone like me – and a lot of other people, I'm sure.

We continue on our tour. The flotsam and jetsam of decades of married life is visible everywhere: dusty books and old magazines, vases filled with dead flowers, worn sofas, and time-darkened photographs. I feel a pang of nostalgia for the life I thought I had with Simon, and sad that I no longer have anyone to amass this kind of history with. But more than that, I'm angry – on behalf of the deceased owners whose heirs won't even come and see the house where they lived.

There are also a few gems scattered among the clutter: some lovely antique tables; a collection of Sevres china and glassware in an ornate floor-to-ceiling cabinet; gilded mirrors in all shapes and sizes. But something seems to be missing and I can't put my finger on it.

'Do the heirs want anything,' my boss asks, or 'would you like us to just get a removal van to clean out all this *junk*.'

The word echoes around the room. Mr Kendall raises his eyebrows.

'The Windham's *belongings* will need to stay here for now,' he says. 'There's an elderly housekeeper – Mrs Maryanne Bradford – who was devoted to the house and nursed Mrs Windham through her last illness. In the last year before Mrs Windham died, she was staying in one of the rooms on the third floor. Some of the things here may be hers.'

'Fine,' Mr Bowen-Knowles says. 'A developer won't care if there's a little clutter.'

'What's going to happen to her?' I say.

Both men look at me.

'Mrs Bradford. Where will she go when the house is sold?'

'She'll need to move out, of course,' Mr Kendall says. 'There's no reason for her to stay.'

'Oh. What a shame.' I feel pang of sadness for the old woman. I read somewhere that having to move house is a major cause of stress and premature death in the elderly.

'Her sister has a cottage in the village,' Mr Kendall assures me. 'She won't have any trouble relocating.'

My boss's forehead cracks into a frown. He moves in front of me like a rook threatening a pawn. 'Let's see the rest of the house, shall we?'

Mr Kendall leads the way up the grand staircase. I feel like Scarlett O'Hara as I trail my hand over the cool marble banister. At the top landing where the staircase divides, I stop. In the centre of the wall is an exquisite, life-sized oil painting of a young woman of about seventeen or eighteen. The background is a blend of murky blacks and greys, and her form emerges like an apparition. Her dark blonde hair is elaborately swept up and tied with ribbons, a few curls cascading around her neck. The bodice of her dress is pale-pink silk with a hint of lace at the neckline. The fabric sweeps out from her waist in shadowy folds, catching the light, and fading back into the blackness. But the most striking thing is the woman herself. Her eyes are bold and arresting, painted the delicate blue colour of forget-me-nots. Her features are soft, with high cheekbones and a delicately shaped nose. Her bow-shaped mouth is drawn up in a half-smile, like she has a secret.

'What a lovely woman,' I say, as Mr Kendall pauses next to me. 'Who is she, do you know?'

'No.' Mr Kendall pauses briefly. 'Though I've often wondered.'

I stare closer at the painting. It's set in a heavily gilded frame that protrudes from the wall a good six inches. There's a brass plaque at the bottom with the date etched in black: 1899. But there's no name, and doesn't appear to be a signature by the artist.

Mr Bowen-Knowles taps his foot impatiently and I have to move on. I follow Mr Kendall through a series of interconnecting rooms – bedrooms, bathrooms, dressing rooms, sitting rooms – on the first and second floors. The rooms all smell of damp, there are bits of flaked-off paint and plaster on the floor, and some of the windows are literally rotting out of their frames. The walls are covered with mildew-spotted wallpaper in garish colours and patterns – and then I realise the thing that's missing throughout the house. Other than the portrait of the young woman in the pink dress, there is practically no artwork anywhere. There are no smoke-darkened portraits of fated ancestors, views of Venice or caricatures of favourite horses or hunting dogs. The only pictures are a few twee landscape prints in a style fit to grace the front window of a charity shop.

The next floor up consists of a long corridor of small rooms – the servants' quarters. The corridor ends abruptly at a white wooden door. I walk towards it, sniffing the air. Instead of the musty damp of the rest of the house, I smell baking.

'That's Mrs Bradford's room,' Mr Kendall says. 'There's a little kitchenette in there.'

I move closer. Cinnamon, ginger... she must be making biscuits, or maybe scones. My stomach gives an almighty rumble. It seems so sad that an old lady who was a loyal employee and who bakes nice things will have to be turfed out. And if we get the instruction to sell the house, then part of my job will be to make sure it happens.

'Whatever she's baking smells delicious.' I say.

Mr Kendall stops me going any nearer to the door with a hand on my arm. 'Let's not disturb her,' he says.

'Oh, of course not.'

We climb yet another staircase that leads to the top of the house, and a huge attic with an oak-beamed ceiling. The space is partially filled with boxes and old furniture, but just below the huge round window, there's an area that was obviously once used as an artist's studio. Two easels are set up near a rack of canvases covered with cobwebs. There's a wooden box of well-used paint tubes, a dried palette of oils, and a wine glass with a dusty residue in the bottom. I can almost smell the ghostly vapours of turpentine; feel the presence of an unknown artist who might return at any second to resume his work.

'I understand that the father – Sir George – was an art collector, was he not?' I run my finger over a stack of old gilded frames, sending up a shimmering shower of dust motes.

'Yes,' Mr Kendall confirms. 'That's right.'

'But there doesn't seem to be much art around – other than the portrait on the stairs.'

Mr Kendall stares out of the oriel window at the acres of parkland below. 'I don't know much about it, but I believe that after the war most of Sir George Windham's collection was sold off to pay for repairs to the house. A few paintings were kept, including a Rembrandt. But that was destroyed when the East Wing caught fire.'

'A Rembrandt was destroyed?' I say. 'That's tragic.'

'Yes,' Mr Kendall agrees. 'It is.'

He seems about to say more, but just then, Mr Bowen-Knowles flashes me another look. I press my lips shut. It's not just Mr Kendall that I have to win over, but my boss too.

'So Ian,' he says in a keen-to-get-down-to-business voice, 'based on what I see, there's a lot of potential here – for the right developer and...' he clears his throat, 'at the right price.'

We head back down a secondary servants' staircase.

'And what, in your professional opinion, would that be?' Mr Kendall asks.

'Well, since the heirs want a quick sale, they could auction it. They might find a buyer, but it's unlikely to get them "top-dollar", so to speak.'

'And what will?'

'Finding the *right* buyer,' Mr Bowen-Knowles says smugly. 'Someone with the cash and wherewithal to jump through the planning and listed building hoops to develop it.' He rubs his chin. 'I'm thinking top-end luxury flats. Swimming pool complex, spa, the works. I saw some outbuildings as we came in – a stables and what-not. Perfect for conversion.'

'Flats!' I blurt out. 'But that would be awful.'

Mr Bowen-Knowles glares at me. This time, I ignore him.

'Surely it should be a family home, with people to love it,' I say. 'That's what it was intended to be. Or else restore it and open it up to the public. And also, we need to make sure that Mrs Bradford isn't displaced too abruptly.'

'Amy...' Mr Bowen-Knowles's voice holds a 'one more word and you're sacked' warning in it.

'I'm sorry,' I say. 'It just seems a shame. There's so much history here. Shouldn't it be preserved?'

Mr Kendall gives me a kindly smile. 'I've been solicitor to the Windham family for years, and yes, you're right, Henry Windham would have wanted the house to be preserved in its original state. But unfortunately, there's no money in the estate for that. And Mrs Bradford will be fine. My job is to sell the house and obtain the highest price possible for Mr Jack and Ms Flora.' He kicks at a cracked stone with the toe of his polished shoe. 'And flats... well... yes, if you can find someone to do a conversion, it would be a good result.' He looks up at me. 'The alternative might be even worse.'

'How?' I challenge.

'There's a rumour going around that a big American developer called Hexagon is buying up land around here for a golf course and recreation complex. "Golf Heritage" they call it – there's one near Minehead.'

'Ah,' Mr Bowen-Knowles says, like he's sorry he didn't think of that.

'There's lots of local support around her for more recreation facilities,' Mr Kendall adds.

I shake my head, picturing this amazing, special house with checked-trouser-clad golfers clomping through it, a pro-shop just off the main hall. Sprinklers watering the lawn and golf buggies zipping over hill and dale. A huge car park out front; a floodlit driving range at the side. Simon and Ashley coming here for a long weekend of Pimm's on the terrace, canoodles on the eighteenth green, 'his and her' massages in the spa. 'Golf Heritage': a historical tragedy.

'What about the National Trust or English Heritage?' I challenge. 'Surely, they must have some say in what happens?'

Mr Kendall shrugs. 'There are lots of derelict old piles around and nowhere near enough money to fix them all. Hexagon can't demolish the place if that's what you're worried about.' He sighs. 'But I'm afraid that they don't have the best reputation for conservation.'

'Really, in what way—?'

Mr Bowen-Knowles holds up his hand to cut me off. 'Has Hexagon made an offer?' he asks.

'Not officially. They threw out a figure, but frankly, it was nowhere near what the heirs were expecting. I told them as much.'

Mr Bowen-Knowles laughs. 'It's an old trick,' he says. 'Force them to auction it and Hexagon will pick it up for a song. Unless, *we* can find you a buyer.'

'And can you?'

Mr Bowen-Knowles nods. 'Having come here today,' he says, 'I'm confident that *Tetherington Bowen Knowles* can achieve the best possible price for the property. In fact, I've got a list of developers who might be interested in viewing it.' He grins smugly. 'And even if we don't find a buyer, our marketing should at least get Hexagon to up their offer.'

'Well, that's good news,' Mr Kendall says, his voice flat. 'For the heirs at least.'

I walk over to one of the tall French windows that looks out onto the back of the house. In the distance, an ornamental lake shimmers in the fading light and a small summerhouse in the style of a Grecian temple glows like a jewel. The gardens are overgrown, but I'm sure they must have been magical in their day. Just like everything else here. Everything that is about to be lost for good.

I follow my boss and Mr Kendall back into the main hall. Mr Kendall points to a door on the wall opposite. 'There's a corridor through there that leads to the East Wing,' he says. 'There isn't much there. It was gutted by the fire.'

'How did the fire start?' I ask.

Mr Kendall shifts on his feet. 'There was an investigation at the time involving a servant, but nothing was ever proved conclusively.'

'But it was an accident?'

'I believe in the end it was an open verdict.'

'Oh.' The English literature teacher in me claws her way to the surface. In *Jane Eyre*, the fire at Thornfield was started by the 'mad woman in the attic' – the first Mrs Rochester. She ended up being killed in the fire, and Mr Rochester lost his eyesight. And then there's the sinister house called Manderley in *Rebecca*. The fire there was started by the psychotic housekeeper Mrs Danvers after she learnt how Rebecca really died. And now, it seems that there's some mystery here involving how nearly half of the house was burned to the ground. I can't help feeling intrigued. 'Can we have a look at the East Wing?' I say.

Mr Bowen-Knowles steps in front of me as if he's trying to hide me like a divan under a dust sheet. 'I think we've seen enough for today,' he says through his teeth. 'The site clearly has huge development potential that we can start marketing right away. I'd like to thank you once again, Mr Kendall, for thinking of *Tetherington Bowen Knowles*.'

'Fine.' Mr Kendall says. He avoids meeting my eyes. 'Provided your commission arrangements are satisfactory, I think we can consider it settled. You can be sole agents for three months. That's all I can guarantee you. If you haven't succeeded in that time, it will either go to Hexagon, or to auction.'

Three months. An imaginary clock shaped like Cinderella's slipper begins to tick inside my head. Three months to find a buyer who will preserve and restore Rosemont Hall. Three months to save it. Can I possibly do it?

While the two of them continue to discuss the details, I gravitate back up the main staircase until I'm standing before the portrait of the girl in the pink dress. From her vantage point above the vast marble hall, surveying her ruined domain, she looks almost lonely. I wonder if in life she was happy – if she was thinking of someone special when she smiled that secret smile. Did she live at Rosemont Hall; find love here? In her hands she's clutching something yellowish in colour, indicated with thick brushstrokes. Some kind of paper, or letters maybe? When I first started going out with Simon, he used to leave me copies of Victorian valentine poems on my pillow, and later on, send me funny little texts to let me know he was thinking of me. If we'd been born in a different era, would things between Simon and me have worked out? There's a sharp pang in my chest as I recall the hurt he caused me; the humiliation. I hope the girl in the pink dress was luckier in love than I was.

'Amy.' Mr Bowen-Knowles's voice jars me back to reality.

'Goodbye,' I mutter to the girl in the portrait and rush down the stairs.

I join the two men. 'Hi, sorry,' I say. 'I was just having another quick look around for the viewings—'

Mr Bowen-Knowles holds up his hand to silence me. 'So as I was saying, Ian, I'll assign my most senior agent, Jonathan Park-Spencer, to handle the marketing *and* the viewings.'

The air goes flat in my lungs. There's no way that Jonathan could ever do justice to this place. I speak up, but my voice sounds small: 'I was hoping that… maybe…'

Mr Kendall's eyes meet mine for an instant. He turns to my boss. 'Now that I've met Ms Wood, I'd like to continue to deal with her.'

I wait for the *but unfortunately, my duty is to the estate*—

'She seems very competent and enthusiastic about the house.'

'Yes, but—' my boss interjects.

'Therefore, I'd like her to be the principal contact – at least while you have the exclusive listing.'

There's a long moment as Mr Bowen-Knowles looks at me like he's hoping the earth will swallow me up. I stand up a little straighter trying to look 'competent and enthusiastic' until the stand-off ends. Finally, Mr Bowen-Knowles lets out a long sigh, his brow withered like a prune. 'Of course,' he says to Mr Kendall. 'Whatever you like.'

My heart leaps in my chest. For a second, I imagine that I feel the atmosphere inside the house shift with a tiny flicker of life. 'Thank you, Mr Kendall.' I say in my most businesslike manner. 'I won't let you down.'

The three of us leave the house and Mr Kendall locks up. A satisfied warmth creeps across my cheeks as he hands me the set of keys. I've succeeded – for now.

I'll be coming back again.

III

Letter 3 (Reply to Letter 2?)

June 2nd (1952)? (hand delivery)

H

    I am delighted that you are home at last, and I am counting the hours until tonight when I will see you again! The months we've been apart have seemed endless. How I long to see your face and feel your fingers on my skin. Because as much as I cherish your letters, when I lay awake alone at night, my mind is full of whispers and doubts. Until you have told your father about us, as you say you will, how can I allow myself to hope?

Seven

Over the next few days I get caught up in a rush of activities around the office. Mr Bowen-Knowles and I seem to have reached an unspoken agreement that my presence is in fact required. I settle into the rhythm of answering phones, typing emails and letters, responding to web enquiries, and springing to life like a puppet whenever prospective clients come in. In the back of the stationery cupboard I find a box of Christmas baubles (in an antique gold colour that looks remarkably like beige) and I use them to trim a little fake tree in the waiting area. The white lights twinkle on and off in my peripheral vision, bringing a tiny bit of cheer to the shortening days.

Despite all my efforts, I still feel a pang of dread each time my boss emerges from his office. When he looks at me, his nose wrinkles like he's tasted something foul, and I sense he's still annoyed that I convinced Mr Kendall to let me take the lead on Rosemont Hall. Not that any more has been said on *that* subject...

I try smiling, then frowning, then ignoring him like the others do. The latter works best – the second time I don't look up when he comes out of his office, he comes over to my desk and instructs me to prepare the particulars for Rosemont Hall. I'm thrilled! I stay late three nights in a row wading through the material Mr Kendall provided on the house, plus seeing what else I can find out about Rosemont Hall and the Windham Family. I can't find much on the slave trader or the gambler, but I have more luck with the modern generation. It's not too difficult to find Arabella Windham's recent obituary in the online archives of the local newspaper. Like a typical old lady, she belonged to the local church and the gardening club. It confirms that she was married to Henry Windham, deceased, and that they had no children. I recall Mr Kendall saying that the American heirs are distant relatives.

Henry Windham's obit from a decade earlier is harder to find, and even briefer than his wife's. It mentions only that he spent time at Eton and Oxford, and refers to his wife, Arabella, his father, Sir George, and the estate that he inherited. I'm forced to conclude that he was a typical young man of privilege, living off whatever family fortunes remained without contributing to anyone or anything.

More interesting, however, is Sir George Windham. I find a short Wikipedia entry on him. He was born in 1900 and attended Eton and Oxford like his father before him and his son after him. He began collecting art in his twenties, and by the time he was thirty, he had amassed a number of valuable paintings. Then, like many idealistic (and wealthy) young Englishmen, in the 1930s he sought adventure by joining the International Brigades to fight the Fascists in the Spanish Civil War. He won a medal for his troubles. During World War II, the house was requisitioned by the RAF, who left it in a miserable state. Topping it all off, a series of bad investments decimated the family fortunes. Sir George died in 1955.

I study the photographs that are embedded into the article. There's a small photograph of a young man with a bold, aristocratic nose that I assume is Sir George as a young man. There's also an architectural drawing of the outside of Rosemont Hall as it must have been when built – its two graceful wings intact and perfectly symmetrical. The final one is a dark, black and white photo of the inside of the great hall, dated 1939. Unlike the house as it is today, in the photo the pale grey walls are covered with paintings. An accompanying caption describes the famous Rosemont Hall art collection, which included several Gainsboroughs, a Caravaggio, and most notably, a Rembrandt called 'Orientale'. I study the photograph, looking for the girl in the pink dress, but I don't see her. I wonder how she alone escaped the fate of the others – the auctioneer's gavel in the late 1940s, or the fire in the East Wing that destroyed the Rembrandt. Once again, I wonder who she was.

I make a note of all my findings so that I can write up a few pages on the history of the house for the particulars. It's exciting to play historical detective. I only wish that I had time to do some real research at a library, not just higgledy-piggledy on the internet. But time is not on my side. I glance over at Cinderella's clock on my desk as the little silver hands move on relentlessly. As I begin writing the particulars, I remember my first sight of Rosemont Hall – its grand silhouette stark and lonely against a grey sky – and I feel a strong sense of responsibility. The house is an important piece of English history that has kept its identity for hundreds of years. It doesn't take a card-carrying National Trust member to realise that such things are worth preserving.

While my research is on track, the other aspects of my marketing campaign get off to a bad start. On the morning of the fourth day after the viewing, I hand Mr Bowen-Knowles the draft text I've composed – 'Historic family home in need of TLC'. He frowns down his nose at me, closets himself in his office for two hours, and finally emerges. He slaps the two pages I've written about the history of the house and the Windham family down on my desk. They're entirely struck out in red pen. He's written instead a heading that says: 'Outstanding green-belt development opportunity for flexible accommodation and commercial recreation facilities'.

'Flexible accommodation?' I say, feeling a strong sense of dread.

'Flats,' he replies with a sniff. 'We're marketing the future potential here, not some crumbling wreck of the past. I want to see a bullet-point list – the 120 acres, a list of the outbuildings that could be developed, the number of en-suite bedrooms that could be converted into apartments, square footage – numbers, not fluff. And what about the photographs, are they back yet? We've got a tight deadline here and need to get this to the printers ASAP. Plus, it needs to be on Rightmove, Primelocation, Zoopla, Country Life and—'

I stare up at him with dismay. It probably should have been obvious, but I didn't realise that I was supposed to arrange the photographs and all those other things. Now I've wasted almost a week of my three months. Tick tock.

'I'm sorry...' my voice catches. 'I didn't know.' Desperate to avoid the sack, I hand him my mobile phone with the pictures I'd taken of the facade. 'I took these,' I say.

The silence seems to last a lifetime. He stares at the photos, flicking back and forth between them with his thumb.

'That one will do.' He hands me back the phone. 'No point printing photos of the inside. The place is a tip. I'll talk to the quantity surveyor about going round...'

I copiously write down all of his instructions. When he finally stops hovering and returns to his office, I let out a long breath.

'Don't worry,' Claire says from across the desk. 'No one gets it right the first time. I'll show you how to upload the particulars onto the websites.'

'Thanks.' I smile gratefully.

'Let's see the photographs, then.'

I hand her the phone. 'Wow.' she says, 'Impressive pile. Haven't seen one of these on the market for a while.'

Jonathan meanders over to Claire's desk. I'm petrified that he'll gazump my first exciting project right from under my nose. Claire shows him the photo.

'Hmm,' Jonathan says with a condescending grin. 'Hope you're not planning your retirement. Looks like a "sticker" to me.'

'A "sticker"?'

'As in, a property that sticks. Your tits will sag to your waist before you sell it.' He laughs at his own vile joke, then swivels his chair around and makes a call on his mobile.

Claire shakes her head and hands me back my phone. 'Don't mind him,' she says. 'Even if it doesn't sell, you might get some good experience showing it. If you're not busy after work, let's go the pub and I'll give you some survival tips.'

'Oh yes.' I say immediately. 'I'd appreciate that.'

*

When the day ends, I've officially made it through my first full week. I'm exhausted from the effort, but luckily, everyone including Claire, shuts down their computer at half four. I rinse out my mug in the kitchen and put it in the cupboard (moving it carefully away from the one that says: 'I'd rather be ... GOLFING'). Jonathan breezes by me on his way out the door without so much as a nod or a wave goodbye, and Patricia does the same. When I return to my desk, Claire has her make-up bag out.

'You ready?' She puckers her lips at the compact mirror.

'Yes, just give me two secs to—'

Mr Bowen-Knowles's door bangs open. He stands at the threshold of his office, radiating the familiar frown. 'Where's Jonathan?' He checks his watch.

'I think he's gone for the day,' I answer. Claire nods as she applies face powder.

'Gone for the...? Well shit.' He glares at me like I'm the one who's buggered off without permission. 'A couple just called – the Blundells. They want to see that new penthouse apartment in Bristol Docks tomorrow. Eleven o'clock. Jonathan was dealing with them.'

I look over at Claire, expecting her to jump at the chance to usurp Jonathan's clients. Instead, she shrugs. 'I can't do it, Mr Bowen-Knowles – Atul's playing football.'

'Shit!' He pulls out his mobile phone from his pocket. I'm sure he's about to phone Jonathan—

'I'll do it,' I say quickly.

Mr Bowen-Knowles looks at me like I have three heads. 'You?'

'Well, why not?' I challenge. 'You said in my interview that I could do weekend viewings. Bristol's not far from me, and I'm happy to take them around the property.'

'You?'

I wait.

'Sounds like a great idea,' Claire interjects.

'Well...'

He checks his watch again like he's hoping something miraculous will happen in the next ten seconds that will enable him to deny my request to help him out. But since nothing does, he ducks back into his office and returns with a few property brochures, a torn piece of notepaper with the client's name and number, and a set of keys attached to a souvenir wine opener. Reluctantly, he hands everything to me. 'Now, just remember,' he says, 'talk the place up. It's a "stunning, ultra-modern penthouse apartment in a top-quality development".' He glares pointedly. 'Don't say anything – anything at all – that might put them off.'

'Hmmm,' Claire says as she puts away her make-up bag, 'the Bristol Docks penthouse. Bit toppy, that one.'

Mr Bowen-Knowles glares and says nothing.

'Isn't that the one where there's been some break-ins? A local gang or something?' Claire smiles at our boss, revealing a set of perfect white teeth.

'Well, obviously she shouldn't mention that,' he snaps, 'or the fact that the residents are suing the developer for faulty wiring and safety concerns with the lift.'

'Or the old lady downstairs who got an ASBO against the previous owners for watching *Newsnight* too loud?' Claire is obviously enjoying this. 'Or—'

'— the ambulance dispatch next door,' Mr Bowen-Knowles beats her to the punchline. 'In fact, don't volunteer any information at all. Just let them inside and look professional.' He hands me the papers and the keys, and I shove them in my handbag.

'Sure,' I say. 'No problem.' At least I no longer have to look 'pretty'.

*

Outside, I punch the air. In less than two weeks, I've managed to turn the theoretical 'odd weekend viewing' into a real viewing with real clients. Claire, however, seems to have a different interpretation of my success. 'That was a lucky escape,' she says, rolling her eyes. 'The way he's taken to you, I'm surprised he didn't invite himself along to the pub.'

I laugh as we walk, certain that she's joking. 'He really hates me, doesn't he? And I thought all that Cheltenham Ladies College stuff was just for show.'

'Oh no, I'm serious. When I started, he didn't speak to me for over two months. It was three months before he trusted me with showing a property.'

'He must be desperate.' This time, my laugh is a little forced. I remember the 'incident' with the magazine under the seat, but decide not to tell Claire.

'Oh, he's desperate all right.' Claire shakes her head. 'He used to be okay, believe it or not. A regular bloke's bloke, good for the odd laugh and a round down the pub. But two years ago, his wife walked out on him. She found him with Sally in the loo at the Christmas party. Since then, he's been your garden-variety bastard.'

I cringe as the image of Mrs Harvey's niece undressed like the page 3 girl flashes into my head. We arrive at All Bar One and push our way through the crowd to an empty table. Claire continues her rant. 'We all thought he'd go crawling back to his wife. But instead, he bought a Porsche and a swish flat with home cinema, sauna and gym – the works. To hear him talk, he's probably got a round vinyl bed with a fur coverlet and a harem of models popping out from underneath.'

I shake my head. Alistair must be ten years older than Simon, but the mid-life-crisis mentality is the same.

'The only one who's got any time for AB-K is Patricia,' Claire adds. 'She's fancied him for years now. And naturally, she's the only one he's never looked twice at. Anything else female has to put up with the odd roving glance here and there, not to mention the sexist digs.'

'Yes, I've noticed.'

'Well, it's a living,' she says. We sigh in unison.

Claire offers to buy the first round. While I wait for her to return with my glass of Rioja, I look around at the bustling throng of young professionals in suits, most of whom would not have been out of place in London. It's a far cry from the long hair, torn jeans and Che Guevara T-shirt crowd I'd grown used to spending Friday evenings with at the 'Hand and Shears' near the college. Suddenly, I begin to feel lonely. I had lots of friends in London, though most of them were 'couple friends' of Simon and me. When I left him behind, I left them behind too. Should I have given up my entire life just to end up here?

Luckily, Claire comes back quickly with the drinks (making me feel instantly guilty when I note that she's only drinking Coke). We settle easily into conversation. She regales me with more stories of AB-K, Jonathan, and the Ghost of Christmas Parties Past. I ask her about her barrister course and tell her about my time at UCL. I get the next round (Cokes for both of us), and end up telling her about Simon. I tell her about the flat that I went to view that seemed so perfect, and the cruel revelation that it might have really been perfect – for Simon and Ashley, not me.

'And did they end up buying it?'

I rake my fingers through my hair. 'I don't know,' I say. 'Everything happened so quickly.' Solemnly, I reveal my great shame – the thrown mobile phone and getting sacked from my job. I recount how I'd tried to talk to Simon when I went back to the flat in Docklands one last time to collect my things – still hoping against all hope that he would tell me that I'd somehow misinterpreted what I'd seen. He didn't – and I hadn't. He did tell me, however, that that the only reason he'd ever thought of looking at flats was because of the text messages from estate agents that I'd signed him up for.

When I've finished my lament, to my surprise, Claire laughs with unrestrained delight. 'That's a brilliant story!' she says. 'And sounds like it was completely worth it. You're lucky, you know.'

'Lucky?'

'Just think – a new start. New home, new job…'

'Well I don't know. It still feels so unreal.'

Claire launches into an account of her own woes: specifically her husband, who can't understand why she doesn't want to live in Birmingham – in a three-bedroom semi – with his extended family from Goa. 'I only see him on weekends,' she says, a bit sadly. 'Maybe someday when I've made it as a barrister I'll be able to buy one of these trillion-pound properties we're supposed to be shifting every day of the week. An "exclusive executive retreat" – or something. Then we can stick his family in an annexe and Atul will have his dad back.'

'Let's hope so.' I feel bad that her situation seems almost bleaker than mine. But then she launches into an amusing account of Jonathan getting drunk at an 'Estate Agents of the Year' luncheon and hitting on Patricia's (now ex-) boyfriend. As someone who's been 'unlucky in love' (as Mum would say), it would seem that I'm in good company at *Tetherington Bowen Knowles*.

We chat and laugh together for a while longer, until the crowd begins to press around our table. I return to the bar and get us two glasses of tap water. Claire downs hers and checks her watch. 'I'm sorry, Amy, but I've got to shoot off now.'

'No problem. I've got to go too. My parents will be worried.'

She gives me a look – like maybe my situation isn't quite as enviable as earlier portrayed – and I blush. As we leave the bar and head back to the office car park, suddenly I remember the viewing tomorrow.

'Claire,' I say, 'is there any trick to these viewings? Am I really supposed to lie like Mr Bowen-Knowles... uhh... AB-K said?'

'Ninety-nine per cent of viewings are a waste of time,' she says. 'So it doesn't really matter what you say. The property will sell itself – or not. Just be yourself.' We arrive at the cars. She unlocks hers while I'm still digging for my keys. 'See you Monday,' she says with a hurried smile.

As she gets into her car and drives away (I'm still looking for my flipping keys), I smile too. One way or another, I'll get through tomorrow. I'll just be Amy Wood – who has just made her first new friend in her new life.

Amy Wood: *Estate Agent*.

Eight

When the alarm goes off the next morning, I'm wishing that I was the Amy Wood who'd had one less glass of wine last night with Mum's cottage pie when I got home from the pub. I've never had a head for alcohol, and on a Saturday morning I should be able to have a lie-in.

But not today.

In the shower, I practise my spiel: 'Hello, Mr and Mrs Blundell. I'm confident that we can find you the *perfect* home...' Water gushes over me. 'Oh my, isn't this such a *stunning* showpiece flat.' Talking the talk seems easy enough. But will I be able to field the challenging questions? 'Neighbours? Oh yes, the downstairs neighbour is lovely. Completely deaf – think of the parties you can have. With plenty of safe street parking for all those friends who'll be flocking over...'

The water goes cold and I turn it off, shivering. I just can't do it. Even if I never sell anything, I'm not going to lie. I may be working in the profession that everyone loves to hate – and with good reason in some cases. But I'm going to be different.

I get dressed and look at the clock: it will take me forty minutes to drive to Bristol, half an hour to show the flat – which means I should be back here by lunchtime. If it's all a waste of time, at least it's only half a Saturday.

Driving through Bristol, I begin to feel better. The city centre has been revitalised – it's vibrant and trendy; the waterfront is bustling with people. Workmen are putting the finishing touches on the huge cascades of white lights strung along the esplanade, in readiness for the big switch-on. I can imagine a hip, trendy couple living in a penthouse flat in the midst of it all. But the Blundells? To me they still seem like Edwardian-semi-material; maybe a mews house at a stretch. But I suspend my disbelief – after all, the customer is always right.

I park the car a few blocks away from the waterfront. A group of teenagers in matching hoodies are loitering across the street from the pay-and-display machine. As the machine spits out my ticket, I debate whether to move the car. But then I see a Mercedes parked a few spaces in front of me. If they can risk it, so can I.

The hoodies cross over to my side of the street and lean against a wooden construction fence. I'm careful not to make eye contact as I walk past, but even so, one of them whistles and a glob of spittle lands on the pavement in front of me. I'm relieved that I'm only showing a flat here, not buying one. Surely the Blundells will feel the same? My erstwhile commission is slipping away like sand through an hourglass.

As I walk along the embankment, the water shimmers in the sunlight. Nearly all the old warehouses have been converted into expensive apartments with shiny glass atria and hothouse flowers in the lobbies. In between are trendy restaurants and chain coffee shops. The quayside is abuzz with people: families with prams going towards the tall ship museums; couples laughing and drinking coffee; elderly people sitting on benches watching the gulls. I find the building: a converted warehouse in yellow brick with a glass atrium. There's a Costa Coffee and Pizza Express in the lobby, and in the centre, an elegant Nordmann pine decorated with silver and purple baubles. There's no sign of the Blundells, so I buy a skinny vanilla latte and sit down to wait for them.

When they don't show after ten minutes, I start to get nervous. After fifteen minutes, I begin to wonder if this is all an elaborate ploy by Mr Bowen-Knowles to test my loyalty. After twenty minutes, they walk through the main door into the atrium. My pulse jolts. The moment has arrived.

'Hi.' I stand up and wave in their direction. Mary Blundell looks startled for a second, like she doesn't recognise me (and why would she?). They walk over.

'I'm Amy Wood, we met once before at my office.' Smiling, I shake hands with them.

'It's good to see you, Amy,' Mary Blundell says. 'I'm pleased it's you showing us around – not that… toff.'

'Mary!' Her husband nudges her with his elbow.

I like them already. I'm glad that it's my job to play matchmaker – find them a 'together home' that suits their life. But could it really be – here?

'It's okay,' I say. 'You've expressed my sentiments on Jonathan exactly.'

Fred Blundell apologises for being late. I ask them if they want a coffee, and they decline – they've got another viewing to get to.

'No worries,' I say. *I will find them the perfect home.* 'Let's go right up to the penthouse.'

We walk over to the lift (which luckily seems to be working) and rumble up to the top floor. The door opens onto a stark white marble foyer. There's a vase on a marble pedestal full of purple and pink orchids. Natural light floods in from a cantilevered skylight. It's all very chic and minimalist, with a fresh smell that says 'conscientious cleaning staff'.

The penthouse is the only flat on the top level. Mary Blundell admires the orchids while I stand in front of the solid walnut door and rifle through my handbag for the keys. Just as I'm about to panic that I've left them in the car, I find them at the bottom of my bag (slightly damp and sticky from my hand sanitiser which has leaked).

Only – they don't fit. I try all three keys. Nothing. Embarrassed, I turn to Fred Blundell. 'Slight hiccup,' I say. 'As you can see, the security is state-of-the-art. I can't even open the door.' I give a little laugh as my hand starts to quiver. The keys are wrong – they must be.

I try all the keys again and then begrudgingly admit defeat. 'I'm really sorry,' I say. 'Let me go down and see if I can borrow a key from the concierge.'

'Do you mind if I have a go?' Fred says.

'Okay, sure.' I hold out the keys, but he doesn't take them. He bends down and examines the lock, then reaches into his pocket and takes out a flimsy plastic card with a V-shaped notch cut in it.

'State-of-the-art,' he says. 'No problem.' He wriggles the card into the door jamb. There's a click; the door swings open.

Fred grins at me. 'Amazing, ehh? Just like in the films.'

'Umm...' I'm about to protest that it's less like a film and more like breaking and entering, but they're already going inside. I swallow my misgivings and follow behind to make sure they don't try any other "special effects".

Inside, the penthouse *is* impressive. The enormous main room is all white with a double-height ceiling and an entire wall of windows looking out over the docks and the city. A modern space-age kitchen with glossy chrome units hugs one of the long side walls. The current inhabitants have furnished the flat all in black leather and chrome, with a few gigantic modern art canvases on the walls. A spiral staircase leads upwards to a mezzanine loft with four en-suite bedrooms and continues up to the roof terrace.

Mary Blundell rushes to the wall of windows. 'It's perfect! Just what I imagined. We've come a long way from Hull, haven't we, Freddie?'

Fred Blundell puts his arm around her waist and kisses her fondly. 'It is wonderful – and so much better than the other one we saw. This one just feels right.'

'It does.' Mary puts her hand on her chest. 'Be still my heart.' She winks at me.

'I'll leave you two to explore,' I say. 'When you're ready, just shout and we'll go up to the roof terrace.'

They seem to have forgotten that I'm there at all. Mary rushes around, opening cabinet doors, looking at the kitchen appliances one by one. To my chagrin, Fred goes over to the elaborate wall inset stereo console, presses a few buttons, and suddenly, a Beethoven symphony floods the entire apartment at concert-hall volume.

'Wow! What a great sound system!' he yells above the booming din.

'Uhh, maybe you should turn that down just a little,' I suggest. 'The neighbours and all, you know.'

'What's that, Amy?'

He presses a button and the room goes quiet.

'Nothing.' I purse my lips.

'Quite the acoustics, ehh? Hope the neighbours are deaf.'

I open my mouth to agree with him, but I just can't do it. The deceit is painful – they're loving the place too much. I, of all people, know that there's nothing worse than finding what seems like the perfect home, only to have it end in disillusion. It's better to end it here and now. 'Mr Blundell, Mrs Blundell,' I say solemnly. 'There are a few things you need to know about this property. It may not be as perfect as you think.'

I proceed to tell them about the elevator, the old woman downstairs, and the street parking situation, complete with personal anecdote about the hoodies I'd encountered earlier.

When I've finished, I watch their faces, expecting the deserved recriminations – Mr Bowen-Knowles could have told them all these things over the phone and saved them a wasted journey. But Mary's excited smile hasn't budged. Fred wanders back over to look at the view. The noonday sun glimmers on the white tower tops of the Clifton Suspension Bridge, just visible in the distance.

'I'm sorry if you were misled,' I say. 'I guess every property has its problems, but I think it's only fair that you should know upfront. It's a shame really – otherwise it really is a lovely flat.'

I wait. Mary walks over to her husband. 'The particulars mention four bedrooms and a roof terrace,' she says, turning back to me. 'I'm dying to see it all – is it okay if we go upstairs?'

'Of course you can – if you still want to.'

Without further ado, they head upstairs. I follow behind at a safe distance, continuing to let the flat 'sell itself'. I take a quick peek into each of the spacious, modern loft bedrooms, each with its own shiny chrome and black marble en-suite.

I catch up with them at the door of the master bedroom. Fred is inside admiring the gigantic fireplace wall.

'And that will be a great space for the big Picasso, won't it, Mary? We may as well enjoy it before we've got to flip it.'

'It sure will.' She grabs his arm affectionately. 'Though let's not count our chickens until it's through customs.'

'Ha,' Fred laughs, 'Piece of cake. He's changed the frame – old wine in new bottles and all that. It will fool the best of them.'

Mary chuckles. 'It's pure genius—'

She spots me and cuts herself off. 'Yes,' she adds, 'it will look great there.'

I retreat awkwardly to the staircase landing. My head is starting to hurt. The Blundells seem so ordinary. But door jimmying; Picassos; old frames; customs? Just what kind of buyers am I dealing with?

When they've seen the bedrooms, we all climb the stairs up to the roof terrace. The wind is bracing, but the 360° view is astounding.

Fred turns to me. 'So, Amy, anything else we should know about before we make an offer?'

'An offer? Really?'

'I think we both agree it's just what we're looking for, ehh Mary? And fifty grand below budget.' He winks at me. 'You only live once.'

'Oh yes, Amy.' Mary grabs my arm like I've just told them they've won the lottery (or at least, successfully managed a heist of the lottery funds). 'It's perfect.'

I hardly know what to say. Didn't Claire and the others say that most viewings are a waste of time? Is this beginner's luck – or are they pulling my leg?

'I can phone the vendors on Monday,' I say. 'What would you like to offer?'

'Why, full price, of course.' Fred looks surprised. 'We wouldn't want to lose it.'

'Isn't that what's normally done in these situations?' Mary asks.

'Well, in this market, I'm sure the vendor will be thrilled.'

'Great, then, it's settled.'

As we head back down the spiral stairs, I can't help but ask: 'And those things I mentioned earlier – about the neighbours, and the lift – they don't bother you?'

'Oh no,' Fred assures me. 'Not a problem – I doubt that the grand piano and artwork will fit in the lift anyway. And as for the little old lady downstairs...' he gives what can only be described as a villainous laugh, 'she's unlikely to be a factor for long.'

'Besides, we won't be here too often,' Mary adds. 'With Fred's job, we travel a lot.'

'I see. Then I'm sure it will be fine.'

The door to the flat clicks shut, locking automatically when we leave. We ride down in the elevator. Instead of shaking my hand, they both engulf me in a three-way hug. 'Thank you so much, Amy,' Mary says. 'You're a lifesaver.'

'Really?' I smile. 'You're welcome.'

I mean, some questions are better left unasked.

Nine

On Monday morning I arrive at the office brandishing a well-earned cinnamon latte and skinny blueberry muffin. I'm still aglow after my viewing success (the only downside was returning to a smashed beer bottle on the bonnet of my car). Everyone is already at their desks, and they look up eagerly as I enter – and immediately look away again when they see it's only me. A few hellos are grumbled.

'Guess what?' I say to Claire as I plunk my bag under my desk. She looks at me a bit foggily.

'What?' she says. 'Have you won the lottery and come to rub it in the faces of your beloved co-workers?'

'No.' I'm slightly put off by her flippant use of 'beloved co-workers'. 'It's just that the viewing went well – the Blundells loved the penthouse flat.' I grin.

Suddenly, all eyes are on me again. This time they linger malevolently.

'That's nice.' Claire smiles without warmth.

'Anyway, thanks for the tips.'

'Just don't get your hopes up, dahling,' Patricia butts in. It's only about the second time she's ever addressed me, and her tone is saccharine with pity. 'Most of them say that. They don't want to hurt your feelings.'

'No,' I protest, 'they really did like it. Mrs Blundell said it was perfect. It's just what they've been looking for – *and* fifty thousand under budget. They told me to ring the vendor and put in an offer.'

'An offer?' Patricia looks at Jonathan.

'Blundell?' Jonathan's voice is low and icy.

'Well yes...' I take a breath. 'It was after you left on Friday that they phoned. Claire was busy, so Mr Bowen-Knowles asked me to do the viewing—'

'The Bristol penthouse?' Jonathan stands up and storms towards my desk.

'Yes.'

'You know, don't you, that the Blundells are *my* clients?'

I stifle a little laugh. Mary Blundell's words come back to me: *I'm pleased it's you showing us around – not that... toff.*

Just before he gets to me, Jonathan swerves and bulldozes straight into Mr Bowen-Knowles's office without bothering to knock. The door slams shut.

I shrug at no one in particular and check my emails. There's one from my former thesis advisor back in London, enquiring hesitantly if I'm 'well', having recently heard the 'news' about my 'unfortunate mishap'. I feel a sharp pang for my former life in academia – like a ghost from Christmas past that I'll never glimpse again. I draft a quick reply thanking him for his concern, and letting him know that I've landed on my feet. Sort of. (And if he hears of any job openings and might be able to put in a word for me, I'd appreciate it.)

The muffled voices coming from Mr Bowen-Knowles's office grow louder.

'Coffee?' Claire nods her head towards the back of the office.

'Okay.' I shrug indifferently, still a bit miffed by her earlier lack of enthusiasm, and grab my mug.

In the kitchen, I pour myself a coffee and one for Claire.

'Great job,' she whispers. 'But you really shouldn't get your hopes up yet.'

'I won't. But the place was right for them – like the proverbial match made in heaven. Surely you must get those sometimes?'

'Sometimes.' Claire shakes her head like it's been a while. 'But lots of things can go wrong.' She takes a sip of her coffee and refills her cup straight away from the pot. 'I remember my first viewing – a cute little cottage in Bradford-on-Avon. The clients walked in the door and it was love at first sight. It was their dream property and was supposed to give them a new start; a new lease of life. I was so excited – for them, and for myself.' She smiles faintly. 'It took them six months to arrange their finances. Finally they were ready to go, so I booked an expensive holiday to Euro Disney for the whole family.' She sighs. 'On the day they were supposed to exchange, the buyer called. He and his wife had decided on a different "new lease of life" – they were getting divorced. The whole thing went down like the Titanic.'

'Oh, that's a shame.' I frown, thinking back on my own experience of finding the perfect flat, but unfortunately lacking the perfect person to share it with.

'But,' she brightens, 'I got over it. Thank God for credit cards – we still went to Euro Disney, though I'm still paying for that trip. The cottage sold through another agent – no commission for me. But enough doom and gloom.' She clinks her coffee cup against mine. 'If you do sell the Bristol flat, it will be a real coup. Those Blundells must be richer than they look – how did they make their money, anyway?'

'I don't know.' My bubble is in danger of bursting. Claire is right: there are so many things that could go wrong. What if they 'can't get the "Picasso" through customs'? What if they can't 'flip it'? And then there's the not-so-simple matter of Jonathan…

Claire is looking at me like she expects me to say something more. 'I don't know much about them,' I say. 'But thanks again for the advice. In fact, I'm sure you're right—'

Mr Bowen-Knowles's door whooshes open, banging against the wall.

Jonathan blusters out, glares at me, and goes back to his desk. He rakes his fingers through his spiky hair, and begins furiously stabbing at his keyboard.

'Amy.' My boss beckons to me.

I square my shoulders and brandish my coffee mug. I walk into his office and close the door.

'Good morning,' I say.

'Sit down.' He begins flipping through a stack of papers.

I do so.

'We've got a situation,' he says.

'So I gather.' I'm determined to stand firm, stick up for myself. The Blundells are my clients now, and I'm not about to let two old boys—

He raises an eyebrow. 'We've got exactly three months to shift this place, right?'

'Sorry?'

'Rosemont Hall.'

'Oh... yes.'

He frowns like I'm completely thick. Did I not just witness Jonathan's tirade? Is my boss going to sweep the Blundell debacle under the carpet? Still, I play along. 'I'll be picking up the brochure from the printers this afternoon, and the details are up on Rightmove, Primelocation, Country Life and Zoopla. I'm happy to help in any way I can.'

'I got an email from Kendall earlier,' he says. 'Apparently his client – Mr Jack? – has his knickers in a twist over this whole thing. He's been in direct contact with Hexagon already.'

'What?' My stomach drops.

'He sounds like one of those American tightwads who's trying to screw us out of our commission. But we're not going to let that happen. Are we?'

'No sir.' I feel like I ought to salute.

He hands me the paper he was reading when I came in. 'This

East Ham CSC & Library
24 hr renewal line 03333 704700
or go to www.newham.gov.uk

ITEMS ISSUED/RENEWED
FOR Mrs Veronica Fiores Usca
ON 03/10/17 17:26:13
AT East Ham CSC and Library (NEW)

Finding home/Westwood, Lauren
90800101064697 DUE 24/10/17
1 item(s) issued

Free Public Wi-Fi is now available at this
branch.
Please speak to a member of staff for
more information.
Thank you - East Ham CSC & Library

is a list of all the people in the last year who've been looking for a country property – two to five million quid.'

I flip through the list. Over two hundred names!

'Ring round to all of them, see if they're still looking, and send out the details to them. It'll be a complete waste of time, but we need to look like we've got our skates on.'

'What about Mrs Bradford?' I ask under my breath.

'Who?'

'The elderly housekeeper who lives there.'

His glare sends a chill through the office. 'What about her?'

'Should I speak to her about moving out?'

'That's Kendall's job,' he snarls. 'We have to assume we're selling with vacant possession.'

'Oh, of course.' I feel a stab of sadness for the old woman whose life in her little room at Rosemont Hall is now nothing more than 'vacant possession'.

He turns away and stares at his computer screen.

'What about the price?' I say. Surely, that's something even he would agree is a valid question.

He fiddles with his right cufflink. 'Excess of two million plus renovation costs,' he says. 'Which reminds me, I phoned the quantity surveyor – he's going round tomorrow morning. He'll estimate the costs needed to get it up to scratch for development – probably gutting the interior.'

I grimace. My boss gives a little smirk. 'He'll be there around eleven. Someone needs to let him in— you. You've got the keys, right?'

'Yes.'

His eyes stray for a second down to my (high) neckline, and he frowns again. 'That's all.' He waves his hand like he's dismissing a servant.

I stand up and straighten the creases from my skirt. 'What about the Blundells?' I ask.

'Oh that.' He swats away my question like a pesky fly. 'Don't let them fool you. That will almost certainly come to nothing.'

'But—'

His phone rings. I turn to leave and walk slowly to the door. 'Oh hello, Mr Blundell,' he says. I wheel around. Mr Bowen-Knowles covers the receiver with his hand. 'That's *all*,' he says. 'Shut the door.'

Resistance is futile. I leave his office.

*

Mr Bowen-Knowles stays closeted away all morning. Jonathan refuses to look at me, and I'm relieved when he finally leaves for a viewing. Meanwhile, I begin the task of cold-calling the list of potential buyers for Rosemont Hall. I phone the first three and leave messages. The next two I reach and begin my spiel, only to find that they've both been sacked from their hedge-fund jobs. The next three have already bought their dream country piles. The one after that – an American – listens to my entire pitch, and then informs me that his country 'fought a revolution to get rid of the Georges', but to let him know 'if you've got any nice English Tudors on the books'.

As I cross each name off the list, I begin to realise that it's a thankless task. To see what I'm up against, I open the internet and type 'Hexagon' into the search engine. The first few results are all emerald-green lawns, modern glass clubhouses, smiling weekend golfers. There's a corporate site that's more of the same, as well as annual reports, shareholders' information, and a picture of a balding man receiving some kind of award for sustainable development. But as I scroll down, I find a few articles that aren't quite so rosy. Hexagon bullying local OAP conservationists; Hexagon 'accidentally' knocking down a wing of an old house, leaving it a ruin. There's also an article on a sad old house called the Parsonage in Herefordshire.

Apparently, Hexagon purchased the site for a water park and promised the council that it would shore up the house. But seven years later, the water park is up and running next door, and there's no sign of any work being done on the house. There's a photo of its once-proud stone walls bowing behind a chain-link construction fence, the roof slateless and sagging. Mr Kendall had obviously done his research when he said that Hexagon doesn't have the best record for conservation. I can't let Rosemont Hall become a pawn in their chess game – it's imperative that I succeed. I close down the websites and pick up the phone again. A dozen more calls and still nothing.

At lunchtime, I invite Claire to go for a sandwich, but she has errands to run. Feeling discouraged, I buy a BLT at Marks & Spencer, and sit down on a bench near the Roman Baths. Tourists are flocking in and out of the Pump Rooms and a group of schoolchildren in bobble hats are singing carols. In front of Bath Abbey, the Bavarian Christmas market is in full-swing. When I'm done with my sandwich, I wander among the little chalets strung with icicle-shaped lights that are selling local products, jewellery and knitwear. I reluctantly avoid the hot glühwein, and instead buy a bag of chocolate-dipped gingerbread for Mum. I end up eating it as I walk. Everything is busy and festive, but all I can think about is how quickly time is passing. Three months – Mr Kendall said that I had three months to sell Rosemont Hall. So how dare this Mr Jack get involved already?

I wrap my scarf tighter around my neck to stave off the cold, and consider this faraway scourge on the future of Rosemont Hall. I bet he has a nice life. I picture him: middle-aged with a beer belly, wearing a baseball cap over his balding head as he mows the lawn at his house in a dusty American subdivision – huge houses on tiny plots of lands, all identical to each other. Mr Jack will drive some kind of fancy 'mid-life-crisis' car – maybe a Porsche – no, a vintage Mustang. In candy apple red.

Roaring off to work each morning while his wife piles the kids into a huge SUV to drop them off at school on the way to yoga class. And at the weekends – of course! – golf at the local country club.

And meanwhile, back in Blighty, a house that he's never seen will continue to crumble; a hollow shell where once there was laughter, warmth and life. The memories it holds will crack and fade like old paint, and one of the finest examples of Georgian Palladian architecture in the South West will end up as little more than a paragraph on a website about England's lost country houses.

Unless I can do something about it.

I throw the empty biscuit package in a bin and head back to the office. I must, as Mum would say, 'keep calm and carry on'.

When I return, everyone is back, and Mr Bowen-Knowles is chatting to Patricia. Five pairs of eyes bore into me as I enter, and a silence descends.

'What is it?' My cheeks flush in the dry office air.

Mr Bowen-Knowles clears his throat. 'It seems that the Blundells were impressed with that flat Jonathan found for them.'

'Jonathan...?' Anger bubbles up inside me.

'They've offered the asking price and it's been accepted.'

Instead of the joy such a proclamation should merit, a noxious cloud descends over the room. 'Fantastic!' a part of me knows I should say. 'I told you so,' is what comes out of my mouth instead.

Mr Bowen-Knowles walks over to Jonathan's desk and gives him a high five. My stomach roils and I think I might be sick. My boss then turns to me, his lips curving downwards into their default position. 'So,' my boss says, 'while this one goes to Jonathan, the good news is that you can stay on permanently – if you want to.'

Claire gives me a surreptitious thumbs-up. I mumble a 'thank you.' I should be happy that I've now got a permanent job.

Here.

I stifle the urge to punch Jonathan on the fake-tanned nose, sit down at my desk, and spend the rest of the afternoon phoning the people on Mr Bowen-Knowles's list. No one in the office looks at me or talks to me, nor I to them.

There's only one thing I can do – keep at it. Surely, success is the best revenge. And when out of the fifty-three people I phone, four are interested in receiving the details on Rosemont Hall, I feel it's destined that, somehow, I'll get my name to the top of the sales chart on the door of the disabled loo. I *can* do this – and eventually I *will*.

After all, Rome wasn't built in a day.

Part Two

'And of this place,' thought she, 'I might have been mistress! With these rooms I might now have been familiarly acquainted! Instead of viewing them as a stranger, I might have rejoiced in them as my own, and welcomed to them as visitors my uncle and aunt. But no,'—recollecting herself—'that could never be; my uncle and aunt would have been lost to me...'

This was a lucky recollection—it saved her from something very like regret.

~ Jane Austen – *Pride and Prejudice*

Letter 4 (Transcription)

Rosemont Hall
June 5th 1952

A

    Seeing you again after so many months was like a glimpse of the sun after a never-ending winter. I will speak to my father about us as soon as I find the right moment. I want to make sure that I do this properly and he realises how serious my intentions are.

    Yesterday, Father surprised me – he says he is planning a ball for my coming-of-age – would you believe it? At first I laughed at the very idea. But reflecting on it, it is a nice gesture and I think one designed to bridge the gap between us. It will be a fitting start to my new life back at Rosemont Hall. I so much want to do him, and you, proud.

    In fact, the preparations have already begun. This morning he stood in the great hall and oversaw every delivery – flowers in crystal vases, wine glasses and champagne flutes, musicians' instrument cases, crates of taper candles, mountains of food and drink. And in his face I caught a glimpse of the father I remember: strong and proud and a patron of the arts. Seeing him like that, I too caught the sense of excitement. It has been so many years since the chandeliers glowed, and the floors smelled of wax and polish. So many years since there was a sense of life about the old place. He's even hired an artist to paint my portrait.

I'll tell you more when I see you. Can you meet me tonight in our usual place?

All my love,

H

Ten

Late morning the next day, I scrape a layer of frost off the car windscreen and drive to Rosemont Hall to meet the quantity surveyor. As I drive up the long, winding approach to the house, once again I'm transported to another era. I'm Jane Eyre glimpsing the stark silhouette of Thornfield, as she contemplates what her new life there as a governess will hold; Elizabeth Bennet touring Pemberley, wondering if she'd been just a tad hasty in rejecting Mr Darcy's tentative advances. In the fragile rays of sunshine, the whole scene has a slightly dreamlike quality – of being familiar and real, but just out of reach. The graceful silhouette of the house is a thing of beauty – a true work of art.

I park the car and get out. Everything is incredibly quiet except for the mournful cooing of a pigeon. It takes me a while to find which key unlocks the door, but finally, the deadbolt grinds open. Inside, the house is even more vast and stunning than I remember – it's like walking through an empty jewel box. It's also absolutely freezing.

I pull my scarf tighter around my neck and up over my chin. The great hall smells of 'old house': thick layers of varnish, dust settled over antique furniture, the sour odour of mice and rising damp. But despite the decay, I feel incredibly lucky to be here. Not many people get to see a house like this, except maybe on television or on a tour. To be here in person is to experience the awe of the proportions, to appreciate the artistry and detail that went into every carved moulding and mantelpiece, the handiwork that makes up every inlaid floor and plastered ceiling.

What would it take, I wonder, to bring the house back to life? To restart its heart and get it breathing again. As I continue walking, the answer seems obvious: people. It would take people. I picture children roller-skating on the marble floors and sliding down the banisters; a man making coffee in the kitchen; a woman baking scones. Gardening on a summer day; a book group meeting in the library; Santa leaving toys under a tinsel-trimmed Christmas tree. Births and weddings, deaths and holidays. Arguments, good-night kisses, homework, DIY, bad jokes, lazy afternoons on the terrace. People going about their lives. People who resonate with the house. People like me.

If the house were mine (and even *I'm* not such a romantic as to delude myself that that could ever happen), I'd be a hands-on type of owner – the kind who's not afraid to go up a ladder to strip wallpaper or repaint a cracked window frame, bleed a radiator, or oil the hinge on a door. (Which is a good thing, I expect, since paying people to do those things costs money.)

I go into one of the rooms off the hall: the library. Every surface is cluttered with papers, mildewed books, and trinkets. Hopefully Mrs Bradford was a better companion to Mrs Windham than she is a housekeeper.

My shoes make footprints in the dust as I walk over to the window. The frame is rotting but the latch is intact. Carefully, I push it open and a rush of cold air stings my face. At the back of the house is a weedy terrace flanked with stone urns. Beyond, overgrown lawns sweep down to a yew avenue, a tangled jungle of a rose garden and eventually the Grecian folly by the lake. The frost on the grass shimmers in the morning light. I fall in love with Rosemont Hall all over again.

As I wander through the rooms on the ground floor, I straighten a pile of yellowing papers here, wipe the dust off a fireplace mantle there. My mind wanders off trying to imagine the place as it once was: a lady sitting in front of the fireplace embroidering; a girl practising a Chopin étude on the pianoforte; a man in riding clothes writing letters at the desk by the window; servants tiptoeing in and out with tea trays, ostrich-feather dusters and the daily post on a silver tray. I can almost hear the whisper of silk and crinolines through the doorway; smell the linseed oil and rosewater perfume. The walls seem to close in around me, as if leaning closer to whisper in my ears.

Eventually, I climb the grand staircase and stand before the painting of the elusive young woman in the pink dress. I lean back against the balustrade and look at her: the bold eyes, the secret smile, the shadowy folds of her dress that seem to appear out of the darkness; so real that I can almost reach out and touch the soft fabric; feel the sheen of silk beneath my fingertips. Was hers a great love story, or a romantic tragedy? The house knows, surely. I close my eyes and listen for a second, but everything is silent except for the noise of a distant drip. I remind myself sternly that it's my job to *sell* Rosemont Hall, not to uncover its history.

A chime echoes melodiously through the hall. Realising that I've lost track of time, I run down the stairs to the main door. The hinges creak when I open it. Standing outside is a young, sandy-haired man with green eyes and freckles. He looks surprised for a moment at seeing me, and then his face sprouts a grin. 'Hi, I'm David Waters,' he says, holding out his hand. 'The quantity surveyor. You must be the Lady of the Manor.'

He winks, and my cheeks flush.

'I wish,' I say, as we shake hands. 'I'm Amy Wood, the estate agent.'

'And here I was expecting the *Honourable Mr Bowen-Knowles*.' He puts on a fake posh accent. 'A nice surprise, I must say.'

It's a surprise that he's flirting so openly with me, and I can't help but feel a little bit flattered – and rusty. I usher him inside. As he looks around the entrance hall, appearing suitably impressed, I give him the once-over. Medium height and build, wearing khaki trousers, work boots, and a tan shearling coat with a crisp pink shirt underneath. He's carrying a notebook with one of those credit-card thin calculators clipped to the front of it. I'm grateful that he's not uptight and stuffy, which was what I'd been expecting. When he's finished looking around the main hall, I get the impression that he's checking *me* out. I'm suddenly conscious that my black pencil skirt is a little tight across the hips.

'So, Mr Waters,' I say, 'I'll show you around if you like.'

'Call me David,' he says predictably. He takes out a pair of wire-rimmed glasses from his pocket, puts them on, and flips his notebook open to a new page of yellow graph paper.

As we embark upon my version of the 'grand tour', I pretend that this is a viewing, and that he's a prospective buyer. He plays along, but each time he writes something in his notebook he frowns. He seems like a plastic surgeon – only interested in defects: many of which I hadn't even noticed until he points them out. There's wallpaper that takes down half a damp plaster wall when he pulls on it; deep cracks in the parquet floor when he moves aside a threadbare old rug; spots of damp and wet rot everywhere; woodworm in the window frames; a wasp's nest in one of the fireplaces. And that's just the ground floor!

In the main bedroom, he moves aside a rickety chair and points to a cracked area of the painted panelling that marks the outline of a door.

Intrigued, I walk over to it. 'Is it a secret room?' I say.

'Maybe.' He winks at me and pulls on a brass ring stuck into the wall. He takes a quick look inside and slams the door shut again. 'Closet.' He fans the air in front of his nose. 'Pheew, something died in there, that's for sure.'

'Oh.' I move on, slightly disappointed.

We go to the next floor up and reach the corridor where Mrs Bradford has her room. This time there's no smell of baking, and when I knock on the door, no one answers. 'I don't have a key,' I say to David, half expecting that like the Blundells, he'll offer to pick the lock.

He shrugs. 'Whatever.' We move on.

Down in the cellar we find a warren of damp, cold rooms: the unmodernised kitchen, pantries and larders with crumbling wooden shelves, and the enormous boiler. David Waters regales me with doom and gloom about probable burst pipes and water leakages. When we find the electric box, he holds me back with his free arm – 'It could be a deathtrap, don't go too close'. My enthusiasm ebbs. David Waters scribbles fast and furiously on his yellow graph paper.

'What is it that you're writing down?' I ask, as we head back to the main hall.

'I'm noting down the structural issues,' he says. 'Then we can look at some options: Mr Bowen-Knowles thought a conversion to flats might be possible.'

'Just that? What about the basic costs to reinstate it as a family home?'

He laughs like I've made a good joke.

'What?' Hands on hips, I stare him down.

'I don't think that's very likely, do you?' he says. 'Given that we're so close to Bath, it might have some value as a development. If not...' he shrugs, 'I don't need a calculator to tell you that the restoration costs will be a lot more than it's worth as a family home – even if you managed to find some rich nutter.'

'Oh.' Visions of 'Golf Heritage' dance in my head.

'Plus, I understand that the planners are keen on developing recreational facilities and low-cost housing around here. With a hundred and twenty acres, someone like Hexagon could make a lot of money.'

'You know about Hexagon?' For me, that name is becoming synonymous with the incarnation of evil in the universe.

'It's part of my job to keep on top of things.'

'And is it part of your job to note down that turning this place into Disneyland for rich golfers would be a crime? This place is an important piece of history. It should be restored.'

Without realising it, I've walked towards him, and am now standing closer than a polite distance. He doesn't step away, and gives me a disarming grin.

'That's not strictly in the job description.' He touches my arm. My skin tingles at the contact. 'But I'll tell you what,' he says. 'You come out with me for a drink tonight, and I'll add your comment as a footnote. Plus, I'll split out the cost of getting the place up to scratch as a single family dwelling – no extra charge.'

'What?' I take a step back.

'Or... another time if that suits you better.'

'No... uhh... tonight is... fine. It's fine.'

'Great.' His eyes linger on my face. I feel my cheeks begin to glow, and not just with the cold.

'I'm going to go have a look at the East Wing now,' he says. 'Since it may not be safe, do you want to wait here?'

'Okay... sure.' Although I want to see what, if anything, is left of the East Wing, I'm too kerfuffled to see it with David Waters. I go with him through the elegant door at the side of the main hall. It leads to a short corridor with a heavy black door at the end. 'I'll meet you in the main hall when you're finished,' I say.

'No problem.'

I return to the main hall and pace the floor. Staring up at the ceiling painting of a Rubenesque goddess of dawn being crowned by nymphs, I take stock. It's been just over two months since I moved out of the rented flat that I shared with Simon. I realise that I'm no longer thinking of the life I lost every moment of the day and in fact, part of me has begun to wonder why I was so deluded into thinking that my relationship with Simon was the be-all and end-all. And now, all of a sudden, other possibilities creep into my mind. I've already got a new job and a new project – this house – to occupy my imagination. Obviously we've just met, but I can't help but wonder – could there be someone out there – someone like David Waters – to begin filling the void that's still left?

While I wait for him to finish his work, I go back into the library to begin sorting through some of the old books and papers – trying to separate them into piles of rubbish/saleable items/personal effects that the American heirs might want. All of those property shows on TV advise that it's important to reduce the amount of clutter before the viewings begin.

In one corner of the room, there's a huge mahogany desk that's absolutely overflowing with papers. The piles of books and papers are so high that they're blocking half of the window, making the room seem dark. Tackling that seems a good place to start. The first thing I see is a stack of telephone bills – the top one dated three years earlier. Arabella Windham must have been a hoarder who saved every bill and scrap of paper.

I move aside the stack of bills and another pile of newspaper clippings – obituaries, recipes, crossword puzzles – to clear some space. Underneath, I find a large, flat book in faded red leather. I open it and discover that it's an old ledger of household accounts. I flip through it briefly. Most of the pages are full of mind-numbing entries for light bulbs, floor wax, petrol, clothing and sundries – silver polish, and the like. In addition to being a hoarder, Arabella – or whoever kept it – must have been quite the penny-pincher.

But when I flip to the older entries towards the end of the book, I find something more interesting. There's a page labelled 'artwork' written in a different, bold, looping hand. It lists entries, going back to the 1920s, of paintings purchased.

I read through the list of artists: Gainsborough, John Singer Sargent, Van Dyck, Matisse, Rembrandt. How amazing it must have been to see the paintings hanging proudly on the walls of Rosemont Hall! Stapled to the last page of the ledger is an itemised auction receipt from Sotheby's for a fine art sale in London in 1951.

Name	Artist	Frame	Condition	Estimate	Sale Price
Matin Rose	Matisse	Orig	Good	3-5,000	4,500
Garden Tea at Petworth, 1899	John Singer Sargent	New	Fair	2-3,000	3,300
Off the Solent	JMW Turner	Orig	Damage to rt corner	4-5,000	5,200
San Pierre aux Roches	Poussin	Orig	Good	6-7,000	5,900
L'Orientale	Rembrandt	Orig	Good	9-10,000	Withdrawn

To me, the prices look ridiculously cheap. But of course, I'm thinking in today's money. And I suppose that after the war there was little appetite for buying art. How sad, though, that Sir George decided to withdraw his Rembrandt from the sale, only to have it destroyed in the fire.

I close the ledger and move it to one side. As I do, I accidentally knock a pile of *Telegraph* gardening sections off the other side of the desk. They fall onto the floor with a thunk. The cloud of dust and mould that rises up sends me into a sneezing fit.

I take a tissue out of my pocket and put it over my nose until the dust settles. When I bend down to pick up what I knocked off, I practically cut my hand on a piece of glass underneath. I move the papers aside and find that the culprit is a broken picture frame. It must have been lying face down at the bottom of the stack.

The sides of the frame come apart when I pick it up – I hope I haven't broken something expensive. The photo inside is a black and white image of a young couple getting married. From the bride's waved hairstyle, fit and flare lace dress, and pillbox hat and veil, I deduce that the photo was probably taken in the early 1950s. I turn it over. Written on the back in faded black ink is: *Henry and Arabella, 1952*. I look at the two people in the picture. Given the soft focus, the angle, and the fading of the photo with age, it's difficult to make out their features, but I note that neither of them is smiling.

I put the photo down on the desk, and something else catches my eye. Wedged between the desk and the wall is a bundle of folded-up, yellowing papers wrapped in what looks like a faded ribbon – it's coated with so much fuzz, dust, and cobwebs that it's hard to tell. Using a pen, I ease it out from behind the desk. When I'm finally able to grab it, I pick up the bundle and blow on it. Big mistake. I start sneezing and coughing all over again.

The ribbon comes apart in my hands. I unfold the paper on top. It's an old letter, dated 1952 – addressed to 'A' and signed 'H'. Arabella and Henry? I skim the text – it's a quaint, heartfelt love letter; saying how much 'H' is looking forward to seeing 'A' after being away at university. He also expresses some worries about his father's health, and waxes poetic about how he's looking forward to a life at Rosemont Hall with 'A'.

I refold the letter. It's all so romantic. I'd love to read more; find out about Henry and Arabella's life here. But do I dare take the letters? They've obviously been behind the desk for many years – I doubt that anyone would miss them – especially since the correspondents are both dead. Surely if I 'borrow' them, no one would mind.

Behind me, footsteps creak over the parquet floor. In a split second, I make up my mind and shove the letters into my coat pocket. When I turn around, David Waters is standing there making a few notes.

'Hi.' He rakes a hand through his sandy hair. 'The good news is the East Wing isn't about to come down on anyone's head anytime soon.'

I smooth down my coat. 'And the bad news?'

'It's causing strain on the main house. There are some huge diagonal cracks – sure signs of major subsidence.'

Subsidence – the dreaded word.

'Unfortunately, it's going to raise the repair costs considerably. And if it's not repaired, then the whole house might start to slowly pull apart. The bottom line is that you'd need to find buried treasure to make a dent in the costs to fix up this place.'

'Buried treasure? As in – actual buried treasure?'

'Either that, or divide it into a whole lot of flats.'

'Oh. Right.'

'So, Amy,' he says, 'I think I've got everything I need now – except your phone number.'

He flips his notebook open to a blank page. Our fingers brush as I take his pencil and write down my phone number. We agree to meet at the *White Swan* in Clevedon. Then he follows me back to the main hall. At the door, he leans in and gives me a kiss on the cheek.

'See you tonight, Amy.' He grins disarmingly. 'Eight o'clock.'

'Eight o'clock.'

Eleven

I retreat to the staircase landing and stand before the portrait of the lady in the pink dress. I stare at her lovely face; her mysterious smile. For a second I think of the letters I found and that maybe they were hers. But they couldn't be, as the letters are from the 1950s and she was painted in 1899.

'So, what did you think of David Waters?' I say aloud to her. 'Should I have agreed to go on a date with him? I mean, technically, it's much too soon to think about "meeting someone".' My words echo hesitantly in the cavernous space of the hall. Pacing the landing, the life I imagined I would have with Simon flickers through my mind like an old-time film: weekend breaks to country B&Bs, browsing second-hand bookshops, having dinner parties and book groups at our lovely little attic flat in Thornfield Gardens. I sigh. We had so much history together that I thought it would be a solid foundation for the future. But in real life, history only goes so far. The memories don't even begin to make up for all that wasted time.

From somewhere below me, there's a creaking noise, followed by a faint tapping – maybe mice? Hopefully not the sound of something about to collapse. I head down the stairs to investigate.

The hall is empty and silent. A draught of chill air sweeps the room. I walk towards the corridor—

An enormous furry beast knocks me to the ground. I scream

and raise my hands to my face. Wet and sticky; I scream again – and I'm pinned down and—

'Captain!' A voice yells.

The giant pauses in my murder and I find that I'm being licked within an inch of my life by a huge Saint Bernard with glassy blue eyes.

'Down boy!'

The dog gives a gruff bark and bounds away down the corridor.

Pulse racing, I scramble onto my knees. An ancient woman appears in the doorway of the East Wing. She's hunched over and standing unsteadily on swollen ankles; stockings rumpled beneath a floral-patterned dress. Her gnarled hands are brandishing a stick – at me.

'Hello?' I say timidly.

'And you are…?' Her blue-grey eyes are sharp and lucid as she peers at me over the top of her half-moon glasses.

'I'm Amy Wood, the estate agent.' I get to my feet and wipe the dog slobber off my face with my sleeve.

She stands silent for a moment, assessing me. Finally, she speaks: 'Maryanne Bradford. Missus.' The lines in her brow furrow and she shakes her head. 'Estate agent. Hmmpff. Vultures more like. I know why you're here. You want to tear this place apart brick by brick.'

I give her my kindliest smile. 'That's not why *I'm* here, Mrs Bradford,' I assure her. 'I've never seen such a magnificent house in all my life. I'd like to find a buyer who will restore it to its former glory. My agency specialises in selling *unique and historic* properties. I'm hoping I can find it a good home – so to speak.' I laugh nervously. 'That's what the Windhams would have wanted… surely?'

'So you knew them did you?'

'No. But—'

'Then don't assume you know anything.' She whistles to

the dog. 'Captain!' From the darkness of the corridor, the dog bounds back, its red mouth dripping drool like the Hound of the Baskervilles. It growls at me, then sinks to the old woman's feet and playfully rolls over onto its back. Its eyes stare past me, and I realise that it's blind.

'Yes, of course,' I say, a bit taken aback. 'Sorry, I didn't mean to imply anything.'

I'd been expecting a nice, grandmotherly, scone-baking old lady, not someone quite so abrupt. But why should she be polite to someone like me? If I was in Mrs Bradford's orthopaedic platform shoes – devoted to the house and Mrs Windham, nursing her through her last illness – I'd be upset too by what's happening. It's natural, I suppose, that she may see me as the enemy.

Mrs Bradford rubs the dog's tummy with her cane, her mouth pursed in a thin line, her eyes assessing me.

'It's a shame, isn't it, that the heirs haven't even been over to visit the house?' I try again to soften her. 'I mean, if I'd inherited a place like this, I'd want to see it, wouldn't you?'

'The *heirs*,' she snaps, clacking her dentures for effect. 'Jack and Flora are good-for-nothing… peasants.' She shakes her mop of silver-grey hair. 'How could they not be – they called in *your lot*, didn't they? They'll never understand – never! It took all these years to put things right, and they've proved that they don't deserve a teaspoon of soil from this place.'

'Um, yes,' I gulp. 'Though I guess it's a big project for someone to take on. I'm told that it's going to take a lot of money to fix up the house.'

She hobbles towards me; the dog slinks along at her feet growling. 'The house is fine as it is,' she says. 'Oh, I know all you young people with your property make-over shows and your white walls, beige carpets and what-nots. But that's hardly what matters, is it?'

'No, it isn't,' I say. 'I think it's the people who matter. Finding someone who will fall in love with the house; someone who will appreciate its history and care about its future. That's what I want to do.'

She looks at me like I'm completely barmy. I sigh – everything I say seems to be wrong.

'You sound like you've been reading too many novels,' she says with a frown. 'But I'll tell you something for free. None of the *people* cared about this house when they lived here. Arabella hated the house – she thought it was too big and draughty. And Henry was Henry. Even Sir George...' She closes her eyes. It's as if her body is standing before me but her mind is somewhere else entirely. 'All those promises, and then... poof! Everything was gone. Up in smoke. And never another word or a how d'ya do.' She snaps her fingers and her eyes pop open.

'You were here in Sir George's time?' I quickly do the maths. If she was here in the 1940s or 50s, then she must be well into her eighties now.

'My mother was the housekeeper here. I practically grew up at Rosemont Hall.'

'How fascinating,' I say. 'You must know so much about the house and the family. I'd love to learn more. I've read a little bit about Sir George Windham. About how he collected art and was a war hero.' I smile. 'He sounds very dashing and illustrious. But that's about all I know.'

'You've read about Sir George, you say?' Her face curdles like there's a sudden bad smell. 'And do you think your history books tell the truth?'

'It was the internet actually—'

'You want to know about him. Well, I could tell you a thing or two – not that it's any of your business.' She sucks in a breath. 'Sir George was no hero, that's for sure. He was a devil.' She bangs her cane on the floor for emphasis.

'Oh,' I say, startled. 'I mean... really?'

'And Henry – he was weak. He never was any match for his father. And Arabella – she was just a pawn in their chess game.' She turns away, shaking her head like it all disgusts her.

I open my mouth to respond, but what can I say? My hand goes unconsciously to the letters in my pocket. The private life of Henry and Arabella is none of my business and I shouldn't have taken them – I'll put them back. Later.

Mrs Bradford begins to hobble off. I follow her at a discreet distance – even if I can't make her like me, I can at least keep her talking. 'I was wondering, Mrs Bradford,' I say offhandedly, 'do you know who the woman is in the portrait – the one on the stairs?'

'Her?' She wheels around, her sunken eyes flaring. 'What do you want to know about her for? You ask a lot of questions.'

'Sorry about that,' I say. 'I'm just curious, that's all. And that picture is so lovely. The frame says 1899. I was wondering if she's Sir George's wife maybe? Or his mother?'

'No!' She waves her stick upwards in the direction of the painting. 'Not his wife or his mother. *She* was nobody. No one at all.'

She pivots on her cane in the direction of the stairs. I hover behind her – I don't want to annoy her with my questions, but she clearly knows a lot about the house and the Windham Family, and I'm eager to learn more. How can I convince her to trust me – that I'm on her side?

Instead of going up to her room, she turns again and begins hobbling back down the corridor to the East Wing, the huge dog plodding beside her. I follow her, anxious to see for myself what still remains after the devastating fire. The corridor is damp and smells of mildew. Mrs Bradford pushes on the door with her cane, and it opens with an unsettling creak. She steps through the door and pauses. Half-turned towards me, she begins to speak again. 'You're curious, are you? You want to know about Sir George?'

I nod encouragingly, keeping my mouth firmly shut. 'The truth was, Sir George needed money,' she says. 'The house was requisitioned in the war, and the soldiers left it a wreck. Sir George sold off his art piece by piece but it wasn't enough. And let's be honest – Henry was never the type who was going to make a fortune by working. So Sir George found another way. He planned the whole thing right from the start. And look what happened.' She hisses through her teeth. 'He was a demon. Those black eyes – it was like they might pierce through your flesh and devour your soul.'

'Planned what, Mrs Bradford?' I say. I'm intrigued, and more than a little unsettled. 'What happened?'

'Lives were ruined, that's what.' She purses her lips like a silent fortress.

I step through the door and immediately stop, aghast at what's before me. The remains of the East Wing are a cross between a bomb site and a tip. There's barely room to walk amid the heaps of charred wood and plaster, broken glass, and the remains of what must have once been tables and chairs that went up in the blaze. Charred rafters dissect the grey sky, and a whole colony of birds has taken up residence in the half-collapsed chimney. Tufts of grass and weeds are growing among the detritus. The rain has long ago washed away the smell of smoke, but not the sense of desolation.

Mrs Bradford turns to me. 'I come here sometimes when I want some peace and quiet,' she says pointedly. 'And to remember things the way they were.'

I nod without speaking, which seems to placate her.

'This was once the grand ballroom.' She gestures with her cane. 'It had a ceiling of glass that let in the starlight. The walls were white with cornices of plaster flowers, and mirrors that reflected the candles a thousand times over. There was a stage for the musicians over there.' She points to a corner of the ruin. 'And the tables of food were set up there.' She indicates with her head. 'The night of the fire was Henry's twenty-first birthday. Everything was perfect – the flowers, the champagne, the music. And the guests...'

She picks her way through the rubble, losing herself in the past. 'Arabella was such a pale slip of a girl – a waif in a green dress. All eyes and hollow cheeks. And the way Henry looked at her... like she was some kind of rare china doll...' She snorts suddenly. 'I remember how the sky turned such a queer shade of red. Angry, like hell had risen up from the ground and swallowed the moon and stars. All those cars with their headlights and not one of them stopping. And then the rain began to fall; black rain – thick and dirty like coal dust.' Her eyes glisten with the memory of towering flames. 'The ash from the fire.'

I keep silent, engrossed in her story.

'And after the fire, Sir George was like a ghost, they say. Walking through the rubble, day and night. Tapping his stick, tap, tap. Muttering to himself and staring at the empty walls where his precious paintings once hung. Luckily, he had the courtesy to die soon afterwards. It's the only good thing he ever did.'

'It sounds awful,' I say with a shudder. 'How did the fire start?'

She looks at me warily, her blue eyes hostile. 'What do your history books say?'

'Well, nothing. I haven't found any mention of that.'

She stops abruptly, looking down at the ground. In front of her is a tight ball of twigs and dried grass – a bird's nest. I look up and see that it must have fallen down from the smoke-blackened beam above.

She pokes at the nest with her cane. Something glints gold in the sunlight.

'I think it's a magpie's nest,' I say. 'There's one under the roof of my dad's shed.'

I bend down and pick it up. 'Look,' I say, 'it's stolen something.' I give the nest a shake. A small gold rectangle has been woven tightly into the nest. I unpick the tangle of twigs and grass and remove it.

'What is it?' she says, peering over her glasses.

I take out a tissue from my pocket and wipe it off. 'It's a cigarette lighter,' I say. 'There's an engraving on it. "To H love A, Happy Birthday".'

She lets out a strangled cry.

'Here,' I say, holding it out, 'do you want it?'

'No!' She recoils with a hiss. The dog suddenly barks and leaps to her side. 'Why is that here? Is this some kind of trick?' Her aged body begins to tremble.

Startled, I shove the lighter into my pocket.

'No – I guess the magpie stole it. I'm sorry if it's upset you. Can I make you a cup of tea or something?'

'I want you to leave,' she says abruptly. 'You don't belong here.'

'As I said, I'm the estate agent, so—'

'Go!'

She brandishes the stick like a cudgel and herds me towards a gaping hole in the collapsed front wall. I scramble over bricks and rubble, desperately trying to stay on my feet. Captain streaks back and circles me, barking and barring his teeth. Mrs Bradford raises her voice: 'Go!'

Twelve

I go. The tyres spit gravel as I drive off, covered with dust and dog slobber. I'm as perplexed as Jane Eyre hearing maniacal laughter in the night; as panicked as the second Mrs de Winter when psycho Mrs Danvers finds her holding Rebecca's nightdress. What did I say? What did I do wrong? The cigarette lighter must have been a gift to Henry from Arabella that got lost many years ago. Why did my finding it upset her so much? I take a deep breath to steady my breathing. As far as Rosemont Hall is concerned, the woman is a living skeleton in the closet.

As I put some miles between me and the house, I try to put things in perspective. Mrs Bradford seemed genuinely upset that the past denizens of the house – like Sir George and Henry – didn't appreciate what they had. And now the house will go to two distant heirs who don't appreciate it either, and have called in 'my lot' to get rid of it. Add that to Arabella passing, and the fact that Mrs Bradford has to move house when Rosemont Hall has been a fixture of her life for so long – it's enough to make anyone a little irrational. If the incident with the lighter is any indicator, she's not going to take kindly to any more change. If I do see her again, I'll just have to keep trying to be polite.

At least the whole kerfuffle has helped take my mind off my upcoming 'date' with David Waters – and my second (and third) thoughts about agreeing to go out with him. While the strain from being chased off the premises by Mrs Bradford might be a reason to cancel, unfortunately, I failed to get his mobile number.

Inside, I explain to Mum that I had a viewing in the area and there wasn't time to go in to the office. I put the bundle of letters and the lighter in my knicker drawer and begin the preparations for my night out. I have a long soak in the tub, shave my legs and pluck my eyebrows, and then have to unpack a number of my boxes looking for an elusive handbag to go with an outfit that I ultimately reject. When I do finally emerge from my bedroom wearing jeans, a V-neck jumper and Ugg boots, Mum asks me where I'm going. Sheepishly, I admit that I'm going out for a drink with a man.

If I'm expecting moral support, none is forthcoming. Mum looks askance at my outfit. 'You don't look like you're making much of an effort,' she says. We argue about it for a few minutes. I end up changing into a vintage red 50s dress I bought at Camden Market. From the moment I leave the house, I begin to worry that it now *looks* like I made an effort.

By the time I reach the car park of the White Swan, my heart is thrumming. But having told Mum what I'm doing, it's too late to turn back.

I'm officially on the rebound.

The air is freezing and I hug my pink scarf and wool coat around me. Inside, the pub is warm and inviting; a cosy wood fire burns in one corner and there's a homely smell of gravy and spicy mulled wine. The bar is draped with a garland of holly and evergreens hung with little Santa and reindeer ornaments. It's an unwelcome reminder that Christmas is less than a month away. Almost three weeks have gone by since the phone call came in about Rosemont Hall. Tick tock.

I'm afraid to look around in case David Waters is already there; or equally, in case he's not. At the same time, I don't want to be blindsided, so I take a cursory walk through the pub, and when there's no sign of him, make a beeline for the bar. I order a glass of mulled wine and a bag of crisps.

The bartender hands me an overflowing glass at the same time a hand touches my arm. I jump, and the wine sloshes down the front of my coat. 'Oh!' I blurt out, 'Uhh… hi David.'

His boyish face looks concerned, his green eyes wide. 'Sorry, I didn't mean to startle you.'

The bartender hands me a towel and I dab at the wet spot. 'No problem.' I force a smile. 'Let me start again by buying you a new one,' he says with a grin. 'Do you want to find a table?'

'Sure.'

He orders our drinks and I head off to find somewhere to sit. All the tables are taken, and the only seat available is a chintz love-seat next to the fire that a canoodling couple are in the process of vacating. It seems much too cosy and romantic for the occasion, but as my heels are rubbing in two places, I hover over the couple until they giggle off into the sunset. I've just sat down and taken off my coat when David comes over with our drinks and a plate of sticky toffee pudding with two spoons. He takes one look at the seating arrangements and the sweetheart neckline of my dress, and it's clear that, for him at least, the seating arrangements are just fine.

'I took the liberty of ordering the house speciality,' he says, indicating the pudding. 'That is, if you want to try it.'

'Thanks.'

Despite the fact that I've already had a hefty supper, the spongy cake and oozy syrup makes my mouth water. Although David Waters could not possibly have known, sticky toffee pudding is my absolute favourite – especially when eating it is a reprieve from making small talk. I take a generous gulp of the steaming mulled wine, all the while conscious that our hips are touching on the sofa.

'You look fantastic, by the way,' he says. 'Even with a garnish of mulled wine.' He holds up his pint of beer. 'Here's to lucky meetings.'

I clink my glass against his. We chat a bit about the cold weather and the local area. As I draw first blood on the sticky toffee pudding, he tells me about his job (he used to be in construction and worked his way up to quantity surveying), his flat (two streets away from the Grand Pier in Weston-super-Mare), and his dog (a yellow Labrador puppy called Stevie). He's polite enough to ask me only a few yes or no questions that I can grunt an answer to in between bites (Q: Did you just move here? A: Uh-huh; Q: And you're enjoying your job at *Tetherington Bowen Knowles*? A: Yuh-huh). Before I know it, only a pathetic little mound of sponge cake with a few spoon streaks of syrup remains on the plate. I set down my spoon, embarrassed.

'Please, finish it,' he winks at me. 'We can get another one if you want.'

'No really. I ate earlier. My mum cooked—' Too late, I catch myself.

'So, you're living with your parents then?'

'Just until I get settled.' I wash down the pudding with the rest of the mulled wine. 'I decided to move here a bit suddenly, you could say. My job in London didn't work out, and here I am.'

He looks at me intently. 'What happened?'

I've been anticipating the question. I've already decided that I'm not going to tell him anything at all: about Simon, or 'Ashley', or the thrown mobile, or my job teaching English – all of which are now ancient history.

'I thought it was time to try something different,' I say simply. 'And as for the job at *Tetherington Bowen Knowles*, I was just at the right place at the right time.'

'I'll drink to that.'

Before I can change my order to a glass of water, David

is up and halfway to the bar. He's smartly dressed in a beige leather jacket, black jeans, and leather shoes. His blonde hair is slightly tousled on top, and his build is athletic. As the wine begins to take hold, vaguely, I wonder what he has in mind for the evening, and why the prospect of whatever that is so far hasn't filled me with terror. After all, he seems normal, and he is attractive in a boy-next-door sense. I don't think we'll be having a deep and meaningful conversation about metaphysical poets, or Mary Wollstonecroft, or houses as characters in fiction, or anything intellectual anytime soon, but maybe that isn't a bad thing.

He returns to the table and hands me a new glass of wine. I take one sip and set down the glass. We still have business to discuss. 'How did you get on with your estimating this afternoon?' I ask.

A flash of disappointment crosses his face. 'I gave my notes to my secretary to type up. I've got pages and pages.'

'I'm sure you have. After you left, I met the housekeeper, Mrs Bradford. She took me to see the East Wing.'

'Quite the wreck, isn't it?' he says. 'Too bad they couldn't afford a bulldozer to clear everything away.'

'Oh,' I say, a little affronted. 'The East Wing was once the grand ballroom. Maybe someone will want to rebuild it someday.'

He starts to laugh, then sees my face and stops. 'Um, maybe,' he says, like he's lying to a child.

I take another sip of my wine and tell him briefly about Mrs Bradford, the magpie's nest and the ruckus over my finding the gold cigarette lighter. 'She seems a little unbalanced by everything that's happening,' I say. 'I suppose she was hit hard by Arabella's death, and the fact that she has to move out. She's pretty old – I feel bad for her.' I stare down at the dark liquid in my glass. 'Anyway, the lighter was engraved "To H from A." I found some old letters between Henry and Arabella too. The house is like a time capsule.' I sigh. 'Mrs Bradford must have a lot of fascinating information about the family – but I doubt she'll tell me. The fact that I'm an estate agent seems to have got us off on the wrong foot.'

He gives me a puzzled look. 'Why are you so interested? It's just a house – and somebody else's family history.'

'I know. It's hard to explain. When I first saw the house, it just seemed special somehow. Like I'd stepped into the pages of a novel. I believe that there can be a strong connection between people and properties. A person can belong to a house just like a house belongs to a person.' I give a little laugh. 'That's what I felt about Rosemont Hall. As soon as I saw it, I knew that it was my responsibility to help save it.'

'Save it?' He looks at me like I'm a few sandwiches short of a picnic.

'Find a buyer for the house who'll fix it up and restore it to its original glory – bring it back to life – not convert it into something else.' I smile at him. 'And that's why I need your help. Anything you can put in your report about the basic structure being sound – like you said – would be helpful.'

He raises an eyebrow.

'I'm not asking you to lie… It's just that Hexagon doesn't have the best track record for dealing with old properties.'

'Well, restoring old properties is expensive and time-consuming. It's easier to build from scratch.'

'Then let them build from scratch – somewhere else,' I say. 'Before I started learning about Rosemont Hall, I didn't realise how many old properties there are out there that are at risk. Historic buildings that are worth preserving. It might sound preachy and sentimental, but I want to make a difference.' I lean a little closer to him. '*We* can make a difference.'

If David Waters is impressed by my poetic activism, he doesn't let on. 'I hope that's not the only reason you're here.' He picks up my glass and puts it in my hand.

'Of course not.' I take a big sip of wine. While he hasn't actually agreed to help me with regards to Rosemont Hall, right now, David Waters is my best ally. And he's made it clear that he's keen on me. I stare at the fire for a minute as thoughts of Simon rise to the fore and recede again. I'm enjoying the long-forgotten feeling of having a man fancy me. And he *is* attractive...

'So, why are you single,' I ask boldly. 'I mean, you are single, aren't you?'

He laughs and leans towards me. 'Yes I am. I guess you could say, I'm looking for the right girl. You?'

'I'm recently... unattached.'

'Ahh, I see.'

He punctuates his understanding by putting his hand on my thigh. I don't remove it. My insides feel like treacle tart.

As I down the second glass of wine, things become pleasantly vague. 'I'm a lightweight when it comes to alcohol,' I hear myself saying. 'As Dorothy Parker says: "One martini, two at the most, three I'm under the table; four I'm under the host."'

'Dorothy who?'

'Never mind.'

He leans in and kisses me. At first I'm startled, and his mouth tastes like beer. Then I worry – it's been so long since I've been kissed properly that maybe I won't measure up. And then I stop thinking and allow myself to relax. Just like riding a bike, you never really forget how. The room swims when we finally come up for air. 'I don't think I can drive home,' I say—

'Do you want to go home?'

'With you?'

He laughs. 'You said it, I didn't.'

'I guess I did.'

I put on my coat and scarf and he walks me out to his car – a red VW Golf. We drive for what seems like a long time. I try not to think about anything at all other than the warmth of the heater on my feet. When the car stops, he leads the way up a flight of stairs, and inside a strange flat where a little yellow dog is sleeping in a basket by the balcony door. I gulp down a glass of water and go to the bathroom to freshen up. I decide to dispense with all of the 'will I, won't I?' arguments with myself and cut to the chase. I take off my dress, and leave it hung up on the hook behind the door.

When I return to the main room, David's eyes widen when he sees me. I think he says something quaint like: 'Wow, you look amazing'. My hands wander over an unfamiliar body, and his skin smells different than I'm used to. The gooey feeling is becoming more like numbness. Part of me wants to go and another part of me wants to stay, and a little echoing voice keeps repeating over and over like a ticker tape: *Rebound Man. Rebound Man...*

*

Late in the night, I open my eyes in a panic, until I remember where I am. I stare into the darkness and listen to the snores coming from the pillow next to me. *Isn't it exciting?* – I try to convince myself. After all, it isn't every day that I have sex for the first time with someone who is not my boyfriend of seven years. *Ex*-boyfriend. Failing that, I try to muster up some guilt, but I don't feel that either. All I know is that my head is throbbing from the wine and I really need to pee.

A luminous alarm clock glows on the bedside table: it's five o'clock in the morning. I think about inventing an exercise regime, or a penchant for sunrises – anything to justify getting out of bed right now, assembling my scattered clothing, and going home where everything is safe and familiar. But I have a vague recollection of David promising to cook me his special 'full English'. Leaving while he's still asleep would surely be rude.

I gingerly remove the duvet and swing out of bed. The outline of the bedroom door is just visible from the light of the clock. The cold air tickles my naked skin as I cross the room and open the door. There's a slight gurgle from the bed behind me. I stand still without breathing until the snoring resumes.

In the hallway, I fumble for a light switch. The brightness hits me like a physical force. The hall serves largely as a repository for sporting equipment. I squeeze past a surfboard, a cricket bat and a set of dumb-bells. There are a number of framed photos up on the wall: David Waters with a group of mates on skis; David Waters in diving gear holding up a dead shark; David Waters playing five-a-side football. He's obviously a sports fanatic – another characteristic that we don't share. There are several doors off the hallway, one of which has an old-fashioned picture of a little boy peeing into a pot. I lock myself in the bathroom, use the loo, and stagger against the sink. The wine is reasserting itself. My heartbeat pounds in my skull, and the four yellow walls begin to spin. I steady myself and stare at a framed photo on the wall above the towel rack: David Waters and a short red-haired man with glasses. They're both wearing white collared shirts and hideous checked trousers. Between them, they're hefting up a golf trophy.

Golf. I lean over the sink and splash water on my face. I'm now both hungover and fully awake. I don't know why it never occurred to me that David Waters might be an avid golfer – after all, a lot of people are. Normally, that would be fine, but not in this case. Not when I need him on side for Rosemont Hall.

I return to the bedroom where at least it's warm. Heading towards the dim outline of the bed, I fail to spot the yellow dog that has entered the room and stretched itself across the centre of the floor. I sprawl across the room and end up flat on my face, setting off a cacophony of yelps. I feel hot stale breath, a cold nose, and a scratchy dog tongue on my back. I shriek. A light switches on.

'Amy?'

David jumps up and pulls the dog off me.

'I'm fine.' I lean over to pat the dog, but it growls – like it wants me to leave. I jerk my hand away.

'Good.' David gets out of bed and helps me up. 'I forgot to mention that Stevie likes to sleep here.'

'I understand,' I say with an awkward laugh. 'I'm just not having much luck with dogs lately. But there's no harm done... I guess.'

He kisses me again and lowers us both back onto the bed. But this time, I smile coyly and shake my head. 'I need to get to work – do you mind if I have a shower?'

'Do you have to leave so soon, babe?'

I cringe inwardly at the generic term of endearment – something I imagine Simon might say to 'Ashley'. 'Yes I do,' I say firmly. 'But don't get up, really, I'll be fine in a taxi.'

'Okay – there's a number by the phone in the kitchen.'

Although I'd planned to take a taxi anyway, he loses more points by not insisting that he drive me (nor has he repeated his offer of a cooked breakfast). I give him a perfunctory peck on the forehead, but he's already nuzzling into the indentation of the pillow that smells like my shampoo, and drifting easily back into sleep.

I return to the bathroom for a shower. The water alternates between freezing and boiling, and I get out more quickly than I got in.

In the bedroom, I reassemble all of my clothes (minus my tights which I can't find anywhere). I make my way to the kitchen (carefully avoiding the dog, which is glaring at me from its basket), find the number of the minicab which is written on a yellow sticky (I note with detached interest that there are two other yellow stickies by the phone with the numbers of

'Susanna' and 'Valerie' written on them with x's and o's), punch the number into my phone and let myself out of the flat.

The morning is wet and overcast as I emerge onto a nondescript street of terraced houses. The wind gusts in my face and I can smell the seafront. I walk towards the esplanade and ring the taxi. My feet and head both hurt, but somehow as I sit on a bench staring out at the leaden-grey estuary, I feel surprisingly serene – like I've been in a train wreck and walked away a different person. David Waters may or may not be the proverbial 'One' – but regardless, I've fulfilled another leg in my post-Simon trinity: new job, new home, new man.

When the taxi pulls up and I get inside, I'm shivering from the cold but smiling too. I take out my phone and scroll down through the list of contacts. I come to 'Simon Work' and 'Simon Mobile' and hit delete. I know the numbers by heart, of course, but eventually I'll forget them. For once, I'm almost glad that there's no going back.

Thirteen

Two hours later when I arrive at the office, everyone is grumbling – even Claire – but no one tells me the reason. Eventually, I discover by osmosis that Mr Bowen-Knowles (working from home) sent everyone (except me) an email saying that in view of poor sales in the last quarter, there will be no Christmas bonuses this year.

'And here I was assuming I'd at least get enough for the airfare to the Maldives...' Patricia complains. She takes a soggy mince pie from a box that someone brought in from Tesco and bites into it, leaving a smear of coral lipstick.

'You haven't sold anything in two months,' Jonathan plays devil's advocate.

'What about you?' Patricia says with her mouth full. 'You would have made bugger all if Claire hadn't split the commission on those condos in Minehead.' She swallows and takes another mince pie.

'Like I had a choice,' Claire mumbles.

'What's that?'

'Nothing.'

As I look back and forth between them, another email pings in, this time to me as well as everyone else. It's an invitation to a company Christmas party with two other branches of *Tetherington Bowen Knowles*, scheduled for next Saturday. If it's intended to boost morale, it has the opposite effect.

Claire shakes her head. 'Doesn't he know that we'd all

rather have a bonus? Who wants a party when there's so little to celebrate?'

Jonathan says something, but I don't hear it because I'm reading the invite details closely. Specifically, the line that says 'Dear colleague + 1'. The dreaded plus-one! As the new girl, I'm obliged to go to the Christmas Party – that much I know. But should I ask David Waters, or some as yet unidentified Rebound Man 2, or just go it alone?

To get my mind off the dilemma, I spend the rest of the morning getting on with my cold-calling. The more calls I make, the more my mood deflates. But then, after leaving three messages in a row, my mobile rings, and a number I don't recognise comes up on the screen. My hopes instantly take flight. Is someone ringing me back about Rosemont Hall?

'Amy Wood,' I answer breathlessly. 'How can I help you?'

'Miss Wood. Ian Kendall here.'

'Oh, hello!' I say, trying to mask my disappointment. 'How are you?'

'Fine.' He clears his throat. 'I've just heard from Mrs Bradford that you were over at Rosemont Hall yesterday.' He pauses. 'I think her exact words were: "some chit of a girl who was asking questions and poking her nose where it doesn't belong".'

'No,' I protest. 'I mean, I was there, but I was just showing the surveyor around. She and her humongous dog nearly gave me a heart attack.' I give an empty little laugh. The cheek of that old woman ringing the solicitor!

'I understand,' Mr Kendall says. 'But do keep in mind that Mrs Bradford is an important beneficiary under the Windham will. She's inherited the artwork and many of the personal effects.'

'Did she inherit the painting on the stairs?'

'Yes.' He hesitates like he's given away something he shouldn't have. 'But that doesn't concern the sale, Ms Wood. And that's what I'm ringing about. Mr Bowen Knowles told you, didn't he, that one of the American heirs, Mr Jack, is very keen to move things along with the sale of the house.'

'We all want that, surely…'

'He's been negotiating with Hexagon directly. I understand they've had a number of conference calls to discuss the terms. Hexagon is definitely interested in the land for their golf course development.'

'But you said that I had three months,' I protest. The Cinderella clock in my head begins to race forward in double time.

'I thought that at the time. But if Mr Jack and Ms Flora can get Hexagon to make an offer they can't refuse, then they'll go with it, naturally. But I thought I should check in with you to find out the status of your marketing efforts. Just to see if there's anything else on the table.'

Steeling myself, I smile down the phone. 'Oh yes, definitely.' The lie escapes my lips in effortless *Tetherington Bowen Knowles* style. 'You can tell your Mr Jack' – I practically spit out the name of this blight on the future of Rosemont Hall – 'that I've been busy making contact with clients whom we know are looking for this sort of property. And there are at least two private buyers who are interested in seeing the house – maybe as early as this weekend. After all, it is a "historic gem with lots of potential for flexible, family accommodation". It's practically selling itself.'

There's a moment of silence at the other end of the phone and I wonder if I've gone too far.

'Fine.' Mr Kendall says. 'You may as well go ahead with that. Hexagon wants to meet with the planners before they make a formal offer. See what kind of hoops they'd have to jump through. They've got a meeting scheduled for next week.'

'Next week? But how can Mr Jack just agree to let them do that? I mean, the estate isn't even probated is it? And Hexagon doesn't own the site. And…' I crawl out onto a narrow limb, 'they won't ever own the site. Please tell your client that I'm going to find a buyer that will fix up the house – or I can tell him myself if you give me his email address.'

'I don't have the authority to do that at this point,' Mr Kendall says. 'But I will speak to him and tell him what you said. And in any case, Amy, I hope you get lucky.' I detect a strong note of doubt in his voice.

'I guess I'd better get to it then.'

'Fine. Oh, and one more thing. The other heir – Ms Flora – is coming over to go through the personal effects at the house...'

'That's good.'

'... to see if there's anything valuable enough to auction.'

'Oh.' So much for hoping that the female heir might have an ounce of sentiment that I could appeal to. I'm all favour of a little decluttering, but from the way Mr Kendall speaks of the heirs, I fear the worst.

I reimagine 'Mr Jack' – the shrewd businessman. Maybe he's a hot-shot investment banker in New York. He'll live in an ultra-modern penthouse apartment on Park Avenue with a doorman in a red coat who tips his hat and calls him 'Sir'. He'll have a driver that takes him to work each morning on Wall Street, wearing his thousand-dollar Armani suit, Bill Blass tie, and Ferragamo loafers. Then dinner and theatre in the evening with his underwear-model girlfriend. And on the weekends? A drive to Long Island or the Hamptons for a little sun and a round of golf. Golf – it always comes back to golf.

And meanwhile, back in Blighty, the last of his family history is slowly slipping away towards the unforgiving oblivion of time. The house will be 'modernised' into something unrecognisable. The girl in the portrait will be dispossessed of her rightful place above the staircase landing, ending up in some new-build banker's mansion in Surrey.

It just seems so *wrong*.

'Anyway,' Mr Kendall says, 'I just wanted to let you know in case you run into her.'

'Thanks,' I say. 'But what about Mrs Bradford?'

'I'll make sure she knows that you may be about the place doing your viewings.'

'Okay,' I say. 'But surely she needs time to adjust to what's happening. She seems to be taking everything pretty hard.'

Mr Kendall sighs. 'It's kind of you to show an interest, but I'm afraid that she's none of your concern. I believe she's already moved out, though she still may be around from time to time.'

'I just feel sorry for her, that's all. Plus, she seems to know a lot about the house and the Windhams. I didn't realise that she was there as a girl when Sir George was alive. She must have seen some fascinating things—'

He clears his throat. 'But as I said, that doesn't have anything to do with you selling the house.'

'Of course – sorry.' I accept the rebuke. It's not my job to learn the truth about the Windhams and Rosemont Hall. It's not my job to spend time there; soak in its atmosphere; or uncover its history. It's not my job to placate displaced old ladies; play tour guide to an appreciative audience; or find someone who will take on the house as a labour of love. It's my job to sell the house to whoever offers the most money for it. Thus, while I've mentally cast Mrs Bradford as the unstable housekeeper, Mrs Danvers, in reality, I'm the one acting irrationally. If the two American heirs, the solicitor, my boss, and the eighty-four people I've phoned don't care about the fate of Rosemont Hall, then I've got no business doing so.

Except, I do.

'Mr Kendall,' I say stoically, 'I completely understand what you're saying. It's my job to sell the house and I need to do so quickly. And I will. We've got a lovely brochure printed up with a nice photo of the front aspect. The quantity surveyor should have his estimate for the repairs today. I've got a lot more people to ring who might be interested, and I will find someone. Just give me a chance. Please.'

He sighs. Fundamentally, I have him pegged as a nice man who doesn't want to see the house gutted any more than I do. But he has a job to do – and so do I.

'I can keep the wolves from the door for now,' he says. 'But not too long. I'll ring you again when I hear from Ms Flora.'

'Thank you, Mr Kendall, for giving me this opportunity.'

'Goodbye Miss Wood.'

The line clicks off.

*

When I return to my desk, everyone is looking at me. 'What?' I say to the collective – they've obviously overheard the entire conversation. Jonathan smirks and shakes his head.

Claire's smile seems forced. The unspoken word seems to reverberate around the office: sticker... Sticker... STICKER.

My face is hot as I sit down, turn the glass slipper clock face down on my desk, put on my telephone headset with a flourish, and continue my cold calls. I leave more messages, talk to a host of people who, despite my hyperbole, are not interested, and two people who ask me to email them the details. No one schedules a viewing. The lie I told Mr Kendall seems to have poisoned my efforts. I take off my headset, my shoulders drooping.

'Fancy a quick sandwich?'

I look up. Claire's face is sympathetic across the low wall that separates our desks.

'I don't know...' I hesitate. 'I doubt I'll be much company.'

'All the more reason to get some fresh air.'

'Okay,' I say. 'That does sound good.'

We put on our coats and leave through the back door. We walk to the main street and buy turkey and cranberry sandwiches at Pret. The town is buzzing with Christmas shoppers, carollers, and tourists traipsing in and out of the Pump Rooms. We find an empty bench and sit down.

'Do you want to talk about it?' Claire coaxes, like I'm a reluctant witness.

I give a little laugh. 'It's so stupid, I know. But it's just that, I gave up a lot to do this job. Well...' I catch myself, 'not gave up exactly. More like lost – or gave away.' I sigh. 'And then when Rosemont Hall came along, I thought that maybe things wouldn't be so bad after all.' I smile sadly. 'I didn't get my happy ending, but I wanted one for the house. But obviously, that was ridiculous. If the American heirs, the solicitor, my boss, and the 102 people I've phoned don't care about Rosemont Hall, then I have no business doing so.'

'Except, you do.'

'Yes.'

Claire takes a thoughtful sip of her coffee. 'Do you want some advice, Amy?'

'Please.'

'It sounds to me like you've got two options. One is to forget about Rosemont Hall. Do your job, make your calls, and let the heirs sell it for a golf course. Focus on reality, move on.' Her smile is brittle. 'Because let me tell you, in this job, your dream is not going to happen.'

'But...'

'We sell houses, not happy endings. Semis, flats, new-builds, terraces – bricks and mortar. To people who want normal lives with a mortgage, a mini-van, kitchen diners, and bi-fold doors onto the garden. We deal with our shitty boss, and make our shitty commissions. Most of us dream of doing something else. And that's what you need to focus on.'

'Hmm.' I eat my sandwich in silence for a moment. 'You mentioned a second option?'

She laughs. 'Well, Amy, in my professional capacity, I really can't advise it.'

'What?'

'Well,' she lowers her voice, 'you could get creative. You're into books, right?'

I nod.

'Then stop thinking Brontë and start thinking Jilly Cooper. There must be loads of country busybodies around there looking for something to do. Start a *Save Rosemont Hall* Campaign. I'm sure people do that kind of thing all the time. Get the nutty housekeeper to rally the troops of local grandmothers – they can fix the place up in exchange for a free venue for bridge night. Ring English Heritage and tell them about the nefarious plot to turn it into a golf course. Write an article about the house for *Country Life*. There's loads you can do. In your spare time, of course.'

'Of course.' I can't mask the excitement from my voice. Claire's words are magic – suddenly the air seems alive with possibilities.

'And if all else fails,' she smirks, 'you can lay naked in the path of the bulldozers.'

I sputter with laugher. 'But I'm supposed to be—'

'Selling the house for the highest price? Then it seems you have a conflict of interest.'

'Yes, it does.' Smiling, I crumple up my rubbish. I can't wait to get back to the office and get started. The job is just a job, but Rosemont Hall needs me. 'Thanks Claire,' I say, 'that makes things a lot clearer. I'll take it all under advisement.'

V

My dear H

I have a birthday present for you that I think – I hope! – will make you happy. I came to see you but you weren't at home. I managed a peek into the ballroom, and you are right about the change that has come over the place! It is as sparkly and shiny as a jewel; I have never seen anything so magnificent!

When I turned around, a shadow fell – your father was standing there, watching me. The look he gave me – I felt like my heart might freeze mid-beat. 'You?' he hissed, like he guessed our secret. I'm ashamed to say that I turned and fled.

A

Fourteen

My new determination lasts the rest of the day and most of the week. In between cold-calling prospective purchasers, I google charities and historical societies in the local area that might be interested in sponsoring some kind of 'Save Rosemont Hall' campaign. I phone a few of them from the car park and talk to the relevant busybodies. There's some polite interest, but none of them think that they can raise the money. Then I try the National Trust, but they tell me that their budget is already stretched, and any acquisition of the house is unlikely. English Heritage confirms that the house is listed, so any alterations will be subject to a consent process. But while the English Heritage chap is sympathetic to my argument that it should remain a family home, he tells me a few hard truths. There are hundreds of 'buildings at risk' all over the country and very little money to restore them. In his view, turning the property into flats or a golf club is better than letting it fall into complete ruin. He points me in the direction of a few relevant websites, and wishes me luck.

None of my results are exactly the silver bullet I've been hoping for, but at least I'm doing something. And when one of my cold calls – to a couple with a whopping budget who are looking to move from Wolverhampton to Bristol – finally pays off, I'm over the moon. I schedule the first Rosemont Hall viewing for the coming Saturday!

As soon as I put down the phone, I mentally go over the checklist:

Make sure Mrs Bradford is (locked away in the attic?) managed;
Bring doggie treats for Captain (half a dozen Big Macs?);
Compile interesting historical information on the house;
Obtain quantity surveyor report;
Get there early and do some cleaning.

After lunch, I get started on #3, reviewing the research I did in my first week. I amass a large bundle of (I think) fascinating information, drawing glares from Patricia for hogging the printer. I'm just about to phone Mr Kendall when my mobile rings again.

The name comes up on the screen: David Waters. My stomach flips, and I rush off to take the call in the privacy of the disabled loo. I know I should be happy that he enjoyed our evening (and has sent me several texts to that effect that I haven't replied to) – and I am – of course. It's just... I'm not sure I've got my head around the 'what next' bit.

'Hi David,' I say. The door bangs shut and I lock it.

'Hi. You haven't responded to my texts.'

'I'm really sorry about that. I've just been in a bit of a flurry over Rosemont Hall. Someone wants to view it on Saturday. This is my first big chance to find someone who might fall in love with the house.'

'Am I going to see you again?' he cuts to the chase.

'Oh yes.' A list of 'buts' flashes across my mind: *but* I'm not ready for a relationship; *but* I think we should take things slower; *but* I've suddenly developed an allergy to dogs; *but* you're into golf... But – then I remember why I can't voice any of those doubts...

'In fact, I was about to ring you.' I say breezily. 'It's our office Christmas party – also on Saturday, in fact. Do you want to be my plus-one?'

There's silence for a moment. 'Well… I guess so.'

'Good.' I ignore the fact that he sounds like he'd rather be having a root canal. 'I'll text you the details.'

'Okey-dokey.'

I cringe. 'Great.'

'And Amy…'

'Yes?'

'I'm looking forward to seeing you again.'

'Me too.' I take a breath. 'And sorry to have to talk shop, but I was wondering about your report on Rosemont Hall – is it ready yet?'

'I'll email it over later.'

His tone tells the whole story – he's annoyed with me; probably with good reason. We exchange awkward goodbyes and I hang up the phone and stare at myself in the mirror. My eyes have dark circles under them from the stress of this job, and my skin seems paler than usual. I'm not getting any younger, that's for sure. I really ought to give David Waters a chance. He's a perfectly nice man, and we had a perfectly nice time. What more can I ask for?

A hard knock on the door alerts me to the fact that I've been hogging the loo for a lengthy amount of time. 'Sorry,' I mutter to a desperate-looking Patricia, and head back to my desk.

*

By the time I get home, I've had plenty of time sitting in traffic to plan how I can make the most of the Rosemont Hall viewing on Saturday. I'll get there early in the morning and do some straightening up before two o'clock when the clients are due. I also want to have a good look at some of the old photographs, and maybe the books in the library. In the last week, I've read and reread the bundle of letters that I found behind the old desk. I feel I know much more about the Windhams and their life at Rosemont Hall than I did before, but there are some missing pieces and unanswered questions too.

That night, before bed, I take the bundle of letters out and flip through them again. The top few are between Henry and his father, mostly discussing Henry's time at university, and his career plans (or lack thereof). Sir George's final letter to his son has a distinct undercurrent of disappointment in it. He talks of his distress at having to sell off his art collection, and about how he's put some plans in place for Henry. I remember how my mum called up Mrs Harvey next door to get me the details of my current job. Presumably Sir George had similar (if probably more illustrious) strings to pull.

Then there's the letters between 'H' and 'A'. The ones in the bundle all seem to be written in the lead-up to the ball that was held for Henry's 21st birthday – the night of the fire, according to Mrs Bradford. The writing is sentimental and old-fashioned – two people expressing undying love for each other, worrying about whether or not their romance will be accepted by Henry's father.

Given the fragile relationship between Henry and his father, it seems somewhat odd that Sir George would organise a ball for Henry's birthday, especially given their reduced financial circumstances. Henry surmises that it's down to his father wanting to 'bridge the gap' between them. One of the letters even states that his father was arranging for Henry's portrait to be painted. But if it ever was painted, then it's not in the house.

The letters between 'H' and 'A' end abruptly – after the engagement was announced, perhaps there was no longer any reason to send each other quaint little love notes. Their happy ending was signed, sealed and delivered.

Or was it? I flip to the last letter, which I've placed on its own in a plastic wallet. It's only a fragment of paper; half of it has been burned away. I read the part that remains:

> *Darling A—*
>   *God forgive me, but I have been such a fool. He means to ruin our plans – but I won't let him. We must play along with this little charade for tonight, but tomorrow—*

The rest of the letter is lost, with only a thin brown edge of ash remaining. What did Henry mean? From the looks of things, it must have been the last letter between them before the ball. The ball that went out in a blaze – literally. What happened between Henry writing this letter to Arabella, and their subsequent engagement and marriage? He must have spoken to his father, stood up to him, and somehow talked him around. Perhaps Henry burned the letter himself so that Arabella wouldn't be upset at how strongly his father objected to their plans. But if Henry or someone else meant to burn it, then why is it part of the bundle at all?

And what about the fire? Was it just an unfortunate coincidence that it happened just as Henry and Arabella were finally able to reveal their love to the world? I put the letters back in my drawer, trying to imagine myself at the ball, as described by Mrs Bradford. The mirrors reflecting the candlelight; the stars visible through the glass ceiling. The scent of roses; the interwoven melodies of a string quartet; liveried waiters serving champagne. A couple dancing together, eyes only for each other. But what of the aftermath? The rising flames blacken my fantasy to a cinder. Whatever the truth is, I can only find it by returning to Rosemont Hall.

Fifteen

On Friday afternoon, I gather together all my papers and research and double-check that I have the keys to Rosemont Hall for the Saturday viewing. I've rehearsed my sales pitch over and over in my head, and I feel ready. This is my big chance to find a sympathetic buyer, and instead of being nervous, I'm quite excited – especially about going to the house early for a nose around.

But at a quarter to five, Mr Bowen-Knowles throws a spanner in the works. He summons me into his office, gives my outfit (cranberry wrap dress from Jigsaw with low V-front) the once-over, and informs me that he has not one, but two additional Saturday viewings for me to do: a cottage near Shepton Mallet, and a semi in Glastonbury.

'Great,' I lie, quickly doing the maths. Even if everything goes smoothly with the first two viewings, I'll still have to rush to make the two o'clock at Rosemont Hall.

'And Amy, I hope these viewings go well, because – you've been here over a month and haven't made a sale yet.' He wrinkles his nose and gives a short laugh.

It's obviously his idea of an off-hand little joke, but all the same, anger surges in my chest. It isn't just that Jonathan and Patricia have been sitting on their arses nearly the whole time I've been here, but the fact that everyone in the office knows that I should have got the credit for the Blundell sale.

'I thought you'd like to know, by the way,' he adds with a little smirk, 'Fred Blundell was arrested two days ago for smuggling stolen artwork into the UK. The only property he'll be buying is an eight by ten cell in Wormwood Scrubs.'

'Oh no!' The moral high ground liquidates under my feet. 'Poor Fred and Mary – they seemed so nice. And keen.'

'Just as well,' he says. 'The vendors have decided to remarket the Bristol penthouse – since the Blundells offered the asking price, they think they can get 3.5 in the new year.'

'Oh.' I hang my head. His eyes follow me as I turn away. I can't face him; there's nothing to say. I'm officially back to square one.

'Amy,' he says as my hand is on the door knob.

'Yes?'

'Here are the keys for tomorrow.' He holds out two envelopes and client intake forms. I force myself to meet his eyes as I take them.

'And Amy...'

'Yes.'

'Good luck.'

Biting my lip, I leave his office.

*

The Blundell incident is a setback (and, I acknowledge, more for them than for me) but I'm determined to bounce back – and I have a plan. First, I bow out of tentative arrangements to go to the pub with Claire. Then I ring Mum and tell her not to expect me for dinner. After work, I creep along in the Bath rush-hour traffic, but instead of turning towards home, I take a detour: to Rosemont Hall.

Rain pelts against the windscreen as I drive slowly through the gates and up the long drive, the trees skeletal in the beam of the headlights. At the top of the low hill, my heart begins to speed up in anticipation of seeing the dark silhouette of the chimneys against the sky.

Instead, the house is ablaze with light.

I slam on the brakes, imagining for a second that the house is on fire. It takes me a second to realise that it's just the lights on inside the house, glowing yellow out of the large symmetrical windows. Someone is inside. Which means that I should turn around and go home. But what if Mrs Bradford is wreaking havoc in advance of tomorrow's viewing? What if she or her huge dog, Captain, goes on a rampage inside?

I pull up in front of the house. A Mercedes that I've never seen before is parked outside. Surely Mrs Bradford wouldn't drive a fancy car (and she looks too old to drive at all). Mr Kendall drives a Beamer so that leaves… who?

As I get out of the car, the cold rain lashes my face. I run across the gravel forecourt and shelter beneath the door architrave. I ring the bell – if necessary I can pretend to be lost. Inside, there's a faint echo of chimes.

I wait. No one comes.

I ring the bell again.

It's all very odd. I could leave, but what if something really is wrong? As I'm about to peek inside the front windows, the door creaks open.

'Oh!' My hand flies to my mouth and I stifle a scream.

Sixteen

It's her – the woman in the painting!

The orange rectangle of light inside the door frames her face as she stares at me with those huge blue eyes that I would recognise anywhere. She's even wearing dusty pink – though as reality begins to dawn, I see that it's a cashmere cardigan rather than a silk gown. Her auburn hair falls loosely around her face but in a long bob rather than curls. Her pink bow-shaped mouth, outlined with dark lip liner, is gaping open at my shocked reaction. I squint like I'm trying to recognise a long-lost friend. It can't really be *her*, so it can only be—

'Ms Flora?' I say.

'Who are you?'

Her voice is nasal and American and immediately I know that I've guessed right: she's one of the two heirs of Rosemont Hall. The one who's come over to strip it bare while her brother, Mr Jack, does a deal with the devil.

'Hi,' I say with a smile. 'I didn't mean to disturb you. I was in the neighbourhood so I thought I would pop around and—'

She puts her hands on her hips. 'And you are?'

'I'm Amy Wood, the estate agent.' I make a half-hearted attempt to fluff my wet hair, and hold out my hand. She doesn't take it. I realise that in my windblown, rain-battered state, I must look more like a tramp than a competent professional. 'Someone is coming around tomorrow to view the house,' I say, trying to salvage my dignity. 'If that's okay with you, that is. I dropped by to make sure everything is in order.'

'Oh?' She raises a perfectly waxed eyebrow.

'Mr Kendall didn't seem to know when you were coming – he thought in a few weeks. So when I saw the lights on, I was afraid that Mrs Bradford, the housekeeper, might be making mischief. But I won't disturb you if you're busy. I can just leave…?'

The woman in the doorway stares at me with her striking eyes as if unable to decide if I'm friend or foe. Had it not been cold and rainy, I might not have cared which way she leaned. But as it is, I'd like to come inside out of the rain.

Warily, she opens the door. 'I guess you can come in, Ms Wood.'

'Please – call me Amy.'

Shivering, I step inside the hallway. It's just as cold inside the house as out. A little puddle of water forms at my feet on the grimy marble floor. The woman stands there, and neither of us seem to know what to say.

'I'm Flora MacArthur,' she says finally. 'Just call me Flora – I hate all that "Ms Flora" stuff the lawyer uses.'

'Pleased to meet you.'

The awkward moment lasts until finally she directs me into the library. I follow her, noticing that she's placed little round pink stickers on some of the furniture and old books.

There's a bitter chill in the room – she's propped the window open with a pile of books.

'I'm selecting things to go to the special auction at Christie's,' she explains. 'Before my brother gets here.'

'Oh, is Mr Jack coming here too?' I stifle a grimace. He's probably planning a meeting with Hexagon to dispose of the property – like a modern-day Mr Jasper in *The Mystery of Edwin Drood* who secretly wishes to ravish his ward. I have no desire to meet him in person. But as I look around at all the pink stickers, I realise that maybe I've been handed a chance on a dusty silver platter.

'I'm sure you and your brother must both be thrilled to have inherited this house,' I fib. 'It's such an amazing place. A truly unique architectural gem. It will be lovely once there's a family to live here again and appreciate it. I'm so glad you've decided to let us market it rather than selling it to developers...' I purse my lips into an exaggerated cringe, '... who will only strip away its character, carve it up, and ruin it.'

She frowns and I fear I've gone too far. 'Didn't the lawyer tell you?' she says. 'The house needs to be sold quickly. The taxes on it are outrageous. And as for who buys it – well – frankly I couldn't care less as long as we get a good price. My brother's in touch with someone who wants to build a golf course or something. He says they sound serious. Fingers and toes crossed that they make an offer.'

I try to reconcile this cold, money-grubbing woman with the young woman in the portrait. Looking closely, Flora is older than I thought when she first answered the door. Faint wrinkles crease her eyes, and her face and neck are late-30s-thin. She's old enough that she ought to be able to appreciate exactly what she's got, but clearly she doesn't – nor does her brother. Aren't Americans, of all people, supposed to be gaga over classic English houses? Lucky me to have found the two bad apples in the barrel!

'Besides,' she says, 'I think the house is hideous. So big and clunky. And cold. I can't imagine anyone wanting to live here. I'm here to sell the furniture and Jack can deal with the rest.' She sticks a pink sticker on an antique mantel clock.

'The house may not be to everyone's taste,' I say through my teeth, 'but a developer will always try to undercut you – I've heard that the golf course people have another possible site on the other side of Little Botheringford. But if you find the right private buyer – well...' I shrug theatrically, 'there are some people who will pay a big premium to get their hands on a place like this. Like the people I'm seeing tomorrow, for example.'

I'm talking knee-deep rubbish, that's for sure. But Flora looks interested.

'What do you mean?'

I give up all pretence of the truth. 'In England, you see, it's all about class. People will often pay over the odds for a status symbol, even if the house is big and cold. Loads of people will be interested – politicians, pop stars, actors – I read some-where that Johnny Depp bought a house near here. Practically a neighbour.'

Flora's jaw creeps down.

'And then there are the foreign buyers: Japanese, Arabs, Russians,' I add. 'They're always looking for something unique and aspirational. Of course, you could make a quick quid – buck, I mean – by letting Hexagon take it off your hands for a song if they think you're desperate to sell.' I shake my head and tsk. 'But you'd be leaving heaps of money on the table.'

'That's not what the lawyer says. He says that it needs too much work for anyone to buy it as a home.'

'I expect his fee for the estate administration is the same either way.'

'Hmmm.' Flora looks around at the room as if seeing it for the first time. 'How much time would it take – to get all that money for it?'

'It's hard to say. The market for country properties is improving a lot. Originally, we'd arranged with Mr Kendall to market it for three months. I've got several interested parties. But a special place like this – it won't sell overnight.'

'Hmmm.'

I decide to push my luck.

'In fact, you might want to wait a bit before clearing everything out. The furniture and artwork might help sell the place – it's the little touches that might tempt the right buyer.' I secretly hope that the girl in the portrait appreciates my efforts to save her home. 'Though I'm all for you clearing out the clutter,' I hasten to add.

She purses her lips. I know I've got her.

'I suppose we could hold off until March,' she says, 'as long as some of the furniture is sold. And as long as my brother doesn't get some ridiculous notion of playing Lord of the Manor before it sells.'

Lord of the Manor. From the little I know about her brother, Jack, that doesn't seem very likely.

'When is he coming over?' I ask nonchalantly.

'Who knows?' She rolls her eyes. 'Jack's in computers. He works in Silicon Valley and teaches up-and-coming tech geeks at Stanford. He's always working on some amazing gadget or another. Or meeting with investors, or shareholders, or helping out some charity. I have no idea when he's going to find time to come over here.'

I consider this new information about Mr Jack. He must be pretty savvy to teach at one of the top universities in America. I reimagine him: skinny with receding hair and pasty skin, wearing a turtleneck sweater, a blazer and cowboy boots. And little wire-rimmed glasses like Bill Gates. He'll drive a convertible accessorised with a lithesome blonde undergrad, and they'll spend their weekends living the California dream: playing eighteen holes at a seaside golf course with the university trustees. It's no wonder that a falling-down old house in England holds no appeal for him. Hopefully he won't bother to come over here at all.

'I can see that all of this must be very inconvenient,' I say.

'Inconvenient?' She sniffs. 'It's a great big pain in the rear. The sooner we've offloaded this place, the better.'

I give her my best smile. 'I'm sure it will all work out. Just give me a chance to do my job. I won't let you down.'

'Why do you care so much?'

'It's my job to get the best price for my clients. But beyond that...' I hesitate – she may not understand, but it seems important to put it into words. 'I feel that the house is special. I used to teach English literature. It reminds me of all the old houses in the books I love. Books like *Jane Eyre*, *Wuthering Heights*, *Rebecca*.' I find myself blushing. 'They may be romantic, but they're classics too.'

Flora wrinkles her nose. 'I think we had to read some of those in high school. They were really boring.'

'I know they're old-fashioned. But the houses are characters just as much as the people. They have personality, and history. It would be a shame if Rosemont Hall was lost to posterity just because something had to be done quickly.'

Her blue eyes narrow.

'And the women in those stories dealt with great obstacles. I think it would be fascinating to learn about the real people who lived here – like the girl in the painting on the landing. You look a bit like her.'

'I do?'

'Yes, haven't you seen it?'

She shakes her head. I gesture for her to follow, hoping I'm doing the right thing. I'm sure that when she sees the portrait, it will be like looking in a mirror. She follows me up to the landing at the top of the stairs.

'Just here.'

I stand aside to give her space. She cocks her head, stares at the picture for a few seconds, and finally, looks at me. 'I don't see any resemblance,' she says.

'No?'

'Honestly, I find it a bit creepy.' She turns away from the lovely girl in the pink dress. 'In fact, I'm glad you dropped by. This place – it gets to you when you're here alone.' She crosses her arms and shivers.

'It does,' I agree, though obviously the house 'gets' to me in a completely different way. I follow her back down the stairs to the great hall. I offer to turn off the lights and lock up. 'You must be dying to get back to your hotel for a nice hot bath,' I venture.

'Well, yes, actually. The flight over here was so long, and then it took forever driving all the way here on the wrong side of the road.'

'Then why don't you leave me to it. I'll just straighten up a bit – the viewing is at two o'clock tomorrow and I want the house to look as good as possible. You did say you're okay with it, right?'

'Knock yourself out. I won't be here – I'm going to London to do some shopping. I've had about as much of this place as I can take. It's so... dead.'

We walk together through the rooms on the ground floor while she tries to remember where she put her handbag. I notice that some of the old papers and magazines have been cleared into black bin bags in a few of the rooms, and there's actually a smell of polish. I practically trip over a heavy upright hoover parked right in the middle of one of the drawing rooms. Someone has definitely been doing some cleaning. Not Flora, clearly, so it must be Mrs Bradford. It seems a strange thing for her to start doing her job now that it no longer matters.

Flora locates her oversized Coach tote and puts on her coat and Burberry scarf, her eyes watering from the chill.

'Can you find your way back to the hotel?' I say.

'Yeah, I think so.'

'Have a good night then, and it was nice to meet you.'

This time when I hold out my hand, she shakes it.

'Thanks,' she says gratefully.

I wait at the door until she's run out to her rental car and the tail lights disappear into the gloom. Then I return to the library. Whoever's been cleaning hasn't made it in here yet. The broken frame with the picture of the newlyweds is face down on the desk where I left it. Rain is seeping in through the open window and pooling on the rotting windowsill. The books that are propping open the window are damp too, and I remove them. The window closes with a bang and a rattle of glass. One by one, I dry the books on my scarf and put them back on the shelves: John Le Carre, Jeffrey Archer, Catherine Cookson, Maeve Binchy. And then the last book – the only one without a title or an author. It's a little larger than a chequebook, with a black leather cover. I open it gingerly, unsure of its age.

It turns out to be a small sketchbook, the pages filled in with doodles and drawings in black charcoal pencil. There's no name or date inside the cover to reveal who the artist might have been, but I flip through it with growing interest. Many of the drawings are rough portrait sketches – young men, children, older women, pretty flapper girls, even a Spanish flamenco dancer. Some of the sketches have names scribbled in the margin: Feldmann, Stein, Rabinowicz. There are also sketches of fancy clothing, like the artist was designing for the theatre. There are beaded flapper dresses with dropped waists, 1930s bias-cut dresses, and jaunty little 40s pencil skirt suits and Homburg hats.

And at the very end, I find a page labelled 'Windham', marked with a folded-over piece of ivory paper. There are several sketches of a dour-looking young man with a thin nose, delicate cheekbones, and a curtain of hair falling half over one eye. I flip over the page, and my heart thuds against my ribcage. *She's* there – in profile and *en face* – the girl in the portrait on the stairs! Her hair is different than in the portrait – tied severely back from her face rather than loose at her shoulders. But the eyes that stare out at me are the same, I'm sure of it. Rendered in muted charcoal, she looks even more like Ms Flora. The rest of the pages in the book are blank. Whoever she was, she was the last person to be sketched by the artist.

I close the book and sit down on an old threadbare sofa with a trail of stuffing that's been gnawed by mice. I consider what I know so far about the girl in the portrait – nothing – and about the Windham family – very little. The letters between Henry and Arabella mention an artist friend of Sir George's who was hired to paint Henry's portrait, using the studio up in the attic. That would have all taken place in the early 1950s. The date on the frame of the girl in the pink dress is 1899, making her well over a hundred years old. So that leaves two possibilities. Either the sketchbook dates back to the time of the portrait – unlikely given the styles of the clothing in the drawings; or else the artist sketched the portrait itself, rather than the original sitter. It's somewhat odd that he sketched her with a different hairstyle, but I suppose he was simply captivated by her face, and those bold blue eyes.

The little book has so piqued my curiosity that I'm a little disappointed that it doesn't hold any real answers. Mrs Bradford said that the girl wasn't Sir George's wife or mother. So who was she?

I slip the book into my bag for safe keeping – I can't risk Flora throwing it out with the rubbish or tossing it in the auction box. As I do, the page marker slips out onto the floor. I pick it up, realising that it's actually a letter that's been folded over and used as a bookmark. Ignoring a momentary niggle about poking my nose where it doesn't belong, I unfold it and read through it:

Rosemont Hall
April 1st 1952

My dear friend—
   I eagerly await your arrival. Has it really been more than a decade since we last saw each other? When I close my eyes I can still smell the scent of gardenia, feel the warmth of the Andalusian evenings on my face, taste the

wine and the salt of sweat on my lips. I've never felt so alive as when we were cheating death every day.

Now that we are soon to meet again, I must warn you that the years have not been kind. I have sold my treasures off one by one, in order to maintain this house. And each time, it's felt like a little death. Only you can help me now, in this, my hour of need.

Be assured that you have been given the finest space in the house, with a view of the parkland, and natural light that floods in through the oriel window. It's everything an artist could want. And you, my friend, are so much more than that.

Please come immediately. I have enclosed money for the fare. We will say that you are here to paint my son's portrait. Your work must be finished before the date we spoke of. I am planning a grand ball for the occasion. And maybe, a few fireworks...

The letter isn't signed, but I deduce that it was written by Sir George. I read through it again. The references to his time in Spain and the sale of his treasures is self-explanatory, but what did he mean by his 'hour of need'? And what about the portrait? There's no portrait of Henry in the house.

I refold the letter and tuck it back into the sketchbook. There's more here than meets the eye, and I'm going to keep collecting any pieces to the puzzle. A puzzle that no one is looking to solve, and pieces that no one will miss. I zip the letter and the sketchbook up in my bag.

I spend another hour looking through some of the old books and papers in the library, but don't find anything else. It's getting late, and with three viewings tomorrow, morning will come all too quickly. I walk through the downstairs rooms off the great hall and shut off the lights. Before leaving, I climb the stairs to the landing and pay one last visit to the girl in the pink dress.

'I told her a few white lies to buy you some time.' I remove the sticker that Flora must have stuck on the frame when I wasn't looking. 'But just how much, I don't know. Don't tell anyone, okay?'

Just for a moment, I imagine that the girl in the pink dress seems to smile a bit more broadly – even conspiratorially – now that she's keeping my secrets as well as her own.

Seventeen

Saturday. I wake up to winter light streaming in through the curtains. Last night's visit to Rosemont Hall and meeting the 'the girl in the portrait' seems like an odd dream. I know it's real only when I check my knicker drawer and find that the bundle of letters, the gold lighter and the artist's sketchbook are all still there. I'd like to sit down and go through everything again; reconstruct the final hours before the ball; look for connections that I might have missed. But I don't have that luxury now. Because all *too* real is the stack of glossy brochures on the nightstand – the particulars for the day's three viewings.

When I emerge from my room, Mum accosts me with a full English (minus the sausages and the stewed tomato). 'You're not leaving the house again, young lady, without a proper breakfast.'

There are worse things in the world than Mum's cooking, so I sit down at the table in the kitchen and tuck in. I'm going to need every ounce of strength today.

'Three viewings?' Mum shakes her head when I tell her my itinerary. 'You've been working six days a week. For what they're paying you, it isn't right.'

'But Mum, if I can sell a property and get a commission, then it will be worth it.' Someday soon I'll be able to buy or rent my own flat and move out, I don't add.

She sips her coffee, looking distinctly sceptical, and I regret having told her that the Blundell deal fell through. However, that was just bad luck. The Blundells prove that, barring unforeseen circumstances, I can sell a property. And since I've done it before, I can do it again. Today.

I down a second cup of coffee and drive to my first viewing appointment: the cottage near Shepton Mallet. The house is in the centre of a small village that is charming at first glance. At second glance, the post office is 'to let', the duck pond is chock-full of floating rubbish, and the pub on the green is boarded up. In fact, the only open business is a garage advertising 'pass or don't pay' MOTs. But on the plus side, there are nice views of open countryside, and the property I'm here to show – Acorn Cottage – is half-timbered and quaint.

I park the car and quickly review my notes. The clients – a Mr and Mrs Wakefield – are retirees looking to downsize. The vendors are a Mr and Mrs Chip.

I make my way through the miniature gate in front of the house and walk up the weedy path. I'd assumed – and hoped – that 'The Chips' would be out during the viewing. But I can hear voices from inside. I tap the tarnished brass knocker on the door. Inside, everything goes quiet.

A minute later, bolts and chains start to jingle. The door opens and a tiny woman (literally – she comes up to below my chin) with stringy black hair stares up at me, a cigarette dangling from her mouth.

'Hi.' I put on my cheeriest smile. 'I'm Amy Wood, the estate agent. Mrs Chip – is that right?'

From behind her, a child screams: 'Mum, Joey did a poo poo in his pants.'

Mrs Chip ashes the cigarette at my feet.

'I'm here to show the cottage,' I say, '– at half nine?'

'Uh huh.' She stands aside and I enter. The room is filled with scattered toys and reeks of ashtrays and dirty nappies. In the centre of the room is an oversized dining table with (I count them) six small children seated around it eating some kind of gruel, and a seventh in a bouncer. One small boy has sick down his front. The unnatural silence is broken when he flings a spoon of slop at the face of a chubby ginger-haired girl across from him.

Mayhem breaks out: 'Stop it Ronnie!'; 'You started it!'; 'Susie called me a wanker'; 'Can I go watch Waybuloo?'; 'Mum, Willy ate a bogey.' Mrs Chip ignores them all, and stares at the television which is blaring with *Bargain Hunt*.

In the height of the fray, the door knocker clunks. The Wakefields – right on time. Unfortunately.

'I'll get it,' I say, though no one is listening. A projectile of goop goes flying in my direction. I barely manage to duck in time for it to whizz past me and splat against the wall.

I hurry to the door and fling it open. A prim, serious-faced older couple are standing outside wearing what at first glance seems to be matching tweed suits and small wire-framed glasses. The woman frowns as the din behind me crescendos.

'Mr and Mrs Wakefield.' I pretend I can't hear the cacophony. 'I'm Amy Wood. I'll be showing you the property – it's a lovely character cottage, don't you think? Can I suggest that we start with the outside?'

From the first, it's clear that the Wakefields are neither impressed, nor amused.

'From the map on your website, we were expecting it to be off the main road,' Mr Wakefield says to me as we stand in the overgrown jungle of a garden.

'And the particulars didn't have any outside photos – I'd no idea that the roof was thatched.' His wife frowns. 'That's a bit of false advertising.'

'It costs a bomb to insure thatch,' Mr Wakefield chimes in. 'I've been in the insurance industry for 40 years, like my father before me. So I should know.'

'Of course.' I smile through my teeth. 'On the plus side, if I'm not mistaken, Mrs Chip is keen to sell.' At least, I assume she is given that her current set-up is like the little old woman who lived in a shoe.

Having exhausted the viewing possibilities of the outside, I usher them inside the cottage, where things have gone from bad to worse. The children have finished their breakfast and are up from the table. Two are fighting over a ride-on Thomas the Tank Engine, and one boy is literally swinging from the net curtains. A mucky-faced girl has her sister by the throat, and two of the older boys are playing 'doctor' with a butter knife. Mrs Chip seems impervious to the chaos, nonchalantly eating crisps straight from a bag with one hand, and smoking a cigarette with the other.

Mrs Wakefield takes one look around and begins to cough.

'Why don't we go upstairs,' I suggest. I lead the way up the narrow staircase.

At the top of the stairs, Mr Wakefield bangs his head on a low beam. 'Bollocks!' he yells, rubbing his head.

'Mummy, mummy, that man said bollocks!'

I cringe inwardly. 'As you'll see, there are three lovely good-sized bedrooms up here and plenty of loft space for storage.'

The bedrooms are packed floor to ceiling with toys and oversized furniture. Everything reeks of smoke. Mr Wakefield ducks and dives under low beams, and Mrs Wakefield walks around with her nose wrinkled up like a pug dog. As we all crowd into one of the tiny rooms, Mrs Chip comes in carrying an enormous pile of laundry. I'm about to suggest that we move on when Mr Wakefield decides to get chummy.

'Why are you selling?' he asks Mrs Chip. All of us ignore a blood-curdling shriek from downstairs.

'My piece o' shit bloke ran off with some tart he met at the school. Me and the kids got a two-bed council flat in Yeovil.'

'Oh,' the three of us say at the same time, for different reasons.

We take a quick peek at the tiny, grimy bathroom that stinks of potty-training-in-progress. Then we head downstairs to the war zone, where little has changed except that two of the children have hunkered down in front of the TV, and one little boy is standing on the table waving a plastic gun at us.

'Uhh, the kitchen, airing cupboard and the sitting room,' I practically shout. 'Lots of original features and potential for renovation.'

It feels like forever as the Wakefields explore the nooks and crannies – crunching plastic toys underfoot, opening over-flowing cupboards – even the fridge. By the time it's finally over, my lip is sore from steady biting. I give Mrs Chip a curt 'thanks', and herd the Wakefields out the door. 'Sorry about that,' I say.

'It's a charming cottage,' Mrs Wakefield says.

'Sorry?' I do a double-take. They hated it – didn't they?

She shrugs. 'Too bad it's on a main road.'

'And thatched,' her husband adds with a disappointed tsk.

'Yes, it is too bad.'

I hand them an extra copy of the particulars, promise to keep in touch, and as soon as they're gone, make a beeline for the peace and quiet of my car.

*

The next viewing is in Glastonbury – No. 12 Orchard Terrace. As I drive into the town, I begin to feel better – the mystical pull of the Tor works its magic. It's said that King Arthur and Guinevere are buried in the abbey. I imagine myself as a knight errant, on a quest for the Holy Grail – my first sale.

I drive past the New-Age shops selling crystals, love potions, indie music and goth clothing in all shades of black. The town centre looks lively and robust. But past the shops and cafés I turn off into a warren of less quaint streets lined with council blocks. Orchard Terrace has a tattoo parlour with three leather-clad bikers hanging around outside. The 1930s pebble-dashed semis are faded and decrepit; several have boarded-up doors and windows filled in with breeze blocks. My enthusiasm evaporates.

I park the car and check my notes. My client is a Mr Patel, a property developer. The house is a 1930s semi that was recently occupied by squatters but has now been cleared out by the police. I roll down the window to take a look.

Every window of the house is broken or boarded up, and the plywood door has a red spray-painted biohazard sign on it. I have a sneaking suspicion that maybe the police declared success a little too early, because there's a booming beat coming from inside the house. *Someone* is home.

This clearly wasn't part of the plan, but I've no time to debate what to do, because just then, a big black car pulls up behind me and an Asian man in a dark suit gets out. I open my door and try to put up my umbrella but it blows inside out. I shove it back in the car.

'Hi,' I say, 'I'm Amy Wood, the estate agent. You're Mr Patel?'

The man frowns and nods his head.

'Honestly, I thought the place was vacant, so I think we should reschedule…' I say the last word to his back. He's already walking swiftly towards the house.

I curse under my breath and follow him to the cover of the leaky porch.

'Someone's inside…' I repeat.

He holds up his hand to cut me off. 'It is of no importance.'

It might be of some importance if we get killed, but it's obvious that he's not going to be put off. 'Okay,' I shrug, and knock hard on the door. No one answers, so I ring the bell. Nothing.

'But you have the key?' my client inquires.

Unfortunately, yes. I fish out the envelope with the keys from my handbag. I unlock the door and shout hesitantly: 'Hello, anybody home?'

Mr Patel pushes past me. He pulls out a laser tape measure. He immediately starts zapping the walls with the little red light, tapping the measurements into his BlackBerry. Cosmetically, the place is trashed – grimy wallpaper hangs off the walls, the carpet is black and ripped, the walls and ceiling are covered with spray paint. I glance at Mr Patel. He's making all sorts of satisfied noises. Surreptitiously, I rip up a tissue to make earplugs. They do nothing to drown out the din.

Mr Patel finishes in the hallway and opens the door to the main reception room. The room has no floor, just joists with rubble beneath. Steadying himself against the wall, he steps out onto the joists. 'Be careful,' I plead, but he ignores me. He skips across the boards, laser measure poised and ready in his fist.

'There are some fine features here that could be restored,' I shout half-heartedly. 'I'd say this house has loads of potential. The rooms are good-sized, and so is the garden. It could be a lovely family home – a real bargain at the price.' It's almost true. Beneath the graffiti, the room does have some nice crown mouldings and an original fireplace.

A rat scurries between the floor joists. I let out a little yelp. Unfazed, Mr Patel keeps measuring. Beyond the remains of the kitchen is an overgrown garden. Rain is streaming in through a gaping diagonal crack in the exterior wall. Mr Patel zaps the crack.

His phone rings and he proceeds to carry on a conversation for (yes, I time it) – seven minutes. Each moment ticking away increases the likelihood that I'll be late for the Rosemont Hall viewing, not to mention the possibility of getting killed.

Finally, Mr Patel puts the phone away. 'Okay, now the upstairs,' he directs.

Clenching my teeth, I go first up the rickety stairs. A

board gives way beneath my feet and I nearly tumble to the bottom. Mr Patel goes past me, brandishing his laser. At the top of the stairs there's a bathroom caked with excrement, and two bedrooms filled with pipes and tubes that resemble a home laboratory. The Chip cottage looks positively pristine in comparison. 'Lovely good-sized bedrooms,' I say. Mr Patel responds by zapping them. He walks to the door of the main bedroom. The music hammers like a ravenous beast trying to escape.

'I think we should skip that one,' I say. 'I can email you the dimensions from the office.'

Mr Patel completely ignores me and throws open the door without knocking. For an instant, I'm terrified. Do I have some kind of liability if he gets murdered? He steps inside the room. I creep over to the door and look inside.

Four very large, very tattooed and pierced men are lying on various filthy sofas and chairs. My heart is in my throat until I realise that their eyes are all closed – they're drunk, or asleep, or stoned, or dead.

I rush over to Mr Patel and grab his arm. 'We need to go,' I shout.

He shakes his head.

Unbelievably, he takes out his laser measure and starts doing his thing. He stands on a sofa next to one of the passed-out men and measures a ceiling rose. I'm feeling panicky and the smell in the room is making me gag – sweat and booze mixed with cigarette smoke and incense. Just then, the CD comes to an end and everything goes quiet. Mr Patel goes to the bay window and measures it, knocking a syringe off the sill in the process. It clatters to the floor and rolls to the feet of one of the men. The man groans and opens his eyes.

'Let's get out of here,' I hiss.

Mr Patel calmly taps the keys of his BlackBerry.

I grab his arm and pull him out of the room.

'What the fuck!—' a loud male voice—

I slam the door and steer Mr Patel away. We successfully navigate a gaping hole in the floor. Mr Patel pauses at the top of the stairs. For an awful second I think he's going to measure something else.

Heavy footsteps; the door handle turns.

'Come on!'

We half tumble down the stairs together. I drag him through the hall and out the front door, slamming it behind us. I scramble for my key and lock the deadbolt from the outside. There's a sudden commotion of voices from inside the upstairs bedroom. An angry face appears at the window.

'Can I see the garden?' Mr Patel stops me with a hand on my arm.

'Ring the office,' I shriek. '—Schedule a second viewing.'

I drag him to the street and bundle him into his car. As the door to the house opens and four angry giants spill forth brandishing beer bottles, I jump back in my own car, shaking all over. I turn on the ignition and floor it.

Eighteen

I put some miles between me and Glastonbury and pull over in a lay-by to catch my breath. I feel like I've aged a hundred years in the last two hours. The last thing I want to do is another viewing. Even – and perhaps, especially – Rosemont Hall.

Thanks to Mr Patel and his laser, I'm running late. The A39 is a red sea of brake lights. By the time I drive through the rickety gates and begin the ascent of the long, winding drive, my heart is in my throat.

The towering monolith of Rosemont Hall, its four chimneys scraping the grey sky, looks forbidding – and lonely. The East Wing is like the skeleton of a vast, beached whale, the burnt rafters slicing the sky into jagged pieces.

The clients should be here by now, but there's no car in the drive. A knot of tension tightens in my shoulders. Are they late too, or have they already come and gone? Or just not bothered to turn up?

I grab my papers and jump out of the car. After the events of the last few hours, I'm now desperate for the loo. I run up the stairs to the front door and wrench the key in the lock.

According to David Waters' report, there's only one working loo in the house. For once, I don't stop to say hello to the girl in the portrait as I dash up the stairs into the Rose Bedroom – which, I assume, was Mrs Windham's.

The bathroom has the same avocado green suite as my parents' bungalow, which makes me feel right at home. But in this loo, the bath is grotty with soap scum, the tiles mildewed, and there's a large hole next to the bath where the floor seems to have collapsed under years of wet feet.

After using the loo, I go to the sink to wash my hands. There are slick strips of rust behind each of the taps, where water is slowly dripping like excruciatingly arrhythmic Chinese water torture. The first tap doesn't turn, and the second tap lets out a trickle of water, and then won't turn off. Worse, the drain seems to be blocked, and water slowly begins to pool in the basin.

With a sigh, I wipe my hands on my trousers and go back out into the bedroom. Even if I tried, I couldn't make it look more dated, faded, and dreary than it already does. The furnishings are a 70s mismatch except for the huge wooden canopy bed that takes up half the room, hung with curtains in a rose chintz pattern.

On the bedside table is a tattered book and a box of tissues. Frowning, I peek at the title of the book. It's one that I know well: *The Tenant of Wildfell Hall* by Anne Brontë. I'm almost positive that it wasn't there on my previous visit. Then I notice that on the bed, the blankets and satin coverlet are rumpled. My skin crawls with the thought that someone might have been sleeping in a dead woman's bed.

As I'm about to leave the room, something else catches my eye: the door cut into the panelling. I remember David Waters saying that it was a closet of some kind. I walk over and pull on the door, wrinkling my nose in anticipation of the smell of dead mouse or mothballs.

Instead, to my surprise, when I open the door, the smell of potpourri wafts out. It's strong, but not unpleasant. I flip the light switch and a bare bulb comes on.

The closet goes back about fifteen feet. It's completely filled with clothing zipped in clear plastic bags, and there's an upper shelf full of hats and even a few elaborately coiffed wigs. The clothing in the bags is like something out of a Victorian pantomime: flouncy gowns, a clown suit, a gentleman's cloak and dagger, a pirate's outfit. A huge spider scurries away from my feet. The whole thing is a bit creepy.

Just as I'm about to switch off the light, I see it: a pink satin dress on a padded hanger; an exact replica of the dress in the portrait. I unzip the plastic and run my fingers over the pale, supple fabric that seems as fresh as the day it was made. The scene in *Rebecca* pops into my mind where Mrs Danvers tricks the second Mrs de Winter into dressing up like one of the paintings for a costume ball, in a similar costume to that worn by the ill-fated Rebecca. The whole party is sent into an embarrassing uproar. And as for Henry's party – well, that ended in a tragic fire. Did the costumes belong to Arabella Windham? Why would Mrs Bradford keep them in such good order when the rest of the house is such a wreck? My neck crawls with goosebumps like I'm intruding on private memories and carefully kept secrets.

I switch off the light and close the door.

The tap is still dripping in the bathroom. I go back in and give it one last good twist to turn it off. As I do, it comes off in my hand. There's a deep gurgling noise, and the next moment, the whole thing erupts and I'm doused head to toe with freezing brown water. I let out a little scream and frantically try to put the broken piece of metal back on. Luckily (if anything about it can be considered lucky) the water fizzles out quickly, and subsides to the original drip. If the house doesn't want its plumbing disturbed, then who am I to argue?

Just then, I hear the crunch of gravel. My clients! I'd practically forgotten about them.

I rush to the window. A silver Aston Martin pulls up in front of the house.

I spring into action, running down the stairs, rifling in my pocket for the paper with the client's name – a Mr O'Brien – leaving a trail of water dripping behind me.

As I reach the door, the car is moving again. It reverses in the drive, like they've taken one look and seen enough.

I run towards the car, waving my arms. 'Mr O'Brien,' I shout. 'Stop! I'm Amy Wood, the estate agent. Please don't leave. I'm here!'

The car stops. The driver door opens and a man gets out. He's wearing a black hooded tracksuit and looks much younger than I expected – about my age, I would say. Other than that he's fairly nondescript. But the woman who gets out of the passenger side is anything but. Tall and bleached blonde, she's wearing a micro skirt, lace tights, and gold stiletto heels. On top, she has on a fitted leather jacket that augments her impressive, oversized chest. Everything about her – nails, make-up, lips drawn in a little red pout – seems in perfect fabricated order.

'Hello Mr O'Brien,' I say. 'I'm really glad you came.'

'It's Ronan Keene, actually,' the man says as we shake hands. 'O'Brien's my agent.' The woman looks at me and sniffs.

'Oh, of course,' I say. Agent?

'And this is my girlfriend, Crystal.'

The woman looks at me with an irritated pout; like I'm a complete moron for not recognising her – or acting more impressed – or maybe it's because I stopped them from leaving – or maybe it's because I'm drenched and dripping from head to toe with rusty water. I rack my brain, trying to recall if I've seen either of them before. If the man is a celebrity, I definitely don't recognise him. The woman looks like someone who could have graced page 3 of the *Sun*, or perhaps a Z-lister from *Celebrity Love Island*. I'm not awed, but I give her a friendly smile. 'Nice to meet you,' I say.

Introductions complete (though I still can't place either one of them), I run back to the car and grab my papers. As we walk to the door, I begin my spiel. 'This house is truly special,' I say. 'It's one of a kind. And with a little TLC, it could be amazing. Every feature is a piece of history.' I point out some of the decorative plasterwork on the outside of the house. The woman wrinkles her nose.

They step inside the front door and crane their necks looking around. I allow them a moment to be 'awed' by the faded grandeur of the main hall, and then enthusiastically launch into a brief history of the house. 'Rosemont Hall was built in 1765,' I say. 'It's one of the finest examples of Georgian Palladian architecture in the region – maybe even the whole country. It's been in the Windham family for over 200 years. The first Windham won the house in a game of whist.'

As we embark upon the 'tour', I watch them closely for any sign that they're awed, overwhelmed or impressed – anything I can connect with. The woman, Crystal, takes out a handkerchief and puts it over her nose as we go through the ground floor rooms.

'Cracking place,' Ronan says. But if anything, he looks slightly puzzled by the surroundings.

'We've had a quantity surveyor around,' I say, persevering with my sales pitch. 'He's just doing a final report on how much the renovations are likely to cost. I know the house is in a bit of a state right now, but just think how much value you could add.'

Ronan shrugs. 'Money's not really an issue, as long as we can do what we like, eh cupcake,' he flaps his elbow at the woman. 'We'd need to be able to put in a full-size swimming pool, sauna, and gym, and clear those fields to build tennis-courts and the football pitch, of course.'

'Of course.' I echo half-heartedly.

'And Crystal wants one of those big open-plan kitchen

diners with bi-fold doors and a breakfast bar,' he adds. 'So we'd want to knock down some walls.' He swings an imaginary sledgehammer.

'The house is listed, so there'd be some restrictions.' I say through my teeth. 'But there's still a lot of scope to put your own stamp on it without altering the basic structure...'

'Is bulldozing it altering the structure?' Crystal asks. She pulls out a compact mirror and reapplies her lipstick. 'Because it's so dark and draughty – it would never do at all.'

'Crystal...' Ronan says, 'you said you'd keep an open mind.'

'But why?' She pouts. 'You know how much I loved that new-build mansion in Gerrards Cross. That pink marble Turkish bath was to die for. And the cinema wing...' She sighs. 'I hate these horrible old houses. I mean – someone else has *lived* here.'

My hand itches to tweak her surgically altered nose. I walk over to the window and look out at the parkland, trying to remain calm and professional.

'Crystal, we've talked about this...'

'Yah know, I mean, why did you have to sign with Rovers? I know the money wasn't as good at Chelsea, but even Man City would have been better. Or Liverpool.'

'Crystal—'

'I'm sure there isn't a nail salon or a decent boutique for miles.'

It's obviously a lost cause. I'm not proud to say it, but I allow a tiny little mean streak in me to come to the surface.

'Would you like to see the kitchen?' I ask, knowing that it's old-fashioned grottiness will horrify her. 'It's in the basement – very spacious, if a little dated.'

'Ugh,' Crystal says. 'No thanks. I'll wait up here.'

Too bad.

I lead Ronan down the stairs. 'It's a big space,' I say, 'you could definitely do something with it.'

He seems almost to prefer the subterranean damp – or maybe he's just happy for a Crystal-free moment. 'It's a nice house,' he says as we enter the first of the cavernous basement rooms. 'It reminds me of my nan's house in County Down. Only a lot bigger, of course. I see that it has lots of potential.'

'Yes it does.' I smile at him, grateful that someone finally seems to 'get it' – on some level, at least. 'It will be a lovely family home once it's restored. The previous owners who lived here were married for over forty years. It's a "together house" – a house for life.'

'Yeah, but that's not really what we want.'

'Oh?' my enthusiasm ebbs.

'Yeah, because I'm never sure where I'll be from one season to the next.'

'Season?'

'The Premiership. You know – football. I signed with Bristol Rovers. We're newly promoted this season.'

'Oh. Well, that is exciting. Maybe I've seen you when my dad… uhh… my boyfriend… watches *Match of the Day*.' (No wonder I've no idea who they are).

'Maybe.' We check out the dank cave that houses the exploded boiler. I try not to picture this lovely house as a football party pad. Hot-tubs, WAGS, gym, football pitch, nail salon. With enough room left over for Crystal's very own live-in plastic surgeon.

Upstairs, Crystal is nowhere to be seen. 'There's two more floors up above,' I tell him, as we make our way back to the entrance hall. 'Would you like to see more?'

'Sure,' he says with more enthusiasm than I had expected.

We start up the stairs, but he pauses on the landing in front of the portrait of the lady in pink.

'Wow,' he says, 'she's something.'

Renewed hope flickers in my mind. Maybe Mr Ronan

Keene, Premiership Footballer, is not an entirely lost cause.

'Yes she is.' I say. 'I love the way she looks like she has a secret.'

An annoyed female voice filters up the stairs. 'Ronan, can we go? I want to buy some flowers for Mummy.'

'In a few minutes,' he shouts. 'Okay,' he says to me. 'You heard that – I've got to leave soon. So, let's see the bedrooms. I assume they're all en-suite?'

We move swiftly back in time through the bedrooms – some 70s decor, some 1950s, some 1930s or earlier. Although the proportions are lovely, I fear that the potential is lost on Ronan Keene. However, when we arrive back at the landing, I have a sudden flash of inspiration.

'I know you need to go,' I say, 'but there's one more room I want to show you – upstairs at the very top. I think it would make a great home cinema.'

He immediately looks interested. 'Okay, let's see it.'

I take him up to the cavernous attic room with the round window in the pitch of the eaves. 'You could use this room for just about anything,' I suggest. 'A cinema, snooker room, a gym – or a pink marble Turkish bath.'

'Yes,' he squints as he looks around. 'I can see that. It's good.'

'RO-NAN!'

'I've got to go.'

I smile and gesture for him to lead the way downstairs. He pauses again at the portrait and shakes his head. I'm about to tell him that I met a real woman who is the spitting image of the girl in the picture, in case he wants to 'trade up', but suddenly from downstairs, Crystal starts screaming.

We both rush down.

'What is it, cupcake?' Ronan shouts.

We run to the library where Crystal is standing on an old sofa; her spike heels have ripped a hole in the upholstery and fluff is coming out.

'I saw a mouse! There!' She points to a tiny hole at the base of one of the bookcases. 'I hate this place. Let's go.'

'Now, cupcake, I'm sure it's more afraid of you than you are of—'

'No! And stop calling me that. We're leaving – NOW!'

Ronan lifts Crystal off the sofa and carries her out to the main hall. Her heels skid on the pitted marble floor as he sets her down. Turning to me, he shrugs apologetically. 'I guess we'd better look at a new-build next time.'

'That's fine,' I say, relieved that Crystal won't be living here. 'There are lots of nice properties out there. I'd like to help you find one that's right for you.'

'That'd be great,' Ronan says.

As we walk to the door I have a sudden brainstorm. 'In fact, 'if you really want modern, I know of a cracking penthouse flat in Bristol. All glass and chrome and views to kill for.'

'Hmmm,' Ronan says. 'What do you think, cupcake? Could you live in Brissy, or is it too near your mum?'

'Anything's better than here,' Crystal moans.

It takes me a few tries to get the door unlocked. I'm secretly pleased that the rain has started up again and Crystal's gelled hair is going flat. She grabs the car keys from Ronan and rushes to the Aston Martin.

'Sorry this wasn't the house for you,' I say. 'But good luck in your search.'

'Thanks.' Ronan glances wearily at the car. 'Sorry to be so… high maintenance.'

'No worries – ring the office if you're interested in the Bristol flat. And if I see anything else come on – new-build mansions and the like – I'll let you know straight away.'

We crunch through the wet gravel.

As we reach the cars, he pauses. 'Hey, Amy, do you think they'd sell that picture? The one on the stairs?'

I stare at him. He really is keen.

'I don't know. I think it goes with the house. But if I hear otherwise, I'll give you a ring.'

'Okay.' He waves and gets into the car. Tyres squelch as they drive off.

I lean against my wet car and let the rusty water trickle down my nose. All my hopes for the day have dissolved like raindrops in the sea. At this moment, all I want to do is get back to my parents' bungalow and have a very long, very hot bath.

Nineteen

As if three terrible viewings aren't enough for one day, there is one additional nightmare in store – the office Christmas party. I return home, sink into the tub, and check my messages: two voicemails and three texts from David Waters asking me when and where to meet. I text him to meet me at the 'Glow Bar' in Bristol where the dreaded event is being held. I put my phone on mute and set it on the edge of the sink. I close my eyes and think back to my visit to Rosemont Hall. For some reason I keep picturing the costumes – such lovely garments, so carefully preserved and looked after. Something else floats to the surface of my mind – something that Fred and Mary Blundell were discussing on their viewing of the Bristol penthouse. A Picasso in a new frame like 'old wine in new bottles'...

I sit bolt upright in the bath, the sudsy water streaming off my skin. All along I've assumed that the girl in the pink dress was painted in 1899, because that's the date on the frame. But what if the date on the frame is a deliberate misdirection, and the portrait is, in fact, a modern painting done to look old?

On my visit to the house with David Waters, I found a ledger that listed Sir George's paintings bought and sold. One of them – a John Singer Sargent, I think – was auctioned off in a frame listed as 'new'. It seems farfetched, but maybe the original frame was taken off that painting and used for the girl in the pink dress. Beyond that, the painter must have been very skilful to replicate the cracked varnish of an old painting, but surely that can be done too. And if the painting is modern, then the girl could be just about anyone.

But there's one person that it's most likely to be. Henry and Arabella were in love and secretly engaged to be married. The pink dress was hanging in a closet in her room. And the letters speak of a painter hired by Sir George to paint Henry's portrait. One by one, the pieces fall into place. Instead of painting Henry, the artist painted Arabella. The painting was still up in the attic studio during the fire, so it wasn't destroyed or sold off. It makes sense that Arabella dressed up in a beautiful Victorian-style ballgown for the party in honour of Henry's 21st birthday. Unlike my original idea, she didn't dress up like the portrait, but rather, she sat for the portrait. And putting it in an old frame lent it gravitas. It was *meant* to fool future generations of onlookers – people like me – into thinking that the portrait was much older. It makes sense too that the painting is the 'birthday present' that she mentioned in her letters to Henry. And when I asked Mrs Bradford if the woman was Sir George's wife or mother, it's no wonder she sniffed disdainfully at me. The young woman in the portrait is Arabella Windham!

I get out of the bath feeling pleased with myself. Everything fits, even down to Mrs Bradford. She was devoted to Arabella Windham, so naturally kept her things in good order, including her 'special dress'. Though if the slept-in bed is any indication, maybe she was a little *too* devoted...

Dad's carriage clock chimes – time to focus on getting ready. I rummage through my closet and unpack more of my boxes to find something to wear. I eventually decide on a vintage pink satin shift dress, with matching heels and shrug. Underneath, I bite the bullet and put on my only surviving pair of lacy knickers 'just in case'.

As I'm standing in front of the mirror wondering whether or not the outline of the underwear will be as visible in a dim-lit bar as it is in my well-lit bedroom, Mum comes in without knocking.

'Oh,' she says, 'that's a lovely dress. You look like a princess – Princess Di. You know, before she—'

'Died?' I can't help but wince. I know Mum means it as a compliment; she's only trying to help bolster my post-Simon low self-esteem. But why couldn't she have chosen Kate Middleton – or even Pippa? Does my dress scream '80s? I'm neither tall nor blonde, nor do I possess any of the statuesque elegance that Princess Di had back in the day.

'Well, yes.' Mum makes a pretext of dusting the ceramic knick-knacks on my bureau. There's a long pause while I brace myself for whatever is coming next.

'You know,' she says eventually, 'if you need some privacy – you know, want to bring someone back here... I mean... your father and I, we're all for it.'

'Mum! Of course I don't.'

'We're both heavy sleepers – we won't hear a thing. And we'd rather know that you're safe than have to go to some stranger's flat.'

'Mum!'

'We want you to meet someone.' She winks. 'Make hay while the sun shines.'

'Mum, I'm hardly going to bring some strange bloke to sleep with me in a single bed on the other side of the wall from you.'

Mentally, I add up my savings plus my meagre wages. Unless I make a big commission, it will be March before I can afford the rent on a half-decent flat.

'Okay, honey, I'm just trying to be helpful.'

'Great Mum. Thanks – I'm sure.'

She dusts for another minute and then leaves the room. She's brought in my thick new novel by Sarah Waters from the living room and set it on the bedside table. How I long to curl up under the covers and escape to a seedy, dim-lit Victorian world.

The book reminds me of the nights I used to spend with Simon, with me reading and him playing games (at least, I think that was what he was doing) on his BlackBerry in bed. The good ol' days. But reality is an office Christmas party in Bristol, escorted by a moderately handsome almost-stranger. On paper, at least, that probably doesn't look too bad.

I do a final twirl in front of the mirror, put on a pair of diamanté earrings, and head for the door. I'm almost there when my dad, sitting in front of the TV watching *Eggheads*, notices me leaving.

'Wow, it's Princess Di,' he says, winking at me. 'Tell Prince Charles that we're dying to meet him.'

'Dad!' I seriously debate changing into something else. 'It's an office Christmas party,' I remind him, 'not a date. Besides, you're twenty-five years off the pace.'

He chuckles. 'Whatever you say, Princess. But looking like that, maybe we'll meet your Dodi Fayed in the morning?'

'Dad!'

'Just kidding. Oh, and just so you know, we'll be out tonight – it's the thirtieth anniversary of the night I met your mum. At your Uncle George's – ha! Can you believe she ever went out with that old todger?'

'No Dad, I can't say I've ever given it that much thought.'

He holds up his hand and points to the television. 'Let's see if the challengers can oust them.'

I stand there patiently while the challengers miss an easy question about Dickens, and the Eggheads take the crown – as usual. I leave my dad hemming and hawing. Just as I reach the door, he turns back to me.

'Well, Princess, try to have a good time. And even if you don't – I'm sure your mum and I will.'

Of that, I have no doubt. The prospect of sleeping elsewhere is becoming more and more attractive. The walls really *are* thin.

I do a quick recalculation to determine if mid-February might be possible on the move-out front.

'Bye Dad.' I force a smile. 'I'll keep that in mind.'

*

I arrive in downtown Bristol, right on time. Then, I proceed to sit in the car for fifteen minutes staring at the cascading white Christmas lights hung between the buildings and fretting about going inside the bar. A thousand objections come to mind: I haven't really 'bonded' with anyone in the office other than Claire, and I'm convinced that Jonathan and Patricia both hate me for some unspecified reason. Then there's the whole issue of David Waters. Unfortunately, absence has not made my heart grow fonder; it's only given me time to conclude that inviting him was probably a mistake.

Finally, I force myself to get out of the car and walk towards 'The Glow Bar'. Half a block away, music, laughter, and chat are spilling out of the bar. It's a chic, swanky joint – all leather and chrome. I pause outside the door and take a deep breath when, all of a sudden, a hand grabs my bottom. 'Hey—' I shriek. Fist raised, I spin around. 'Stop that!'

The hand belongs to my boss, Alistair Bowen-Knowles. He stands there grinning at me like a Cheshire Cat. Over his usual shirt and tie, he's wearing a tacky knit snowman jumper with an embarrassingly phallic carrot nose. It's obvious that he's made an early start on the drinking part of the evening. An attractive blonde woman is hanging onto his arm. Conveniently for him, she's peering into a tiny compact mirror and fixing her lipstick and doesn't notice anything untoward.

'Tessie,' he slurs, turning to his date. 'Meet our newest addition, Amy Wood.'

'Pleased to meet you.' My face burns.

'Charmed, dahling.' Tessie says. Her voice is deep and she shakes my hand with claw-like fingers. For a second, I wonder if she was once a man. 'Are you here all alone?' she warbles.

'No,' I say firmly. 'I'm meeting someone – he may already be inside.'

'Well, let's go and look for him, shall we?' Alistair says. 'First round's on me.'

He steers me around (his hand on my back this time) and the three of us enter the bar. I push my way through the crowd towards a cordoned-off area in the back. A big banner trimmed with a gold garland is taped to the wall: *Happy Christmas from Tetherington Bowen Knowles*. It's a relief to spot Claire taking a glass of champagne from a roving waitress.

'Hi.' I make a beeline over to her. She's dressed in a lovely teal blue sari, accessorised with a handsome Indian man in tow – her husband, I presume.

'Oh hello, Amy.'

She introduces me to Raj, the husband, and then leaves to go to the loo. He gives me a dead-fish handshake and I stand there trying to make small talk. Unfortunately, I can't remember anything she's told me about him other than that he's from Birmingham. I make a brief comment to Raj about how Simon and I once went up north to Edgbaston to do the Tolkien Trail, but he looks blank and says they live up near Walsall.

It feels like we've been standing there talking forever, and saying absolutely nothing. I'm dying to get away – go dance, go home, go look for David Waters, but I don't want to be rude. Raj speaks in a monotone, and tells me in great detail about his family's Indian restaurant. Then he regales me with details of the '68 VW Beetle he's restoring. Then he tells me about the pedigree Alsatian he wants to buy for his son. I can't get a word in edgeways, even if I had something to say about any of his topics of interest. Across the room, I see Claire laughing with a few women I don't know but I assume must be from the Cardiff office. I want to join them but stay where I am, nodding and umming in the right places.

I'm concentrating so hard on the non-conversation with Raj that the next thing I know I'm holding two empty glasses of champagne – one in each hand. My quota for the entire night is gone in the first fifteen minutes.

I shift my weight from side to side, pleased that I'm still secure on my feet. But a second later, a waitress comes around and suddenly I'm holding a new glass – this one full. A cold hand grabs my arm. 'Oh!' I scream. The glass goes flying, spilling champagne all over Raj's shoes before shattering on the floor.

Like a needle ripping across a vinyl record, all conversations stop and everyone turns to look at me. I look up at a horrified David Waters.

'Hi,' he says. 'Looks like I've made an entrance yet again.'

'Looks like you have.' A small army of waitresses and bar staff rushes over and attacks the mess with towels and brooms.

We move away from the wreckage. David gives me a little kiss, but I turn my head and it ends up somewhere in my hair. 'You look great,' he says, appreciatively taking in my dress.

'So do you. Love the jumper.' Over his pink shirt he's wearing a kitschy red jumper with a knit white beard and black knit Santa Claus belt, nicely filled out by his athletic torso.

'Yeah, seemed appropriate.'

Before I can reply, Mr Bowen-Knowles (sans Tessie) swoops over to us.

'David Waters,' he says in a distinctly 'superior' tone. 'How nice to see you.'

'Hello Alistair. Great party.' David moves closer to me and takes my arm. 'Love the jumper.'

'Ditto. I didn't know you were Amy's guest.'

'Well, she was nice enough to ask me.'

'I see.'

They stand squared off against each other, Christmas jumper-clad chests thrust out – a pissing contest if I've ever seen one. I'm curious as to how far back these two go. Certainly, I'm not vain enough to think that they're actually fighting over *me*.

'And how's your handicap?' Mr Bowen-Knowles asks.

'Up to six now. You straighten out that left cut yet?'

'I'm working on it. But I don't believe you're at six.'

'Well, fancy a round to prove it then – and you can put your money where your mouth is?'

Golf. They're talking about golf. I almost choke on my rapidly dwindling champagne. My date and my boss are planning a golf weekend.

'How about next weekend?' my boss says. 'You still a member at Minehead?'

'Yeah.' David seems to lean away from me a little. 'It's still my favourite course – for now.'

'Brilliant.' Alistair raises his glass. 'Put it in the diary.'

Maybe it's a trick of the twinkling Christmas lights, but the room has positively started to spin. I grab a glass from the tray of a roving waitress and drain it. There may be other golf courses in Minehead, but the one that I know is there for sure is 'Golf Heritage'.

'Amy?' David grabs my arm as I teeter away a few steps. He steers me to a chair and sits down opposite keeping hold of my hand.

I pull it away. 'I didn't know you and Alistair were such good golf buddies,' I say.

'Oh, not really.' He shrugs. 'We play from time to time. That's how we met.'

'And I suppose you'll be happy when Hexagon guts Rosemont Hall to build another 'Golf Heritage' and you can run your golf carts through the wreckage.'

His boyish face hardens. 'That's not fair, Amy.'

'No?' I inhale sharply. 'I read your report – line by line. You're right, someone will need to find buried treasure to fix it up. Whereas… a golf course – now there's a good option.'

He shakes his head. 'I'm just doing my job, Amy. You know that. And if it does become a golf course, then at least the site will be open to the public – you should like that.'

'I've read the articles about Hexagon and their "sustainable developments". I'm sure you have too.' I stare him down.

'Look, babe,' he says. 'Do we have to talk about this now? This is a party. Let's go dance.'

He points to a cleared space across the room where Alistair is in the process of mauling Tessie to the tune of 'It's Raining Men'. Claire and her husband step into the fray and join them.

I shake my head. 'No David, I'd rather not.'

He purses his lips, obviously taking my refusal as a personal rejection. 'Why did you invite me tonight?' he asks. 'Because you needed a date for your work party, or because you wanted to grill me about my report? Clearly, you weren't seeking the pleasure of my company.'

He's got me there, and I do feel a little ashamed of my behaviour. David Waters came here in good faith, as my guest. He didn't come to talk about work, and I'm the one who's putting a damper on the evening. 'Look David,' I say, smiling shakily. 'I'm sorry. I've had a little bit too much champagne to dance. But I'd like to sit and chat – maybe a glass of water might help.'

'Fine. I'll go get you one.'

'Thanks.'

He gets up and heads to the bar. As soon as he's gone, I head to the Ladies' loo to splash cold water on my face. I'm in the toilet cubicle when I hear the loo door swoosh open. Water begins to run. Hoping it's Claire, I come out.

'Oh!' I cry.

It's Alistair Bowen-Knowles – in the *Ladies'* loo. He's standing at the sink, his tie pulled out of his jumper, rubbing at a spot on the silk with a paper towel.

'Ah, Amy,' he slurs. 'Just the person I want in a crisis. Can you come help me with this stain?'

With some trepidation, I walk over. He holds the tie out to show me – a splash of red wine. He drops the tie and grabs my hand. 'I wanted to tell you, Amy Wood – you're doing an awfully good job for someone so new.'

He thinks I'm doing a good job? First I've heard of it—

'Well, I—'

He leans in and kisses me lightly on the cheek. The champagne is definitely getting to me, because it doesn't even make me flinch.

Of course, he doesn't just stop with a peck on the cheek. He pecks a little line of kisses in the direction of my mouth. The snowman's nose flattens against my side. I have the overwhelming urge to laugh out loud – this can't possibly be happening. For a second, I go limp, which catches him off guard. I push him away.

'I don't think this is a good idea.' I flatten myself against the sink.

'Why not? It's Christmas. No strings attached right?'

Anger and alcohol mix in my veins. I grip the edge of the sink. 'Two reasons really. One, I don't want to, and two, I feel... oh no—'

I pirouette on the spot, and retch into the sink.

'Shit Amy!' he yells.

'No,' I sputter. 'It's sick.'

I stay there for a moment, my head bent over the sink. Alistair thrusts a towel in my direction. I wipe my mouth and run water in the sink, hoping Alistair will get the hint and leave. But as soon as I straighten up, he's there again, weaselling up to me. He rubs his hand in little circles on my back. 'There, there,' he says, like he's comforting a skittish horse or something. The hand on my back creeps around to my front. I wheel around to push him away, but at that second, the door opens again and Tessie comes inside. She screams, and I scream, and everyone comes running. And they see me standing there panting, my hands raised in crash position, my boss standing guiltily close to me. People are pointing at me, and I point at Alistair. My face in the mirror is as red as Rudolph's nose. And Jonathan is laughing and David swoops up and grabs me by the arm.

Cold air hits me in the face. I'm outside a fire exit being dragged away by David, and, I notice, Claire.

'Are you all right?' she asks me.

'Yes, but it wasn't my fault – Mr Bowen-Knowles—'

'Don't worry,' she says. 'That happens sometimes when he gets drunk. Don't take it personally.'

'But how can he just – do – that? It's awful. What if no one had come in?'

'I don't know,' David says angrily. 'What if no one had come in?'

I stop and stare at him. 'What? You think I led him on— ? That's ridiculous.'

'Anyway, I think the evening's over.'

'Yes,' I snap. 'I'll call a cab. I want to go home.'

David steps forward. 'I'll take her,' he says to Claire.

Claire looks at me. I hang my head, realising that I've left my handbag in the toilet. I don't have my mobile phone or any money. 'Whatever,' I say.

After Claire retrieves my handbag, I'm bundled into my coat and David's car. I know he's angry, and I'm angry, and I never should have come to this stupid party in the first place, let alone bring a plus-one. We drive in stormy silence all the way to Nailsea.

By the time we near my parents' bungalow, I'm quite sober and a more than a little sorry. After all, technically, it isn't David's fault that it turned into a miserable evening (actually, we were there for just over an hour) and that I'd had too much to drink.

The outside of the bungalow is trimmed with a riot of multicoloured Christmas lights, white icicle lights, and this year, Dad's outdone himself with a tableau of near-life-sized light-up plastic figures: Santa, Rudolph, and – oddly – the baby Jesus, next to the door.

As David slows down to let me out, I put my hand on his arm. 'I'm really sorry about tonight, David. I know you're angry – and you've every right to be. But would you like to come inside for some hot chocolate?'

He looks at me, and I can tell he's debating whether to tell me where to go. He looks at the house – behind the garish display, the windows are dark. My parents and their anniversary night, I recall with foreboding.

'Okay,' he says.

Still slightly nauseous, I fumble around for my keys. We walk to the door and the automatic light flicks on like it's caught me in the act of doing something untoward. I glance over to the house next door – the curtains in Mrs Harvey's kitchen window twitch and she gives me a little wave. Then she disappears, no doubt to phone her friends at the Scrabble club to tell them that Amy Wood brought a bloke home when her parents were out.

I unlock the door and push it open, making the wreath wobble precariously. I usher David inside and turn on the lights. Suddenly, I'm aware of things that I usually don't notice: the smell of cabbage and English Leather soap that's a dead giveaway of 'ageing parents'; the fibre-optic tabletop Christmas tree that Mum keeps plugged in 24/7; the fading floral, slightly threadbare sitting-room suite with crochet-covered throw pillows that are not ageing gracefully. And then, I feel ashamed of being ashamed. Not for my parents – they have the perfect right to live in whatever manner they see fit – but rather, for myself. I'm the university-educated, grown woman, who's having to be escorted back to her parents' house by her date.

David Waters takes off his coat and walks towards me with a come-hither look on his face – like he's now looking forward to the 'kiss and make up' part of the evening. I teeter backwards. All of a sudden, everything feels wrong.

He reaches out for me.

I sidle away towards the kitchen and start babbling over my shoulder. 'I'm so cold – I'll just put the kettle on. Chocolate, I thought, unless you'd prefer coffee? And maybe you can turn on the gas fire? I'll make enough chocolate, I mean, coffee, for my parents too – I'm sure they'll be home any minute now, and they'll be happy to meet you... or, if you don't want – which I completely understand – we can, uhh, do this another time and—'

'Amy.' I wheel around as he comes into the kitchen. 'I don't want any chocolate or coffee. I didn't want to talk to those people at the party, and I didn't really want to dance or sit and chat at that bar. I just want to be alone with you.' He draws me close and kisses me full on the lips while simultaneously unzipping my dress and pulling it down at the front. I will myself to sink into his embrace but my body automatically stiffens. He stops kissing and fumbling.

'I'm sorry,' I say. 'I'm... it's just that... I'm not feeling...'

'Oh.' He holds me at arm's length. 'Of course, you're still feeling sick.'

'Well, yeah, I am. Plus...'

'Plus?'

'Plus... this is all going a little fast for me.'

'Fast? We've been out exactly twice.'

'Yes, but I'm just not sure. To be honest, I'm feeling a bit of pressure.'

He takes a step back. 'What is it? The golf? That damned house?'

I wince. 'It's not any of that. In fact, it's not you at all – you seem like a great guy. It's me—'

He holds up his hand, and his lip curls downwards into an ugly expression. 'Don't worry,' he says. 'I get it. I'll just get my coat—'

'Amy, is that you?' A voice. My *mum's* voice.

'Hi Mum... just a minute—'

'Oh!'

To my great horror, Mum appears in the kitchen doorway with Dad at her side. They're both giving me – and David – the once-over. David looks flushed and dishevelled like he's *coitus interruptus* instead of *coitus rejectus*. My dress is hanging off me, my bra showing, and my face hot, and the kettle begins whistling at full pitch.

I rush over and turn off the hob. But by then, Mum has taken charge.

'I'm sorry we interrupted you,' she coos to David, drawing him conspiratorially by the arm. 'It's our anniversary. We had a very nice dinner and thought that we'd have an early night – if you know what I mean?' She actually giggles. 'Love the jumper, by the way.'

'We weren't expecting you and Amy back so early,' Dad says, 'but since you're here, we're just so pleased that she's met a nice chap.'

I cringe. 'Actually, Dad,' I say, 'David was just leaving. He has a dog that needs—'

'Don't worry, Mr and Mrs Wood,' David cuts in (in a way that is clearly meant to torture me further), 'the dog will be fine. I've been looking forward to meeting you and dying for that chocolate.'

'Yes, Amy, sit down and be polite.' Mum addresses me like I'm one of her five-year-olds. She draws David away into the sitting room. Dad follows them, humming 'Some Enchanted Evening'.

Resigned to my fate, I spoon chocolate powder into four mugs. I stall for as long as I can, putting biscuits on a plate, finding the sugar bowl and four spoons, and putting it all on a tray. Unfortunately, by the time I bring everything into the sitting room, Mum, Dad and David are getting on famously. Dad is consulting David about the garden shed he wants to tear down and rebuild, and David is offering suggestions. Then Mum asks his opinion on some fabric swatches for new curtains. David goes along with all of it – he winks at me over his cup of chocolate, clearly enjoying my discomfort.

I sip my chocolate and eat too many biscuits, as the conversation turns to holiday plans, Christmas jumpers, party games, and more specifically Scrabble – my parents' favourite. Before I can voice an objection, the single malt Scotch is out and the Super Scrabble rotating board is on the table.

'No,' I groan. No one pays any attention.

We all draw tiles to see who goes first. My head is half-nodding in sleep and I just want to crawl into bed – alone. But everyone else is going strong, and Mum gives me a little kick under the table.

I draw the high tile, which means that I go first. I take six more terrible letters – ending up with a J, Z, E, two U's, an S and an X. I take a minute to wordsmith the possibilities, but in the end, I'm forced to increase my humiliation further with – SEX on the double word score.

'Heh, heh,' Dad jokes. 'I guess that's what you two kids would rather be up to, ehh?'

'Dad!' I want to curl up in a ball and die.

'Well, I'm sure we'll have you both beaten in no time and then you can get on with it. Are you okay on the sofa bed?'

'Just write down my twenty points, okay?'

David makes a crack about my parents' bed being more comfortable and everyone laughs but me. The three of them come up with a spontaneous new rule – extra points for every naughty word.

Mum has the next clincher with 'TOSS' and David manages somehow to make 'SHAG'. I'm hoping that at least all the S's are gone when Dad makes a coup using one of Mum's S's and the next thing I know, 'PENIS' has entered the fray.

The three of them rollick with laughter, slapping each other on the back. I silently palm a few tiles, trying to make the game go faster.

My next turn, I make 'BANKER' and everyone frowns. I'm obviously a party pooper. When someone offers to trade me a 'W' for the 'B', I push my rack of letters away and stand up. 'That's it!' I say. 'I'm going to bed.'

The laughter fades. Mum looks embarrassed. Dad and David both look annoyed.

'I've had a rough day and a lot to drink. I need sleep.'

David stands up. 'I've had a lovely time. But I should be going.'

'No,' Dad practically pleads. 'Stay to finish the game. I haven't had this much fun since Amy's boyfriend... I mean – ex-boyfriend... heh, heh... took me go-cart racing...'

'Well, if you insist.' David smiles triumphantly and sits back down. I go over and give him a little obligatory peck on the lips.

'Thanks for an interesting evening,' I manage.

'Sure,' he says. 'See you around.'

He doesn't look at me as he lays down his next word: 'SUCKS'.

Twenty

On my way to work on Monday morning, I amuse myself by trying to decide which of the weekend debacles was most humiliating. From the three disastrous viewings, to the Christmas party and its aftermath, it's impossible to pick a winner. But surely, it's statistically impossible for everything to go wrong forever.

As I walk into the office and nod to my colleagues, immediately I sense a collective flashback to the shenanigans at the Christmas party. I sit down at my desk and turn on my computer. Claire asks me if I made it home all right after the party. 'Yes, thanks,' I say, my cheeks hot with embarrassment. I go about the business of checking my emails. Before I've even deleted the day's spam, Mr Bowen-Knowles's office door bangs open. He blusters out, without a hint of regret or apology, and gets straight down to business.

'Amy,' he says sternly, 'I've just had a Mr Patel on the line. You showed him a property over the weekend?'

Everyone looks at him, then at me. I shudder at the memory of what I've tallied as the fourth most humiliating experience of the weekend: getting chased out of a crack house by squatters.

'That's right,' I say.

'Well, he's just phoned with an offer. Sounded fairly genuine to me. The financing is already in place and he wants to exchange this week, if possible.'

Although I recall all too well Mr Patel's enthusiasm with the laser measure, still, I'm stunned.

'He said you convinced him that it had great potential.'

'I did?' I practically choke. 'I mean... yes, I did.'

Mr Bowen-Knowles's lip curves up in what might be construed as a smile. Not the wolfish, lecherous grin I've seen from him before, but one that is almost genuine. One that, despite his behaviour at the Christmas party, almost smacks of respect. And I realise that for better or for worse, this job is for real, and I can do it. I look around: Claire is smiling; Jonathan is glaring; Patricia is putting on lipstick.

Mr Bowen-Knowles comes over and shakes my hand. Then he heads back into his office. I sit back in my chair, my hand smarting from his firm grip. I may or may not ever get my name on the top of the sales chart. I may have made a complete arse of myself at the Christmas party, but I wasn't the only one. I may have sent a decent bloke packing without so much as a proper goodnight kiss. I may be living with my parents and causing them perpetual disappointment because I haven't inherited the Scrabble gene. But none of that matters right now. What's important is that I've made a sale. And that's something I can be proud of.

*

After the dose of good karma, the morning goes by quickly, and soon it's time for lunch. Claire invites me out for a sandwich. We sit outside the Assembly Rooms, watching the tourists, and she fills me in on the Christmas party antics that occurred after I left: Mr Bowen-Knowles moved on to snog Patricia under the mistletoe; 'Tessie' left in tears and got her own taxi; Jonathan punched someone from the Cardiff office over a slur to his rugby team. I decline to fill her in on the later events of my evening. Still, I like the way she's non-judgemental, and sees me as a co-conspirator rather than just an object of gossip. By the time we return to the office, my sides hurt from laughing, my hands are freezing from sitting outside, and the day has a general winter glow about it.

Until about an hour after we return from lunch, that is.

I'm sitting at my desk going through a few enquiries that have come in over Rightmove. I refill my coffee in the kitchen and when I return, Mr Bowen-Knowles is hovering over Claire's desk. Immediately, the glare he was directing at her gets turned full beam on me.

'Amy,' he says, crossing his arms. Stiff upper-lipped, I follow him inside his office and close the door. He tells me to sit down. I sit down. He sits at his desk and frowns at a piece of paper in front of him, then at me.

'A Nigel Netelbaum phoned from Hexagon,' he says. 'You were out so I took the call. They're going to send through the offer for the Rosemont property. If we do the legwork, we should be able to pocket the commission even though Kendall's client – that idiot "Mr Jack" – negotiated the deal. At least, you'd better hope we can, or else it's all been a colossal waste of time.'

I open my mouth, but can't speak, as the cracks in my heart begin to widen.

'Anyway, they're sending someone round to have a look at the house. Since they aren't going to be able to knock it down, they want to see what they're in for.' He shrugs. 'They're hoping to make it into the clubhouse: pro shop, fine-dining restaurant, cigar parlour, members only VIP lounge.' His face turns wolf-like as he outlines the possibilities. I imagine that he's mentally practising his swing for his first round there with David Waters.

'But if that doesn't fly with the English Heritage antis and the local blue-hair brigade, then they'll build the clubhouse on the other side of the property. It's the land they're mainly after anyway. The planners have hinted that if they at least shore up the house so it doesn't fall down and fence it off out of the way, they'll be able to get permission for the other stuff they'll want to build: floodlit driving range, car park, groundsmen houses, machine sheds, etc. The planners seem pretty happy just to let them run with it.'

'But what about my three months to find a buyer?' I croak. 'A buyer who will restore it as a family home? Or... or even flats?'

Mr Bowen-Knowles laughs in my face. 'Come on Amy, get a grip. If Hexagon wants to buy the place, then good riddance. As long as we get our share,' he adds. 'Besides, you've had plenty of time to make something happen with that place. Your efforts to date have been... let's be frank... industrious, but also ineffectual.'

'That's not exactly true—'

'You've had what – two viewings?'

'One,' I mutter. Cinderella's clock has short-circuited, and all too soon, struck midnight. I can feel the chill seep into my bones as my dress shreds to rags and my golden coach turns back into a pumpkin.

He shrugs like he's not surprised. 'Either way, I realise that you're the only one around here who's shown much of an interest in getting the sale. So I'm going to allow you to stay involved – if you want to.'

'Yes,' I whisper.

'Someone will ring you to arrange the viewing – probably mid-Jan. Until then, pull everything together: the site plan, the surveyor's report, the probate petition. We'll want to have everything ready to go once they make a formal offer. And get in touch with Kendall – make sure that his "Mr Jack" agrees in writing that we get our commission. These Americans can be such hard-arses.' He wrinkles his nose. 'You can also help me with the paperwork on the Glastonbury place and...'

I stop listening. After all, what's the point? I should be happy that he's getting me involved and making me a part of things – wasn't that what I was celebrating earlier? But now I feel like I've crashed into a cement wall. Once Rosemont Hall is gone with me failing to save it, I'll be left, if I'm lucky, with the odd Mr Patel or two in between failures like the Blundells and all the rest—

'Amy? Have you heard a word I've been saying?'

Given that 'no' is not an acceptable answer, I settle for a hoarse laugh. 'Sorry Mr Bowen-Knowles,' I say. 'I'm happy to help out in any way I can.'

*

I seek the sanctuary of the disabled loo to hide tears that appear from nowhere as soon as I leave my boss's office. I stay there until I begin to calm down, drying my eyes on a piece of rough toilet tissue. When I emerge, Claire is in the kitchen. 'Are you all right, Amy?' she asks gently.

'Fine.' I shrug off the question.

'Did he say something about the Christmas party?'

'No. It's Rosemont Hall.'

She opens the cupboard, pushing aside the 'I'd rather be… GOLFING' mug.

'That was always going to be a long shot, Amy,' she says.

'I know. It's just all got away from me so quickly. And Mr Bowen-Knowles is annoyed because we might not get any commission.'

'Hmm, that would be bad.'

'And the old woman hasn't moved out – at least, I don't think she has. She may be a bit unstable, but I feel sorry for her, and…'

Mr Bowen-Knowles's door bangs open.

'Amy—' he bellows.

Good grief, what now?

'Yes?' I say wearily.

'You need to go back to the house in Glastonbury — now,' he orders. 'The police are on their way. They're going to clear out the junkies once and for all. Go there and make sure they don't damage the house – we need to preserve Mr Patel's investment.'

As the day goes from bad to worse and in order to safeguard Mr Patel's dubious "investment", I end up ducking clubs of broken beer bottles and police crossfire (in truth, all I do is sit in my car for what seems like hours while the police have an orderly raid, arrest the four squatting thugs, and do all the paperwork, including taking a statement from me and my new best friend Mr Patel), once again, I rue the fateful day that I ever set foot in the offices of *Tetherington Bowen Knowles*.

Part Three

As I stood there hushed and still, I could swear that the house was not an empty shell but lived and breathed as it had lived before.

Light came from the windows, the curtains blew softly in the night air, and there, in the library, the door would stand half open as we had left it, with my handkerchief on the table beside the bowl of autumn roses.

~ Daphne du Maurier – *Rebecca*

VI

Letter 6 (Fragment)

A—

    God forgive me, but I have been such a fool. He means to ruin our plans – but I won't let him. We must play along with this little charade for tonight, but tomorrow—

Twenty-One

In real life, there are no happy endings – only ups and downs and new beginnings, and loose ends, and a few laughs, and many tears. This I realise during the course of the next few weeks, which fly past in a blur. Christmas comes and goes (my parents and I exchanging gifts of socks and bath smellies), then New Year's Eve (my parents lamenting my poor taste in having jettisoned the most willing Scrabble player they've had in years). The holidays make me think of all the things that might have been with Simon, but, like the ghost of Christmas yet to come, turned out to be only in my mind. It's a letting-go of a sort, and I feel more than a twinge of sadness. But I get through it.

As a break from the festivities, I begin transcribing the letters I found. The hours leading up to the ball and Henry's cryptic last letter niggle in my head like an itch I can't quite scratch. I look through the sketchbook again for any clues as to who the artist was, but there are none. All I know is that the artist was captivated by the image of Arabella Windham in her pink dress, and that he was most likely Spanish.

The keys to Rosemont Hall remain at the office, locked in a desk drawer. Viewings grind to a halt during the holidays, and in the new year, I'm kept busy dealing with people interested in putting their homes on the market. Just before the new year, I rang up David Waters (who hasn't called me since our Scrabble night) and apologised for my behaviour. Admittedly, it was a relief when it went to voicemail. But as the days pass and he doesn't ring me back, a tiny flicker of doubt sets in as to whether I let him go too easily.

He finally rings me back when I'm at the office. We make the obligatory small talk and harmless flirtations, so I automatically assume that he might be wondering if I've changed my mind about seeing him again. I almost do change my mind. But just when I'm about to suggest that we go out for a friendly beer, he asks to speak to Mr Bowen-Knowles. I realise that he's not pining after me, and in fact, didn't even ring to speak to me at all.

'Oh, so you want to schedule another round of golf, then?' I joke to hide my embarrassment.

'Actually...' his tone is deadly serious, 'it's not a golf round that we're planning, but the golf course. I'm going to work on some costings. It's potentially a great business opportunity for me if I can crack into golf course development.'

'Just a minute, I'll see if he's available.' Choking out the words, I transfer the call to my boss. In a way, I'm relieved. Nothing else could have done more to convince me that I no longer require the services of David Waters on either a personal or a professional level.

Things begin to look up when, a week later, Mr Patel completes on the Glastonbury house. My name goes straight to the top of the sales chart on the door of the disabled loo. It's a good thing too – especially since everyone is murmuring about double-dip recessions. The winter days gradually begin to lengthen, and although I have several promising client viewings of 'character cottages', 'charming semis,' and even a 'top-notch barn conversion', I'm not one jot closer to finding anyone to rescue Rosemont Hall.

The long shadow of the meeting with Hexagon's representative hangs over my head. Every phone call to the office; every email enquiry kindles my worries. Each night when I go home, I feel a sense of relief, like a prisoner having received a stay of execution. Each morning when I come into the office, I experience the same creeping dread that today might be the day.

Then, on a grey Wednesday afternoon the last week in January, the axe falls.

I return from a lunch-hour spent browsing the last of the sales to find a telephone memo on my chair: *Meeting confirmed for Rosemont Hall, Saturday January 31st 11 a.m. Mr Faraday.*

Hexagon. At least now they have a name. I drop my other work and make one last Herculean effort to find an alternative buyer. I check all the website cookies for people who have clicked on the property particulars and phone them. But thanks to David Waters and his repair estimate, the precious few who might be interested are immediately put off. As a last resort, I even ring up Ronan Keene, the footballer. I'm surprised when he answers himself, and even more surprised when he remembers me.

'Hullo Amy,' he says. 'I'm glad you called, in fact, I've been meaning to ring you.'

'Oh, well, that's nice.' A splinter of hope pricks my heart.

'Yeah. We looked on your website at that other place you mentioned – in Bristol. Crystal's very excited. She thinks it might just be the place for us. What was it you said? – our "together home".'

'Great.' I cross them off as 'possibles' for Rosemont Hall, but business is business. There's a right property for everyone, and I want to find it for them.

'You know the one I mean, yeah? The penthouse apartment?'

'I certainly do.' An image forms in my mind of Fred Blundell sitting in jail. He and Mary had been so excited on their one viewing – when they'd found 'the right home' for them. And promptly lost it again. Criminal or no, I know how that feels. I wish things – a lot of things – had turned out differently.

'It's very much a showpiece flat,' I tell him. 'Ultra-modern, lots of light, great for entertaining. And brand new,' I emphasise. 'Not pre-lived in. I'm sure you and Crystal will love it.'

I gush a little more about the Costa Coffee and Pizza Express, the pool and gym in the basement, and the roof terrace. He seems delighted with my descriptions. We make arrangements for a viewing. I feel confident that I'm well on the way to matching up Ronan Keene and Crystal with their perfect flat. But as for Rosemont Hall, I've singularly failed.

Twenty-Two

The dreaded day dawns bright and clear with a dusting of snow on the ground. I give myself plenty of extra time to drive to Rosemont Hall because the roads are slick, and cars are skidding all over. I'm so early that I stop off in Little Botheringford for a coffee and muffin to calm my nerves. There's a twee little tea shop called the 'Cup o' Comfort' that looks welcoming and smells delicious. There's nothing like fresh baked scones with currants and cinnamon to perk up a cold morning. I park the car in a loading zone and run in. The tea shop is nearly full with older people and families taking advantage of the £3.95 full English advertised on a blackboard outside. A rather harried, white-haired woman serves me a huge scone that's dripping with fresh butter on a willow-patterned plate. There's an embarrassing moment when I remind her that I've asked for it to take away, and she purses her lips and chucks it into a paper bag. The 'Cup o' Comfort' doesn't have any takeaway cups either, so I decide to skip the coffee.

By the time I emerge from the café, the sun has disappeared and the sky is a strange purple-brown colour that means more snow. I begin to hope that Hexagon's stooge will be put off by the weather and not turn up. If he does turn up, I'm secretly glad that the place will not be looking its best.

With the hour upon me, I drive the rest of the way to the house. There's already a good four inches of snow covering the drive. However, my car ploughs through it easily, so undoubtedly, if this Mr Faraday is so determined, he'll be able to make it too.

When I pull up in front of the house, I've still got a few minutes before the viewing. I go inside and deliberately scatter some of the papers and books so that it looks even more cluttered than it is. I note that more of the rooms look and smell clean, and there's a bag of knitting next to one of the threadbare sofas. I tiptoe up the stairs to Arabella's room, but thankfully there's no sign of Mrs Bradford. The book is gone from the nightstand, and the bed has been remade. Back downstairs, I go from room to room pulling the curtains shut, making the house seem dark and forbidding. Not that my efforts to jinx the viewing will make one jot of difference to a golf course developer. Feeling chilled to the bone, I decide to wait in the car, where at least there's a working heater.

Mr Faraday is late. I sit staring at the house through foggy windows. Twenty minutes go by. The knot in my stomach begins to loosen slightly – if I left now, surely I'd be in the clear. At the very least I could inconvenience Mr Faraday, put him off, make him schedule another viewing.

Just then, a car drones in the distance. I watch in the mirror as it tops the rise of the hill. A blue Vauxhall Corsa – a slightly newer model than mine. Not the flash sports car or monster SUV I'd expected a Hexagon executive to drive.

The car pulls up next to mine. A man jumps out – I glimpse a red ski jacket and dark hair. I walk a few steps towards his car.

'Mr Faraday? I'm Amy Wood the—'

I stop.

He stops.

Our eyes meet.

'—Estate Agent...' I finish to break the remarkable silence. In an instant, the world has shrunk into a bubble around me and this stranger. He stares back at me, his sharp-chiselled face framed by soft, dark brown hair. I begin to shiver, but not with the cold.

'Hello,' he says, his voice deep and penetrating. 'I'm sorry I'm late. Thanks for coming out in this weather.'

I blink hard and, immediately, time comes rushing back. I remember who I am and what I'm doing, who this man is, and why this can't possibly be happening.

'Oh, no problem.' I stammer. 'It's my... pleasure.'

I can't meet his eyes – a soft blue-grey like the winter sky. Looking past him, I hold out my hand. He takes it and our fingers touch. He's smiling at me; the puffs of our breath mingle as he speaks: 'To be honest, I wasn't expecting this snow. The rental car's not really cut out for this weather...'

A few things register: Accent = American. Our hands = still together.

I jerk mine away.

Twenty-Three

I don't like him. He's anathema to everything I believe in. He's an unfeeling Neanderthal who's come to ravage a piece of history. I'm *determined* not to like him.

It's just...

I'm acutely aware of his presence as we trudge through the snow towards the front door. I don't speak – I can't speak. I know I should start talking my spiel about the house. Try to appeal to his humanity, if he has any. But the words won't come.

As we reach the front door, he points to the frost-caked stone crest above.

'Is that the family crest?' he asks.

'Yes.' I look up at the stone lintel to avoid glimpsing the face that might bewitch me. 'The house came into the Windham family in the early 1800s – not long after it was built. I believe the owner added it then. It's eroded, of course, but originally it was a dog and unicorn.' I purse my lips. He can't possibly be interested.

'A dog and unicorn?'

'It stands for fidelity and virtue.' Infuriatingly, I blush.

'Fidelity and virtue.' He says under this breath. 'That's odd.'

'Odd?'

He turns towards me. I take a quick step back.

'I guess that's the wrong word.' He laughs lightly. 'It's just that I wasn't expecting the place to be quite so...'

I exhale a long breath as a wave of relief passes over me. The place is way too rundown for anyone to bother with. Hexagon can develop a golf course somewhere else. I can go home now and try to forget that I ever laid eyes on this man who's—

'... beautiful.'

'Beautiful?' Warmth oozes through my veins. 'You really think so?'

He laughs again. 'It's obviously a bit of a fixer-upper, but the outside is pretty amazing. I guess maybe because you're English, you see these things every day and don't notice them anymore.'

'Well actually...'

'Where I'm from, ancient history starts about 1900,' he says. 'I was never that interested in exploring Europe – it's a typical American attitude, I'm afraid. We've got our own history, and lots of interesting things in our own country. And when I learned about European history at school, all they really focused on were the wars, the beheadings, and Henry the Eighth's six wives. None of it seemed very "real", if you know what I mean.'

'No... I mean – yes.' I fumble in my handbag for the keys. 'And I suppose people can play golf anywhere.'

He raises an eyebrow as if studying me. He seems to come to some unreadable conclusion. 'I guess that's true,' he says. 'Though I don't play myself.'

'Really?' I narrow my eyes, assuming that he's joking.

'No – never got into it. What was it that Mark Twain said? "Golf is a good walk spoiled"?'

I stare at him, in surprise. 'Yes,' I say. 'That's right.' I turn the key and the lock grinds open. All this must be a ploy – some dirty little trick of Hexagon to catch me off guard; lull me into a false sense of security.

We step inside the hallway. It's freezing, but even so, the air seems unnaturally heavy. I loosen my pink cashmere scarf and drape it over the staircase banister. I wait while Mr Faraday looks around the room. He lets out a low whistle.

'This place really must have been something in its heyday,' he says. 'Can't you just picture it? Ladies in silk gowns, gentlemen in top hats. Servants scurrying about... Amazing. I mean, you see places like this on TV and read about them in books. But to actually be here... it's completely different.' He smiles wistfully. 'If the house could talk, I bet it would have some interesting things to say. You can practically feel the history crackling in the air, can't you?'

'I... well...' No. *This* man, of all people, cannot possibly be the one person who understands.

'But— I see now that the surveyor hit the nail on the head,' he says. 'It would cost a small fortune to fix up. No – make that, a *large* fortune.'

'You know, I definitely agree. This place is a money pit.' I raise my hands in futility. 'A huge, unwieldy white elephant. And although the surveyor's report says it would cost at least three million pounds just to get it to comply with Building Regs...' I lower my voice, 'I happen to know that he was just being generous. I'm sure Hexagon would be better off building their golf course somewhere else. The only way this place is going to be saved is if someone buys it to fix up – as a labour of love.'

I take a breath and gear up to lie in grand *Tetherington Bowen Knowles* fashion. 'Besides,' I say, 'no matter who your friends are in the planning department, you'll be tied up in red tape for ages. There's an army of old ladies in the village ready to challenge any change of use. They'd rather see it crumble to the ground than have a golf course here. And I also heard that there are some protected bugs near the village. And bats – there are loads of bats that live up in the eaves. Developing this property as a golf course would be nothing but hassle and headache, let me tell you.'

'Well, I guess that's good to know.' He gives me a puzzled

frown. 'But aren't you supposed to be selling the place?'

'Oh,' I laugh coyly. 'Yes, I am. But I don't want to lead you up the garden path. I think it would make someone a fantastic family home – someone who loves it and has the wherewithal to restore it. It's just the merits as an investment that I question.'

'All property is an investment,' he says. 'If you live in it, develop it, rent it out – whether you keep it or sell it, it all has investment consequences. And this place…' he waves his hand to take in the great hall, 'it *is* a money pit. I did a little research myself when I first saw the surveyor's report. Apparently, with a listed building, it's incredibly hard to make any alterations, and every material used for restoration has to be old and authentic. That will put most people off. It's too bad really. I seriously doubt you'll be so lucky as to find someone to take it on as a "labour of love".'

'You never know.' I smile. 'There's a right house for everyone, and a right owner for every house. Someone who belongs to the house as much as the house belongs to them. I'm working on finding the right combination for this house.'

'You're like a house matchmaker, is that it?' His eyes dance with amusement.

'Precisely.'

He doesn't answer, and instead walks into the first drawing room off the main hall. He opens the curtains and a puff of dust engulfs us. In addition to the mess I've contributed to, I notice another pile of old papers and newspaper clippings on a sofa that wasn't here last time. There's a pair of half-moon glasses next to the pile – Mrs Bradford's. Mr Faraday takes one look around the room, then goes over to the newspaper clippings and picks up the top one. It's a page of obituaries.

'I'm sorry for the mess,' I say. 'The housekeeper, Mrs Bradford, is a bit shaken by everything that's happened. It's too bad really, but between us – she's a bit barmy.'

'A bit barmy?' He laughs. 'I like that.' He skims over the

obit and sets it back on top of the others. 'Do you know if Mrs Windham died in the house?'

'Oh yes.' Actually, I have no idea whether or not Mrs Windham died in the house, or whether it might have been Mr Windham, or neither, or both of them. But I seize what might be another opportunity to put him off. 'Right upstairs in the main bedroom. I think the body was here for a few days before anyone discovered it. Luckily, the smell has dissipated.'

Mr Faraday doesn't respond. Instead, he walks through to the next room: the blue salon. He looks around and touches things – marble mantles, old books and photos, the carved panelling – almost reverently. He's lost in thought. Maybe he's picturing all the rich men in collared shirts drinking whisky and smoking cigars in the parlour after their eighteen holes. But somehow, I don't think so. Still, he is who he is and we are where we are.

It takes the better part of twenty minutes before we've walked through one wing of the downstairs and return to the great hall. 'Interested in seeing the upstairs?' I ask cheekily. 'It's even more of a tip.'

'Sure,' he says with a shrug. The warmth has gone out of his voice. I begin to feel strange – like I'm the one betraying the house, not him.

I lead the way up the stairs and pause by the portrait of the young woman. I rub my fingers along the frame as if to say 'hello again'.

He stops beside me and looks the painting up and down, then at my hand, which is still touching the frame. Sheepishly, I withdraw it.

'Who is she? Do you know?' He leans in and studies the brushwork.

'Not for sure. But I think it might be Arabella Windham.'

'Those eyes...' he says. 'She looks familiar somehow. And what's that in her hands? Paper or letters, maybe?' He takes a step back, still analysing the painting.

'I don't know,' I say. 'Maybe you'll discover the answer when you start ripping the house apart piece by piece.'

As soon as the words come out, I can't believe I've said them. Mr Faraday looks shocked.

'I'm sorry, that was totally out of line,' I say. I turn away and walk to edge of the staircase landing. The time-worn banister is smooth under my hand. I look out over the elegant hallway and give a half-hearted laugh. 'You must think I'm the barmy one. I've obviously grown too fond of this place...' I can't even finish. It all sounds so silly, and I don't know why I'm bothering to explain. But something about this man seems to demand it. 'It should be nothing to me,' I add. 'I'm just the estate agent. But this house is special. I'd so like to see it go to a family that loves it – or else preserved and opened up to the public. I hate the idea that yet another great English House is about to be changed into something beyond recognition. I'm sorry.'

I look at him out of the corner of my eye. He's staring at the picture like he hasn't heard me.

Unable to bear his presence, I leave him there and go into the first bedroom. This one doesn't have a working loo or a closet full of costumes, but it does have the same clutter spanning decades – some as far back as the 1930s. On the mantle, there's a photograph of a young couple standing on either side of the queen, and a photograph of the same man standing next to Winston Churchill. I pick the photograph up and blow the dust off the frame.

I sense Mr Faraday coming into the room after me. I set down the photograph and look up. His eyes seem to pierce my skin and see inside the depths of my soul. To my great shame and dismay, I almost hope that he does recommend to Hexagon that they pursue development of the property – so that I might have a reason to see him again.

He comes over and picks up the photograph I just set down and looks at it intently. 'I admit that things are not quite what I had expected. I can almost see where you get your romantic notions from.' He sets down the photograph. 'But unfortunately, reality is something quite different. The public will get to enjoy the estate – the members of the golf club, at least. There are worse results, surely.'

'I just wish I had more time.'

'That's something you don't have.' He goes over to the grotty en-suite bathroom and peers inside.

I don't know what to make of his comment, but my stomach feels liquid. I'm confused and flustered, and this man is entirely the cause.

He comes back over to where I'm standing. 'You're obviously a passionate person, Miss Wood, and I admire that. But maybe you're also too quick to judge a book by its cover.' He smiles like he's won a victory over me, and at that moment, I do hate him a little. I maintain a discreet distance as he walks through the rest of the rooms on the second floor. He doesn't speak and seems to be lost in thought, touching a damp spot here, a crumbling window frame there.

We go up another flight of stairs. He quickly tours some of the servant's bedrooms and we head up into the attic. He walks over to the huge, round window, at the centre of the house, and looks out at the view over the parkland beyond. I walk over and stand beside him. Far below where we're standing, the fountain crumbles in the forecourt, and beyond, the long tree-lined drive snakes downwards from the house into a little valley. A cloud of dust rises, and I can almost see Rochester riding furiously towards Thornfield, his horse wild-eyed and lathered, straining at the bit; when all of a sudden, he encounters Jane Eyre on the path—

'Damn,' he mutters beside me, and I realise that there is no horse and no Lord of the Manor, just a car coming up the drive. Immediately, I snap back to my senses.

'If you'd like, Mr Faraday,' I say, making every effort to

sound professional, 'you can take your time looking around and I'll go down and see who it is.'

'Fine.' He smiles at me. I get a sense that he sees everything – from my ridiculous fantasies with him in a starring role to how much I wish they could be true. And I can't bear to think that he might be laughing at me, thinking I'm pathetic and eccentric – or worse.

'Fine,' I repeat. I leave the room and the spell that he has cast over me, rushing down the stairs two at a time. As I reach the lower staircase landing and the portrait of the lady in the pink dress, the front door creaks open and slams shut. Immediately, I tense up. The last thing I need is a visit from Mrs Bradford and Captain. I head quickly down the stairs to stop her at the pass.

As I reach the bottom step, a woman enters.

'Oh, hello,' I blurt out.

It isn't Mrs Bradford, but rather, the Windham heir, Ms Flora. I had no idea that she was back in town. She looks as polished and perfect as before, this time wearing a dark green Burberry coat, black stiletto boots, and a black pashmina.

'Hello, Miss Wood.' She unbuttons her coat. 'How are you?'

'I'm fine, Mrs MacArthur,' I say, returning the smile. 'I'm just showing around one of the executives from Hexagon. We won't be much longer – is that okay?'

She raises an eyebrow. 'Hexagon? You must be joking.'

'No, not at all—'

'Actually, Miss Wood,' she interrupts, 'you can go now. I'll lock up the house. I need to speak to my brother in private.'

Twenty-Four

Brother?

As soon as Flora says the word, the penny drops. Mr Faraday is not, in fact, an executive from Hexagon, but the second American heir – Mr Jack – and now that I know the truth, it seems blindingly obvious. I rewind the sequence of events: my boss telling me that an executive from Hexagon was planning to schedule a viewing at some unspecified point in the future, me jumping to the conclusion that Mr Faraday was said person. But though the wires were crossed, Jack Faraday must have guessed my mistake – how dare he deceive me like that?

Finally, I have a good reason to hate him.

But when a few seconds later he comes down the grand staircase, his sheer *je ne sais quoi* hits me all over again. I feel like Jane Eyre after she's been half-flattened by Rochester's horse and lashed with his whip. His blue-grey eyes flick from me to his sister.

'Hello Flora. Glad you could join us.' He sounds anything but.

'Sorry to blow your cover. But I'm not going to let you play Lord of the Manor.' Tension crackles in the air between them. She turns to me like she's dismissing a servant. 'Can you see yourself out?'

I look from her to Jack. He shrugs like Flora's in charge and it's nothing to him anyway. 'Thanks for showing me around,

Miss Wood,' he says. 'It's been interesting. I'll call your office tomorrow, okay?'

'Sure, no problem,' I say through clenched teeth. I hurry to the door and practically run to the car.

*

'Shit, shit, shit!' As soon as I'm out of sight of the house I bang my fist on the steering wheel. I can't believe some of the things I said: *Luckily, the smell has dissipated*!

And to be fair, while Mr Faraday didn't come clean and say that he was co-owner of the house, in fact, he never denied it either. He might even have assumed I knew. *Aren't you supposed to be selling the place?*

Shit. I take my foot off the accelerator. The view of Rosemont Hall in the rear-view mirror will surely be my last.

Twenty-Five

After two sleepless nights and a miserable Sunday afternoon spent helping Dad demolish the old garden shed, when Monday morning rolls around, I still feel furious, embarrassed, and every other negative emotion in between. I seriously debate taking a sickie. But in the end, I can't stand the thought of sitting at home stewing in my juices while Mum potters around and Dad waits for the Argos delivery of a new pre-fab shed. Besides, since I'm obviously going to have nothing more to do with Rosemont Hall, I may as well give Jack Faraday a piece of my mind if he does ring the office.

Jack Faraday. I think back to all my ludicrous imaginings of him: fat and middle-aged, a New-York ball-buster; Bill Gates – all golf-playing, and all based on nothing at all. Whereas in reality, I now know that he's devious, underhanded, and... beautiful. Every nerve in my body tingles when I recall the sound of his voice; the electric moment when we shook hands.

Which is just ridiculous.

I try to force him from my mind with a cup of hot coffee and a piece of toast. It doesn't work. How could he, of all people, be the one person who feels a connection to the house? And feeling that connection, how could he betray it? He's even worse, much worse, than I thought.

And so much better.

I change my outfit three times, but I'm no less distracted.

Then, as I'm about to leave the house, I can't find my pink cashmere scarf, which was a birthday gift from the first and only class I taught. I'd be sorry to lose it. I've a vague recollection that I wore it to the Rosemont Hall viewing. It's another freezing morning, so I grab one of my mother's chunky knit snoods instead. I'll call Mr Kendall to arrange to get it back – sometime when I know for sure that Jack Faraday won't be there.

At the office, I try to lose myself in the task of checking the latest property stats on Rightmove. I'm not going to think about him. Full-stop.

Mid-morning, an email I wasn't expecting pings in. It's from my former graduate thesis advisor. It twigs that I asked him a few months ago to send me information about teaching jobs he heard about, but that he hadn't responded before now. He's attached an advert for a job opening in Edinburgh, teaching literature at a private school for girls. 'Happy to put in a word for you,' his note reads. I stare at the screen, the realisation dawning about how much my life has moved on over the last few months. I think of the Blundells, David Waters, Hexagon, and Rosemont Hall. For all the toil and trouble I've encountered at *Tetherington Bowen Knowles,* I have a strange notion that for the first time, I've been experiencing life, not just reading about it. And then there's Jack Faraday. I shiver at the memory of the brief, fleeting 'realness' of him.

Get a grip! I scold myself. My fingers tap out an email to my former advisor: 'Thank you! The job sounds perfect. I'll definitely send in my CV'.

The phone rings. I stare at the blinking light on the switch-board. It's *him* – I just know it.

The light stops blinking but doesn't go out. From the bowels of Mr Bowen-Knowles's office, I can hear his muffled voice – he's picked up the phone. I've missed my chance to do damage control. But that's fine, because I'm not going to think about him.

The phone rings again. My heart leaps into my mouth. Maybe *this* is him.

I jerk the phone off the cradle. '*Tetherington Bowen Knowles*, Amy Wood speaking.'

It's Ronan Keene ringing to schedule a viewing at the Bristol flat. We go through all the details and arrange it for that same afternoon. Which is fine by me. Anything to get my mind off – *other things*.

When I hang up the phone, Mr Bowen-Knowles's line is still lit. The suspense is killing me. I stand up. 'Anyone for Starbucks?' I say. Over the last few months, my willingness to do the coffee run has somewhat defrosted the hearts of my colleagues, but today, I just need to clear my head.

Everyone orders their usual (skinny double decaf latte for Patricia; lemon poppyseed muffin and Earl Grey tea for Jonathan; Americano for Claire) and I leave the office practically at a run.

The day is grey and foggy, but nonetheless, Bath is buzzing with tourists and shoppers. The traffic crawls by, people push past me, and I feel like I'm in a bad dream where I'm being chased through the woods but my feet are too heavy to run. The dreadful mistake I made on Rosemont Hall continues to loom in my mind. As does the delicious and unscrupulous Jack Faraday.

I enter Starbucks and take my time staring up at the chalk-board. 'Next please,' the barista says with disinterest. I place the office order and add a mint hot chocolate for myself. As I wait at the coffee bar, I'm startled by a tap on my shoulder. 'Amy Wood – is that you?'

I turn around. It's Mary Blundell. She smiles at me, looking fresh-faced and rosy from the cold. She's wearing an old coat and a knit scarf similar to my own, and once again I'm struck by her homely openness that seems in such direct odds with her being married to an art thief and falling in love with an ultra-modern penthouse flat.

'Hi Mary,' I say with real enthusiasm, 'how are you getting on?'

'Fine – we're fine.' By some unspoken cue, we both collect our drinks and sit down together at a little table by the door.

'I can only stay a few minutes,' she says. 'I'm on my way to London to visit Fred at Pentonville.'

'And is Fred doing... okay?' I figure I can ask since she brought him up.

'Yes, he's good. He's using his time inside to finish up a business plan for a new gallery we hope to open.'

'Really?'

'Yes. The prison has a good library, and he's making lots of good contacts.'

'Oh,' I say, a bit less enthusiastically. 'How interesting.'

'We were both gutted to lose the flat in Bristol,' Mary adds. 'As soon as Fred's out, I'll ring you. We'd still love a flat like that – on a bit of a smaller budget.' She winks.

'Sure.' I smile. She may have criminal associations, but still, I'd like to help her and Fred find their perfect 'remand home'. I decide to come right out and ask her how her husband got into his – 'business'.

Mary sips her coffee thoughtfully. 'Fred always loved art,' she says. 'Did you know – he studied to be a painter in Madrid.'

'Really?'

'Yeah. But he was rubbish at it. His flatmate had an uncle who was an artist. *Tio Francisco*. The uncle was a hero during the war – World War Two. He helped wealthy Jewish families smuggle their art to safety from the Nazis.'

'Wow,' I say. 'That *is* interesting.'

'But after the war, *Tio Francisco* had to go back to more mundane things. Art smuggling and that sort of thing. He taught his nephew, Fred's flatmate, the tricks of the trade. They started a business together.'

'And it's been… uhh… lucrative?'

'No risk, no reward, Amy,' she says good-naturedly. 'Fred's a good man. He sees it as his mission to help make sure great art gets appreciated.'

'Umm… how's that exactly?'

'Well, let's face it – who do you think will appreciate a great piece of artwork more – a collector who loves it and is willing to pay for it, or your average member of the public day-tripping through a museum?'

'I admit I've never thought of it that way.'

'It's all a matter of perspective.' She grins. 'You say "tomato" and all that—'

Just then, her phone beeps in her pocket. She rummages for it and frowns at the screen. 'Sorry Amy, I should go. Flipping French postal workers – always striking when you need them.'

I don't dare ask her what she means. With a conspiratorial grin and a little wave, she walks briskly out of the café.

*

Everyone's coffee is cold. Back at the office, I dole out the goods and collect money (today I end up short-changed by 22p). Mr Bowen-Knowles's phone line is still lit and his muffled voice seems louder than usual. Meeting Mary Blundell was temporarily distracting, and it was interesting to hear about Fred's art 'career'. But I still have the Jack Faraday debacle to deal with. I sit down at my desk, skim through my emails, and wait for the inevitable to happen.

The inevitable takes exactly seven minutes to occur. I'm sipping the last of my hot chocolate when Mr Bowen-Knowles's door opens with a smack against the wall.

I look up. He frowns at me with his usual irritated disdain.

'You,' he points, 'in here.'

I am thus summoned.

All eyes are on me as I embark on the familiar walk of shame. Though the Christmas Party 'incident' has never been discussed, mentioned, or repeated, fleetingly, I wonder if my colleagues think I'm putting in a little 'overtime' behind closed doors.

'Sit down.'

I thus obey.

He sits down opposite me, steeples his fingers, and frowns.

'While you were *out* just now, Ian Kendall rang about Rosemont Hall. I understand you had quite a mix-up.'

'Yes, you could say that.' My anger begins to simmer. 'But you could also say that the viewing was arranged under false pretences. I may not have the right accent, or have gone to the right schools, but my time is not worthless.' I stare him boldly in the face. 'Saturday was a waste of time – I'm hardly going to sell a property to someone who owns it already, am I? So if you or Mr Jack Faraday are unhappy with what happened – well...' I stop just short of telling him where to go.

Mr Bowen-Knowles sits back in his chair and appraises me. I furiously calculate the odds that his next words will send me packing. I'm too angry to care, although I *do* care – more than I want to – about a great many things.

He makes me wait. His phone rings. He ignores it.

'Jack Faraday would like you to ring him,' he says. 'I gather that he came over here to see the house before it's sold and didn't have a key.'

'You said that Hexagon was sending someone around,' I say heatedly in my own defence. 'But no one's rung me. I assumed that this Jack Faraday was their rep. It was an honest mistake.'

He waves his hand. 'Look, this "Mr Jack" is a moron – that's obvious. I'm as annoyed as you are.'

I doubt that, but I'm surprised that he's taking my side.

'You've done as well as could be expected – that old pile was never going to sell. And most importantly, you *looked* like you were doing your job.'

'Oh...?'

'Yeah. Mr Kendall rang to let us know that Hexagon came in with a formal offer this morning. It's on the low side, but Mr Jack talked them up from the original figure. He's going to accept it – cut his losses.'

I wring my hands together, struggling to stay composed.

Mr Bowen-Knowles fiddles idly with his cuff-link. 'But because we did the viewings, we're going to get partial commission. The Hexagon rep is going to ring to sort out the paperwork – I doubt he'll bother to go round the place now. It's now all down to the numbers, the plans, and, of course, the cash.'

'I see.' I stand up. 'Thank you, Mr Bowen-Knowles. Thank you for telling me.'

My chest aches and my breathing is shallow as I walk out of his office feeling like I've been diagnosed with a fatal disease. I grab my handbag from my desk and leave through the back door – desperate to get away from the office. There's the Ronan Keene viewing in Bristol – but it's not for several hours yet. I get in the car and start driving.

As I leave Bath, I think of all the literary heroines I've encountered over the years. All of them had to cope with bad things happening – tension is a necessary part of good literature. I wonder if I'm an Elinor Dashwood in *Sense and Sensibility*. Even when she thinks she's been jilted by Edward, she bears her sorrows with a stiff upper lip. Or maybe I'm a Jane Eyre – she votes with her feet when she discovers that Mr Rochester already has a wife who is deranged and locked in the attic.

I honk the horn hard at a lorry that is overtaking as two

lanes merge into one. At least I've no penchant to be an Emma Bovary or Anna Karenina. Topping myself would be too messy.

I drive on, but rather than take the turn-off to Bristol, I take a detour. To Rosemont Hall. If no one is there, I'll just pop inside quickly and see if I can find my scarf.

When I reach the gates I drive slowly, knowing this is my last visit here. I try to memorise the details and that first view of the house when the road tops the crest of the hill. The huge silhouette against the sky always makes my heart beat a little faster.

But today, the view is marred by another huge silhouette: a removals lorry backed up to the front door. I slam on the brakes, skidding across the grassy verge.

In addition to the removals van, there are two cars – Jack Faraday's hired Vauxhall and Flora's Mercedes. Two burly men are loading something heavy into the back of the lorry.

I do a swift three-point turn and floor it back to the main road. Once I'm outside the twisted iron gates, I discover once and for all which kind of romantic literary heroine I would be: the kind who when faced with adversity, pulls her car over to a lay-by, puts her head against the steering wheel, and cries.

*

I may have lost both battle and war, but I still have a flat to show in Bristol. Maybe if I sell enough penthouse flats in Bristol to footballers, someday I'll be able to afford a little flat in a historic house conversion next to a golf course.

Perish the thought.

While the car is stopped, I remember that I'm still supposed to ring Jack Faraday. I dig in my handbag, throwing out the contents on the seat. At the bottom, I find the yellow sticky with the information for the 'Hexagon viewing': Mr Faraday's mobile number.

Knowing that he's busy directing removals men to bin his deceased relatives' precious belongings lends me courage. I dial the number but nothing happens. I try again, adding a US prefix. The phone begins to ring.

At first, the line clicks and I assume it's going to voicemail. But a second later, his voice sends a very strong, very unwelcome surge of adrenalin through my body.

'Jack Faraday.'

'Oh, hello,' I stammer. 'It's Amy Wood. The estate agent.'

'Amy...' His brusque tone becomes warm. 'I'm glad you called.'

'Mr Bowen-Knowles said you asked me to ring you?'

'Yes, yes. I... just a second.'

A commotion erupts in the background (a woman's voice yelling: 'No! The one with the sticker, not that old thing!').

The phone is then muffled. I wait.

'Sorry, Amy,' Jack says a moment later. 'It's not really a great time for me to talk, but listen, is there any chance you can come over to the house tonight? Say around seven?'

I hesitate, wishing the blood would stop rushing in my ear. 'I can do that,' I say, 'but I'm not sure—'

A loud crash echoes in the background.

'Shit!' Jack's voice. 'Sorry Amy – did you say yes or no? I think you left your scarf here.'

'Well, yes, but—'

'Great, I'll see you around seven.'

'But—'

The line buzzes.

I roll down the window to let in the cold air. The lay-by reeks of urine. A car whizzes past.

Jack Faraday wants me to stop by so that he can return my scarf – nothing more, nothing less.

So why are my palms clammy and I feel like I might hyperventilate?

I should probably ring him back – tell him to give my scarf to the solicitor and take his lovely, ruined house and stick it somewhere unpleasant.

But I do nothing of the sort. Instead, I put the phone away and drive off towards Bristol with a silly grin on my face.

Twenty-Six

The idea of seeing Jack Faraday again – even if it's only for him to return my scarf – fills me with a guilty, thrilling terror. Despite my best efforts, he's there in my mind, drifting just below my conscious thoughts. There was a spark there when we met; an understanding on some primordial level. It's ridiculous; it's annoying – and it's incredibly distracting.

When I meet Ronan Keene at the Bristol penthouse (this time with the right keys), I'm so on edge that I even greet Crystal with a friendly kiss on the cheek. She instantly stiffens – like I've mussed up her carefully applied foundation; but her bee-stung lips give a little smile: 'How've ya been?' she even asks (though she clicks off in her stilettos to send a text before I can answer).

I'm pleasantly surprised when they both instantly like the flat: the building, the location, the view, the floor-to-ceiling glass walls. For me, it's not the same buzz I had showing the flat to the Blundells, especially knowing how gutted Mary was that she and Fred had lost the flat. But it's out of my hands, and all I can do is my job.

Of course, there are quite a few things that Crystal finds fault with: the double-width bathtub is too small; the carpet on the top floor is hideous beige (and 'wouldn't white look so much better?'); the alcove in the master bedroom is only big enough for a 72-inch screen rather than a custom home cinema. But overall, she's much more enthusiastic than I'd expected.

Ronan doesn't say much, but I get the feeling he's eager to end what must be a very painful search with Crystal in tow ('I know it isn't perfect, cupcake, but remember, we'll only be here a few times a month anyway').

I praise the place to the moon, downplay the defects in grand *Tetherington Bowen Knowles* style, and eventually, leave them on the roof terrace mulling things over. I flop onto the ultra-chic cowhide sofa in the main living space to wait for them.

My mobile phone rings: it's Claire checking to make sure that I'm okay. She goes a bit quiet when I tell her where I am (keen clients being hard to come by). But she wishes me luck

Ronan and Crystal stay outside on the roof terrace for a long time. I check my watch – at this rate, I won't even have time to go home and get changed before the evening. On the other hand, why should I? I'm wearing a nice suit, and I really don't want to face my parents and their over-zealous questions about where I'm going, who I'm meeting (and whether he or she plays Scrabble). I even debate going back to the office – anything to get my mind off seeing Jack Faraday again.

Finally, Ronan and Crystal come back inside and have another look around the downstairs. Ronan asks me a few questions about service charges, parking, council tax, and whether the furniture is for sale. I have a competent answer prepared for everything.

'This place has given us a lot to think about,' he says as we ride down the (newly replaced) lift. 'We'll definitely be in touch soon.'

'Thanks,' I say. 'I'll look forward to hearing from you.'

We shake hands and go our separate ways. I grab a coffee at Costa and sit down at a little table. The clock on the wall reads 5 o'clock.

Two hours to go before…?

Twenty-Seven

I grip the wheel with sweaty palms as I pull up in front of Rosemont Hall. The lights are on downstairs, the windows glowing like jack o' lantern eyes.

The removals lorry and the Mercedes are gone, but the blue Vauxhall is still there. I park next to it but stay in the car, gathering my courage. When I finally do get out, my knees are so shaky that I can barely totter in my heels through the mucky gravel. I manage to make it up the cracked stone steps to the front door. Holding my breath, I ring the bell.

Within seconds, the door opens. Jack Faraday's smile has the air of amusement. His face is too craggy to be considered classically handsome, I suppose. His blue eyes are sharp and intelligent, and I feel like they could penetrate the fog of my deepest dreams. I immediately experience a stirring in parts of me that I thought were long dead.

'Hi Amy.' He holds out my scarf. My heart plunges – is that it then?

He gestures for me to come inside. 'Come on in – it's freezing out there.'

I put the scarf in the pocket of my coat and move past him into the great hall. In the centre, a table is set up with a white paper cloth and plastic plates for two. In the centre of the table is a large brown bag – the room smells of Chinese food. Two electric radiators stretched to the end of their electrical cords are set up at either end of the table.

I stand there, stunned.

'I wanted to apologise for offending you,' Jack says. 'I should have told you who I was right away. But by the time I realised that you thought I was someone else, it seemed too late to tell you. Besides...' the laughter is back in his eyes, 'it was interesting to see your sales technique.'

'I should be the one to apologise. I had no right to say those... uhh... things.'

He gives a little smirk and I blush. 'Anyway,' he says, 'I hope we can call a truce. And do some damage to this Chinese takeaway.' He grins. 'I'm told it's the best in Little Botheringford.'

'You mean, the *only*.' I automatically grin back. I'm tingling all over, and not just from the warmth of the radiators.

'Can I take your coat?'

'Thanks.' I unbutton my coat and hand it to him. He hangs it on the newel post of the staircase, then gestures for me to take a seat.

'Since you love this place so much, I thought we could have a picnic in here,' he says. 'Unfortunately, as you know, cooking anything in the kitchen is out of the question. And as far as I can tell, there isn't a supermarket for miles. Otherwise I would have whipped up my special chilli con carne, extra spicy.'

'Do you like to cook?' I ask, pleasantly surprised.

'Sometimes. But nothing too fancy. I can do Mexican pretty well – that's all in the sauce. And I like making Italian food with home-made pasta. And I live near the ocean, so I like making things with fresh fish. Anything seasonal, really. That's the secret – fresh ingredients.'

'I can make chicken curry,' I say. 'But that's about it. When I lived in London, I did a lot of takeaway, I'm afraid.'

'Well, I understand that too. I don't bother to cook when I'm working late, or when I'm eating alone.'

Alone as in no wife or girlfriend? I can't bring myself to ask. 'And where is it that you live?' I say instead.

He rummages in the bag. A bottle of wine and two glasses appear in his hand.

'California,' he says. 'I've got a nice Victorian house in a little town called Carmel-by-the-Sea. The house was built in 1899. Practically ancient – for California.' He smiles. 'It's painted light green with dark green gingerbread trim. There's a holly tree out in front that's as old as the house. It's trimmed in the shape of a bell. And from the top floors, you can see a little strip of ocean. There's a balcony in front called a widow's walk. It was built for a sea captain's wife – so that she could go out and see if her husband's ship had returned.'

'It all sounds lovely,' I say truthfully.

'I thought you'd like to hear about the details. It shows that I'm not a complete architectural and historical Neanderthal, I hope.'

'No,' I risk a little laugh. 'I guess I was wrong.'

He opens the bottle of wine and pours some into a glass.

'Your sister said that you're in computers,' I say. 'And that you teach at Stanford. That's impressive.'

'Is it?' He hands me a glass to taste. I sniff it like I know what I'm doing and then take a little sip and nod.

'Well, I think so. Stanford is a great university and all.'

'Yes, it is,' he agrees, pouring the wine into both glasses. 'And I'm lucky to have the job. It's fun. Some of those kids are so smart that I'm not sure who's teaching whom. We're working on a new design for micro-processing board circuitry.'

'Umm, what's that?'

'Basically, components found in all microchips,' he adds. 'That's what my company did before I sold it. Now I'm mostly freelance.'

'I'm not quite sure what to say.'

He laughs. 'Don't worry. I don't expect you to be interested in computer chips. Business is business, and I make a point not to mix it with pleasure.'

My cheeks flare with warmth. He looks at me intently and takes a sip of his wine.

'What most people don't realise is the creativity that goes into even simple devices. It's that creative part that I enjoy now more than anything. If my team succeeds with this patent, it could be revolutionary.'

As I'm trying to take this all in, he clinks his glass to mine.

'But I must be boring you silly,' he says. 'Sorry about that. It's just habit. We computer geeks don't get out much.'

'I'm not bored.' How can I be when each detail adds to my mental picture of him? I want to know everything about him. I want—

'Good.' He smiles like he's read my mind.

I swallow hard. 'And what do you do when you're not working?'

'Well,' he takes a sip of wine, 'after my wife died, I kind of shut off from everyone and focused on work mostly. It's only in the last year or so that I've enjoyed doing anything again. I suppose most of my hobbies are solitary – art galleries, walks by the sea, reading books – nothing too exciting. I guess a geek is as a geek does.'

'I'm sorry about your wife,' I say. 'Not that sorry is any good in these situations.'

He swirls the wine in the glass. 'Maybe not. But I'm getting past it. It was cancer. She's been gone for three years now.'

Frowning, he takes a handful of plastic cutlery out of the bag. I want to reach out and grab his hand – comfort him somehow. His story has plucked a chord that resonates inside of me. My loss was nothing compared to his, but still, I know what it's like to have one's world and one's life turned upside down. I feel like I've known Jack Faraday for much longer than just hours. It's strange and implausible, but it's like he's been there all along.

'It was awful, of course,' he says, 'and time isn't the great healer that people say. It's like you're waiting every day for something to happen. Some days, you wait for the person to come back. Other days, you're waiting to forget. Months pass, then years.' He sighs. 'And then one day, out of the blue, a stranger with an English accent called up looking for a "Mr Jack and Ms Flora". At first I thought it was a wrong number. But it turns out that my sister and I had inherited a crumbling mansion in England. It didn't sound like the thing I was waiting for... in fact, the whole thing sounded like a damned nuisance.' He shakes his head and passes me a plate. 'But the lawyer, Mr Kendall, seemed like a decent guy. He told me that he'd met an estate agent who was passionate about the house – and finding a buyer who would restore it. I admit, I was very sceptical.' He gives a little laugh. 'In fact, I pictured you as looking like that woman – what's her name? – Camilla Parker Bowles – tweed suit, sensible shoes, big hair.'

'Really?' I laugh too.

'So you can imagine that when I finally met you, I was pleasantly surprised.'

'Me too,' I say. 'I won't even go into what I thought you might look like.'

He smirks. 'Bill Gates, maybe?'

I grin. 'Something like that.'

'Well, I guess we were both wrong. But enough about me. Tell me about Amy Wood.'

'Oh... uhh...' Nerves robotically commandeer my body. I should make up something interesting about myself – pretend I'm an Olympic triathlete or studying to be a barrister or a brain surgeon, or campaigning to save polar bears. But Jack has been honest with me; I decide to tell him the truth.

'I used to teach in London...' I begin. I tell him about my

former job, and then move on to the juicier bits: viewing the flat that I thought could be our perfect home, discovering the truth about Simon and Ashley, getting sacked, and moving back in with my parents, in their 1970s two-bed bungalow. My life… warts and all.

Jack listens to my every word, slowly sipping his wine. I take a little sip from my glass to moisten my throat, determined not to get too intoxicated to drive.

I come to a pause and he shakes his head. 'Sounds like you've had a hell of a time.'

'Oh,' I shrug breezily, 'it did hit me pretty hard. But it feels like ancient history.' With him sitting across the table, it feels true.

'Sounds like you're better off without your ex but it is a shame about your job. English literature…' his eyes twinkle. 'I should have guessed. This place is straight out of a novel, isn't it?'

I nod, disconcerted by his insightfulness.

'Maybe *Jane Eyre* or *Pride and Prejudice* – something like that.'

'You've read those?'

'Hasn't everyone?'

'No,' I say. 'I don't think so.'

'Well, my wife had all those books. After she died, I went through a phase of reading the classics. They may be old-fashioned, but the themes still resonate today, don't they?'

I nod.

He leans in on his elbow, staring at me as if something doesn't compute. 'And then you became an estate agent?'

'I didn't plan on it. I mean, who would? I don't know what it's like in America, but over here, they have a certain… reputation.'

He laughs. 'Tell me.'

'I'm afraid there's a certain tendency to, shall we say, over-state the good and downplay the bad.'

'You mean they lie in order to get a sale? Yeah – they do that everywhere.'

'I guess so.' I sigh. 'And of course I would rather be teaching literature, or history – anything, really. But I was lucky to find any job around here and I was determined to make it work. Then on my first day, when the solicitor called about Rosemont Hall, it seemed like fate. When I saw the house, all I could think about was how much I wanted to find someone who would bring it back to life.' I shake my head. 'It sounds naff, but I feel a strong connection with Rosemont Hall.'

'I can tell,' Jack says. His lips narrow. 'Despite the fact that you were trying so hard to make me hate the place.'

'Well that's because...' I stop.

His smile fades. He takes the food containers out of the brown bag. 'Shall we eat?' he says.

A cold wave of reality hits me. This man may not be from Hexagon, but he is not some kind of romantic hero. He is not going to restore and nurture the house that's been handed to him on a silver platter. In fact, he's the one who contacted Hexagon in the first place. In between creating his revolutionary microchip, cooking chilli con carne, reading the classics, and taking walks by the sea, he's been dealing with the devil. Whatever happens to Rosemont Hall – if it becomes a golf course, or just crumbles away to dust – will be entirely down to Jack Faraday.

He opens up the white cartons of steaming food. 'I got chicken, beef, and vegetarian. A little of each?'

Biting my lip, I nod. He scoops the food onto my plate.

'Flora and I are selling the house.' Looking at me intently, he hands over the plate. 'To Hexagon. It seemed the best result under the circumstances.'

I take a bite of chicken chow mein, but it turns to paste in my mouth. The whole evening is a pointless charade – with any romantic happy endings purely the product of my imagination.

Not that I had the right to expect anything different. For one evening, as Flora said, Jack Faraday is playing *Lord of the Manor*. I let him play me in the process.

'I can't agree that it's the best result,' I look him squarely in the face. 'If you gut this house and turn it into a golf clubhouse or flats, it will be lost forever. It will, Jack…' I set down my fork. 'And all the computer chips in the world won't be able to save it once it's gone.'

He rests his chin in his hand. 'Okay, Amy Wood, you're the estate agent. Tell me – what's the alternative?'

'Well…'

I should have the perfect answer prepared. I should have the perfect buyer lined up. But I haven't found that person. The failure doesn't just rest with Jack Faraday. It rests with me too.

'Once it's fixed up it could be self-supporting,' I grasp at straws. 'Lots of estates like this are. It would make a lovely home for the right person, or perhaps be opened up to the public.'

Jack Faraday looks for a second like he's about to laugh in my face. Instead, he folds his arms and sits back. 'And how do you propose that it gets "fixed up", as you say? I'm sure you've seen the figures just to get it watertight, not to mention the rest of the work, plus the annual upkeep. Then there's the inheritance taxes and other debts of the estate.'

'There are grants and things, and bank loans, and…'

I trail off, completely embarrassed. After all, if *I* had inherited Rosemont Hall, even with the best will in the world, I couldn't afford any of those things.

Jack sighs. He picks up his glass and takes a sip of the wine, savouring it on his tongue for a moment before swallowing it.

'Tonight before you got here, Amy, I spent a couple of hours here in the house, just walking through the rooms. As I told you the first time we met, before I came over to England, I had never really had much time for history. My life was all about the future. But being here, it feels like something inside me has opened up. And the house – well, it seeps into you, doesn't it? It's that comfortable feeling of having eaten a big meal at Christmas and then sitting before a roaring fire with a glass of wine, surrounded by the people you love most.'

'*You* feel that way?'

'Don't get me wrong, I mean, it sounds crazy. I don't think you can just turn up at a place and have it feel like home.'

'But it does, doesn't it?' I whisper.

There's a long moment. My heart begins to kindle and flare up with a dangerous fire – that thing called hope.

But then Jack turns away, severing the connection. Slowly, he turns back and shakes his head. 'I admire your passion.' He sighs. 'Don't think I don't. But real life is more complicated than fiction. In this case, there are no heroes or villains – I hope you can see that.'

The lid on Pandora's box shuts firmly. Hope? Silly me. 'You're right, Jack,' I say. 'Life is complicated. I'm sorry that I've wasted your time.' I push my chair back and get ready to leave. It's the only thing left that I can do.

Suddenly, the lights flicker overhead. We both look up at the cobweb-laced chandelier. There's a loud popping sound and the whole house goes dark. The hum of the heaters stops. Everything is deathly quiet.

'The heaters must have blown a fuse.' I grip the table to orient myself.

'Amy... wait,' Jack says softly. His hand finds my arm.

I jump up. 'Thanks so much for dinner, Jack. It's been great.' I take a few steps in the direction – I think – of the newel post with my coat. 'I don't think there's much you can do about the lights tonight. The cellar's a bit of a maze – probably best to leave it until tomorrow. Oh, and the housekeeper, Mrs Bradford – I think she might still be living in the house some nights – just so you know.'

'Really? She told me she'd moved out.'

233

'Oh, you've spoken with her? Well, anyway, I don't know.'

My heels echo on the marble. The staircase isn't where I thought it was.

'Let me help you.' Jack says. He flicks on a tiny pen-sized torch.

'I'm okay—'

My heel catches one of the cracks in the marble tiles. The next thing I know, the cold floor comes up fast and hard against my face.

'Owww!' I yelp. The darkness is spotty before my eyes.

Strong arms help me into a sitting position.

'Amy! Are you hurt? Your ankle?'

I can just make the outline of my heel – half-twisted off. But nothing is seriously damaged other than my pride – and my foolish illusions.

'I'm fine,' I say. 'I just need my coat.'

'Sure, I'll get it.'

His arms release me, and he goes over and gets my coat and scarf. I will myself to get up and leave, but my ankle *does* hurt – a little. But more than that, there's a strong force deep inside me that's battling for me to stay.

Jack wraps the coat around my shoulders and plunks down beside me. I'm acutely aware of his proximity. He flicks the tiny beam of his torch absently over the floor.

'It's bad timing,' he says with a little laugh. 'After all this time, I finally meet someone, invite her to dinner, and forget the candles just when they would have come in handy.'

I process the salient piece of information: *meet someone.*

'Don't worry, Jack. It was a nice surprise – thank you. I hope I haven't offended you.'

'No Amy, you haven't. I hear what you're saying about the house. And part of me agrees with you. But it isn't just about the money for repairs and upkeep. There are other things – other people in my family who have been hurt over the years. I can't explain it to you. Not in a way that would make any sense. But I think it's best if our family is shot of this house.'

'What do you mean?'

The circle of light from his torch begins to fade. His hand brushes my cheek as he leans very close to me and whispers in my ear.

'It's a long story. But know this – I'm sorry if you're disappointed about the house – disappointed in me. I'm sorry for a lot of things... but not for this—'

And there in the darkness, his kiss sends lightning bolts of electricity through every nerve in my body. I want to melt into him, and our lips mould together like they were made to stay that way. His fingers are magic as they slowly trail down my neck, and my body is screaming to end what seems like years of drought. But, at the same time, my mind is screaming at me to stop, I can't do this, it will end in tears, I'm betraying Rosemont Hall, *and*...

He stops and draws back. My hands are on his chest and I've pushed him away.

'I can't...'

I pull on my coat and scramble to my feet. I whip off the offending shoes and run stocking-footed across the cold marble.

'Amy, wait. I didn't mean to—'

The slam of the door drowns out his words.

Twenty-Eight

I haven't just made the biggest mistake of my life. I haven't ruined a perfect evening. And I know this because...

Reason eludes me as I nearly slam into the back of a lorry at a roundabout. Certainly, I've made lots of mistakes before – too many to count. Mistakes like not having a candid discussion with Simon about where our relationship was headed; or acting on impulse and committing an assault with mobile phone; or moving back to Somerset; or kissing Frankie Summers at age fourteen when he was at home with chickenpox. But running away from Jack Faraday is not another disaster of my own making.

In fact, the more I think about it, the more certain I am that I made the right decision. I was bowled over by the moment, and it was right to step back before I was swept away into the abyss of... what I really wanted to happen.

The miles between me and Rosemont Hall flash by. Jack Faraday is not a friend – of mine, at least. Rosemont Hall will be turned into a golf course, for the gleeful enjoyment of people like David Waters, Alistair Bowen-Knowles, Simon, and 'Ashley'. Jack said himself that it's not about the money for repairs and upkeep. After all, he teaches at Stanford and works in Silicon Valley. He's successful, from the sounds of it. He could save Rosemont Hall if he wanted to.

When my mobile phone rings, my hands jump on the steering wheel. Should I pull off the road, answer it, and if it's Jack, give him a piece of my mind? Or should I pull off the road, turn around, rush back to the house and pick up where we left off? I nearly skid as I look for a verge that doesn't exist. The call goes to voicemail; I drive on. The lights of Nailsea shine cold and white in the distance.

Jack Faraday is nothing to me – and it's going to stay that way. He'll go back to America and his nice life in Carmel-by-the-Sea.

Leaving me...

Here.

My mobile rings again. I screech to the side of the road and scramble for it in my bag. It rings off before I can grab it. I turn it off, my hands unsteady as I drive the rest of the way home.

Mum and Dad are still up watching the news when I get back. I refuse the offer of a cup of tea, have a quick shower, and get into bed. I try to read a little; then turn out the light and put a pillow over my head. It doesn't matter who called. I toss and turn and pop in my earplugs.

The suspense is killing me. I sit bolt upright, creep out of my room and grab my handbag. I smuggle it back into my room and take out my phone. Three missed calls. Biting my lip, I check the number.

Yes! My heart does a jig of glee. I turn off the light and lie in bed, trying hard to recover the mixture of confusion and outrage I'd so carefully concocted on my way home. But it's no use. I close my eyes and snuggle into the duvet, my body still tingling from the memory of his kiss.

*

After a night of pleasantly disturbing dreams, I wake up the next morning in a fog of disbelief. How could I have run away from Jack Faraday? How could I have been so utterly stupid?

It takes a cold shower and most of the drive to work before

I can once again focus on the anger I feel towards Jack. He's hiding something about Rosemont Hall, I'm certain of it. Why didn't I get more information when I had the chance? Why on earth didn't I stay?

The day gets worse when I reach my desk and listen to my voicemails. The first is from the PA to one Nigel Netelbaum, Director of Regional Development for Hexagon UK. He wants an appointment to discuss the paperwork for Rosemont Hall. I hit delete.

The next message is from Mr Kendall asking me to ring him as soon as possible. I stall – make some coffee, run out and grab a muffin, eat it slowly at my desk. While I'm at it, I google Jack Faraday.

There are a lot of hits. Jack Faraday is officially a rich and successful computer geek. I find a picture of him in the *San Francisco Chronicle* giving a $100,000 cheque to a cancer charity. There's another article on the sale of his company with figures involving more noughts than I can count on one hand. I was right all along: Jack Faraday has the money to keep Rosemont Hall and save it.

But he isn't going to.

As I close down the website, my phone rings. I recognise Mr Kendall's number.

I grab the phone. 'Hi Mr Kendall,' I say. 'I was just about to ring you.'

'Hello Amy.' He sounds cordial as usual, if a little chilly. He tells me that since we're no longer instructed on the sale of Rosemont Hall, I don't need to deal with Hexagon; he'll take care of Nigel Netelbaum himself. All he needs from me is the keys back as soon as possible.

'Sure,' I choke, 'I can drop the keys by your office.'

'All right then, if—'

I cut him off. 'You know, Mr Kendall, I tried to convince Mr Jack that he should keep the house – it's part of his family heritage and all that. I think he could afford to fix it up, if he wanted to.' I give a weak laugh. 'But I couldn't persuade him.'

Mr Kendall sighs – he obviously thinks I've got way too big for my knickers. 'Not everyone is like you, Amy. Why should Mr Jack and Ms Flora – two people who have their own lives in America – want to keep a house that they've never visited before – maybe never even knew existed.' He begins to sound perturbed. 'You may not know it, but they're running out of time before they will have to pay the estate debts and the first instalment of a whopping inheritance tax bill.'

'Oh.'

'Besides, not every family history is a happy one. The Windhams may have owned a grand house, but in the end, it's just a house. What about the people who lived there – aren't they more important? And believe me—' he pauses as something beeps in the background.

'Yes...' I coax. 'Please... I'd really like to know more. So I can understand.'

'Sorry Amy, I've got another call that I need to take. You know – don't worry about dropping off the keys. I'll send someone round later today.'

'No really, it's—'

The phone clicks off.

My chest feels like a black hole, but for the rest of the morning it's filled with other matters. Ronan Keene phones, and (miracle of miracles) puts in an offer on the Bristol flat. I ring the vendor myself and come back with a counter-offer, engage in some toing and froing on the price, and finally an agreement is reached. My co-workers are hanging on with bated breath while I close the deal. By the time I get started on the paperwork, once again my name is heading to the top of the sales chart on the door of the disabled loo.

That *should* make me happy. I *am* happy. So why don't I *feel* it?

I check my mobile, hoping Jack might have rung again. He hasn't. I debate ringing him. I don't. After all, what's the point? Jack Faraday will go back to America. Rosemont Hall will be sold. I'll still be here at *Tetherington Bowen Knowles*.

Unless I do something about it.

Luckily, I know just the thing. It's as if the universe has sensed my wayward path and is now catapulting me in the right direction. I've been playing estate agent and old-house advocate for long enough. It's time for me to go back to my true vocation – teaching literature. If nothing else, it's much less painful than real life.

I spend an hour dusting off my CV and writing a cover email to the headmaster of the school for girls in Edinburgh. I wax lyrical about how I've always been inspired by setting as a 'character' in fiction, and how I'm looking forward to exploring with my students works that evoke the wilds of Scotland – *Rob Roy, Ivanhoe*, the poetry of Robert Burns. By the time I've written my piece, I've almost managed to convince myself. *Almost*. My throat is tight as I press send.

At lunchtime, Claire asks if I want to grab a sandwich. I don't much feel like it, but I'm desperate for someone to talk sense into me. As we stand in line at Pret, I tell her the latest on Rosemont Hall (leaving out certain relevant details about my dinner with its reluctant heir).

As expected, she's less than sympathetic to my plight. 'God, Amy, you've really got to get a grip,' is what she says.

'Yes – I want to. But how?'

'Well, you can start by facing the facts. If the house is sold, then it's sold,' Claire says. 'It may be a shame, but no one's died... I mean, other than the last owner. But *you* need to move on. The heirs have every right to sell it if they don't want it.'

'I know, it's just...'

'It's just what?' She cocks her head, frowning. 'There's

something you're not telling me. Is it the old lady who's been turfed out? Or something else?'

I realise that someday, Claire is going to make one hell of a barrister. 'Well, there is one other thing that might be worth mentioning...'

'Yes?'

'The heir: Jack Faraday.'

'What about him?'

'We had dinner. And a long talk.'

'Dinner?'

'I think I might be falling for him.'

Claire's mouth becomes a lip-lined 'O'. 'Please say you're joking.'

'Well I certainly don't want to! I despise him: he could save the house if he wanted to. *We* could save it.' I tell her about what Jack Faraday said. About walking through the house and having the history seep into his bones. I tell her that he feels a connection just like I do.

'But he's not going to save it, Claire. None of it makes any difference.'

'That's his prerogative, I guess. But for the record, did he say why not?'

'He said that people in the past had been hurt.'

'Which means what?'

'I've no idea.'

'Then ask him! Come on Amy – this isn't the nineteenth century. You have to stop thinking like Jane Eyre and start thinking like Ruth Watson – you know, the woman with the big beads who used to be on *Country House Rescue*?' She tsks. 'You're a beautiful, professional woman with a great sense of dedication. Make a business plan for saving the house and present it to him. And if he still says no, then you can always get down on your knees and beg.'

241

A plan – a business plan? Why didn't I think of that before?

'Get the facts down on paper,' Claire says. 'Crunch some numbers. Show him how the house can make a profit on its own – if it can. Convince him that he's better off keeping it than selling. If he's a techie, then he ought to appreciate things like that.'

'Yes,' I say brightly. 'Numbers. That's what I need. But how do I get them?'

Claire rolls her eyes. 'Haven't you learned anything from our delightful boss? Make them up. All you need to do is get something down on paper. A spreadsheet. Something that will get him thinking.'

'I've never written a business plan before, but I can give it a try.'

'I'll cover for you at the office – tell them you're taking one of my viewings. Go to the library – find a book. There must be loads.'

'Thanks Claire. I owe you big time.'

'I won't forget.' We smile at each other and eat our sandwiches.

Claire is a genius. After lunch we go our separate ways – she back to the office and I to the tourist information office. I pick up some leaflets on historic homes in the area that are open to the public – like Longleat House. They have a zoo and a safari park, loads of activities for kids, eateries, gift shops – it looks like the place is definitely paying its way.

Maybe Jack and I could go and visit the places together and I could convince him of the possibilities. I picture us in a little open-top car, driving through country lanes, my hair tied up in a scarf, him wearing his red jacket and sunglasses. We'd visit Longleat in the morning and Sudeley Castle in the afternoon, stopping for lunch at a rambling little country pub where we'd sit outside in the garden and Jack would sample the local bitter. And at night when the sun went down, neither of us would want the day to end. We'd have supper together in the restaurant of his hotel and talk about our day, and all of the plans we could make for the future of Rosemont Hall. And gradually, we'd make more plans of our own – little trips we could take, other places to see... and one thing would lead to another, and—

'Hey, watch it,' someone yells.

I look up and realise that I'm in the middle of a crossing, about to get run down by a 'Hop on, Hop Off' open-top city tour bus. A group of Japanese schoolgirls snap me with their iPhones. At least if I'm flattened, there will be plenty of witnesses.

My fantasy in tatters, I walk down the road to the public library. The librarian points the way to the relevant section. I grab a book called *Business Plans for Complete Idiots* and a free table. I tackle chapter one: *Brainstorming*. I take out my notebook and begin jotting down a few ideas.

I come up with a fairly long list of things that could be developed at Rosemont Hall to turn a profit. At the very least, it could have a tea room with locally sourced organic produce, a children's adventure playground, garden walks and treasure hunts, paintball boot camps, and the real money-spinners: weddings, corporate away-days, film shoots.

It's a good start. The next section of the book covers budgeting expenses and forecasting revenue. My eyes glaze over at the examples they give of double-entry accounting systems, ledgers, and profit-and-loss statements. Writing a credible business plan is going to take a lot more research and know-how than I can gather in one afternoon, and I'm already up against it timewise with Hexagon waiting in the wings. My 'can-do' mood begins to deflate rapidly. I shove the notebook back in my handbag and wander through the library until I find the local history section. Being surrounded by history books makes me feel instantly better. One of the shelves has a whole section on local places of architectural interest. I find an old hardback book on Little Botheringford, the village nearest to Rosemont Hall. The publication date is 1950 – before the fire, I note. The book contains a three-page section on the house.

The print is miniscule and I have to squint to read it. A lot of the information about the architecture I already know from the internet. But I'm intrigued by three black and white photos included with the blurb. The first one is a photo of two men in a mountain pass. The caption reads: 'Sir George Windham and Francisco Walredo, Spain 1937'. I stare at the photo. I've no idea who Walredo might be, and the text doesn't say. I jot down the name to look it up later. In the photo, Sir George is smiling, but his eyes are dark and murky as pools of ink. What had Mrs Bradford said? *The eyes of a demon.* The back of my neck prickles with goosebumps.

The second photo I've seen before – it's of the inside of the great hall at Rosemont Hall, circa 1939, the walls covered with paintings. The caption describes the famous Rosemont Hall art collection. 'Most of the artwork was sold off after the end of World War II to pay for repairs to the house', it reads. 'However, a few key collection pieces, including "Orientale" by Rembrandt, were retained by the family.

The final photo on the facing page is dark, and the painting it shows is dim and shadowy, except for a few shimmering rays of light that reveal the figure of a man dressed in a Chinese-style robe. It's a picture of the Rembrandt! Even in miniature, the details of the painting – the folds of the fabric, the brocade on the jacket, the fall of light on the planes of the man's face – are vivid and otherworldly. It must have been a stunning sight to see that painting hanging in a place of pride at Rosemont Hall. It's no wonder that Sir George wanted to keep the painting even after all the rest of the art was sold off. It must have been his pride and joy. But in holding onto it, he unwittingly contributed to its destruction.

I close the book and put it back on the shelf. The Rembrandt was lost in the fire, and the house is about to suffer its own sorry fate unless I can conjure up a miracle. And maybe not even then.

My mobile vibrates in my bag. I take it out and check the screen. It's nearly three o'clock and I have four missed calls from the office.

I leave the library and rush back to work. Everyone looks up when I enter like I'm some kind of prodigal daughter.

'A Mr Kendall came here looking for you, Amy,' Claire says. 'He wanted to pick up some keys but we couldn't find them.'

In fact, I did completely forget that Mr Kendall was coming by for the keys to Rosemont Hall. Keys which are currently safe and sound at the bottom of my handbag.

'Sorry about that,' I give Claire a wry smile. 'I forgot. I'll drop the keys off at his office later.'

'He says someone will be at the house tonight. He asked if you can drop them there on your way home.'

'I'll do that.'

Someone. My heart thumps hard in my chest.

Twenty-Nine

In the early evening, I drive to Rosemont Hall. My palms are sweaty on the wheel as I turn off the road and drive between the sagging iron gates. While my previous visit far exceeded any expectations, tonight, I'm expecting no miracles.

The sky is streaked with pink and gold, and the outline of the house looks lonely and forbidding. Two vehicles are parked in front: Mr Kendall's Beamer and a gargantuan black Range Rover. No Vauxhall Corsa – no Jack Faraday. As much as I want to want to forget him, I unwittingly taste the sharp bile of disappointment.

I park next to the Range Rover, pull my pink scarf tightly around my neck, and walk to the front door. As I'm about to knock, it opens. Mr Kendall is standing there (apparently he doesn't need my set of keys *that* badly), and behind him, a shortish man in a pin-striped suit. Something about him looks familiar, and everything else – from his ginger-hair (looking suspiciously like a comb-over), to his golf club print tie and rhinestone-chip cufflinks – makes my hackles rise. A single word comes to mind...

Hexagon.

'Hello Ms Wood,' Mr Kendall says. 'Thanks for stopping by. We were lucky to catch Mr Jack before he left for the airport – he let us in.'

'Oh.'

Jack is gone. I'm suddenly awash with anger – at myself.

Why didn't I return his calls? Why did I let him go?

Mr Kendall turns to the ginger-haired man. 'I don't believe you two have met,' he says. 'This is Amy Wood, the estate agent.'

The man's fleshy face lifts into a smile. 'Hello there,' he says. 'Nigel Netelbaum, CEO of Hexagon plc.'

'Hello.' I croak. I realise why he looks familiar. I've seen him in a photo in David Waters's flat. The two of them were standing together holding up a golf trophy. I force myself to shake his hand.

'We're just finishing up,' he says. 'Helluva place, isn't it? Must have really been something once upon a time.'

'It's still really something,' I say wistfully. 'For a little while yet, it still is.'

'Yeah, O-Kay.' He raises an eyebrow like he's humouring me, then turns back to Mr Kendall and asks him something about the paperwork. His accent is American like Jack and Flora's – the conspiracy theorist in me begins to wonder if it's all some kind of nefarious transatlantic plot. The two men talk and I stand there feeling like an outdated piece of furniture cluttering up space. I should hand over the keys and leave – there's no reason for me to be here. But I keep a tight grip on the key ring.

'Right then…' Mr Kendall is saying, '… that all sounds good. We'll send over the draft contracts early next week.'

The two men shake hands. Mr Netelbaum gives me a little wave and a 'cheerio' as he goes down the steps and climbs into the Range Rover. The vehicle roars to life and he reverses in a three-point turn. I watch the vehicle until it disappears into the gloom.

'So that's it, then?'

'That's it.' Mr Kendall lets out a long sigh. 'He's just doing his job, Amy. We all are.'

I shrug like I'm not bothered. 'Sorry I wasn't in the office earlier,' I say. 'I guess subconsciously I don't want to hand these over.' I place the heavy ring of keys in his hand. They're no use to me now.

'Thank you.' He tucks the keys into the pocket of his overcoat. 'Jack forgot to leave me his keys. He and Ms Flora are on their way back to America. You just missed them. I doubt either of them will be back.'

I don't trust myself to reply.

'Would you like a last look around?' Mr Kendall offers. 'Since you love the place so much?'

He stands aside so I can enter. For the first time, I have no desire to go inside. The house seems cold and dead: an empty shell where my heart once lived. And I can't even pretend that it's all down to meeting Mr Netelbaum and seeing him seal the deal.

Jack is gone.

Mr Kendall raises an eyebrow expectantly. 'Unless you need to be somewhere—'

'No.' With a sigh, I walk past him into the main hall. I'll see the house one last time, then try to start the process of forgetting. 'I've no other plans.'

He flicks the light switch and the chandelier illuminates (minus about half its bulbs that blew out during the power surge). I circle slowly, taking a last look at the grand staircase, the marble floor, the cool stone walls, the exquisitely decorated ceiling. Despite everything that has – or hasn't – happened, I want to remember every detail.

The power is back on, but other than that, everything from my evening with Jack has been cleared away, as if it never was. Even the heaters are gone. Last night, I didn't notice that in the other rooms off the great hall, most of the furniture and bric-a-brac had been removed. Now, more than ever, a once-loved home feels cavernous and forbidding. I peak into the library. Even the books have been cleared off the shelves. All that's left is dust and mice droppings.

But there's one thing that does cheer me up a little. The painting of the lady in the pink dress is still hanging in her place on the staircase landing. As long as she's there, I feel a tiny flicker of hope that, somehow, Rosemont Hall can be saved.

Mr Kendall follows me up the stairs and we stand together in front of the painting. 'She's quite stunning, isn't she?' he says.

'Yes. It's Arabella Windham, isn't it?' I half-turn to him. 'All along it's been her, watching as everyone tramps through her house, talking about her things like they're just some old lady's rubbish.' I purse my lips.

'Arabella? Is that who you think she is?'

'Yes, I do.' I explain briefly about the costumes I found. I avoid mentioning the sketchbook and the letters, which are still safely ensconced in my knicker drawer. If anyone misses them, I can always post them back.

Mr Kendall frowns. 'But I've always assumed that the painting was old. It says 1899 here on the frame.'

'But frames can be changed, can't they? New wine in old bottles and all that.'

He shakes his head. 'I don't know, Amy. I've been their solicitor for about twenty years – Arabella was already well into middle age when I knew her. But she had light brown hair and brown eyes.' He points to the face of the girl in the painting. 'Not blue like hers.'

'Oh.' I take a step back. The only photo I've seen of the young Arabella was the blurry black and white wedding photo, where it wasn't possible to make out the colour of her eyes. But now, I realise that it's obviously not the same girl. All of my sleuthing – thinking that I was so clever to discover the historical joke that Henry and Arabella must have played – has been pointless. If there is a mystery as to who the girl in the portrait is, I haven't solved it.

'Anyway,' Mr Kendall says, 'whoever she is, most likely she won't be going far.'

'What do you mean?'

'All the art in the house was left to Mrs Bradford, not Flora and Jack,' he explains. 'That's why that painting is still there. When the house is sold, Mrs Bradford will have to take it away.'

'Oh. Is she going to sell it?'

'I've no idea.'

Mr Kendall turns and slowly walks the length of the landing. It's as if he too is trying to imprint the house on his memory. 'If this place does become a golf clubhouse,' he says, 'then at least Hexagon will be required to keep the fabric of the building. Maybe it won't be so bad. Lots of people will be able to enjoy the house, not just one family.'

I shake my head. 'You don't believe that.'

'Of course I'd prefer it to be left intact. It's a national treasure – too bad the National Trust didn't want it.'

'You checked too?' I smile wryly.

'Yes, I did. A while back, when Mrs Windham was ill. I was told that the Trust has its hands full – during the last recession, a lot of the *nouveau-pauvre* walked away from their stately homes, leaving them to rot.' He stops walking and puts his hands on the railing, leaning over to look down at the great hall. 'And even were that not the case, this place needs too much work. It's a money pit.'

'They could open it up to the public.' I say, all too aware that I'm grasping at straws. 'With the right business plan, Rosemont Hall could be self-supporting. A wedding venue; a tea shop and restaurant; organic garden shop – the whole estate would draw in loads of people if it was advertised properly.'

Mr Kendall shakes his head. 'That requires a huge outlay of up-front cash. No bank will lend on a wing and a prayer – not anymore. And as I mentioned before, there's a large inheritance tax bill that the heirs are responsible for. The first instalment is due next month. Eighty thousand pounds. And that's only the beginning. The total bill is closer to a million.'

'A million pounds in taxes?'

'Yes, that's right.'

The truth seeps through my veins like freezing water. I remember what David Waters once said: *It will take buried treasure to save this house.* No amount of number-crunching about tea rooms and adventure parks is going to make any difference.

'You have to remember that the crown always gets paid first out of an estate before any remainder can be distributed,' he says. 'The house and land are the only assets with any value. If the heirs don't sell, they'll still be liable for the IHT. Imagine getting a phone call out of the blue that you've inherited a crumbling mansion in England. And by the way, please can you pay a million pounds for the privilege.'

I look at the young woman in the portrait, my eyes blurry with tears. 'It's hopeless,' I whisper.

She smiles back, keeping her secrets.

'Anyway, the heirs were very relieved to get an offer from Hexagon. At least they can walk away with the debts cleared.'

'Of course.' I turn away from the painting, my head hung low. It was ludicrous of me to think that Jack might want to keep the house even if he could afford to. How relieved he must be to be shot of the whole inheritance palaver, and everything and everyone associated with it. Everyone – including me.

Mr Kendall gives my arm a fatherly pat. We stand there together, leaning against the carved railing. It helps to know that he's feeling sad too about the fate of the house. But I suppose that ultimately, he's right – both of us have a job to do.

A noise from below breaks the silence. Mr Kendall and I look at each other. Keys rattle; the front door opens and closes. Then, the sound of whistling.

Mr Kendall goes back down the stairs just as Mrs Bradford enters the great hall, clunking her stick in time to the music.

Behind her, she's dragging a plastic trolley full of grocery bags – like she's setting up camp in the house.

'Hello, Mrs Bradford,' he says loudly. 'You're keeping well I trust?'

The last note peters out. Looking past Mr Kendall, she lifts her gnarled hand and points her cane at me. 'What's *she* doing here?'

'She's with me.' Mr Kendall intones like he's talking to a child. 'I'm sure you remember Amy Wood. The estate agent.'

I go down the stairs, keeping a smile drawn on my face. I'm sure we both remember all too well our previous encounter when she and her dog ran me off the property, and then she called the solicitor to complain about me. But I remember my resolve – she's an old woman going through a difficult time, and I'm going to be polite.

'Hello, Mrs Bradford. It's nice to see you again.'

'Is it?' she says. Her blue eyes look hollow and haunted.

'All the cleaning you've been doing is really making a difference. The house is really starting to scrub up well.'

'Well it's high time,' she says. 'Now that *she's* finally gone. Out with the old and all that.'

'Yes, I suppose so.' The thinly veiled reference to Arabella's passing is somewhat disturbing.

'I hope you're not tiring yourself out, Maryanne,' Mr Kendall says. 'After all, it's a big house.'

'Pah,' she says. 'I've never felt better.'

She starts to drag her trolley towards the kitchen stairs. Mr Kendall and I exchange a look.

'I think the power is back on,' I say. 'In case you were planning on doing any cooking.' I point to the trolley.

'Well you would know, wouldn't you,' she says snippily. 'Since you're always here snooping around; poking your nose where it doesn't belong.' She looks smugly at my shocked face. 'Taking a few souvenirs for your trouble?'

'Really, Mrs Bradford—'

Mr Kendall steps forward and cuts me off. 'Amy and I are here to do our jobs,' he says gently. 'And Ms Flora had a removals van around to take away some things. But everything that belongs to you is still here, so don't worry about that—'

I purse my lips guiltily, keeping shtum.

'Oh, I'm not worried.' With a pointed look at me, Mrs Bradford chuckles, and keeps plodding onwards. At the edge of the great hall, she trips on a cracked tile. Her stick quavers like she's about to go down. I run over and help to steady her.

'Here, at least let me help you with the trolley,' I say.

I expect her to lash out and tell me where to go. So I'm surprised when she leans on my arm and says: 'All right.'

She regains her balance and lets go of my arm. 'Hand me that bag, will you,' she says, pointing at the top one.

I do so. Immediately I see that it's not, in fact, groceries in the trolley, but cleaning supplies. She takes out a can of Mr Sheen and some old rags. She sprays some on a rag, and leaning on her cane, begins going up the steps one by one, dragging the rag over the banister.

The whole thing is ridiculous to watch on one level, and heart-breaking on another. Instantly, I grab another rag out of the bag, spray on some Mr Sheen, and begin polishing the white marble balusters.

'Uhh... Amy,' Mr Kendall says, 'I think we should go now.'

'I'd like to have a word with Mrs Bradford first, if you don't mind.' I set my chin firmly. 'Alone.'

He raises an eyebrow and checks his watch. 'I have to be back at the office for half six,' he says. 'So you've got five minutes.'

'I'll meet you out by the cars.'

*

I continue to polish as Mr Kendall walks out the front door.

The only sound is the thud of Mrs Bradford's cane as she makes her way up the stairs, and the swish of the dust rags.

'They're going to turn Rosemont Hall into a golf course,' I say. 'I couldn't find a buyer to save it. So it will go to Hexagon.'

From above me on the stairs, Mrs Bradford tsks. 'A house is just a house,' she says.

I steel myself, determined to find a chink in her armour. 'Is it? So you don't mind leaving here for good?' I shrug. 'I'm glad to hear it – because I was worried you might be upset.'

I can feel her looking at me, but I focus intently on the baluster I'm working on. I'm aware that she's reached the top of the stairs, and has stopped polishing.

'What does it matter what I want or don't want?' she says. 'I'm just an old lady who was looking after another old lady.'

'Good. So you don't mind having to relocate? Silly me...' I give a deliberate little laugh, 'I was worried that Rosemont Hall might feel like home to you.'

She mutters something under her breath. It sounds like 'more than you know'. Her knuckles are white as her hand reaches for the banister. She strokes it like the smooth cheek of a baby. And that's when I know that I'm right. Mrs Bradford does care about the house.

'Anyway, I wanted to make sure you knew what was happening. Once the probate decree comes through, things are bound to happen pretty quickly.'

'I did everything I could,' she says. 'But I knew in my heart that it wasn't meant to be.'

I glance at her. Her eyes are clouded over. She's not answering me but talking to herself.

I keep silent.

'And the worst part was all those years of nothing. Not a letter or a how d'ya do.'

She wheels around suddenly to face the painting. My heart

almost stops as she brandishes her stick at the girl in the pink dress.

'Stupid, that's what she was. Stupid.'

'Oh,' I say, alarmed. 'Why was she stupid, Mrs Bradford?'

'She fell in love with the wrong person.'

'Oh.' I consider this.

'And who is she?' I ask.

Mrs Bradford ignores me and turns away from the painting. A moment later, it's as if the demon has passed. She begins polishing the dado rail like nothing is amiss.

'My daughter thinks it's a good idea that I won't be able to come here anymore.'

I stop polishing and look at her. It's hard to know if she's speaking to me or not. I contemplate the fact that Mrs Bradford has a daughter. She seems like such a lone, stalwart figure that I hadn't even thought of her as having family other than the sister in the village.

'She thinks it was a bad idea that I ever came back here at all. But then again, what does she know?'

'Your daughter?' I say. 'Is she local?'

'No of course not,' she says sharply. 'She lives in America. She's Jack and Flora's mother.'

'Their mother?' I look up in surprise. 'So you're their grandmother?'

'So you worked that one out, did you?'

'Sorry,' I say, 'I had no idea. Mr Kendall said that the heirs were distant relatives. I didn't know you were related to the Windhams.'

She shakes her head like I'm an idiot child. 'Of course *I'm* not related to them.'

'But the house...?'

'Who else were they going to leave it to? They had no children, and no relatives.'

'I don't know. But you have to admit – it sounds like something out of a fairy tale – a faithful servant inherits the castle...'

She wrinkles her nose.

'I mean... not that you're a servant...' I add quickly.

'It was no fairy tale,' she snaps. 'It was payback. And *I* didn't inherit it. Unfortunately.'

'Amy?' Mr Kendall's voice is icy as he calls up to me. 'We need to go now.'

'Just one more minute,' I shout back.

'You heard the man – off with you now,' Mrs Bradford flicks her dustcloth in my direction.

'I will, but I was just wondering one more thing.' I gesture at the painting of the girl in the pink dress. 'What are you going to do with *her*?'

'Nothing.' She leans against the wall heavily like the weight of her years is suddenly pressing upon her.

'I suppose she belongs where she is,' I say with an uncomfortable little laugh. 'Stupid or not, she fits that spot so well – the spot where the Rembrandt used to hang. Right?'

Mrs Bradford doesn't answer.

'Maybe Hexagon will buy her and let her stay.' I brush the heavy frame with my fingers. 'But if not, I had kind of a silly thought,' I say. 'If you were thinking of selling it, maybe you'd let me know. I have a little money saved up.' I purse my lips. 'Not much, and actually, I'm supposed to be using it for a down payment on a flat – or a rental deposit. My boyfriend dumped me, you see, and I'm living with my parents,' I prattle on, a last-ditch effort to shake some information out of her.

'Anyway, it's such a beautiful painting, and you only live once, don't you? No harm in asking and all that?' I give an awkward little laugh. 'Though I'm sure it's out of my league. I'm a nobody too, you see. And I've also fallen in love with the wrong person.' I can feel myself blushing. 'Just like the girl in the picture. Maybe that's why I'm drawn to her.'

Her stick is still as she peers at me over the top of her glasses. She doesn't speak, but I can feel her looking at me.

'Anyway, I'd better go now.' I begin walking down the stairs hoping that she'll stop me. She doesn't.

Until I reach the bottom step.

'Why do you care so much?' she says. 'What is it that you want? The painting, or something else?'

'I wanted to save the house,' I say, shaking my head. 'But I failed. The only thing I still might be able to do is preserve its memories. The girl is part of that, surely.' I sigh. 'I thought that maybe, you, of all people, might understand.'

She sucks a breath in through her teeth. 'All I know is that Rosemont Hall is my home.'

'Not any more, Mrs Bradford.' I shake my head. 'I'm really sorry, but not any more.'

*

The freezing rain mirrors my mood as I close the heavy door to the house behind me. Mr Kendall is sitting in his car, the windows steamed up. He rolls one down and gestures for me to get in the passenger side. I do so.

'Well, Amy,' he says, 'it's been great working with you. I'm sorry things didn't work out the way you wanted, but...'

'... but that's life,' I finish for him.

'I'll give you a call when the probate decree comes through, and if you can get me your part of the paperwork as soon as possible, I'd appreciate it.'

'Of course,' I say. I make a move to get out of the car. But I just can't let go.

'What about Mrs Bradford?' I say.

'What about her?'

'Should I come back tomorrow? Check that everything's okay and that she knows what's happening? Check that she really has moved out?'

'No.'

The single word is final; the judgement is passed. My involvement with Rosemont Hall has ended. I turn to him and we shake hands. Bowing my head, I get out of the car. 'Goodbye, Amy,' Mr Kendall says, 'and good luck.'

I open my mouth to speak, but the words are lost on the wind. I get into my own car and follow him down the dark, winding drive. I'm leaving Rosemont Hall...

For the last time.

Part Four

Restore to me that little spot,
With grey walls compassed round,
Where knotted grass neglected lies,
And weeds usurp the ground.

Though all around this mansion high
Invites the foot to roam,
And though its halls are fair within --
Oh, give me back my HOME!

~ Anne Brontë – 'Home'

Thirty

It's over. There's nothing I can do.

Except, there is one little fingernails-gripping-the-edge-of-a-cliff thing that I can do. I can phone Jack. After all, I've had three missed calls from him after our… meaningless-and-never-to-be-repeated encounter. He'd tried to talk to me before he flew off into the sunset.

I could phone Jack. After all, it's rude not to.

But I'm not going to.

This becomes my new mantra each morning as I enter the office, checking my emails first thing to see if there's any word about the Edinburgh teaching job. Mr Kendall is right: I need to move on. I need to forget all about Jack Faraday and Rosemont Hall, turfed-out old ladies, mysterious paintings, buried secrets, and happy endings. The reality is that I'm a 31-year-old single woman working in the profession that everyone loves to hate. I've shown that I can adapt, even excel in a new environment. I've 'earned my spurs' and proved myself. But I never intended this to be my 'forever job'. I need to focus on an alternative future.

By Friday morning, the week is almost over, but I've made very little progress getting Rosemont Hall and Jack Faraday out of my mind. I've tried everything – even attempting to raise the ghost of what I once thought I felt for Simon – in the early days, at least. But all I can muster up is a feeling of annoyance with myself that I couldn't see the wood for the trees. What I feel for Jack is totally different – and totally pointless. There's only one thing for it – I must banish Jack Faraday from my head. At my desk I turn on my computer and answer a few emails and enquiries. Jonathan rolls into the office late, gloating about a big sale he's made of a new-build mansion in Cheddar. I ignore the chat around me and print out some documents related to the sale of the Bristol flat.

THIS IS MY REALITY.

By late morning, I've had it.

I grab my handbag and mobile and sneak out the back door to the car park. I sit in my car, bite my lip, and dial the number. *His* number.

On the third ring, the dashboard clock catches my eye – it's 11:30 a.m. UK time, which means that in California it's—

I fumble frantically to hang up the phone, but it's too late. A groggy male voice answers: 'Hello?'

'Uhhh.'

'Who is this?'

'Jack?' My voice is a squeak.

A long pause.

'Amy? Is that you?'

'I'm so sorry Jack, I didn't realise that it's the middle of the night there. I'll ring back. I'll—'

'Amy, why didn't you return my calls?'

I hear movement like he's sitting up, then a click – a light switch? Just hearing his voice makes me dizzy with desire. Which is stupid. *Stupid.*

'I didn't know you were going back to America so soon.'

'Yes – but I did try to call you. Something came up here in connection with work. I had to get back immediately. Otherwise, I might have stayed a few more days.'

A few more days. But then he would have been gone just the same. In a way, I'm probably lucky. Except, I don't feel lucky – not one bit.

'I wanted to apologise.' I limp along. 'I heard about the inheritance tax. Of course you couldn't keep Rosemont Hall with so much debt hanging over it. I was vain and naïve to think otherwise, I'm sorry.'

'The inheritance tax? Yes, the solicitor did phone about that. Great business for the state, or the queen, or whoever. But how did you find out?'

I launch into an account of my meeting with Mr Kendall, our conversation, and the newfound cleaning proclivities of Mrs Bradford.

'I didn't realise that she was your grandmother,' I say. 'I mean you didn't mention it.'

'Sorry,' he says. 'I just assumed you knew. But anyway, the truth is, we're far from close.' He sighs. 'I never really understood her obsession with Rosemont Hall.'

'To be honest, I'm a little worried about her,' I say. 'I think she's more upset than any of us realise. Change can't be good for her at her age.'

'She's moved in with her sister,' he says. 'Aunt Gwen has a very nice cottage in the village. When I last talked to her, she seemed fine.'

'Of course,' I say. 'Sorry. I'm being stupid. You know best about her, I'm sure. And besides, no matter who you sold the house to, she'd have to leave, wouldn't she?' I laugh sadly. 'Vacant possession and all that. And as it stands, the sale is all going ahead as you planned. Mr Kendall has the draft contracts drawn up for Hexagon. I met Nigel Netelbaum briefly – that man you were in contact with. I'm sure your grandma will be all right and I've bothered you for nothing—'

Jack begins to laugh softly. 'Amy Wood, I must say – you're so different to anyone I've ever met before.' His voice is warm, like a purring cat. 'The night we had dinner, I felt very strange – like I'd known you for a long time. Seeing you, it was like a door was open before me. To some imaginary place that's totally different from my real life. A place full of passion and mystery – and just a little bit of the – what was your word? – "barmy" about it.'

I don't dare to breathe.

'For a minute I thought that maybe things happen for a reason – that to get on with my life I had to travel halfway around the world to a crumbling old house in England. That maybe some things aren't rational, but we still just have to go with them.'

'Yes?' I say breathlessly.

'And then you ran off and slammed that door in my face.'

'I'm sorry,' I lament. 'I didn't mean it like that— really. I guess I was just... I don't know. Overwhelmed. Scared too. I just wasn't expecting anything like that to happen. I wish... well...' I can't bring myself to say what it is that I wish.

He's silent for a few seconds, and I wonder if I've revealed too much. 'I thought a lot about things while I was on my way to the airport and on the plane back to California,' he says. 'I thought how much I'd like to experience more of the world, get outside the sunny little bubble I live in. I had this crazy fantasy that you and I could go around and explore England together – maybe in one of those nippy little English cars. What are they – Minis?'

'Yes.' I whisper, bubbling inside. 'And?'

'And... part of me wishes that things had turned out differently.' He sighs (or maybe it's a yawn). 'But coming home, reality hit pretty hard. I realised that my life may not be extraordinary, but at least it's familiar. My only regret is that I didn't get to know you better.'

'Yes.' It's like I've been slapped in the face. 'Me too.'

'Well...' he gives a forced laugh, 'I'll deal with Gran. You don't have to worry about her. And I'll call you, okay – next time I'm in town. I'll plan a longer trip – maybe in the summer.'

'Okay, Jack. I'll… I'll talk to you. Sometime.'

'Goodbye, Amy.'

I turn off the phone and sit there staring at nothing.

Thirty-One

The devil makes work for idle hands (or in this case, it's Mr Bowen-Knowles masquerading as said demon). The next morning I arrive late at the office (terrible traffic, and long line at Starbucks), and find a stack of papers on my desk. My boss is hovering in the waiting area, straightening the home decor and *Country Life* magazines on the table – my job. As soon as I sit down, he comes over to me.

'Amy...' his tone is brusque, 'I need you here at 9 a.m. – not ten past.'

'Sorry.' I take a long sip of my latte, hiding behind the cup,

'There's a couple who want to view some properties this afternoon. Everyone else is busy, so you'll do it.'

'Fine.'

'The details are there.' He indicates the papers on my desk. There are two brochures, and two Google map printouts. Like a proverbial bad penny, both of the properties are in villages within a few miles of Rosemont Hall.

I manage to get through the morning occupying myself with trivial things like returning phone calls, typing up client intakes, managing the online listings – all of which I can do in my sleep. Before I know it, it's well past noon. I gaze at Cinderella's glass slipper on my desk, and calculate that I've survived three more hours of life-without-Jack. Only a countless number left to go.

Mr Bowen-Knowles comes out of his office and checks the

gold watch on his wrist. 'You still here?' He frowns. 'You'd better get your skates on.'

'I was just leaving.' I grab my coat and my handbag and head out the back way, a sickly smile on my face.

Just out the door in the car park, I run into Claire. 'Oh Amy, I think I've just sold a whopper of a flat.' She grins from ear to ear. 'This could be the one I've been waiting for. The mortgage is already in place and they want to exchange this week!'

I give her a quick hug. 'That's great, Claire. I'm so glad.'

'Do you want to have lunch? On me?'

I shake my head. 'I'm off to do some viewings. Mr Bowen-Knowles is already growling at me for running late.'

'Well, you go knock 'em dead. The market really is picking up.' She beams. 'Maybe it'll be your lucky day too.'

'Maybe. Thanks, Claire.'

I don't spoil her mood by telling her the truth – it would take more than luck to turn my day around. It would take a miracle.

*

Things do not improve when I get to my first viewing and re-alise that the house-hunters are my old friends the Wakefields: Mr & Mrs 'Thatch-costs-too-much-to-insure', from the ill-fated visit to the Chip cottage.

When I get out of the car, I'm about to make a joke about main roads and thatch, but it's clear from Mrs Wakefield's expression and her husband's handshake, that they don't even remember me. I don't bother to remind them of our previous encounter.

Remarkably, the viewing goes off without a hitch. The two cottages I show them both have solid slate roofs and substantial front gardens on quiet country lanes. Mrs Wakefield makes the appropriate noises that she's pleased, and her husband seems happy enough to follow her lead. By the time we leave the second property, I even find myself thinking that if the job was like this all the time, it would be almost enjoyable.

Feeling brave, I invite them for a cup of tea in Little Botheringford – walking distance from the second cottage. We stroll together down the tiny high street.

I smell the 'Cup o' Comfort' tea room a half a block before we reach it. Home-made bread, a touch of cinnamon – scones fluffy and thick with strawberries and mounds of fresh cream. After days of not feeling very hungry, suddenly, I'm starving.

A bell tinkles on the door as we go inside. There's a nice big table by the window, and we sit down. The curtains and tablecloths are matching chintz, and little doilies nestle underneath the willow-patterned cups. Only two of the other tables are occupied. The white-haired proprietress takes her time sauntering over to us, and we order tea and scones all round.

The Wakefields are quite familiar with the local area. I take out a map and have them point out their search radius. Mrs Wakefield points to a few neighbouring villages that they like. I promise to keep my eye out for new properties coming on to the market.

Then, Mrs Wakefield points to a big green patch on the map: one that I know all too well.

'There's a big country estate here,' she says. 'The owner's widow died a few months ago. Winford? Winslow? – something like that. Maybe it will open up to the public – it looks like a great place to walk the dogs.'

I don't even bat an eyelid. 'It's Windham, actually. The house is called Rosemont Hall. Unfortunately, it's destined to become a private golf course – unless you can find a Good Samaritan with a spare million or four...'

'I'm afraid not.' Mrs Wakefield sips her tea.

'Hey, I know that place,' Mr Wakefield says. 'I've been in insurance for forty years, and so was my father before me.'

'Really?' I act surprised.

'Dad worked for Lloyds in their Bath office. He investigated all kinds of claims – flushed out fraudsters like a flock of grouse.'

'Oh?'

'He always said that Sir George was one of the worst.'

'Sir George Windham?' I lean forward in my chair. 'What do you mean?'

'He was a war hero, so no one was going to doubt his word in any official sense. But it was common knowledge that he was a wily old bastard. Dad couldn't prove it, but he always thought that Sir George set that fire himself.'

'The fire in the East Wing?' I breathe a little faster.

'You know your stuff, don't you?' He takes a bite of his scone. 'Sir George tried to pin the blame on some poor servant. But no one believed that.'

'Why would he set fire to his own house?'

'The house wasn't insured but some painting was. A Renoir, I think.'

'A Rembrandt?'

He shrugs. 'Maybe. It was the only one he'd kept when the rest of his collection had to be sold off. The painting was destroyed in the fire – so he said anyway. He made a hefty claim under the insurance.'

'What do you mean by "so he said"?'

His wife checks her watch. 'Peter, we should be getting home to the dogs.'

'Okay,' he says to his wife. 'But it's not often I get a captive audience.' He smiles at me.

'But what about the painting?' I ask quickly. I grip the edge of the tablecloth. The puzzle pieces swirl around in my head faster and faster, refusing to come together. Sir George planning something. Henry and Arabella assuming it was the ball and unveiling Henry's portrait. But what if it was something else entirely?

Mr Wakefield chuckles. 'Search me. The funny thing was – no one at the party remembered seeing it hanging in the ballroom that night.'

'The Rembrandt wasn't in the ballroom? Well, I suppose that makes sense. I mean, I saw an old picture of the great hall. That's where it usually hung... right?'

'Sorry – I don't know.'

I think aloud. 'I suppose the Rembrandt might have been moved out of the great hall, if that's where Henry's portrait was supposed to go. Except, there is no portrait of Henry. Just the girl in the pink dress.'

Mrs Wakefield taps her husband on the shoulder. 'Peter, I think we should wrap up now...'

'Wait,' I say holding up my hand, 'what did your father find? Was there any wreckage – some kind of fragments of the painting?'

'The whole place was a wreck,' Mr Wakefield says. 'I do know that they found a gold cigarette lighter. Sir George said the servant used it to start the fire.'

'A gold lighter!' My mind stops whirling, centring in on the first time I met Mrs Bradford. The insurance people must have returned the lighter to 'H', it got mislaid, and ended up woven into a bird's nest.

'In the end,' he continues, 'Dad held things up in red tape. We're kind of good at that in my business. Heh, heh, heh.' He winks. 'Sir George died before anything was paid out. I don't think the burnt bit of the house ever did get fixed up.'

'It didn't,' I confirm.

'The insurance company never did close the case. An open verdict – that's what it was left as.'

'And what about the servant? Did they arrest anyone? Why would someone do that—? Why would Sir George, of all people, do that?'

'Peter…' his wife says again. 'Sorry Ms Wood – my husband can tell his stories all day.'

'Really, I'd love to know more.'

'You'd make a pretty good insurance investigator yourself, young lady,' he says. 'Whew, I'm worn out with all those questions.'

'Sorry.' I am sorry – that I won't be finding out anything more from him today.

'No worries,' Mr Wakefield says, standing up. 'And we'll ring you about those cottages.'

'Oh, yes.' I get to my feet realising that I'd completely forgotten about my 'day job' and their property search. 'And I'll keep you posted if anything similar comes on the market.'

'Sure, great.'

We shake hands, and the bell tinkles as they leave the café.

*

I sit back down at the table to consider what I've just learned. Sir George was planning something – something that involved his Spanish artist friend. It wasn't Henry's portrait, because as far as I know, no portrait of Henry was ever done. And the portrait of the girl in the pink dress: Arabella – or whoever she is – I still don't know for sure if the painting was done in 1899 or the 1950s. Those eyes – they're familiar somehow. I tap my fingers restlessly on the table. Rosemont Hall hasn't given up its secrets, and pretty soon it will be too late. I have to find out more. But how?

The white-haired woman comes back over to my table and I ask for more hot water. I should go back to the office and see if there are any more properties that might suit the Wakefields. But the gas fire is warm and cosy and if I can just think it all through again —

'I heard what that man was talking about.'

Startled, I look up. The white-haired woman sets a pot of hot water down on my table.

'He was talking about Rosemont Hall.' She stacks the plates of crumbs left by the Wakefields. 'About the fire, and Sir George.'

'Yes, he was.' I stare up at her.

'He doesn't know the half of it.'

'What do you mean?' I shift eagerly to the edge of the chair. Maybe today is my lucky day after all.

The woman puts her hands on her hips. 'When I was a girl, my mother worked up at the house. Sometimes we used to play there, and when I got older, I worked there when they needed extra help for the parties. They were the most fancy parties and balls you could imagine – Sir George liked to recreate the old days before the wars.'

She stares at the flickering gas flame. I swallow back a thousand questions, afraid that I might put her off.

'There were so many beautiful people there. My sister and I were mad about the men – ex-soldiers and officers, bankers, politicians up from London. But we were nobody – only the hired help. Sir George ran the house like it was the 1850s rather than the 1950s – everyone in their place.'

She starts to wipe down a nearby table, but a shadow falls over her face.

'Sir George was a devil.' She shakes her head. 'So was his son, Henry. People like us meant nothing to them.'

'What do you mean?'

The old woman clams up like she's just remembered she's talking to a complete stranger. She frowns at me. 'Why are you so interested anyway?'

'I'm interested in local history, that's all.'

The little bell on the door tinkles and a woman with a pram comes inside. Silently, I curse.

The white-haired woman greets the new customer. They

chat for ages about the village school bake sale. I pour more hot water into the teapot, and wait.

At last, the pram woman leaves. The proprietress flips the sign on the door from 'open' to 'closed'. She sighs like a hard day's work is finally finished. Then, she turns around and sees that I'm still there.

'I'm closing up now, will you be wanting anything else?'

'I'd like you to tell me more about Rosemont Hall. I thought maybe I'd...'

At that moment, an idea strikes me.

'... write a book about the history of the house. The things that aren't mentioned in the archives. The nameless women who lived and loved there. I'm a teacher – or, at least, I was. I can't save Rosemont Hall, but I can preserve some part of its history.'

Now that I've voiced the idea, it seems like a no-brainer. Why didn't I think of it before? Writing about Rosemont Hall is right up my street – provided there's something to write about. Which I'm increasingly sure there is.

'But I need to uncover more information,' I say, thinking aloud. 'A story that will really bring the place alive.'

The woman looks at me like I've sprouted a second head. I don't care. My chest feels fizzy with excitement. I can go home and start right away.

'Hmm.' The woman shakes her head. 'I'm not the one you should ask. If you want colourful detail, my sister knows a lot more.'

The bell on the door tinkles again. We both look up.

'This must be your lucky day. Here she is—'

I barely hear the words. I stare at the old woman who's just come in. She looks at me and frowns, her eyes – her forget-me-not-blue eyes – sharp and piercing. And suddenly I guess the truth – that's been staring me in the face all along.

Thirty-Two

Mrs Bradford hobbles in leaning on her cane. The huge Saint Bernard, Captain, pads in behind her. When she sees me, her face remains impassive and she nods almost politely. Captain, comes over and licks my hand like today I'm friend, not foe.

'Hello,' I say, staring at her wizened face like I'm seeing it for the first time.

'This is my sister,' the proprietress says. 'As I say, she's the one you should be asking your questions.'

'We've met, actually.' I feel like I've been flattened by a very large bus.

The cane points in my direction. 'Amy Wood,' Mrs Bradford cackles, 'Estate agent.'

The dog lays down at my feet and I scratch his shaggy head, still staring at the old lady.

'Estate agent?' The proprietress looks at me with suspicion clouding her face. 'You said you were writing a book.'

'Um... yes, I am – in my spare time.' I grip the edge of the table, bracing myself for an outburst from one or both of them about 'poking my nose where it doesn't belong'.

To my surprise, Mrs Bradford starts to laugh. 'A book, is that it?' She hobbles over to a table across the room from me and manoeuvres herself into the chair. The stick waves in her sister's direction and clatters to the floor. The dog growls and picks it up in his mouth to give it back to her. 'What is it? Some kind of two-penny romance with you as the heroine, I suppose.'

'Actually,' I say through my teeth, 'it's a history book.'

'A history book.' She raises a bushy white eyebrow and chuckles again. I've no idea what could possibly be so funny. 'Get another cup of tea for Miss Wood, will you, Gwen.' She gestures for me to join her at her table. I stand up and move over to the empty chair, as her sister goes off with an irritated tsk.

'Please, call me Amy,' I say.

She waves off my request with a gnarled hand. 'So, what is it that you want to know today? Let me guess – all about that painting on the landing. Who that girl is; what her life was like. What her secrets are.'

'It's a stunning painting,' I say. 'And the artist has really captured something of the subject – she's beautiful certainly, but more than that too, I think.' My eyes lock with her familiar blue ones – or rather, with those of a girl – many years younger – in a pink dress.

The laughter fades from her face. 'So you've finally guessed, have you, Amy Wood?'

'It *was* you all along, wasn't it?' I shake my head. 'How silly of me not to have seen it.' Of course it's her – right in front of me, staring me in the face. No wonder Jack thought she looked familiar. And Flora – her granddaughter – is her spitting image.

Mrs Bradford sighs. 'Maybe it isn't so obvious looking at her pretty face – innocent dope that she was. But give yourself another sixty years and the trouble I've seen and see how you fare.'

I sit forward, leaning on my elbows. 'Tell me the story, Mrs Bradford. How did you come to be painted like that?'

'You mean how did a lowly girl from the village come to be hanging on the wall in the big house? Just say it, Amy Wood. You won't be the first.' She sits back in her chair, her lips pursed like a sphinx.

'Okay,' I say, 'if you like.'

Her sister returns with a tray and sets it on the table. With a cursory frown, she takes up the story. 'A trunk full of costumes was delivered,' Gwen says. 'Sir George wanted everyone to dress up in period costumes for the ball – even the hired help. We were supposed to dress as kitchen servants, but then we found a whole room of beautiful dresses and costumes that belonged to Sir George's late wife. We couldn't resist trying on the beautiful gowns. They were fabulous – made of silk and satin, taffeta and chiffon. Trimmed with pearls, lace and sparkly beads – what girl could possibly resist?'

'I understand completely,' I say. I doubt I could have resisted either. 'When was this?'

Gwen looks at her sister before answering. 'It was a week or two before the last ball,' she says. 'The one that Sir George held for Henry's 21st birthday. Sir George had an artist friend there – some Spanish chap – handsome too. He was working in the studio in the attic. He was there to paint Henry's portrait, I think. But he had an eye for the ladies. He took a shine to Maryanne. He sketched her, and then did that painting.'

'The sketchbook,' I say, stealing a glance at Mrs Bradford. 'I came across it in the library the night that Flora was there. I umm... took it for safe-keeping. It's at home in my drawer along with the lighter.'

'Hmmff, I thought as much.' Mrs Bradford crosses her arms. Other than the sunken blue eyes, her pudgy, lined face bears little or no resemblance to the girl in the painting.

I shake my head. 'I just can't believe it was you...' I trail off, only just realising that I've spoken aloud.

'Well, Amy Wood, it's the truth.' Mrs Bradford nods firmly. 'I was the girl in the pink dress – and a hot and scratchy thing it was too, let me tell you.' She chortles. 'And those costumes are still there in the house – in the closet off the Rose Bedroom. But of course, you found them too.' She lifts her chin. 'Oh yes, I noticed.'

I smile uneasily. At least I was right about the pink dress – it wasn't a replica of the dress in the painting, it was the real one.

'Anyway, now you know.' She shrugs. 'No big secret.'

'But when I asked before, Mrs Bradford, why didn't you just say it was you?'

She sniffs. 'You asked if she was Sir George's wife, or his mother, or Arabella – someone posh and important. You never dreamt it might be a nobody like me – though that's what I told you the first time you asked.'

'Well, you have to admit, it does seem a little strange. I mean, if the artist was there to paint Henry's portrait, then how come he never did?'

'He said, "Henry was no picture",' Gwen says with a little laugh. 'An eye for the ladies, that's what he had.'

'It seems odd that he never did what he'd been commissioned to do,' I say. What did the letter say that I found? Something along the lines of *we will say that you are here to paint my son's portrait*. 'But maybe Sir George wasn't all that bothered?'

Mrs Bradford snorts like I'm stating the obvious.

'And what about the Rembrandt?' I say. 'It used to hang in that space, didn't it? The man I was talking to earlier said that it wasn't in the ballroom the night of the fire. Do either of you remember seeing it there?'

The obnoxious ring of my mobile cuts off my question. I fumble frantically in my bag to turn it off, but it's too late. Gwen looks at her watch, then at me. 'I'm closing up now,' she says. 'We've got choir practice.'

'Wait,' I say. 'You can't go yet.' I find my phone and jab at the mute button.

Nonplussed, Mrs Bradford whistles through her dentures. The dog jumps up, his head and tail high like he's standing to attention.

The phone rings again in my hand. Cursing under my breath,

I check the screen – my parents' number is blinking on the display. Mrs Bradford hoists herself to her feet. The phone rings and rings. I have to answer it.

'Amy!' Mum shouts frantically in my ear. 'Please... come home right away. Your dad's had an accident.'

The blood drains from my face. 'I'll be there in twenty minutes, Mum.' I hang up the phone and stand up.

'I have to go now,' I say to Mrs Bradford. 'But please will you tell me the rest of the story another time?'

Ignoring the question, Mrs Bradford hobbles off towards the loo in the back, thumping her stick, and chuckling her head off.

Thirty-Three

I prepare myself for the worst: Dad's been hit by a car; or had a heart attack; or a stroke, and I'm too late and he's dead. I should have been a better daughter: providing them with grandchildren, or at least doing something with my life that they could brag about to their friends at the Scrabble club. I should *not* have muted the phone the first time Mum rang. All the way home my heart is in my throat. I turn into the lane expecting flashing ambulance lights, wailing sirens, and gaggles of curious onlookers.

When I rush into the house and find Dad sprawled on the sofa watching a repeat of *Antiques Roadshow* with Mum holding a packet of frozen peas on his ankle, I'm relieved – of course! – but also a tiny bit perturbed.

'Dad fell off a ladder putting pigeon spikes on the shed,' Mum explains. 'He fell into the lilac – otherwise, he might have broken something.'

I kneel down beside the sofa and give Dad a kiss on the cheek. 'I'm glad you're okay—'

'Shhh,' he waves his arm, 'let's hear the valuation.'

I look at the TV. Fiona Bruce is wearing a green leather coat and tight red jeans. Beside her is a rotund, bearded man whose face is pouring with sweat.

'The good news is the vase does have the mark from Occupied Japan...' the bow-tied valuation man says.

'That man is hoping he can sell that vase to build an extension so his mum doesn't have to go to a home,' Mum says. 'Isn't that sweet?'

'*But I'm afraid that the chip in the base means it won't fetch much more than two hundred at auction...*'

The rotund bloke looks crushed. I stand up and offer to make supper.

'That would be nice,' Mum says (making me feel bad for not offering more often). 'I've thawed some sausages, plus, these peas.'

Sausages! Peas *a la* Dad's ankle!

'Actually, I was thinking I might do something different, like... uhh, chilli con carne—'

'Shhh.' This time Mum holds up her hand. 'This one looks interesting.'

I roll my eyes and start heading to the kitchen.

'*I've had my eye on this painting all day...*' The valuer says. '*Tell me how you came by it.*'

I hover at the door. There's no denying that I'm a sucker for *Antiques Roadshow*.

'My grandmother died, and I inherited it...' a young woman is saying. 'She was Jewish and she lived in Germany before the war. Luckily, she got out.' The camera pans to a painting of two children playing at the seaside.

'You could make one of those curries—' Dad says, struggling to sit up.

'Shhh. Dinner can wait. I want to hear this.' I grab the remote off the arm of the sofa and turn up the TV.

'A genuine Mary Cassatt!' the valuer says. 'And a lovely one at that. But you said there's more to the story?'

'A friend of a friend put my grandmother in contact with a Spanish artist who was also an expert smuggler. Walredo, his name was. He helped her hide it. Here's a photograph of her house...'

Oh my God. Walredo – the man in the photo with Sir George.

I never did look up the name. My heart begins to thunder in my chest. I move closer to the TV. The woman holds up a black and white photo of a painting. But it's not the Cassatt. It's...

'*That's fascinating. You mean, they hid the Cassatt to smuggle it out of Germany...?*'

... a portrait of a Spanish flamenco dancer painted in a style that's remarkably similar to one I've seen. She seems to melt out of a background darkness, and dominate the canvas with her dark eyes and strong presence.

'*Yes, that's right...*' the woman smiles. '*The Nazis never found it.*'

A painting that hides a secret.

'*It was pure genius to hide it so well...*'

Buried treasure that could save a house.

'*... and the story you've told me makes it worth even more...*'

And at this moment...

'*I'd say you could easily be looking at seven figures...*'

I know where it is.

Thirty-Four

Sir George might have been a devil, but he was also devious and shrewd. His beloved Rembrandt wasn't sold or destroyed in the fire – he made sure it was carefully hidden. And then, he died without letting anyone in on the secret. It's been right in front of me – and everyone else – all along.

All through dinner with my parents, followed by a game of three-handed bridge (Dad pulls the invalid card, so I can hardly refuse), I'm more and more convinced. In fact, the day I had coffee with Mary Blundell, I should have started putting two and two together. But I didn't, and now I've lost precious time. The sale to Hexagon will complete as soon as the probate decree comes through – any day now. But if I can find the painting, maybe there's still a chance to stop the sale.

There's only one little problem niggling in my head – I no longer have the keys to Rosemont Hall.

*

Of all the things I thought I might be doing as an estate agent, breaking and entering did not figure high on the list. Nevertheless, the decision comes easily. After the game, I settle my parents in front of the TV to watch *Wallander*, telling them that I've got a headache and am planning to get an early night. I change my clothes in my bedroom, then sneak out to the garage and find Dad's torch. Luckily my car is parked a little way down the road, so my parents don't hear me as I get in and drive off.

I reach my destination shortly after ten. Just as I'm about to turn into the drive, I slam on the brakes. The old stone pillars have been reinforced with new brickwork and the ornate iron gates have been rehung. They now meet firmly in the centre, shut with a heavy chain and padlock. Obviously, someone has got wise to the fact that leaving Rosemont Hall vacant is a security risk. Now, they're making an effort to keep people out – people like me.

I park the car in a lay-by and turn off the lights. There's no traffic at this hour, and disguised in my black leather jacket, leggings, black trainers and knitted woolly cap, I blend in with the darkness.

No sooner am I out of the car, when a police car passes, its blue lights flashing. I flatten myself against the prickly hedgerow and take a few deep breaths. There's nothing to fear – I'm not here to steal anything. I haven't done anything wrong.

Yet.

The gates tower over my head, black and imposing. I try to climb the iron scrolls but can't get a good foothold. Instead, I follow the old stone wall a few metres from the gate. The wall is overgrown with brambles and ivy, and I find a place where the top stones have collapsed and I can scramble over. I thunk to the ground on the other side right into a nest of stingers.

The moon breaks through the clouds as I brush myself off and begin the long walk to the house. The wood is dark; the bare trees spindly and sinister like skeletons. It takes the better part of twenty minutes before I top the last hill and then Rosemont Hall is before me. The windows shine black in the distance like glassy pupils – seeing all. Seeing me.

Gravel crunches under my feet as I reach the front of the house. A tiny shape runs across my path – a mouse or a squirrel. My heart begins to pound faster.

I try the front door, but of course it's locked. I make my way around the side of the house. The paving stones are uneven and I have to flip on the torch. I creep up the gracefully curving staircase that leads to the back terrace. There are plenty of broken windowpanes, but unfortunately, none of them are at a level where I can reach a latch. I shine the torch over one of the sets of French doors that lead into the green salon. Clenching my teeth, I knock the torch hard against a cracked pane near the handle. The glass shatters. I unlatch the door and slip inside the house.

I'm now officially a criminal.

Inside, darkness swallows the beam of the torch. The parquet floor creaks and groans with my every step, as if protesting at the illicit entry. I grope my way through the green salon to the great hall, not daring to turn on the lights. I tiptoe up the main staircase and stand before the portrait.

Now that I'm here, I'm not quite sure what to look for. I half-wish that I'd brought Mary Blundell along for some tips. I shine the torch over the painting. The oil paint glimmers, accentuating the shadows and the folds of the pink dress like moonlight. She truly is beautiful – though I'm still finding it hard to imagine that the lady is really a young Mrs Bradford. I try to visualise the ball she spoke of: the ballroom in the East Wing lit by candlelight, well-coiffed ladies swirling around with handsome men in old-fashioned costumes. The portrait painter sketching a young woman as she tries on costumes before the ball: her neck long, shoulders soft and white, the silk clinging to her body like a second skin.

The frame is thick and ornate, the gold partly rubbed off and dust in the crevices of the moulding. I shine the light over the date on the plaque that was meant to fool everyone: 1899. It's the frame from the John Singer Sargent painting sold a year earlier at auction. It seems so simple – but then, I suppose the best deceptions usually are.

I set down the torch and try to lift the painting off the wall.

But it's almost as tall as me, and very unwieldy. Something thumps to the floor from behind the heavy frame. For a second I'm worried that I've broken something, but I lower the painting back to the wall and it's still firmly affixed in place. I pick up the torch and shine the light over the bundle by my feet. At first I think it's a book that's missing a cover, but then I look closer and realise that it's a stack of airmail envelopes bound together with an elastic band. I pick it up, squinting in the dim light. The envelopes are addressed to a 'Miss A Reilly'. I haven't heard the name Reilly before, but surely it's Arabella like the other letters that I found?

And then I hear it: gravel crunching; the noise of a car engine. The blood freezes in my veins. Although it can't be – there's a car outside.

I shove the bundle of letters into the inside pocket of my jacket and switch off the torch. I can't see headlights, but the sky in front of the house lightens.

There's only one thing I can do – hide. I flatten myself against the staircase and begin inching down, my heart thundering. If I can just make it to the East Wing corridor then I might be able to keep out of sight until whoever it is goes away.

A cracked piece of marble gives way beneath my feet. I tumble down the last few steps; the torch clatters to the floor of the main hall splaying batteries. A car door slams. Terror grips me – is it Mrs Bradford? Or the police who drove past earlier? I'm not sure which is worse. Leaving the torch on the floor, I creep across the main hall to the front windows.

The car's headlights penetrate the darkness like the eyes of a cat, then go off. A door opens; a pencil torch flicks on. A dark silhouette of a figure opens the boot, takes something out, and closes it again. Another tiny light goes on – a BlackBerry or mobile. The intruder is composing a text message as they walk to the front door. Definitely not Mrs Bradford or the police.

I leg it to the door that leads to the East Wing corridor and pull on the handle. The door sticks; I pull with all my strength. Nothing – it's locked. Panic rises in my throat. I'm trapped in the open. The lock of the front door jangles as a key is turned. The hall is dark – if I can just stay absolutely silent, I might be able to slip out the front door—

The door opens. From the pocket of my jacket, my mobile beeps. I stifle a gasp and fumble for my phone. It's too late.

The beam of the visitor's torch jerks across the floor towards my feet. A deep and familiar voice cries out.

'Who's there?'

Thirty-Five

Jack Faraday.

Oh my God, it's Jack Faraday! It can't be. But it is.

I cower against the wall, gripping my phone. Escape is now impossible. The beam of light flicks upward to my face. I put my hands in the air – I'm guilty!

'Amy? Amy Wood? Is that you?'

I shield my eyes with my arm. 'Oh, hi Jack. Umm, I left my uhh…' I lower my hands. His skin glows like marble in the near-darkness. My body begins to quiver in all those unmentionable places. I realise how much I've cocked things up. It's not like Jack and I have a future, but now, he must think I'm, at worst, a criminal or, at best, a nutcase – or the other way around. The one saving grace is that I didn't throw my phone at him.

'Amy, what are you doing here?' His voice chills the air.

I slump to the floor, defeated. 'I'm breaking and entering with an intent to poke my nose where it doesn't belong.'

He frowns – probably deciding whether or not to call the police.

'It's the painting – the one on the stairs,' I say. 'I had a hunch that I needed to follow up…' I swallow hard. 'I'm sorry.'

He's silent for a moment, his eyes shiny and penetrating. 'Any idea where the light switch is?' he says.

'By the door, left side.'

I struggle to my feet and dust myself off.

Jack Faraday goes over to the door and flips the switch.

Harsh light from the dusty, bare-bulbed chandelier floods the hall. But a second later, a loud pop makes us both jump. The chandelier goes out and everything is black. Unlike last time when the sudden darkness promised everything, this time he keeps his distance.

'Another damn fuse,' Jack says. 'Unless you've get a good torch, we'd better get out of here. And you can tell me exactly what the hell is going on.'

Thirty-Six

The atmosphere is glacial as he drives me to the main road where I've left my car. I try – and fail – to make a bit of idle chit-chat: 'When did you arrive?' 'Early this morning.' 'How was your flight?' 'Fine.'

I'm heartbroken over the unspoken questions I want to ask: 'What are you doing here?' 'Why didn't you ring me?' 'What next?'

Things improve marginally when he drops me off at my car. 'Now, I still want that explanation,' he says gruffly, 'and you can buy me a drink for good measure.'

'Sure.' Hope kindles inside my chest.

'You can follow behind.'

'Okay.'

He rechains the gates as I get into my own car. I follow him to the White Horse Inn just outside Little Botheringford. My palms are clammy on the steering wheel. I know the place – a traditional Elizabethan country hotel with diamond pane windows and wisteria vines growing up the front. We park our cars and go inside. At all times I'm conscious of his proximity – and his distance. Inside the bar area, a few tables are occupied. I point to a small table in the corner.

'What would you like?' I say.

Jack shakes his head. 'I was joking about you buying.' His tone is anything but light. 'What would you like to drink?'

'Red wine, please,' I croak.

He goes to the bar. I take the opportunity to nip to the loo. My reflection in the mirror is appallingly dishevelled: my eyes have dark circles underneath, my hair is dusty, my lips are chapped from the cold. I look less like a cat burglar and more like something the cat dragged in. Not that it matters. The disappointing reality is that there was never anything between Jack and me. Now, I'll explain myself and then leave. I've only got to endure his painfully attractive presence for maybe half an hour, max.

I go back to the table as Jack arrives with the drinks. He sits down, his face like carved stone. 'Okay, now start talking. And you'd better make it good.' He crosses his arms. 'Convince me not to call the police – and your boss.'

I grip the stem of my wine glass. 'It's the mystery of the girl in the painting. I've solved it… or, at least I think have.'

'What mystery? What are you talking about?'

Jack Faraday is judge and jury as I sum up the details of my 'research'. I start by recounting what Mrs Bradford and her sister told me – about how young Maryanne came to have her portrait painted – and finish with my hunch about the painting. He listens in silence, his face and thoughts unreadable.

'So I went there tonight,' I finish. 'But I'd already given back the key.'

Jack frowns. 'Let me get this straight. You saw something on television – what was it again – *Antiques Roadshow*?' His raised eyebrow says it all. 'It made you think there might be a missing Rembrandt hidden somewhere in the house – a painting that everyone thought was destroyed in a fire? And no one's discovered it over all these years until you came along?'

'I know it sounds—'

'Crazy?'

I hang my head.

'So you felt you needed to go to the house dressed like a burglar, and break a window to get inside?'

'I wanted to look for the painting. It's not like I was there to steal anything.'

'So having got inside, did you find this priceless missing Rembrandt?'

'Well… no. I didn't really have a chance to look. But I did find these.' I reach into my pocket and set the bundle of letters on the table. 'They were in the gap between the frame and the wall. I just wanted…' I trail off, defeated, 'I don't know… to find something worth saving before Rosemont Hall was lost.'

'Lost?'

'It was my fault.' My voice quivers. 'It was my job to sell it. My job to find someone who would restore the house. Bring it back to life.' I stare at the letters and the untouched wine in my glass, dark red like old blood. 'You said once that I was like a house matchmaker. Only, this time – when it was most important – I failed.'

He picks up the bundle of letters and stares at the name on the front: 'Miss Reilly'. He makes a point of tucking them away in his jacket pocket and looks at me in silence.

'I'm not some kind of deranged nutcase, Jack. Really, I'm not.'

Having said my piece, I await sentence.

He drains his pint and turns the empty glass around in his hand. 'You wanted a happy ending,' he says.

'Sorry?'

'A happy ending, like in one of your classic English novels.'

I look at him. Every cell in my body shivers and realigns itself, like leaves growing towards the light. How can he possibly know me so well? How will I ever get over the ache of sitting across the table from him knowing that there's no future. Tears spring to my eyes.

'Yes,' I say. 'That's it exactly.'

And I pray that he'll make it happen, but instead, he stands up and walks over to the bar. And the tiny part of me that isn't in love with him, hates him a little. By rights I should just leave. But I don't.

He returns to the table with a second pint, and (I'm pleased to see) a glass of water for me. 'You could have just called me,' he says. 'If you'd told me about your "hunch", maybe you could have saved yourself the trouble of breaking and entering.' He fiddles with the beer mat. 'In fact, when I saw you there, I thought maybe...' he hesitates. 'Maybe you got my text.'

'Text?'

'I sent you a text earlier. You didn't get it?'

'No – I...' I reach for my handbag – my phone must be somewhere.

'Never mind,' he says. 'I'll just tell you. It was to let you know that I was in town. I wanted to surprise you. I guess I did.'

My breath catches. 'But when we spoke, you said that your life was familiar. I thought that meant you were gone for good.'

'I was.' His aquamarine eyes bore into me. 'I had some important work to do on the patent that couldn't wait. I flew home just like I'd planned. But as soon as I got there... and you called me in the middle of the night...' He shakes his head.

'What?'

'I went to my home. I went to my meetings. I went to work. But familiar was no longer enough. Nothing felt right. Something happened when I was here. Something completely unexpected.'

I sit frozen in my chair.

'I realised that I had unfinished business. Something more important than computer chips or patents. Much more important. So I booked myself onto the first flight to London. I didn't know if you'd even see me, after the last time.'

'Me?'

'Yes, Amy. You.' He stares at me intently. I can feel a flush creeping up my neck.

'And then you didn't respond to my first text. I figured that was my answer. I paced the room for a while but I couldn't sleep. So I decided to visit the place that most reminded me of you – Rosemont Hall.' He shrugs. 'When I got there I sent you another text – you know – the tell-tale beep.' He gives me a half-smile. 'When I saw you there with your torch, I thought you'd come after all.'

He narrows his eyes beneath his long dark lashes. 'But now, I realise you were a burglar.'

'No, Jack! I didn't get your message.'

'So the question now is...' he pauses, probably to make me sweat a little more, 'if you had read my text – asking to see you – what would you have said?'

'I would have said that I was a complete idiot before – running away like that. And I've regretted it every moment since.'

He moves his chair closer and takes my hand.

'Spoken eloquently, like an English teacher.' His soft laugh sends delicious shockwaves through my veins. And at that moment, my appetite for mystery disappears, leaving room for nothing except him.

'No, Jack, I'm just an estate agent.'

He smiles and draws me close, his breath ruffling my hair. 'In that case, Amy Wood, *just* an estate agent,' he whispers in my ear, 'I'd love to hear more about your sleuthing. But maybe we can continue this little chat upstairs.'

He stands up and takes a room key from his pocket. This time, I can't even imagine running away. I leave my drink on the table and follow him out of the bar.

Thirty-Seven

From the moment I enter his room, I'm lost. We come together with the urgency of two travellers in a desert seeking an oasis. His kiss is hard and searching, his hands delicate as they remove my clothing and explore my skin. The bed is a large four-poster; and we fling ourselves onto it. I pull him over me and he shudders as I run my fingers through his hair and over his chest. Together we fumble with the zip on his trousers. 'Amy,' he whispers, and then the words are lost as our lips come together and speak their secret language.

And when we finally lie still in each other's arms, Jack whispers in my ear, 'I didn't think I'd ever find this again.'

'I can't believe it either,' I whisper.

'Well, believe it,' he says, and after that, neither of us have the opportunity to speak for a while.

*

Tennyson wrote that it's better to have loved and lost than never to have loved at all. I spend the night and all the next day with Jack. Somehow, the logistics get sorted: I phone in sick to work, breakfast arrives on a tray and we eat it together at the little table in his room that looks out onto the village green. Then we're back in bed and the duvet is warm and Jack's skin is warm; and his mouth is soft and yielding; his hands confident and demanding. I want it to last, but of course it won't. I know that there's no future and that when we say goodbye, it will be forever. There are still unanswered questions and unspoken topics between us: the house, the painting, the family secrets. But cocooned in his hotel room, a universe of two, I put all that out of my mind.

Finally, we sleep for a few hours, tangled in the sheets and each other's arms. When I wake up, it's late afternoon. A cold fear grips me. I don't want this to end.

Jack feels me stir and rolls over.

'Amy...' he says, stroking my thigh under the blankets.

'Hmm?'

'We should go while it's still light.'

'Go?' My heart freezes.

'I assume you want to go have a look for that painting. We can't count on the lights working.'

'You mean... you don't mind?'

I roll over. His face is grave.

'I don't know anything about lost paintings, portraits, old letters, or anything like that. You have to admit – it sounds pretty far-fetched. And the house will be sold, Amy – make no mistake. I don't want you here under false pretences. But if you need to go back there one more time – to say goodbye or whatever, then I'm not going to stop you.'

I shiver with regret. The hands of the clock are winding down so fast. I don't want things to end. But that's precisely what's going to happen.

'I don't know, Jack.' I run a fingernail delicately over his chest. 'Maybe it's better if I don't go back there. You'll return to America, and I'll go back to my life. I might wish that things were different, but the truth is...' I turn away so he can't see the tears in my eyes, 'you've already given me more of a happy ending than I ever could have hoped for. I just want to enjoy *this* – while it lasts.'

He brushes a piece of damp hair off my face but doesn't

try to correct me. 'That's not the Amy I know,' he says. 'What about your hunch?'

'In the end, the house will be sold.' I choke back a sob. 'As you've pointed out, it's really none of my business.'

Jack sighs. 'It's complicated, Amy. And I don't know how much Gran has told you.'

'Not a lot. Just snippets here and there.'

'I don't know the whole story either – far from it. But I do know that for her, bygones are not bygones.'

'What do you mean?' I prop up on my elbow.

He looks at me with his arresting blue eyes. 'When Flora and I were kids, Gran used to come and visit us every Thanksgiving and Christmas. Sometimes we'd sneak out of our bedrooms at night and sit on the stair landing listening to the adults. Gran would have a few drinks, and then start talking about England where she came from. Something about a big mansion, and how something happened to her there.' He pauses. 'She always said that America was the land of opportunity. There wasn't all this business about class and family heritage.'

He fingers a lock of my hair, but his eyes are far away.

'Her story was a bit garbled and pieced together, but I gather that when she came over to America – in the 50s, I guess – she was pregnant with our mom. It was just like something out of one of your classic novels. She'd been seduced by Henry Windham.'

'Seduced?' I pull away, stunned. 'By Henry? But... I thought, I mean... the letters! He was in love with Arabella. Wasn't he?'

'Probably, I don't know,' Jack says. 'Or maybe all that came later. All I know is that Gran was a nobody – just a girl from the village. But incidentally, her maiden name was Reilly. She could be the "Miss Reilly" on the letters you found behind the painting.'

I sit bolt upright as the possibilities explode in my mind like fireworks. I'm thinking not of the letters behind the painting, but about the original letters I found in the library. Reilly. Maryanne Reilly. 'A'—?

'Did your grandma ever go by "Anne" by any chance?' I say breathlessly.

He furrows his brow. 'I don't know. Once when we were little, Flora called her "Granny Annie". She flew off the handle and said never to call her that again.'

The fabric of time that I've carefully constructed in my mind rips apart. All along I assumed that the original letters I found were between Henry and Arabella. I never considered another possibility. All those benign, innocent love letters that I thought were written between a future husband and wife – who were married to each other for over forty years. *They never had any children.* And now it seems that all along, the great love story of Rosemont Hall never existed. Not between Henry and Arabella, at least.

'The other letters I found – the love letters I told you about. They were between "H" and "A". Arabella, I'd assumed. But maybe I've been wrong all along. Could they be between Henry and your grandma?'

'It's possible, I guess.' He frowns, as if it's all too much to process at once. 'I'd like to read them. Are they still at the house?'

A blush rises to my cheeks. 'Actually, they're at home in my knicker drawer.'

He laughs. 'Of course they are.'

I laugh too, but my brain is still whirring. 'The letters I found stopped just before Henry's 21st birthday party. That was the night of the fire. That must be significant. Do you know much about her past? How she ended up in America, for example?'

Jack narrows his eyes. 'As I'm sure you can imagine, she's not really the type to be open about that kind of thing.'

I nod. I *can* imagine.

'I don't know all the details, but she gave birth to my mom

not long after she arrived in America. She settled in New York and found work in a big hotel – told them she was a widow, I think, to avoid the stigma. It must have been difficult with a baby – I don't know how she managed it. But she ended up marrying the hotel manager, Tim Bradford. Grandpa Tim. He was great,' he smiles. 'Taught me how to ride a bicycle and build a tree house – stuff like that. We even took apart an old Radio Shack computer together. They were married for a good many years before he died.'

'He sounds like a good guy.'

'They didn't have children of their own. But my mom grew up and married my dad. Then Flora and I came along. That should have been the end of it – a happy ending, if you like. But it wasn't.'

'What do you mean?'

He stares up at the beamed ceiling. 'Gran always talked like she hated her life in England. So you can imagine how surprised we were when she pitched up one Christmas and said that she was moving back there.'

'Did she give a reason?'

'Just the usual – homesick for her own country and all that.'

'So what happened?'

'She left – just like that.' He snaps his fingers. 'We didn't hear much from her – just cards at birthdays and Christmas. But once or twice I heard my mom arguing with her on the phone. Later on, Flora and I found out that her main reason for going back to England was to confront Henry Windham once and for all. All through the years she'd been so angry that he got her pregnant and just dropped her. That he never even tried to contact her.'

'I can see why she'd be angry. I think she said something to me about "never a letter or a how d'ya do".'

'But it didn't stop there. What she really wanted him to do was rewrite his will to leave Rosemont Hall to her. And if he didn't, she threatened to tell Arabella about Henry's child. Arabella was unstable, I believe. Paranoid because she hadn't given Henry an heir.'

'So she blackmailed him!' I try to reconcile this with the old woman I know. It's not that hard to do. But on the other hand, if Jack's account of what happened to her is accurate, maybe she was justified.

Jack nods. 'Henry was a bit senile by that time. But he didn't doubt her word. I don't know if he ever loved her or not, but he'd never forgotten her.'

'Well that's something, I guess.'

'And anyway, he did change his will. But he left the house to Flora and me, not Gran. He also gave Arabella a life estate – so that we would only inherit the house after she died.' He shakes his head. 'Gran was livid, but what could she do? She stayed on at Rosemont Hall because she insisted that it was her home. And now...' he pauses, choosing his words. 'Let's just say, she's not very rational when it comes to Rosemont Hall.'

Ignoring the obvious understatement, I nod.

'My mom first spoke to Ian Kendall when Henry Windham died. He told her about the inheritance and the life estate. He also told her about what Henry did, and about Gran "applying some pressure" to get Henry to change his will. Mom was disgusted with the whole thing – still is. She told me that when she was growing up, Gran would rave sometimes about Rosemont Hall, and how Arabella had stolen the life she should have had.

'Mom didn't want anything to do with the place or the Windham family. To her, Tim was her dad. He'd worked his way up from nothing, and it was ingrained in her – in all of us – to do the same. She was no gold-digger – she didn't need or want anything from the likes of Henry Windham.' He shrugs disdainfully. 'Flora and I felt exactly the same – it was family history best forgotten. Plus, at the time Henry died,

I'd just finished my engineering degree. Flora was married and had started a small fashion boutique. We had our lives in America. What were we going to do with a crumbling old pile in England?'

What indeed?

'Anyway, Arabella was alive for some years. Gran worked as her housekeeper and companion until she died.' He shakes his head. 'They probably made each other miserable, for all I know.'

'Remarkable. I thought Mrs Bradford was devoted to Arabella.'

Jack runs his finger along the line of my jaw. 'So that's it,' he says. 'The whole story.'

'It's all so terrible – yet fascinating – at the same time.'

He nods. 'Though as far as I know, Henry Windham and Arabella were content in their marriage. At least until Gran tried to make things difficult. And I guess she had her reasons – a ruined life and a broken heart.'

'Yes. It's hard to know who to feel sorriest for.' I pause, considering. 'And there's one other thing too.'

'What's that?'

'The fire.' I tell him about what Mr Wakefield told me. That a servant was blamed for the fire, but nothing was ever proven. 'Do you think she had anything to do with it?'

Jack frowns. 'Gran is strong-willed, that's for sure. But I find it hard to believe she would do something like that.'

'Me too. I can't see her wanting to harm Rosemont Hall.'

'But if she was accused, it would explain why she left England. I guess the only person who knows for sure is her.'

'Yes,' I say. 'You're probably right.'

Jack rolls onto his back. 'So now, the house will be sold. Flora doesn't want it. I didn't either...'

He stops talking and seems to be debating with himself. For a dreadful moment, I worry that he's about to get out of bed and go on his way. 'The sale should complete in a few weeks,' he says. 'Then the debts of the estate can be paid.'

'But surely you know that your grandmother wants you to keep the house?' I recall Mrs Bradford's past ravings about the house being torn apart brick by brick, and about how the heirs were 'peasants' not to appreciate the place.

He gives me a sideways glance. 'Of course she's tried the "you should appreciate where you came from" lecture a few times. Then she tried the "I worked so hard to get this for you and you're just throwing it away" card.' He shakes his head. 'I'm afraid those kind of arguments don't work very well with me. I guess Gran and I aren't on the same wavelength. Maybe we never will be.'

'Maybe not.' I sigh.

'Anyway, I've got a meeting with Mr Kendall tomorrow. I'll drop off the letters to Gran on my way. I guess Henry must have wedged them behind the painting. Unless Gran put them there herself.'

I nod.

'And then I'm flying home – to America. I'm a non-exec director of my former company, and we have an important board meeting coming up. This was just a bit of a whirlwind visit.'

'Yes, Jack,' I choke.

'Hey,' he says cupping my chin with his hand. 'Don't look so glum. Now that I've seen you again, I hope this will be the first of many whirlwind visits.'

'Okay,' I say, snuggling into his chest.

He strokes my hair. 'So once again, I'll ask you – do you want to go to Rosemont Hall now and have a look at that painting?'

'Right now?'

'Well, maybe not *just* now...'

My answer dies on my lips as he covers them with his.

VII

Letter 7 (unsealed envelope addressed to 'A Reilly')

(Transcription) (Dated June 27ᵗʰ 1952)
Rosemont Hall

My darling—
    My hand is shaking as I write these words. You were right all along – my father guessed our secret plans and set out to ruin them. I should have known from the moment that SHE arrived – some simpering little girl with a rich daddy and dreams of being Lady of the Manor. But I'm ashamed to say that I was still labouring under the delusion that Father meant to honour me, not marry me off. Why did I not suspect that he was capable of such cruelty? Why did I think I was a match for his cunning and ruthlessness?
    This morning, I went to tell him once and for all that you and I will marry. He laughed in my face. He told me that he burnt the note I sent you – telling you that at the ball I was planning to play along with my father for the sake of appearances, and then renounce everything in the light of day. My heart aches thinking of the torment that last night must have caused you!
    But I told him that none of that mattered – and there is nothing he can do to keep us apart. And then he dropped his bombshell – his 'belief' that you started the fire. My father said that he found the lighter you gave me for my birthday in the

wreckage. Such tosh! But the constable was all too happy to believe him.

I know that you have done nothing wrong – that you would never lift a finger to harm your beloved Rosemont Hall. I am told that you have fled to safety. My darling, I will try to clear your name – find out who really set the fire. And then you can return. I want you with me forever, as we have planned all along. Write and let me know that you are safe. Write that you love me still.

—H

Thirty-Eight

I return to Rosemont Hall, no longer a burglar; and in fact, a different person in so many ways. I have to pinch myself as Jack and I approach the house in his hire car because it feels like I'm with the right person coming home to the place where I belong. I glance over at him, trying to burn his profile into my mind. For when he leaves – tomorrow. And in an instant, the fantasy shatters, leaving a dark, empty hole inside.

'You ready?' Jack glances over at me.

I bite my lip. 'Yes, let's do it.'

Though I'm still dressed in my burglar black, this time I enter much more respectably through the front door. I follow Jack up the stairs to the landing. He seems to have caught my enthusiasm for the mystery. He stands back from the painting of the girl in the pink dress and studies it thoughtfully.

'She was so beautiful,' I say quietly.

'And you're sure it's really Gran?' He cocks his head.

'That's what she told me.'

'I guess she does look a little bit like Flora.'

I laugh, remembering how Flora saw no resemblance to herself.

'It all fits, Jack,' I say. 'Everything points in one direction.'

'Yeah, you keep saying.' He gives me a sideways glance. 'But now that we're here, before we go lifting paintings and removing heavy frames, can you just run me through it again?'

'Of course.' I explain how Sir George met the artist Francisco

304

Walredo during his time in Spain during the Civil War. The two of them became friends. The names in Walredo's sketchbook – Feldmann, Stein, Rabinowicz, etc. – were most probably Jewish clients who, prior to WWII, commissioned him to 'hide' their precious artwork so that it wouldn't be stolen by the Nazis. Then, a decade later, the time for heroism had passed. Sir George had been forced to sell his beloved paintings, and *Tio Francisco* had gone back to smuggling and petty art crime. But when it came time to part with his most beloved painting, Sir George wrote to his friend for help in his 'hour of need'. The Rembrandt was withdrawn from the auction, the original frame was removed from the John Singer Sargent and replaced with a new one. Walredo came to Rosemont Hall, ostensibly to paint Henry's portrait to put over the Rembrandt. But instead, he painted a young beauty who had caught his eye – Maryanne Reilly. He painted her in a style that he used for his other 'overpaintings' – the same style as the one on the *Antiques Roadshow* that hid the Cassatt.

Jack frowns and hangs on my every word. 'And he went to all that trouble so that he could keep the painting, but also collect the insurance money?'

'Which was never paid out.'

Jack stares at the painting in silence for a minute. 'Well,' he says finally, 'although I haven't actually seen the infamous knicker drawer evidence, it all sounds pretty convincing.'

Blushing, I cross my fingers behind my back. We just *have* to find something.

Jack's hand brushes mine. 'Okay, so let's see if you're right.'

He motions to me to take one side of the painting while he takes the other. I grip the ornate gold frame tightly and stand on tiptoes to steady my side while he lifts the painting off the wall. There's a sharp cracking noise and a rain of white plaster as together we stagger forward under the unexpected weight and ease the bottom edge of the frame to the floor.

I keep the frame upright while Jack kneels down and studies the back of the painting. There's a heavy piece of board bolted to the back and a wire used for hanging. I scan the piece of wood for any marks of identification, but there's nothing.

Jack pulls a Swiss army knife out of this pocket. 'Good thing I was a Boy Scout,' he says. He finds the right tool – a tiny adjustable wrench – and starts loosening the first of the bolts.

'Be careful,' I say. My stomach feels suddenly queasy. Are we about to find an important 'lost' Rembrandt? Or just a pretty picture of a girl in a pink dress? 'Do you think we ought to leave it to an expert?'

Jack laughs softly. 'I have — You.' He hands me the first of the bolts.

It takes him the better part of a quarter-hour to loosen all the bolts. They clink together in the pocket of my coat. When the last bolt is off, he tries to pry the board off with a small screwdriver, but it's wedged too tightly into the edges of the frame. I watch as Jack the Engineer analyses the frame again and finds a weak spot in one of the mitred corners.

'I'm afraid we might have to do this the hard way,' he says. He inserts the screwdriver to pry the frame apart. I look away. The wood and nails give way with a loud crack and a cloud of dust. The long side of the frame comes loose, hanging onto the bottom by a few nails. He wrenches it all the way off. I move around the painting to his side.

'Look!' I say fizzing with excitement. 'There are two canvases – one behind the other.' In fact, there's a sandwich of various layers of thin plywood, cloth, scrim and wadding behind the top canvas. It was clearly done by an expert framer – or art smuggler.

'Well I'll be damned.' Jack gives a low whistle. He runs his fingers reverently over the layers. 'Quite a clever feat of engineering, I'd say. It's like one painting has been hermetically

306

sealed behind the other. You'd never have any idea that it was there.'

He puts his Swiss army knife back in his pocket. 'Now, I think we ought to leave the rest to the experts. What do you think?'

'I completely agree.' As much as I'd like to see the unveiling of the second canvas, I know that Jack's right – it needs to be done with proper tools by proper art restorers. I'm suddenly conscious of the cold and damp. The paintings need to be moved to safety as soon as possible.

'Okay. Grab your end.'

Together, we lift the heavy frame and double canvases and lean them against the wall. Then we both stand back without touching, but with palpable electricity flowing between us. The girl in the pink dress stares back at us, her smile as inscrutable as ever.

'I wonder if *she* knew what she was hiding.' I say softly.

'Grandma Maryanne?' Jack says. 'It's hard to say. But if she'd tell anyone, it would be you.'

I laugh, assuming he's joking. But he shakes his head.

'I'm serious,' he says. 'Before I came to the house that night and found you "burgling" it,' he smiles playfully, 'I stopped by the cottage and saw Gran. I was worried about what you said – that she was struggling to adjust to moving out of Rosemont Hall.'

'Yes. Is she okay?'

'I think she's accepted the situation, though she's not happy about it. She wouldn't say very much. As I said, we aren't that close.'

'That's too bad.'

'But she did tell me that she'd met "a lovely girl who really seems to care about the things that matter".' He smiles. 'I'll spare you the "... and why can't you be more like her?" part of the conversation.'

'Thanks,' I say, secretly pleased that at last, Mrs Bradford seems to have recognised that I'm on her side.

'And who knows? Maybe Henry guessed the truth – after all, he left the painting to her.' He reaches over and laces our hands together. My chest wells up. 'It's so sad. I mean all that time she was the housekeeper here, looking up at her own portrait. And Arabella – how much did she know? I will ask your grandma. I'd love to know more…'

'That's my Amy,' Jack laughs and squeezes my hand.

My Amy.

I lean in and give him a kiss on the cheek.

'Anyway,' he says, kissing me back, 'the past is the past, and we may never know the whole story. But whatever it is, I'd say that today, you've helped to write a pretty important new chapter of it.'

*

Racing too fast, the clock winds down, and suddenly, my time with Jack is over. We leave the house together and he drives me back to the hotel to get my car. He gives me one last, searching kiss in the car park. 'I'll call you before I head off to the airport,' he says, as our lips reluctantly part.

My heart ripping in two, I just smile and nod.

'And I'll let you know what Sotheby's say about the painting.'

'Thanks.'

'In the meantime, let's not tell Gran about your "hunch", okay? Let's get the results first.'

'Of course, Jack.' My voice quavers.

He touches me on the chin. 'Come on, Amy, let's see a smile. Everything's going to be fine – you'll see.'

'Yes, Jack.' I swallow hard. 'But I really don't see how…'

He stops me with another kiss.

'I *will* see you soon.' His breath in my ear makes me quiver all over. But I must stop it. Jack is off to see the solicitor and then back to America. He says I need to trust him – that he'll come back soon, that we'll keep in touch... and after that, who knows what might happen?

But I know what will happen. He'll go. I'll stay. It was nice – lovely, actually – while it lasted, like the proverbial candle burning at both ends. The end of 'Jack and me' is bittersweet. Just like real life.

'Goodbye,' he whispers.

He slams the car door. I give him a limp wave and reverse out of the car park. My hands tremble on the steering wheel. Finding what might be a lost Rembrandt has left me completely drained and exhausted (not to mention late for work).

I pull over to the kerb in the village and gather all the Rose-mont Hall particulars from the passenger seat and the floor. I shove them in an overflowing rubbish bin by the post office. The photo I took of the house is forever etched in my mind, along with my vision of what it could be if someone took on the labour of love. *If.*

But that someone won't be Jack.

And it won't be me.

*

When I return to the office, my colleagues greet me with their usual pained indifference. Jonathan checks his watch when I enter and gives a little smirk. Patricia fakes a concerned look when I plunk down at my desk.

'I hope whatever you had isn't catching, Amy,' she says.

'Me too.' I'm aware that my eyes are red and I look rubbish. 'But with a bad case of swine flu, you never know.' I blow my nose loudly for effect.

She looks horrified but I ignore her. Just then, Claire comes in from the back, breathless and smiling.

'Oh Amy,' she says, 'did they tell you my news?'

'Hi Claire. No... but I'm sure Patricia was just about to.'

She puts her handbag on her desk and sits down. 'I've got a pupillage in Birmingham – with a really top chambers! I gave notice this morning – I'll be leaving here in two weeks.'

'That's great!' I go around to her desk and give her a hug. 'Fantastic!'

I ask her all about her new job, and she happily launches into an account of her interviews, the people she'll be working with, and the crown prosecution work that she'll be doing.

Of course I'm very happy for her. But I also wonder when this painful spate of goodbyes is going to end. I look around at the others in the office, wishing it was one of them leaving rather than Claire.

After our chat, I sort through my post and emails. I've received loads of requests for property details, two viewings have been added to my calendar, and four people want valuations to put their homes on the market. I try to concentrate; try not to think about Jack; try to do my job as best I can.

But inside my chest, there's a gnawing hollowness that won't go away. My skin still tingles with the ghost of Jack Faraday's touch. The phone rings and I forget to answer it. Emails come in and I just stare at the names on the computer screen. Mr Bowen-Knowles comes out, starts speaking to me in his usual nasal drone, leaves me a pile of papers, and I've no idea what he's said.

Late in the day, a large brown envelope is delivered to me by courier. It's from Mr Kendall's firm. There's a compliments slip attached to the top: *Mrs Bradford didn't want these, so Mr Jack said to give them to you. Yours, Ian Kendall, Esq.*

I quickly shove the envelope in my handbag. I don't want any questions – I can't answer them.

As I'm about to leave for the day, Jack phones. He's at the airport waiting for his flight. Our conversation is brief, and I feign cheerfulness and bubbly faith. But hearing his voice so far away, the cracks in my heart grow a little wider.

I tell him that I received the envelope from Mr Kendall with the letters inside.

'Gran was in one of her moods,' he says. 'I got another earful about not respecting the family history and Rosemont Hall.' He laughs uncomfortably. 'You probably agree with her.'

'Maybe a little bit.' I manage a laugh.

'She took some convincing even to let me get the painting looked at by an expert in London. She thought I was trying to sell it even though it was left to her. I tried to tell her that wasn't the case – I only wanted to see if it needed restoring or preservation.' He sighs. 'I guess Flora and I haven't been the best grandchildren in the world.'

'She's a one-off, your grandmother.'

'That's putting it nicely. Anyway, I'd better go. They just put up the gate info. I'll call you.'

'Okay.' I can't bring myself to say goodbye so I quickly hang up the phone.

I sit at my desk in the empty office staring at the four beige walls. Focus on the present, breath by breath. Focus on the positives: the painting will be delivered to Sotheby's in London for examination by an expert. As for what that expert will find, I have a pretty good idea. As for what my future holds...

I shudder to think.

Letter 8 (unsealed envelope addressed to 'A Reilly')

Rosemont Hall
August 30th 1952

Darling— I married her. Last weekend, in a ceremony in the village church before my father, 120 well-wishers, and a God that doesn't exist. There really was no choice. Please let me explain...

A fire investigator came from Lloyds – a local man called Wakefield. He immediately questioned my father's well-rehearsed charade. He found the gold lighter you had given me in the wreckage. But he also found traces of accelerant that he believes started the fire. 'How could a servant do this without being seen?' he asked. There was something about him – he was not a man to let the matter lie.

My father instantly confronted me – nearly begged me – such a pathetic thing. He needed the protection of HER father who is a Lord. The family association would place him above suspicion. And he showed me the true state of the estate finances – much worse than I ever could have suspected. All I could think about was that if I didn't marry, I would have to sell Rosemont Hall. And how could I allow that to happen? Even though I may never see you again – I must try to accept that now – it is still your home. You are the mistress here – your vision haunts every corner of the house.

My father says that you have gone to America – the land of opportunity. He said that if I marry without a fuss, he will give me your address. If only my letters can reach you, then perhaps there is still hope. I believe the insurance man will declare an open verdict – he won't implicate father directly, but he won't pay out either. When that happens, you can return and I will have this sham of a marriage annulled. In the meantime, there will be no children – I will make certain of that.

You trusted me once and I betrayed you. I dare not ask again. But you have only to say the word and once again I shall be yours.

Thirty-Nine

At home, Mum and Dad are in the lounge watching *Midsomer Murders*. I slip past them into my room and take the brown envelope out of my handbag. Slitting it open, I remove the bundle of letters addressed to 'A Reilly'. The envelopes each have an American address and a stamp, but no postmark – they were never sent. Nonetheless, each one is slit open along the top. Someone has read them.

As I'm about to open the top letter, I suddenly feel like I'm riffling through someone else's dirty laundry, or else, 'poking my nose where it doesn't belong'. When I read the original letters between 'H' and 'A', I assumed that both correspondents were deceased. But now that I know the truth, really, I've no right to be looking at letters addressed to Mrs Bradford – even if she doesn't want them.

I retie the letters and set them on top of the bureau. I lie back down on my bed and pick up a book from the bedside table. After a few seconds of staring at the page, I realise that I'm holding the book upside down. How can I concentrate on reading fiction when the truth is staring at me from across the room?

Maybe I'll just read one or two. I close the book and stand up. After all, someone's opened them already. Maybe they might contain something important. If I don't look, I'll never know – and neither will Mrs Bradford. I take the stack from my bureau and sit on the bed.

It isn't until five in the morning that I finally turn off the light.

Letter 9 (unsealed envelope addressed to 'A Reilly')

Rosemont Hall
1ˢᵗ April 1953

My darling—

I now accept that I may never see you again. I curse the long years ahead. Without you here, I hope that the old house crumbles to the ground. It has become a prison, my marriage a life sentence.

Overnight my father has turned old. He walks through the wreckage, tapping his stick like a blind man, cursing and talking to himself. Sometimes, he talks to his last beloved painting – the Rembrandt – as if it's still hanging there on the empty wall. The insurance man refuses to settle the claim. He thinks that my father has spirited the painting away. He can't prove anything, but too many questions remain unanswered.

Cleverer still is my wife's father. He carefully hid the fact that Arabella's fortune was nowhere near as much as promised. We've put every penny into fixing the roof – there's nothing left over to restore the East Wing.

In spite of everything, there is one comfort that remains for me. My father's friend, the painter, left behind an unexpected and most precious gift. A framed canvas, almost life-sized, discarded in his attic studio. A picture of a girl in a pink dress – the silk clinging to her body in a way that makes me ache for her. She's clutching a bundle of letters, and I can see the love shining from her eyes. I had no idea that you sat for him! Perhaps that was the surprise you were so eager to tell me. In any case, the painting is so lovely and lifelike that it has become my fondest salvation and my greatest torment.

I carried it out of the attic and hung it on the stair landing. My father took one look at it and began to cackle like a madman. I've seen him stop and stand in front of it, staring like he's trying to see through the pigment and canvas. Like it somehow holds the key to what his life has become.

Perhaps you think it is cruel of me to have hung up your portrait – and to taunt my wife every time she sees it. But if she minds, she has never said. Every night I give her a sisterly kiss on the forehead and we go our separate ways to bedrooms at the opposite ends of the house. Poor Arabella. None of this misery is her doing.

But be that as it may, I would gladly trade her life for a single moment with you, my love. I suppose that makes me just as much of a demon as my father.

Forty

As the sky begins to lighten through the net curtains, I carefully refold each of the letters in turn, barely able to swallow from the lump of tears in my throat. After Henry's marriage to Arabella, the letters reduced in frequency as Henry's despair and resignation came home to roost. He never 'made anything of himself' without Maryanne at his side – as far as I can tell, he had a job as a minor civil servant at the local council, which would hardly have provided much money for the upkeep of a house like Rosemont Hall. His life seemed to settle into a kind of muted rhythm. He continued to give an account of certain key events – the death of his father; a near-miss for Arabella when she cut herself on a rusty blade and got blood poisoning. This event was not explained in detail, but it leads me to wonder about the depth of her own despair at her marriage.

Some of the later letters went on to speculate about what Miss Reilly's life might have been like after she fled, and where she might have disappeared to. And why she never sent an answer to the years of love letters she must have received. Henry concluded that her silence was down to her own superior internal strength, and the supposition that her life had in fact turned out well. I sigh. Did he ever suspect that in all the time that followed, she had never received his letters?

And all the while – over forty long years of his marriage to Arabella, the house gradually fell into a worse and worse state. He speaks of the cracks in the plaster, the leaks in the roof, the woodworm, and the gathering layers of dust like they are somehow a comfort to him. It was like the crumbling walls of Rosemont Hall were absorbing his lifelong pain of a broken heart.

My eyes are red and puffy from lack of sleep and deciphering Henry's tiny, deliberate handwriting. His words of love echo in my head – sometimes poetic, but ultimately futile.

And I even spare a thought for Sir George – a 'devil' by all accounts. I reread the letter he sent to Henry that was in the original bundle of letters. It must have been written just before Henry came home from university. There's a sense of loss in his words, as he speaks of selling off his art, and his grand 'plan' for Henry to 'restore the family fortunes'. In the end, Sir George's schemes failed miserably and ruined many lives, including, it would seem, his own. And if I'm right about the painting we found, then I agree with Henry's assessment that his father was a little mad. I suppose that by entombing his beloved Rembrandt, Sir George thought that he could keep it for himself out of reach of the world. Perhaps just knowing it was still there in the house was enough for him. Didn't Mary Blundell say something about art collectors valuing their treasures more than casual viewers do? Not that I believe that for a second, but then again, I've never owned anything anywhere near as valuable or beautiful so as to be able to judge.

And what if Jack and I hadn't found the painting – would another treasure have been lost forever? Because even if I do end up saving the Rembrandt, I still haven't saved Rosemont Hall.

I refold the letters and put them back in the envelope along with the lighter, the sketchbook, and the original bundle of letters from my knicker drawer. I get dressed and slip out the back door before Mum can ply me with a breakfast I couldn't possibly stomach. Half-dazed, I drive to work and park the car. But instead of going into the office, I walk for twenty minutes to the other side of Bath.

I stop in front of a golden-stone facade. Next to the door is a brass plaque with an engraved name. I ring the bell and speak to the receptionist. I'm buzzed in and walk into an immaculately painted hallway with original Georgian coving and staircase. I walk up to the first floor.

Mr Kendall's office has the warm, comforting look of a gentleman country solicitor's. There's a spacious waiting area with bookshelves on one wall, filled with neat, leather-bound law books in tan, burgundy, and green. His assistant is a middle-aged woman with glasses, who greets me when I enter. 'Mr Kendall is on the phone,' she says when I tell her my name. 'But he might be able to fit you in before his next client arrives. Would you like some coffee?'

'Yes, thank you.' I sit down on one of the leather chesterfield sofas and thumb through the latest *Country Life*.

It's half an hour before Mr Kendall is finally off the phone. He comes out of his office and immediately sees me sitting there.

'Mr Kendall, this young lady...' his assistant begins.

'Thank you, Colleen. I'll see Ms Wood now.'

I stand up. We exchange greetings. He ushers me into his office and I sit down in a comfy leather chair across from his large antique banker's desk. We make a bit of small talk – about his office, the weather, the local property market.

'I came to see you about the letters.' I cut to the chase.

'Yes, what about them?'

'Has Mrs Bradford read them? Did she hide them in the hollow behind the painting?'

Mr Kendall sits back in his chair. 'No. She denied knowing anything about them. And I believe her.'

'So who put them there? Henry Windham?'

'More likely it was Arabella.'

My hunch confirmed, I let out a long sigh. 'Are you certain?'

He steeples his fingers like a wise sage. 'I was the family solicitor. To many people that means more than just a lawyer.

Confidante, therapist – confessor. Arabella and I had tea together once or twice a year.'

'So she knew then? That all those years her husband was in love with someone else; wanted a life with someone else? That he continued to write love letters to Maryanne Reilly even after they were married? And Arabella made sure that they were never sent?'

'That's the gist of it.' Mr Kendall does his best to sound lawyerly and indifferent, but the sad look in his eyes tells the truth.

'So Maryanne Reilly – Mrs Bradford – never knew that Henry tried to find her?'

'Perhaps not.'

'That poor woman!' I blurt out 'And poor Arabella and Henry... and—'

I stop. The past is the past. Henry and Arabella are dead. Mrs Bradford is bitter and unstable. Rosemont Hall will become a golf clubhouse and conference centre if it's lucky, and crumble to dust if it isn't. Either way, the walls will forget what they know, and the voices they once heard will fade away.

Mr Kendall chuckles. 'Strange isn't it, Ms Wood, but also, in a way, fitting. All along, you've been the one who's shown the most interest in Rosemont Hall. You're the best person to preserve what we know of its history. At least that's what Jack said when I told him his grandmother didn't want the letters. He's entrusted them to you.'

I sit up straight in the deep, leather chair. 'I'm sure that's very noble. But I can't take them. You once told me that the house was less important than the people who live in it. The others are dead, but Mrs Bradford is still alive. After all, if I was her...' and suddenly it strikes me how alike we are – both loving men who were unattainable to us, and both loving Rosemont Hall. 'I'd want to know the truth.'

Mr Kendall shrugs. 'As far as the estate is concerned, the

letters passed to Jack when Mrs Bradford didn't want them, and he said to give them to you. What you do next is up to you.'

I stand up. 'Thank you for clarifying that, Mr Kendall. You've been very helpful.'

'It's been a pleasure.' He stands up and we shake hands.

'Yes it has.'

Just as I'm at the door, he stops me. 'Oh, and Ms Wood, one more thing.'

'Yes?'

'The final probate decree is supposed to come in this week. Please can you let Mr Bowen-Knowles know that the sale of Rosemont Hall should be able to complete immediately after?'

'Of course. We'll have our part of the paperwork ready.' I swallow hard.

As I leave Mr Kendall's office and walk back to mine I have a strange sense of anticipation and foreboding, like somewhere, a wave is building up and about to crash over my head. I text Jack saying that I've read the letters, and can he please ring me. At the very least, I want to keep him informed (and remind him that I haven't stopped thinking about him). I get an almost immediate reply: 'Will phone later. Love, Jack.' I reread the last two words about ten times. Then I do a quick directory search on my phone. For the 'Cup o' Comfort' tea room in Little Botheringford.

Forty-One

The little bell on the door jingles as I enter. The teashop has a cosy glow about it, and the gas fire is on. There's a heady smell of baking and coffee, and on the counter is a fresh lemon cake and a tray of chocolate and salted-caramel flapjacks. It's just after three o'clock, and luckily, no one in the office even looked up when I fibbed that I was off to do a viewing.

I've wrapped the letters in a plastic bag for protection. Mrs Bradford's sister, Gwen, whom I spoke to on the phone to arrange the meeting, blinks like she's seen me before but can't quite remember.

'Hello.' I set the bag on a table by the fire. She walks over and I order a pot of tea for two and a plate of cake and flapjacks. I grab a newspaper from the rack, sit down at my table, and wait.

When the bell tinkles again, I close the newspaper. The hunched-over woman with unruly grey hair and swollen ankles looks at me with piercing blue eyes: Maryanne Bradford – the girl in the pink dress – paramour of the late Henry Windham – grandmother to Jack and Flora – the housekeeper with an axe to grind. And behind her pads Captain, her faithful, blind Saint Bernard.

She hobbles towards me, her cane thumping across the floor. The dog lets out a low growl, then a sharp bark. If my heart hadn't already been thundering, it is now.

'Captain,' she rasps. 'Down.'

The huge dog whimpers, his pink tongue hanging out. He

slinks on his belly under the table and lies down on my feet. Unable to stand up for fear of losing a leg, I stay seated, the bundle of letters in my lap.

Her eyes never leave my face. She scrapes a chair across the floor. Her joints creak as she lowers herself down like an old-fashioned lift.

'It's good to see you, Mrs Bradford,' I say. 'Are you well?'

She chuckles. 'As can be expected at my age.'

I smile back, remembering what she said to Jack. We aren't exactly friends, nor exactly allies, and yet, who knows? Maybe one day, we could end up being both.

I put the bundle on the table. 'These belong to you,' I say. My hands fumble to untie the pink ribbon.

The lines on her face deepen, all companionability gone. 'I told Jack I didn't want them,' she says.

'Just hear me out – please. They were written after you went away. But they were never posted.'

Her mouth purses tightly, but her lower lip quivers ever so slightly.

'You were upset because Henry never wrote to you,' I say. 'But actually, he did.'

She clenches her gnarled hands into fists. 'Don't mention him to me,' she snaps. 'He was just as bad as his father. Worse, in fact, because he was weak – and stupid too. He thought he could outplay his father at a game of human chess. But there was never any doubt who was the more cunning and shrewd.'

'Maybe so, Mrs Bradford. But the letters confirm that his feelings for you were real.'

She tsks angrily. 'Feelings – what use are they in the real world? When I was a girl, I loved staying awake late at night reading silly books. Some people might call them classics – *Jane Eyre*, *Pride and Prejudice*, *Wuthering Heights*. But I call them dangerous. They gave girls like me the wrong notion. That life was some kind of grand "rags to riches" romance, and if we looked pretty and talked clever, then we'd have the world at our feet.'

'Yes,' I gulp. 'I guess you could see it that way.'

'I thought that because I had a pretty face, I was somehow entitled to something better than my lot. I told you that I practically grew up at Rosemont Hall. It was my *Pemberley*, my *Thornfield*, my fairy-tale castle. You know?'

I nod, knowing all too well.

'Back then, Henry was just another freckle-faced, snot-nosed boy. At age twelve, he went off to boarding school. When he came back for school holidays, I barely recognised him. He'd become a proper young man. And I was just the daughter of a servant.

'When I was sixteen, Henry came upon me reading a book in the rose garden.' She wrinkles her nose. 'It was *Jane Eyre* if you want to know. We got to talking – about books and things. I knew he was interested in me, but for a long time, I played hard to get. I remember every second of that summer.' She smiles dreamily, her mind far away. 'He would chase me through the gardens and steal a kiss under the weeping beech tree. I was "his Annie" – he's the only person who's ever called me that.'

'Annie,' I whisper. 'A'.

'But no matter what the books promised, there was never any hope for Henry and me. Never.' She glares at me like it's all my fault.

'I know it's painful, Mrs Bradford, but please hear me out.'

She curves her lips over her dentures like she's tasted something sour. After a long moment, she sits back obediently in the chair.

'You thought that Henry never gave you another thought. But he did. I think that Arabella must have intercepted Henry's letters before they were sent.'

She hisses but says nothing.

I summarise the salient points: Henry loved her. He wanted

her to live at Rosemont Hall. He didn't throw her over willingly. If she came back, then he would leave Arabella – have the marriage annulled. But none of what Henry wanted ever happened. I leave out how devastated Arabella must have been when she found out. In the end, it seems, it's her story that won't ever be fully told.

As I speak, Mrs Bradford's face, hard-set with years of resignation, begins slowly to soften. In fact, her whole body slumps in her chair.

'All those years…' she says, 'I loved him. I never forgot him. Or forgave him neither.'

'I can understand that.' My throat wells up as I think about her tangled and tragic life. She may have been the villain when it came to blackmailing Henry, but she was a victim too – one of several, it seems.

She puts a hand over her mouth and rests her elbow on the table. She stares at the bundle of letters, but doesn't touch them.

'I'm sorry,' I murmur.

Suddenly, she raises her wrinkled arm and sweeps the letters off the table. They flutter to the floor like wounded doves. Captain jumps up and yelps, his hackles raised.

Mrs Bradford calmly sits back and pours herself a cup of tea.

'You were *his Annie*,' I say. 'He never stopped loving you.'

'What does it matter now?'

'It matters to me,' I say. 'Tell me your story.'

She analyses my face. For a second, I'm worried that I've spooked her. I want to look away, but I force myself not to.

'All right.' She plops four sugars into her tea. 'I suppose I should be grateful that you're here and you're interested. That's a lot more than any of the rest of them ever were.' She sighs. 'You've earned the right to know the whole story.'

I smile encouragingly. *Maybe friends…*

She looks down at her tea, stirring it slowly. 'Henry and I sent each other little notes,' she says. 'It started as a silly game

– using initials only in case they were ever intercepted. But as time went on, everything got more urgent. We just *had* to see each other, and when we couldn't, we just *had* to tell the other everything.' She smiles. 'I lived for those notes; for his words spoken from the heart. When he returned from university that last time, we met up in the attic of the house. It was our special place.' She pauses for a moment, lost in the memories. 'One thing led to another, and all of a sudden, I was pregnant.'

She plops an extra sugar cube into her tea and watches it dissolve. 'I was so besotted with Henry that I didn't even stop to think that it might be a bad thing. He'd promised me the world, you see. Or at least, Rosemont Hall. He was always writing how we belonged there together and he wanted to grow old with me there. I bought it, hook, line, and sinker, let me tell you. But there was one tiny little detail that never seemed to get sorted.'

'His father?' I venture.

'His father.' She sniffs.

'Henry had been waffling for weeks – promising to tell his father about us. But each letter he wrote me had another excuse as to why he'd kept quiet. I suspected that he was losing his nerve. And until Henry came of age, Sir George could revoke his inheritance. But it was more than that. Henry adored that old devil, who never gave him the time of day. Henry was like a lapdog – always there to lick his father's boots, no matter how often he got kicked.

'And then the preparations for the party began. I suspected Sir George was up to something – he wrote to Henry as much. Henry thought that the party was the surprise. And then, when the artist turned up, he thought the portrait was the surprise. But I knew – or should have known – otherwise. Because why on earth would Sir George spend every last penny on an extravagant party for the son who was a disappointment from start to finish?'

She purses her lips and stares down at her cup. 'Henry said his father had "plans" for him, but he was too thick to guess what they might be. I guessed that someone was coming to the party that he wanted to impress. Sir George couldn't afford to have regular servants, but he hired some girls from the village to make it look like he did. I got myself taken on as a temporary servant for the party.

'You already know about me and some of the other hired girls trying on the costumes we'd found upstairs. It was great fun pretending we were ladies – and I almost told them my secret – that soon I would be Mrs Henry Windham: the real lady of the house.' She shakes her head.

'Then, when the others went back to work, I tiptoed up the back stairs to the attic. I was still wearing the pink dress I'd tried on – I wanted to surprise Henry by looking like a real Lady of the Manor. Instead, it was me who was in for a surprise.

'I found that our attic had been taken over by an artist – some Spanish chap that Sir George knew from the war. He was there to paint Henry's portrait, though he never did it. I stood and watched him work for a few minutes and was about to leave when he spotted me. He beckoned me inside and started to fuss over how lovely I looked, and how he wanted to sketch me. I was flattered, of course, so I let him. I had no idea that he was going to do a painting of me. All I was hoping was that Henry would come as he'd promised. I twisted his note in my hand until it was practically in shreds. But when I finally did hear footsteps on the stairs, suddenly I felt afraid. I jumped up from the chair and hid behind the door.'

'What did you see?' I coax.

'It was Sir George, not Henry,' she says. 'He looked around him with his demon black eyes like he half-suspected that some-one was watching. The artist took out a canvas and they stood and pored over it together. I remember thinking it odd at the time – the canvas was white and blank – there was no painting on it.'

'A blank canvas?' I lean forward in my chair.

'Yes. But Sir George was examining it as carefully as if it was the Mona Lisa. They spoke in low voices, but I heard Sir George say: "It does look good – I'd never even know it was there. But are you sure it won't be damaged?"

'"Zere will be no damage," the Spanish chap said. "You know I am zee best."'

'What do you think they were they talking about?'

'I've no idea,' she snaps, dropping the bad accent. 'But I knew it was something I shouldn't have overheard. And when Sir George finally left, he looked right at the place where I was hiding. It chilled me to the bone. As soon as his back was turned, I slipped out and ran down the back stairs. I can still feel those dark, demon eyes boring into my back as I went.'

She takes a breath and continues. 'After that, I knew that Sir George was onto us. I'd turn around and there he'd be, watching me. I tried to see Henry, but his father kept him busy, running errands and entertaining guests.

'I knew the game was up for Henry and me the minute Arabella arrived at the house for the party, looking like some kind of pale, fragile, porcelain doll all dressed up in her finest clothing. I served tea to her and her father while Henry and Sir George were closeted up in the study together. She was so frail and simpering – all huge eyes and sharp cheekbones.' She lets out a snort of disgust. 'Her father was singing Henry's praises and talking about how he'd pay for a lavish wedding for them. But the look on her face…' She chuckles. 'It seems like the news came as a shock to her as well.'

'Anyway, I went back downstairs and told the cook that I was ill. I went home to think – I suspected that if Henry's father wanted him to go from lapdog to pedigree stud hound, he'd do it. I was devastated and angry – I wanted to hurt them. I decided that I had to go back for the party – that, whatever happened, Henry would have to look me in the eye.'

'It sounds awful,' I whisper.

'That night, I dressed up in a maid's costume just like Sir George wanted us to. I blended into the background, bringing up the serving trays and filling glasses of champagne. Everyone was decked out to the nines – I've never seen so many sparkling gowns in my life. It was as if the wars had never happened and we weren't in the twentieth century at all.

'Then, in the middle of the dancing, Sir George silenced the musicians and said he had an announcement to make. Henry came forward, leading Arabella by the hand – a mousey little waif in a green silk dress.' She sniffs. 'Sir George announced the engagement. Henry smiled at his bride-to-be. He looked contented – even pleasantly surprised. I knew it was all over.' She shakes her head. 'But I'd come prepared, you see. I'd brought with me every little simpering love note that Henry had ever written to me. I put them on the tray of drinks that I carried into the ballroom. When they made the announcement, I dropped the tray, the notes scattered everywhere.' She chuckles softly. 'It was less than they deserved, but it certainly disrupted the moment.

'A quarter of an hour later, Sir George came down to the kitchens. He grabbed me by the arm and pulled me into the pantry. I still remember the stink of his breath against my face.' She grimaces.

'He had a letter in his hands – the last one that Henry wrote to me. "Whatever you're playing at, it stops now," he said. He took out the gold cigarette lighter that I'd given Henry and lit the edge of the paper. We stood there together watching it burn. Then he dropped it and ground out the flame with his foot.

'"It's rubbish," he said. "Just like you are." Then he thrust a purse into my hand. "Your train leaves tomorrow at 7 a.m.

You'll go to Portsmouth. There's a boat in the afternoon. To New York. You'll be on it."

'"No!" I screamed. "Henry loves me. He went along with your silly party, but he won't marry HER."

'Sir George laughed in my face. He called me a few more nasty names and pushed me. I slipped and fell to the floor. I knew that if I lost the baby, I'd lose everything. I lay there on the ice cold floor, very still.

'"You will be provided for if you leave now. And if you don't..." He didn't need to finish the threat. He slammed the door and left me on the floor, shaking. The last ember went out on the paper and everything was pitch-black.'

'But that's terrible,' I blurt out.

She eyes me like she's pleased that I'm affected, while she no longer is.

'Terrible?' She shakes her head. 'So many things in life are terrible.' She takes a sip of her tea.

'I lay there until I was sure I hadn't lost the baby. Then I changed out of the maid's costume, put on my own clothes, and went home. There was no sign of Henry – he didn't come to try and find me. Most of the guests had left or were leaving. They passed by me as I walked all the way back to the village. That walk is the thing I remember most clearly. The lights of all those fancy cars going past me, but no one stopping to offer me a ride.

'But by the time I got near to the village, there were lights and sirens going the other way – back towards the house. The sky turned an awful shade of deep red. I didn't know at the time, but the East Wing was burning.'

'So you didn't start the fire?'

'Of course not.' She glares at me. 'I was still stupid enough to cling to the hope that I might live at Rosemont Hall. I loved that house. I'd never do anything to harm it.'

'Sorry.'

'I was up all night,' she continues. 'I didn't want to believe that it was all over, and if it was, I didn't want to let Henry off that easily. I wanted to confront him – make him tell me to my face that he no longer loved me and wanted me to go away. But just before dawn, someone knocked on our door. My sister answered. I heard the words: "constable", "fire", and "a few questions". Sir George had stitched me up.'

'It's criminal!' I say.

'It was convenient. There was nothing I could do. I had to think of the baby – I couldn't go to jail for something I didn't do.'

'Of course not. And the lighter that the surveyor found – that was the one you gave Henry?'

'Yes.' She shrugs. 'All those years and suddenly it shows up. Along with you.' She stops talking and stares into her empty tea cup. 'Anyway – that's it. I left.'

Tears of indignation well up in my eyes. She must have felt so lost in those terrible days after the fire: all alone on a slow boat to America, holed up in steerage with a fatherless baby in her belly and grief in her heart. 'I'm so sorry,' I say.

She looks up at me, the steel back in her face. 'The rest is history…' she makes a sweeping gesture with her hand. 'And now, Amy Wood, you know it.' She begins to lever herself out of the chair with her cane. Captain – I'd almost forgotten he was there – jumps to his feet and crouches behind her, growling in his throat.

'But that's not the end of the story, is it, Mrs Bradford?' I say. 'You came back to England, all those years later. Why did you do that?'

With a tetchy sigh, she sits back down in the chair. Captain lies at her feet, eyeing me like I might be lunch.

'I came back because this is where I belong. But I waited too long. Henry was an old man.'

'What happened between the two of you?'

'*She'd* had her claws into him for all those years. Arabella. She hated Rosemont Hall – thought it was too big, too draughty,

332

too empty – the two of them knocking about like old bones. She didn't care if it fell to ruin. It's no wonder that he suffered a stroke.'

'But when you saw him, didn't he mention the letters that he wrote? Did he ask you why you never responded?'

She shakes her head. 'It wasn't like that. By the time I returned, he barely even knew me. I guess...' her bold voice wavers for a second, 'that I must have changed too. I wasn't "Annie" anymore – not the one that he still had in his mind.'

'You were apart for a long time.' I bow my head, thinking how empty and hollow those years must have been.

'Yes,' she muses. 'A lifetime.'

'But he did leave the house to Jack and Flora.'

'And do you think he did that out of the goodness of his heart?' She lets out a brittle laugh.

'No, but...' I hold my breath, recalling Jack's suspicions of blackmail.

'He extracted his price, believe me.'

'And what was that?'

'That Arabella never be told about my daughter, of course. And that I stick around until Arabella died and look after her.'

'So that's why you did it?'

'Can you think of any other reason?'

'Yes.' I smile wistfully. 'Because Rosemont Hall is your home.'

She raises a bristly eyebrow but says nothing.

'You had to come back, didn't you? Despite the terrible thing that happened to you, you came back here. Henry loved you – his letters prove that. He didn't think you set that fire. He wanted you to live with him – at Rosemont Hall. But it couldn't be. Sir George hurt him too. Hurt everyone, from the sounds of it.'

'So?'

'So you braved the humiliation and the upheaval. The thousands of miles and all the years. You did what you had to do in order to come back to Rosemont Hall. Its heart resonates with yours. You can't just let it go.'

'Well it's not my choice, is it?' Her tone is sarcastic, but her eyes are shiny and moist.

'I think you need to tell them your story – Jack, Flora, your daughter. You deserve to have them know the truth, and they deserve to know. Yours was the great love story of Rosemont Hall.'

'They're not interested,' she says. 'It's ancient history.'

'It's not ancient history. It's *their* history! The house is part of you, and it's part of them too. Like it or not.'

She stands up, leaning against her cane, her hand quavering with the strain of her years. Captain gets to his shaggy feet, standing loyally by her side.

'You're a dark horse, Amy Wood, that's for sure. You clearly read too many novels, but your heart is in the right place.' She sighs. 'But for me, it was never about the house. It was Henry that I loved – I was no gold-digger; or home-wrecker neither. And in the end, it was no great love story, was it? Henry made his choice all those years ago. All I did was make sure that he did the right thing and left the house to his true heirs – the flesh and blood that he never knew he had.'

'I understand.'

'And in return, it seemed right that I respected his last wish that someone take care of Arabella. By then, we were just two old ladies. We drank sherry, played backgammon, watched *Countdown*, and saw who could do the crossword the quickest. What came before hardly mattered. We were content enough together.' A tear dribbles down her cheek. 'I miss her.'

I reach out and give her gnarled hand a squeeze.

Smiling sadly, she squeezes my hand back and then withdraws. 'I said much the same to Jack when he came to give me the letters. He spouted some drivel about how he was finally starting to understand how I felt about Rosemont Hall.'

'Jack said that?'

'He never would have realised it on his own. I think someone opened his eyes.' She chuckles. 'Now, I wonder who that could have been?'

Her blue eyes meet mine. She knows about Jack and me.

'Um, right,' I mutter, my cheeks glowing pink.

'I told him that I'm settling in to the cottage, thank you very much. I have a comfortable chair in front of a cosy inglenook fireplace; a reading lamp with a green glass shade; a brass bed with a handmade quilt; and an Aga that actually works.'

'It sounds lovely.'

'And she has a TV with Sky,' she adds proudly.

'Great.' I smile.

'Though... I can hear Gwen snoring through the wall...'

'Oh – well, here...' I dig into my handbag and find a new box of earplugs I bought. I set it on the table in front of her. She looks down at it warily, then picks up the box and puts it in the pocket of her bulky cardigan.

'Thanks,' she says. 'Why don't you stop by for a cuppa sometime?' As soon as the words are out of her mouth, she looks surprised she said them.

'Okay,' I say. 'I'd like that.'

'I can always use someone handy with a dust rag to help reach the high shelves.'

'Sure!' I grin.

She turns to leave, manoeuvring herself around the bits of paper on the floor.

'And what about the letters?' I say.

'Keep them,' she says with a wave of her hand. 'Shove them in an attic, burn them, or read them out at my funeral. Or use them to write your history book. Send me a copy when it's done – if I'm still alive.'

'But don't you want to know how Henry felt about you in his own words?'

Her toothless laugh seems almost sad. 'Henry Windham is dead and gone. And the house, well...'

She shrugs. The huge dog slinks behind her as she clomps across the room and out the door. Her words hang in the air like restless spirits.

And the house, well...

Part Five

There is a spot, 'mid barren hills,
Where winter howls, and driving rain;
But if the dreary tempest chills,
There is a light that warms again.

The house is old, the trees are bare,
Moonless above bends twilight's dome;
But what on earth is half so dear–
So longed for–as the hearth of home?

> ~ Emily Brontë – 'A little while a little while'

Forty-Two

I feel once again like I've failed at something important, though, in truth, I don't know what more I could have done. I pick up the scattered letters and put them back in the bag. Mrs Bradford's story has shaken me to the core. It's tragic that 'the girl in the pink dress' lived her whole life regretting a failed romance. Is it my fate to do the same?

After paying the bill, I say goodbye to Gwen and leave the café. The next day I go to work, and the day after that. With each day that goes by, I feel like I'm holding my breath.

A few days after my chat with Mrs Bradford, I'm putting concealer under my eyes in the disabled loo after a sleepless night, when my phone rings.

It's Jack. It's the first time he's called me since he left England to return to the States. Just hearing his: 'Hello? Amy, is that you?' on the other end of the line turns my knees to jelly. But the connection isn't great, and he sounds as far away as he actually is.

'Amy,' he says, 'I'm sorry I didn't call you sooner. I wanted to have some news first.'

'Yes?' I breathe in sharply.

'You won't believe this. Or actually… what am I saying? You of all people *will* believe it.'

'Can you speak a bit louder?' I cup my hand around the earpiece.

'You were right! Damn it, Amy, it's a Rembrandt. An honest-to-God real Rembrandt. Called "Orientale".' Jack pronounces it 'Ori-ENT-al. 'The expert has been working round the clock. He's done all kinds of tests and research on its provenance. There's absolutely no doubt.'

I hold the phone away from my ear. I wait for the flood of happy vindication to sweep over me.

It doesn't come. Instead, I feel an intense regret, like Rosemont Hall has finally given up its last secret. The final thread in the tapestry is complete. But the end is already starting to unravel.

'It's amazing, Amy...' Jack is saying. 'You really did find buried treasure – a lost Rembrandt! And to think I doubted you. We haven't known each other long, but already, I've learned that when you say something...'

I love you! The words scream out inside my head as the thing I want to say but I can't. If I've learned one thing from Mrs Bradford, it's that words – whether written on paper or said over a telephone line – don't make a difference when it truly matters. 'Anyway,' he continues, 'so I need to talk to Gran – see what she wants to do with it. It needs a bit of cleaning and restoration, but once that's done it will be worth a lot of money.'

'That's wonderful, Jack,' I hear myself saying. 'I'm so pleased that it's been found. It would have been so tragic if a great work of art really was lost.'

Tell him! You have to tell him.

'I'm going to suggest that she donate it to a museum,' Jack continues. 'Maybe the Tate Britain or the National Gallery. It should be given back to the public. Don't you agree?'

'Yes.' I swallow hard. 'I do. That's surely the best result. Then everyone can enjoy it.' My voice catches.

There's a pause. 'Amy? Are you all right? You sound a bit strange.'

'No, Jack, I'm just overwhelmed by the news. And... everything really.'

'Okay,' he says, giving the tiniest of hesitations. 'Anyway, I'm just on my way to a meeting now, but I wanted you to be the first to know. You're incorrigible, Amy Wood. Incorrigible, and amazing.'

'So are you, Jack,' I manage. 'And thanks for telling me...'

'Amy?'

I press the hang-up button with my thumb as the tears begin to roll fast and furiously down my face. 'I love you,' I whisper into the dead line.

Forty-Three

I half-expect something miraculous to happen – like a curse has somehow been lifted from Rosemont Hall. Mrs Bradford has found out the truth about her lost love, a valuable painting has been recovered. After our conversation, Jack emailed me with the name of the expert in case I wanted to speak to him myself. I make a note of the number, but I don't call. Even days later, I still find it difficult to make sense of everything that's happened – or, in reality, not happened.

Because Rosemont Hall is still going to be sold to Hexagon. Jack still lives in America. I haven't told him how I feel because what's the point? I'm still living in my parents' bungalow, working at *Tetherington Bowen Knowles,* hardly any closer to my original goal of getting my own flat, or going back to teaching. All I have to show for my experience is the memories – and the story that I've uncovered.

Which is why one evening after work, I begin writing everything down. I start with the strange premonition I had from the first phone call with Mr Kendall about Rosemont Hall. That somehow, my life would never be the same.

I go on to describe my first impressions of the house: its beauty and grandeur, my sadness that it's become a white (well, grey and decaying) elephant, and most of all, the strange connection I've felt with the house and its history.

I also begin writing Maryanne Bradford's story down, as

much word for word as I can. I transcribe the letters I found and put everything in order so that the story they tell – the schemes, the deceptions and misconceptions, and ultimately the hopes that were never realised – are preserved. I couldn't save Rosemont Hall, but I can make sure that the truth comes to light. Surely Mrs Bradford – and the other unsung, undocumented women of Rosemont Hall – deserves no less.

Mum comes in from time to time bringing me cups of tea and plates of biscuits. She doesn't say anything, but I can tell she's happy to see me in my element – writing – rather than working at a stodgy old estate agency. I keep writing late into the night, and by the time my head starts to droop over the keyboard, I've got thousands of words. I go to bed feeling tired, and far from happy, but at least I'm moving forward.

The next day at work, and the next, I keep waiting. Something is going to happen – something...

Three things do happen, but not what I was expecting.

First, I get an instruction from a new client to market and sell another Bristol Docks flat. This one is a quarter the size of the penthouse, but when I visit it, it has the same feeling of light and space, plus a great view of the USS Great Britain. I return to the office feeling upbeat. The flat will surely sell itself, and maybe even prompt a bidding war.

I phone the photographer to arrange the photos for the particulars. No sooner have I hung up the phone when it rings again. It's Mary Blundell. She tells me that Fred has been released (apparently, the Picasso was a forgery, so his sentence was reduced on appeal from art smuggling to failure to declare an item at customs). They're in the market for a property. Their budget is now a modest £850,000 (the Picasso forgery was clearly worth *something*) – but that's close to the asking price of the new Bristol flat. Within two hours, they've 'found' some extra cash, made an offer of the asking price, and the vendor has accepted. I'm over the moon! It just goes to show that there's a right home for everyone, and I'm proud that I've helped them find it.

Even better, I calculate that once the Blundells complete on the flat and I'm paid my commission, I'll have enough money for a down payment on a flat. A modest flat, small, and quaint, maybe with a few original features like a ceiling rose and a fireplace.

Just as I've started to check through the files to see if there's anything like that coming to market, the second thing happens.

A call comes in on my mobile from a number I don't recognise. It's the headmaster of the school in Edinburgh. They want to interview me for the teaching position. With everything that's happened, I barely even remember sending in my application.

'Your former advisor says that you'd fit in perfectly at our institution,' the man says. 'That you're bright, and funny, and that you live every moment of the books that you teach.'

'Um, thanks...' I say, noting how different this conversation is from the one I had that fateful first day with Mr Bowen-Knowles. 'I never wanted to leave teaching, but... I assume you know about "the situation"?'

'You mean that you got sacked?' He gives a hearty laugh. 'I like a lass who stands up for her principles. Not that I approve of revenge via mobile phone—'

'It was more like poor aim.' Finally, after all these months since it happened, I manage a chuckle.

'Anyway, we like strong women role models here. When can you come up for a proper interview?'

We settle on a day and time, and I thank the headmaster for considering me for the position. By the time I hang up the phone, my mind is awash with possibilities. I could have another new start, this time in cold, grey, historic Edinburgh. I could rent a flat in an elegant row house made of soot-stained stone, sew tartan curtains for the windows, buy some antique furniture off eBay and take a course in restoration. I could leave behind the world of 'flexible accommodation', 'prime development opportunities' and 'exclusive recreational facilities' and return to my true calling. I'd surround myself with like-minded colleagues with lilting accents, and I'd go back to reading, teaching, and 'living' the books I love. I'd work hard at being a positive role model for my students, taking it upon myself to ensure that each "lass" I teach can "stand up for her principles". In my spare time, I'd hold little soirees for my new friends on Burns Night and Hogmanay. Eventually, maybe I'd meet someone.

Meet someone. That prospect makes me feel like I've severed a limb and am slowly bleeding to death.

As a distraction, I login to my personal email and look for the original message with the Edinburgh job description. Surely, I owe it to myself to give it a shot. At the very least, being back in academia should help me get my book published... that is assuming I can muster the will to finish it. Idly I skim over the new messages, deleting the huge amount of spam that has accumulated since I last checked the account. And near the bottom I see a message that's like a chill wind from the past. The subject is 'Hey Stranger' and it's from Simon.

My hand on the mouse hovers the cursor between 'open' and 'delete'. I do a quick catalogue of my feelings, and discover that I feel nothing. Whatever my present woes may be, Simon no longer figures. I open the message:

Hey Amy, how are things? I hope you're well. I just wanted to say I'm sorry about what happened. For you to find out about Ashley and me the way you did was really not on. You'll be interested to know that we didn't buy that flat – it was outrageously small for the price don't you think? In fact, Ashley's gone back to America – apparently her 'Daddy' found some Ivy boy for her to marry – his father owns a hotel chain or something, so she's off to become the next Mrs Bigwig, spending her weekends at the tennis club or on the golf course, or whatever people like that do. I don't mind that she's gone, but I do miss you, babe. You were a bit mad, but in a good way. We had some good times, didn't we? Anyway, I'd love to hear from you. Maybe we can have dinner or a drink sometime – and then see what happens? My new email address is below.

Luv and kisses,

Simon

Instead of counting up the number of things about the email that infuriate me, I calmly hit delete. Simon's a shit, and I'm well shot of him. In a strange way, I can see why Mrs Bradford didn't want to read the letters from Henry. As they say, you can't step twice into the same river. Some things are well and truly in the past.

And other, more important things are quickly slipping away from me in that direction. Just as I'm about to shut down my computer for the day, a reminder pops up on the screen. Tomorrow morning I'm scheduled to go to Mr Kendall's office. Hexagon is signing the paperwork to purchase Rosemont Hall. Despite my best efforts, there's been no miracle, no fairy-tale ending.

This, after all, is real life.

Forty-Four

I arrive at Mr Kendall's office at a quarter past ten the next morning. The completion meeting is scheduled for half past. Mr Kendall's assistant, Colleen, gives me a kindly smile. 'He'll be right with you,' she says. 'He's just finishing up a call.'

I sit on the edge of the leather sofa. Idly I flip through the stack of *Country Life* magazines, but I'm not in the mood to read about rich people and their posh houses. Where are Mr Netelbaum and his henchmen? Shouldn't they be here by now? I check my watch. They're late.

The main door opens. My stomach plummets. But it's only the postman. He chats with Colleen and hands her a stack of letters. My eyes are glued to the door. I want to get this over with so I can leave. Where the hell are the men from Hexagon?

I drum my fingers on my knee, then take out my mobile and check for messages. There are none.

I pull out a pen and a small notebook from my handbag while I'm waiting. I keep meaning to start a 'life plan' now that I'm once again back to square one – and it seems like now might be as good a time as any to put pen to paper.

The blank page stares back at me. I start trying to jot down a few bullet points:

- finish book on Rosemont Hall
- look for flats in Edinburgh
- apply for mortgage

- nail Edinburgh interview
- join internet dating site

One by one I cross out the things I've written. In truth, I'm feeling numb. I still have some grieving to do and I'm not quite ready to pull myself together just yet or face another 'new future'—

The door opens. A small army of men in dark suits enters the office. Every muscle in my body tenses up. Nigel Netelbaum runs a hand through his greased-back ginger hair and gives me a nod. 'Nice to see you again, Amy,' he says. 'Let me introduce you to my colleagues.'

But I'm already staring at one of his 'colleagues'. The sandy hair and boyish grin that once seemed endearing, but now seem more like a scary clown.

David Waters.

'Hello Amy.' He has the nerve to wink – at me, but also towards the group. He's obviously told all of his new buddies about our past 'association'.

'Mr Waters,' I say through my teeth. 'I see you've got a new job.'

'Yes,' he says smugly. 'I'm working full-time for Hexagon now. The design for the new golf course and clubhouse at Rosemont Hall is almost done. It's going to be all glass and mod cons – with a Georgian facade. Everything behind the front is going to go.' He smiles like he's thrusting a knife into me. Which he is. 'I was going to ring and tell you,' he adds, 'but somehow, it didn't *come up*.'

I give him a pained smile and force myself to make the further round of introductions. There are several names that I don't catch – but I think there's a CFO, a COO, and a couple of directors. Two of them have golf club ties. After the round of handshakes and exchange of business cards, I have the overwhelming urge to douse my hands with sanitiser.

'Hello, everyone – sorry to keep you waiting.' Mr Kendall appears in the doorway of his office. For the first time since we've met, he seems a little flustered. I know that he's also sad to be seeing the back of Rosemont Hall. Though, when Hexagon completes, presumably, he'll be paid. That might go a long way to making him feel better. Lucky him. I force myself to walk the few metres across the floor to the conference room.

'Please help yourselves to coffee and biscuits.' He gestures to the conference table. It's empty except for the coffee service and food. Where is the paperwork? I want to get this over with and leave as soon as possible; get on with my scribbled-out life plan.

The others help themselves. David Waters holds out the plate to me, still grinning wolfishly.

'No thanks.' I look away.

Mr Kendall hovers by the door. He's making me nervous – why isn't he sitting down with the rest of us?

He clears his throat. 'Thank you for coming, gentleman – and Ms Wood.' His glasses have slipped down his nose and he pushes them up.

'Of course,' Mr Netelbaum interrupts. His voice sounds unnaturally loud. 'We're all very excited about this project. Thanks to David here, the planners are more or less on board for our design, and we should be up and running in a few months.' He laughs.

'And if the whole thing falls down first, we won't have to bother,' David adds.

He looks at me.

I glare at him.

'Yes, well, umm...' Mr Kendall clears his throat again. 'I'm afraid there's been a slight last-minute hiccup.'

'Pardon?' Mr Netelbaum frowns. 'What's that?'

Mr Kendall begins to pace. 'Well, you see, one of the heirs has got cold feet.'

'Cold feet? What's that supposed to mean.' Mr Netelbaum suddenly morphs into the wolf at the door.

'About selling. To you – Hexagon – that is.'

I grip the edge of the table.

'What?' Mr Netelbaum slams his coffee cup down on the table. 'What do you mean – *to us*? We've been in discussions with Jack Faraday. Where the hell is he? Get him on the horn.' His minions scramble for their BlackBerries.

'Mr Jack is sorry he can't be here today,' Mr Kendall says. 'Believe me, he would have liked to be. But the truth is, we've received a higher offer. A better offer.'

I stifle a gasp.

'That's outrageous,' Mr Netelbaum stands up angrily. 'We're signing the paperwork now. The funds are all approved and ready to be wired. They can't just back out.'

'Actually they can,' I cut in. 'No contracts have been exchanged yet, so technically, the heirs can sell to whomever they like. I'd say you were gazumped.'

Mr Kendall nods sheepishly.

'You!' Nigel Netelbaum turns the force of his anger at me. 'You've been playing us all along. Don't think I don't know it. David here – he's told us all about you. That you were opposed to us from the start. And how you were even willing to take your clothes off to get him onside. You're nothing but a back-stabbing little tart.'

'How dare you—'

'Gentleman, that's really not called for,' Mr Kendall says, calmer now. 'I agree it's an unfortunate situation, but in the end, they just didn't feel that your plans were the right outcome for Rosemont Hall. The house has been part of their family history for 200 years, and they've decided that they *do* care what happens to it.'

I feel like I'm floating above the table.

'So I think we're done here,' Mr Kendall says. 'My secretary will validate your parking on the way out.'

'Take the house and shove it up your ass,' Mr Netelbaum practically spits. 'Come on,' he gestures to his colleagues. 'We've wasted enough time here.'

The army of suits rises en masse and storms out. David Waters' face is red and he doesn't look at me.

'Have a nice day,' I say brightly. 'Good to see you again, David.'

The group goes back out to the waiting area. A door slams.

Mr Kendall and I both let out a breath. He sits down opposite me, takes out a handkerchief, and wipes his brow.

'Sorry about that,' he says. 'It really was a last-minute thing. I didn't have time to cancel with them or tell you.'

'But Mr Kendall, I don't understand. Was that all true? Has there really been a higher offer?' My elation turns to silent panic as I realise that things are now even more unsettled. What will the house become now? Flats? A conference centre? Nothing?

He sits back and steeples his fingers. 'Everything I said was true. The offer was confirmed yesterday. I've been up most of the night preparing the new paperwork. It's one of your clients, as it turns out.'

'One of *my* clients?' I lean forward. 'What are you talking about?'

'Well, maybe not a client exactly, but the buyer is insisting that any commission goes to you.'

'Commission? Me?'

'It was you that convinced them to make the purchase. Here, have a look.'

He stands up and goes over to the credenza at the side of the room. He takes out a thick stack of papers and sets them in front of me. He points to the cover page. 'This is the charter of the new Rosemont Hall Charitable Trust,' he says. 'Not all the paperwork has been filed, of course, but once the financing is confirmed, all that will be left is to dot the i's and cross the t's.'

'But… I don't understand.'

'You sure you don't want something to drink?' He opens another door of the credenza and takes out a decanter of brandy and two glasses. He pours and hands me one. I don't refuse.

'Now, I'll explain…'

And my eyes widen as he talks about the new charitable trust that is buying the house. 'So you see,' he says to sum up, 'the trust benefactor decided that the house should be saved. It will be restored and opened to the public. That's the idea anyway. There are still lots of details to be sorted out in the final business plan – the idea is to make the house self-supporting once it's restored. Tea rooms, adventure play-grounds, wedding and film bookings – whatever. As for the details, that's where you come in.'

'Me?'

'Of course.' He looks surprised that I'm so dim. 'Didn't Jack mention any of this?'

'Jack?'

The truth dawns like a desert morning.

'Well, of course. Maryanne Bradford is the principal bene-factor. She'll be funding the purchase of Flora's share of the house with the proceeds from the Rembrandt when it's sold at auction next month. Jack has decided that he will be keeping his share. He will be the main trustee in charge of operations.'

'Keeping his share?' My heart feels like it's going to catapult out of my body. Jack Faraday is keeping Rosemont Hall. Jack Faraday and Mrs Bradford – who will be able to buy her share of the house because of the 'buried treasure' that I found. Jack Faraday wants me involved with sorting out the details. Jack Faraday wants *me*.

'Amy?' he says. I realise that my mouth is gaping open like a zombie. 'Would you like another brandy?'

'Yes please – I think I need it.'

Forty-Five

Two brandies later, I leave Mr Kendall's office in a minicab. I'm tipsy, overwhelmed and still trying to make sense of all the emotions swirling around in my head. The world looks different as we whizz by buildings and people. It's bright and clear; full of life and colour. Full of potential for a future I couldn't even have dreamed of. Enthusiasm is fizzing in my veins as I ponder the things that Mr Kendall has told me.

Apparently, Jack and his grandmother envision me taking charge of the trust and renovating the house. Then it will open to the public. I'll be a paid employee of the trust – full or part-time, depending on what I choose (or – if I choose to accept, as he put it). But clearly, Mr Kendall doesn't know of our past 'association', so I can't ask the real questions that are burning in my mind: does Jack intend to live over here, at least some of the time, and if so, does that mean he wants something more than the few nights we've had together? And why the hell didn't Jack tell me all this himself (I try to summon the appropriate level of indignation on this point, but frankly, I'm feeling way too happy to do so)? There's clearly a lot I need to think about, and a lot of details to be ironed out, but for now, none of that matters. The pieces are falling into place – I'm on the verge of a future I could hardly dare to dream of.

I've saved Rosemont Hall!

Just as the taxi pulls up in front of my parents' house, my

mobile rings. I hand a wad of cash to the driver and pull the phone out just in time.

It's him. My hand trembles with excitement as I hit the button. 'Hello!' I say, breathlessly.

'Amy,' he says in that lovely deep voice of his, 'how are you? I hear there was quite a bust-up at the lawyer's office over my little surprise.'

'Yes, there was!' I beam. 'And everyone was certainly surprised. But how—? Why—?'

'Well, I'll fill you in on everything when I see you next. I'm going to arrange a trip for spring break and then the whole summer – we could go on that tour we talked about. But for now, let's just say, Gran and I had a long heart-to-heart. She told me her whole story – fascinating stuff, and heart-breaking too – just like something out of one of your books.' I can sense his grin. 'But ancient grudges and broken hearts aside, she says that the place is her home. She asked me not to sell up.'

'Good for her!' I can't help saying.

'Yeah. I mean, she's happy living in the cottage with Gwen. But she still wants to be able to visit the house. Talk to it, clean it, wander through it – whatever the heck she does there.'

'I can understand that.'

'Yeah,' he laughs. 'I'm sure you can.'

'Anyway, for the first time, we were actually having a conversation about what she thought and felt, not what *I* should feel or do. It worked wonders. I think we're well on the way to understanding each other much better. And that's all down to you, Amy.'

'I'm just so shocked – in a good way, I mean...'

He laughs. 'She wanted me to give you a message. Something about how "maybe the great love story of Rosemont Hall is yet to come". Does that mean anything to you?'

'Umm, yeah. Thanks.' I shiver inside with delight.

'Good, well, I guess it's one more anecdote to add to your book. How's that going, by the way?'

I step out of the cab, grinning from ear to ear. 'Great,' I say. 'It's going great. You know, Jack, I've discovered that writing it is a lot easier now that I've stopped worrying about the ending.'

Epilogue

One year later...

The grand opening of Rosemont Hall is held on a Saturday in late May. The day before, the last of the scaffolding comes down, the caterers set up in the brand new kitchen, and a huge marquee is erected on the south lawn to house refreshments for the hundreds of people – locals, press, bloggers, and lovers of old houses from all over the country – that are expected to be there.

I spend the day in a flurry of activity: chasing florists; confirming directions; stapling books of tickets; making sure there are signs pointing the way to loos and parking, dusting for the tenth time the portrait of the girl in a pink dress. She's been cleaned and restored, and still hangs in pride of place above the staircase landing. But she's alone now. The Rembrandt she hid for so many years has been auctioned – and luckily, it was bought by Tate Britain. So now it too will be on view in London for the whole world to appreciate.

I stay at the house late into the night trying to put into order the final wave of chaos. I want everything to be perfect – just the way all of the fated ancestors would have wanted.

By the time I return to my parents' bungalow (I've been far too busy to look for my own flat), I'm tired and elated, nervous and happy, all at the same time. The past year has flown by, and it's been downright exhausting – project-managing builders, restorers, craftspeople, painters, plasterers, gardeners, English Heritage, the local council – not to mention a number of *very distracting* visits from Jack.

The house has been fixed up top to bottom, inside and outside. It will take a few more seasons for the garden to be back to its best, and a few of my grander ideas like the adventure playground, the organic tea-room and farm shop aren't quite off the ground just yet. And while the East Wing has been shored up and stabilised, it will be a while before the restoration of the ballroom begins.

Nonetheless, I feel proud of what I've achieved so far. Restoring Rosemont Hall has been the most exciting adventure of my life so far, and I've thrown myself into learning everything from the ground up. I'm looking forward to the next phase – running tours, writing leaflets, teaching people about the house and its history – helping to create *new* memories and history here. And while sometimes amid the dust and chaos of construction, I've missed the staid and well-settled world of teaching literature, now, when I walk through the beautifully proportioned and stately rooms of Rosemont Hall, I know I've chosen the right vocation.

And when Jack phones me from the airport and asks me if everything is ready for the grand opening, I can honestly say that barring any surprises, it is.

The morning of the grand opening dawns bright and crisp. Dad's wisteria casts a purple glow outside my bedroom window and all the birds in the garden are chattering that summer's almost here. I dress in old clothes in case I have to muck in with any last-minute jobs, but I have a new dress (red silk sheath with matching heels and fancy hat) in a plastic bag to take with me. Mum cooks me breakfast and I give her and Dad a kiss (and a 15-minute fully interactional walk-through of the map to Rosemont Hall – my dad is rubbish with directions), and then I'm off.

Even a year on, when I drive through the freshly painted iron gates and glimpse Rosemont Hall from a distance, I still get the same electric thrill as the first time I saw it. Only now, instead of a sad and forbidding edifice riddled with dry rot and unhappy secrets, to me it seems transformed – just as I am. The brickwork on the outside has been thoroughly cleaned and repointed, and the nymphs now frolic in a playful spray of water in the fountain. The hedges have been trimmed, and the beds replanted with roses and bee-friendly flowers.

I park at the edge of the widened gravel area – the temporary parking area until the new car park is completed out of view of the house. I get out of the car and savour the silence, the sunlight, and the feeling that I'm in the place where I belong.

I enter the house and spend the next few hours handling some last-minute mini-disasters that require my attention: scones from the 'Cup o' Comfort' that didn't rise; two temp waitresses who haven't turned up; a power failure in the posh Portaloos; a loose paving stone by the front door.

I deal with each of them in turn, and manage to sneak off and change into my dress just before the camera crew of *Country House Rescue* arrives. Over the last year, the new presenter has helped me perfect the business plan for Rosemont Hall and the show has generated nationwide publicity for the newest local tourist attraction.

I leave the crew to set up and give the volunteer guides a final briefing. I talk them through the draft historical guide to the house that I've written, and show them the glass cases where the Windham letters and the artist's sketchbook have been preserved. When that's finished, I relax for a few minutes and sample all the food in the marquee.

It's not long before the office staff of *Tetherington Bowen Knowles* (minus Claire, but including Mrs Harvey's niece, Sally, with a rosy-faced toddler tucked in a pram) arrives. Alistair Bowen-Knowles greets me with a handshake and a brief glance down at my chest. Jonathan sniffs and commandeers a roving waitress with a tray full of champagne flutes. As he passes them around, I reflect for a moment on how much I owe to my beloved former work colleagues. Without their indifference to that long-ago telephone call from Mr Kendall, I wouldn't be where I am today. When everyone has a glass, I raise mine and propose a toast: 'Here's to estate agents,' I say, 'and to finding our clients the perfect homes.'

'Hear hear.'

We clink our glasses together and I feel a little twinge of nostalgia. But it only lasts a second. Alistair Bowen-Knowles, Jonathan, and Patricia all are off to schmooze some of my former clients that have come for the occasion: Ronan and Crystal (the latter resplendent in a hot pink mini-dress and matching fishnets); Mr Patel; Mary and Fred Blundell. The band starts playing, and more and more people arrive: the Wakefields (who have found a lovely little cottage only about a mile away); and then, my parents. Mum gushes to anyone who will listen about how the restoration of Rosemont Hall is all down to me.

'Thanks, Mum, but really, it wasn't just me,' I say. 'Lots of people helped out.'

'Nonsense,' she says. 'Credit where credit is due. And make sure that boyfriend of yours takes you out for a nice dinner later.' She winks at Dad. 'We were hoping to have the bungalow to ourselves for tonight.'

'Oh, I'll definitely be *very* late,' I say, hiding a shudder. Now that the renovations are over, I really need to get back to searching for a flat...

A little later, Claire arrives with Raj and her son in tow. 'Well, well...' she gives me a hug, 'I'm starting to see why you fell for this place. It really is quite something.'

I hand her a glass of champagne. 'It is,' I say, smiling broadly.

'And how are you coming on with the book?' During the

last year, Claire has indulged me by reading some of my draft chapters. Her honest, no-holds barred, Earth-to-Amy comments have sometimes stung a little, but I've come to accept that – just occasionally – I need help getting my head out of the clouds.

'It's good – I think. I sent it off to three agents last week. Fingers crossed and all that.'

Rolling her eyes, she gives me a quick hug. 'I'm sure it's better than good, Amy. Remember, you just have to believe it here.' She taps her chest. 'You deserve good things.'

'Thanks Claire, but there is one important thing missing.' I make a point of checking my watch. Everything seems to be going to plan, but secretly, I'm worried. Jack's flight was due to arrive at Heathrow at 6:55 a.m. It's nearly 2 p.m. and there's still no sign of him.

'You mean the dashing hero?' Claire shrugs. 'I wouldn't worry. It's his house – he's sure to be here.'

I don't bother to correct her – the house belongs to the trust, and to all the people of this fine land. Jack Faraday, however, still has a right to live here under the charter documents, and a suite of as yet unrestored rooms on the first floor has been allocated to him. Mrs Bradford also has the right to a room in the house, but so far, she's decided to stay on with Gwen. I visit her at least once a week for a 'cuppa' (and to dust the high shelves), and she comes and goes from the main house as she pleases. She's been teaching me how to bake scones and also how to sew cushions and curtains. She's also an invaluable source of information about how the house looked back in the day. Sure, she talks to herself, and sometimes has two-sided arguments with Arabella; she's tried to run more than one workman off the project; and Captain, her humongous St Bernard, just adores sleeping in the canopy bed on the first floor, rumpling the blankets and chewing old books (in fact, he was the culprit all along). But those things aside, I think we've earned the right to call each other friends. And who knows...

I'm keeping my fingers crossed that, someday, we might even be *family*.

As I'm dealing with a minor crisis of a spilled glass of red wine on a freshly polished parquet floor, I spot her hovering around the bar with Captain slobbering at her feet. She's cackling to the bartender, who keeps refilling her glass with an amber colour liquid. Although it's not on the bar menu, I'm pretty sure it's whisky.

She catches my eye and waves her cane at me. 'Amy Wood,' she half-shrieks. 'Poking your nose into anything and everything, as usual, I see.' Her smile is crooked but warm. 'Sit down, have a drink. Enjoy yourself!'

'Thanks.' I take the drink she hands me and we clink glasses. But in truth, I'm too on edge to relax or enjoy myself. Jack still hasn't arrived. It's increasingly difficult to keep smiling and making small talk. The band is playing swing tunes and people are dancing. One or two guests begin to leave.

'Now off with you,' she says. 'And keep your chin up. If a thing is meant to be, then it will be.' She gives my hand a squeeze and turns back to the bartender. I weave my way through the crowd, hoping, by some miracle, what's 'meant to be' is that I'll spot Jack. I don't. Instead, I see Mr Kendall. He waves at me with the programme of events in his hand and I walk over to him.

'It's amazing what you've done here, Amy,' he says, beaming. 'You've saved the place single-handedly. It's going to be a real success now, I can tell.'

'Not single-handedly.' I blush. 'Jack and Mrs Bradford's money helped a lot.'

'Yes, but it took more than money. It took the right person – someone to perform a genuine labour of love. From the start, it's like you belonged here, just as much as any marble floor or fancy fireplace. You're a proud feature of the house, Amy.' He smiles. 'And certainly... original.'

'Well—' I grab a glass of champagne (only my second of the day) from a tray, 'thanks a lot for saying that. I just wish—'

Maybe the bubbly goes down the wrong way, or maybe the emotions of the day have finally taken their toll. But suddenly, I'm sputtering and fighting back tears.

'What?' Mr Kendall looks concerned.

'I just wish Jack were here. He was supposed to be here at noon. I don't know what happened.'

'Ah,' Mr Kendall says. 'Jack.' He sighs.

'What? Is something the matter?'

'Well, you know Jack...' he raises an eyebrow, '—he's always full of surprises.'

Something in his manner sets off a cascade of panic in my chest. 'You mean he's not coming?' I can barely swallow, but somehow manage to drink down the glass of champagne. 'All this— and he's not coming?'

Mr Kendall shakes his head. 'I believe he was detained. That's all I know. But anyway, you've still got to attend to the business at hand.' He points to something on the programme of events. 'It's 2 p.m. According to this, it's time for you to give your speech.'

He takes me by the arm and steers me up towards the podium. He's right – it's my job to get up on stage and thank everyone for coming, but I just can't do it – not right this second. I—

It's too late. The band stops playing and the dance floor begins to clear. I'm standing there at the edge of a vast space with Mr Kendall at my arm.

'No,' I whisper, 'I need a minute.'

Mr Kendall squeezes my arm. 'Come on Amy, this is your moment.'

I know he's right. I step forward and tap the microphone.

'Ladies and gentlemen,' I say. Everyone looks up at me and my nerves vanish. I feel a warm flush of pride, knowing that I belong up here. *I can do this.*

'I'd like to welcome you all to the grand opening of Rosemont Hall and thank you so much for coming today.' I scan the faces of friends and strangers alike, and can't keep from smiling. 'For those of you who don't know the whole story, let me just say that a little over a year ago, Rosemont Hall was a house in peril – no offense to any golfers in the room.'

I enjoy the laughter that filters through the crowd.

'But after a lot of hard work, put in by a number of dedicated people, I honestly think that we've achieved the best possible result for this national treasure.'

My estate agent friends give a little cheer. And then suddenly, my mind goes blank. Jack should be here. The next part of my prepared speech is about him.

'And, umm... anyway, if I tried to thank everyone that made today possible, we wouldn't have time for any more drinking or dancing,' I say. 'But rest assured, each and every one of you are playing your part in the ongoing story of Rosemont Hall. Especially...' my voice falters. I sense Mr Kendall take a step closer to my side for moral support—

And at that moment, the door flaps at the back of the marquee part and Jack steps through. His smile is devastating as Mr Kendall gestures him to the front.

And then he's there – at my side. My knees go weak with joy.

'I don't want to steal your thunder,' he whispers in my ear. 'But I'd like to say a few words. Is that okay?'

I nod, my hand trembling as I pass him the microphone.

He gives it a tap and then begins to speak. 'For those of you who don't know me, I'm Jack Faraday. While some people may say I've got no right to be here...' he winks at his grandmother, Mrs Bradford, who downs a shot of whisky and clacks her dentures in response, '... sometimes, things turn out a little differently than one might expect.'

There's a smattering of laughter and murmuring in the crowd.

'A year ago, I would have done just about anything to get

shot of this place. To me it was a decaying white elephant on the wrong side of the Atlantic from everything I knew. Whether it became a golf course or just crumbled to dust was all the same to me. But then, like Saul on the road to Damascus, someone opened my eyes. Someone with a passion for history and heritage, who was willing to fight for the things that matter. Someone who cares not just about houses, but about people too. Someone who is the heart and vision behind the new Rosemont Hall. Ladies and gentlemen, please raise your glasses to Amy Wood.'

'Hear hear!' There's a general hum in the crowd and the clinking of glasses. Jack takes my hand and smiles at me. I feel warm all over – a cosy sort of warmth like my heart has curled up in front of a fireplace. But just then, Jack lets go of my hand and taps the microphone again. The crowd goes quiet.

'But there's one additional piece of business that I'd like to settle while Amy's up here in front of you all,' he says.

I look at him quizzically. We've both said our pieces, and I'm anxious to leave the stage.

'When I first met Amy, she thought I was going to tear Rosemont Hall apart brick by brick – and she hated me for it.' He winks at me and my insides liquefy.

'In fact, ever since then, I've given her a lot of reasons to be annoyed with me, infuriated, and generally pissed off,' he grins, '– not least of which because I was very late today.'

The crowd chuckles when I nod my head.

'But just like Amy's been preparing for this day, I'd like to assure her that I was delayed due to some preparations of my own.'

Someone (Dad!) whistles.

'Because apparently, some jewellers in London don't open until eleven o'clock.'

Everyone including me gasps as he takes out a small velvet box. 'So, in spite of all the water under the bridge, Amy, I hope that you can still find it in your heart to love me, even half as much as I love you.'

He opens the box – there's a ring of pink and blue sapphires surrounded by diamonds and seed pearls in a Victorian setting. My hands tremble as he slips it on my finger. 'It's not a family heirloom,' he says. 'But I hope that someday it will be. Amy Wood – will you marry me?'

And there, right there in front of my guests, the staff, my parents, my former co-workers, Mrs Bradford, the TV cameras, God and everyone, I grab him by the collar and kiss him silly.

He's laughing as we finally come up for air. 'So what do you say?' he points the microphone in my direction. 'Has Rosemont Hall got its love story? And have *you* got your happy ending?'

'Yes!' My heart is bursting with joy. 'Oh yes.'

And the crowd cheers as Jack leads me off stage and out the back of the marquee. The band starts up again and I can't feel the ground beneath my feet as we walk across the lawn to the front of the house. And I still can't speak as he waves goodbye to the visitors behind us, and takes me by the hand into the house. He leads me through a door marked 'Private' and up the back stairs; laughing and stealing kisses. And in that moment, overwhelmed by love and desire; I know that I've been given such an incredible gift.

I'll be coming here again. I'll be coming... *home.*

THE END

Author's Note and Acknowledgements

Rosemont Hall is a fictional house, but there are thousands of historic houses that have been lost or are in peril in the UK. For more information about country houses at risk and an archive of these lost treasures, please see Matthew Beckett's excellent blog and website: thecountryseat.org.uk. Other invaluable resources include the National Trust, the Landmark Trust, and English Heritage, whose many employees and volunteers work tirelessly to preserve our heritage and make it part of our future.

This book was inspired by my family's three-year long quest to find our perfect home, which took in a 100-mile radius of London and made us the bane of numerous estate agents – I very much applaud the spirit and positivity of estate agents everywhere who, day in and day out, deal with people like us, and the ups and downs of matching people and property. Any mistakes I've made in describing such a difficult job are purely my own.

There are many people who have helped and supported me to ensure that *Finding Home* 'found a home'. I loved writing this book – which is a good thing, since it took me over six years. In 2012, the opening chapters were short-listed in the 'Undiscovered' Competition at Novelicious.com, and it was this tiny kernel of success that helped keep me going through the long, dark night of a writer trying to get published.

I hope you'll forgive me a little 'Oscar' moment as I have

many people to thank. First, my writing group: Ronan Winters, Chris King, David Speakman, Francisco Gochez and my dear friend Lucy Beresford. We've been going for ten years now (in various incarnations), and we've laughed, argued, cried, and drank a lot of red wine. Second, I'd like to thank my agent, Anna Power, for sticking with me *through* ups and downs, and introducing me to the amazing Caroline Ridding and her team at Aria (Head of Zeus) who had a vision for the novel, and the courage to back an unknown horse.

Next, it goes without saying – which is why it's so important to say it! – thank you to my family – the unsung heroes. Living with a writer means tolerating an entire cast of 'imaginary friends' that you haven't met and can't interact with. I know I'd struggle to do it! Your love and support mean everything.

Finally, I am grateful to current and future readers of *Finding Home*. There is nothing more satisfying to an author than introducing our beloved characters to their audience. It's you that truly brings them to life.

Lauren Westwood
Surrey 2016